#1 New York Tim .ber

"Popular romance writer Debbie Macomber has a gift for evoking the emotions that are at the heart of the genre's popularity."
—*Publishers Weekly*

"It's clear that Debbie Macomber cares deeply about her fully realized characters and their families, friends and loves, along with their hopes and dreams. She also makes her readers care about them."
—*Bookreporter.com*

"Debbie Macomber is one of the most reliable, versatile romance writers around."
—*Milwaukee Journal Sentinel*

"Readers won't be able to get enough of Macomber's gentle storytelling."
—*RT Book Reviews*

"Bestselling Macomber...sure has a way of pleasing readers."
—*Booklist*

"It's impossible not to cheer for Macomber's characters.... When it comes to creating a special place and memorable, honorable characters, nobody does it better than Macomber."
—*BookPage*

"Macomber is a master storyteller."
—*Times Record News*

DEBBIE MACOMBER

Summer Weddings

Father's Day and *Daddy's Little Helper*

/IMIRA

/ll MIRA™

ISBN-13: 978-0-7783-6864-9

Summer Weddings

Copyright © 2025 by Harlequin Enterprises ULC

Father's Day
First published in 1991. This edition published in 2025.
Copyright © 1991 by Debbie Macomber

Daddy's Little Helper
First published in 1995. This edition published in 2025.
Copyright © 1995 by Debbie Macomber

Recycling programs
for this product may
not exist in your area.

For questions and comments about the quality of this book, please contact us
at CustomerService@Harlequin.com.

TM is a trademark of Harlequin Enterprises ULC.

Mira
22 Adelaide St. West, 41st Floor
Toronto, Ontario M5H 4E3, Canada
MIRABooks.com

Printed in U.S.A.

Also available from Debbie Macomber and MIRA

Blossom Street

The Shop on Blossom Street
A Good Yarn
Susannah's Garden
Back on Blossom Street
Twenty Wishes
Summer on Blossom Street
Hannah's List
"The Twenty-First Wish"
  (in The Knitting Diaries)
A Turn in the Road

Cedar Cove

16 Lighthouse Road
204 Rosewood Lane
311 Pelican Court
44 Cranberry Point
50 Harbor Street
6 Rainier Drive
74 Seaside Avenue
8 Sandpiper Way
92 Pacific Boulevard
1022 Evergreen Place
Christmas in Cedar Cove
  (5-B Poppy Lane and
  A Cedar Cove Christmas)
1105 Yakima Street
1225 Christmas Tree Lane

The Dakota Series

Dakota Born
Dakota Home
Always Dakota
Buffalo Valley

The Manning Family

The Manning Sisters
  (The Cowboy's Lady and
  The Sheriff Takes a Wife)
The Manning Brides
  (Marriage of Inconvenience and
  Stand-In Wife)

The Manning Grooms
  (Bride on the Loose and
  Same Time, Next Year)

Christmas Books

Home for the Holidays
Glad Tidings
  (There's Something About
  Christmas and Here Comes
  Trouble)
Christmas in Alaska
  (Mail-Order Bride and
  The Snow Bride)
Trading Christmas
Christmas Letters
The Perfect Christmas (includes
  Can This Be Christmas?)
Choir of Angels
  (Shirley, Goodness and Mercy,
  Those Christmas Angels and
  Where Angels Go)
Call Me Mrs. Miracle
The Gift of Christmas
A Country Christmas
  (Kisses in the Snow and
  The Christmas Basket)

Heart of Texas

Texas Skies
  (Lonesome Cowboy and
  Texas Two-Step)
Texas Nights
  (Caroline's Child and Dr. Texas)
Texas Home
  (Nell's Cowboy and Lone Star
  Baby)
Promise, Texas
Return to Promise

Contents

Father's Day

1

"I can't believe I'm doing this," Robin Masterson muttered as she crawled into the makeshift tent, which was pitched over the clothesline in the backyard of her new home.

"Come on, Mom," ten-year-old Jeff urged, shifting to make room for her. "It's nice and warm in here."

Down on all fours, a flashlight in one hand, Robin squeezed her way inside. Jeff had constructed the flimsy tent using clothespegs to hold up the blankets and rocks to secure the base. The space was tight, but she managed to maneuver into her sleeping bag.

"Isn't this great?" Jeff asked. He stuck his head out of the front opening and gazed at the dark sky and the spattering of stars that winked back at them. On second thought, Robin decided they were laughing at her, those stars. And with good reason. There probably wasn't another thirty-year-old woman in the entire state of California who would've agreed to this craziness.

It was the first night in their new house and Robin was exhausted. They'd started moving out of the apartment before five that morning and she'd just finished unpacking the last box. The beds were assembled, but Jeff wouldn't hear of doing anything as mundane as sleeping on a real mattress. After waiting years to camp out in his own backyard, her son wasn't about to delay the adventure by even one night.

Robin couldn't let him sleep outside alone and, since he hadn't met any neighbors yet, there was only one option left. Surely there'd be a Mother of the Year award in this for her.

"You want to hear a joke?" Jeff asked, rolling on to his back and nudging her.

"Sure." She swallowed a yawn, hoping she could stay awake long enough to laugh at the appropriate time. She needn't have worried.

For the next half hour, Robin was entertained with a series of riddles, nonsense rhymes and off-key renditions of Jeff's favourite songs from summer camp.

"Knock knock," she said when it appeared her son had run through his repertoire.

"Who's there?"

"Wanda."

"Wanda who?"

"Wanda who thinks up these silly jokes?"

Jeff laughed as though she'd come up with the funniest line ever devised. Her son's enthusiasm couldn't help but rub off on Robin and some of her weariness eased. Camping was fun— sort of. But it'd been years since she'd slept on the ground and, frankly, she couldn't remember it being quite this hard.

"Do you think we'll be warm enough?" she teased. Jeff had used every blanket they owned, first to construct the tent and then to pad it. To be on the safe side, two or three more were piled on top of their sleeping bags on the off-chance an arctic frost descended upon them. It was spring, but a San Francisco spring could be chilly.

"Sure," he answered, missing the kidding note in her voice. "But if you get cold, you can have one of mine."

"I'm fine," she assured him.

"You hungry?"

Now that she thought about it, she was. "Sure. Whatcha got?"

Jeff disappeared into his sleeping bag and returned a moment later with a limp package of licorice, a small plastic bag full of squashed marshmallows and a flattened box of raisins. Robin declined the snack.

"When are we going to buy me my dog?" Jeff asked, chewing loudly on the raisins.

Robin listened to the sound and said nothing.

"Mom...the dog?" he repeated after a few minutes.

Robin had been dreading that question most of the day. She'd managed to forestall Jeff for the past month by telling him they'd discuss getting a dog after they were settled in their house.

"I thought we'd start looking for ads in the paper first thing tomorrow," Jeff said, still munching.

"I'm not sure when we'll start the search for the right dog." She was a coward, Robin freely admitted it, but she hated to disappoint Jeff. He had his heart set on a dog. How like his father he was, in his love for animals.

"I want a big one, you know. None of those fancy little poodles or anything."

"A golden retriever would be nice, don't you think?"

"Or a German shepherd," Jeff said.

"Your father loved dogs," she whispered, although she'd told Jeff that countless times. Lenny had been gone for so many years, she had trouble remembering what their life together had been like. They'd been crazy in love with each other and married shortly after their high-school graduation. A year later, Robin became pregnant. Jeff had been barely six months old when Lenny was killed in a freak car accident on his way home from work. In the span of mere moments, Robin's comfortable world had been sent into a tailspin, and ten years later it was still whirling.

With her family's help, she'd gone back to school and obtained her degree. She was now a certified public accountant working for a large San Francisco insurance firm. Over the years she'd dated a number of men, but none she'd seriously consider marrying. Her life was far more complicated now than it had been as a young bride. The thought of falling in love again terrified her.

"What kind of dog did Dad have when he was a kid?" Jeff asked.

"I don't think Rover was any particular breed," Robin answered, then paused to recall exactly what Lenny's childhood dog had looked like. "I think he was mostly...Labrador."

"Was he black?"

"And brown."

"Did Dad have any other animals?"

Robin smiled at her warm memories of her late husband. She enjoyed the way Jeff loved hearing stories about his father—no matter how many times he'd already heard them. "He collected three more pets the first year we were married. It seemed he was always bringing home a stray cat or lost dog. We couldn't keep them, of course, because we weren't allowed pets in the apartment complex. We went to great lengths to hide them for a few days until we could locate their owners or find them a good home. For our first wedding anniversary, he bought me a goldfish. Your father really loved animals."

Jeff beamed and planted his chin on his folded arms.

"We dreamed of buying a small farm someday and raising chickens and goats and maybe a cow or two. Your father wanted to buy you a pony, too." Hard as she tried, she couldn't quite hide the pain in her voice. Even after all these years, the memory of Lenny's sudden death still hurt. Looking at her son, so eager for a dog of his own, Robin missed her husband more than ever.

"You and Dad were going to buy a farm?" Jeff cried, his voice ebullient. "You never told me that before." He paused. "A pony for me? Really? Do you think we'll ever be able to afford one? Look how long it took to save for the house."

Robin smiled. "I think we'll have to give up on the idea of you and me owning a farm, at least in the near future."

When they were first married, Robin and Lenny had talked for hours about their dreams. They'd charted their lives, confident that nothing would ever separate them. Their love had been too strong. It was true that she'd never told Jeff about buying a farm, nor had she told him how they'd planned to name it Paradise. Paradise, because that was what the farm would be to them. In retrospect, not telling Jeff was a way of protecting him. He'd lost so much—not only the guidance and love of his father but all the things they could have had as a family. She'd never mentioned the pony before, or the fact that Lenny had always longed for a horse....

Jeff yawned loudly and Robin marvelled at his endurance. He'd carried in as many boxes as the movers had, racing up and down the stairs with an energy Robin envied. He'd unpacked the upstairs bathroom, as well as his own bedroom and had helped her organize the kitchen.

"I can hardly wait to get my dog," Jeff said, his voice fading. Within minutes he was sound asleep.

"A dog," Robin said softly as her eyes closed. She didn't know how she was going to break the bad news to Jeff. They couldn't get a dog—at least not right away. She was unwilling to leave a large dog locked indoors all day while she went off to work and Jeff was in school. Tying one up in the backyard was equally unfair, and she couldn't afford to build a fence. Not this year, anyway. Then there was the cost of feeding a dog and paying the vet's bills. With this new home, Robin's budget was already stretched to the limit.

Robin awoke feeling chilled and warm at the same time. In the gray dawn, she glanced at her watch. Six-thirty. At some point during the night, the old sleeping bag that dated back to her high-school days had come unzipped and the cool morning air had chilled her arms and legs. Yet her back was warm and cozy. Jeff had probably snuggled up to her during the night. She sighed, determined to sleep for another half hour or so. With that idea in mind, she reached for a blanket to wrap around her shoulders and met with some resistance. She tugged and pulled, to no avail. It was then that she felt something wet and warm close to her neck. Her eyes shot open. Very slowly, she turned her head until she came eyeball to eyeball with a big black dog.

Robin gasped loudly and struggled into a sitting position, which was difficult with the sleeping bag and several blankets wrapped around her legs, imprisoning her.

"Where did you come from?" she demanded, edging away from the dog. The Labrador had eased himself between her and Jeff and made himself right at home. His head rested on his paws and he looked perfectly content, if a bit disgruntled about having his nap interrupted. He didn't seem at all interested in vacating the premises.

Jeff rolled over and opened his eyes. Immediately he bolted upright. "Mom," he cried excitedly. "You got me a dog!"

"No—he isn't ours. I don't know who he belongs to."

"Me!" Jeff's voice was triumphant. "He belongs to me." His thin arms hugged the animal's neck. "You really got me a dog! It was supposed to be a surprise, wasn't it?"

"Jeff," she said firmly. "I don't know where this animal came from, but he isn't ours."

"He isn't?" His voice sagged in disappointment. "But who owns him, then? And how did he get inside the tent with us?"

"Heavens, I don't know." Robin rubbed the sleep from her eyes while she attempted to put her garbled thoughts in order. "He looks too well fed and groomed to be a stray. He must belong to someone in the neighborhood. Maybe he—"

"Blackie!" As if in response, she was interrupted by a crisp male voice. "Blackie. Here, boy."

The Labrador lifted his head, but stayed where he was. Robin didn't blame him. Jeff was stroking his back with one hand and rubbing his ears with the other, all the while crooning to him softly.

With some effort, Robin managed to divest herself of the sleeping bag. She reached for her tennis shoes and crawled out of the tent. No sooner was she on her feet than she turned to find a lanky man standing a few yards from her, just on the other side of the three-foot hedge that separated the two properties. Obviously he was her neighbor. Robin smiled, but the friendly gesture was not returned. In fact, the man looked downright *un*friendly.

Her neighbor was also an imposing man, at least six feet tall. Since Robin was only five-three, he towered head and shoulders above her. Instinctively, she stiffened her back, meeting his dark eyes. "Good morning," she said coolly.

He barely glanced in her direction, and when he did, he dismissed her with little more than a nod. After a night on the ground, with her son and a dog for bedmates, Robin realized she wasn't looking her best, but she resented the way his eyes flicked disinterestedly over her.

Robin usually gave people the benefit of the doubt, but toward this man, she felt an immediate antipathy. His face was completely emotionless, which lent him an intimidating air. He was clearly aware of that and used it to his advantage.

"Good morning," she said again, clasping her hands tightly. She drew herself to her full height and raised her chin. "I believe your dog is in the tent with my son."

Her news appeared to surprise him; his expression softened. Robin was struck by the change. When his face relaxed, he was actually a very attractive man. For the most part, Robin hardly noticed how good-looking a man was or wasn't, but this time...she noticed. Perhaps because of the contrast with his forbidding demeanor of a moment before.

"Blackie knows better than to leave the yard. Here, boy!" He shouted for the Labrador again, this time including a sharp whistle loud enough to pierce Robin's eardrums. The dog emerged from the tent and approached the hedge, slowly wagging his tail.

"Is that your dog?" Jeff asked, dashing out behind Blackie. "He's great. How long have you had him?"

"I'll make sure he doesn't bother you again," the man said, ignoring Jeff's question. Robin supposed his words were meant to be an apology. "He's well trained—he's never left my yard before. I'll make sure it doesn't happen again."

"Blackie wasn't any bother," Jeff hurried to explain, racing forward. "He crawled into the tent with us and made himself at home, which was all right with us, wasn't it, Mom?"

"Sure," Robin answered, flipping her shoulder-length auburn hair away from her face. She'd had it tied back when she'd gone to bed, but it had pulled free during the night. Robin could well imagine how it looked now. Most mornings it tended to resemble foam on a newly poured mug of beer.

"We're friends, aren't we, Blackie?" Jeff knelt, and without hesitation the dog came to him, eagerly licking his face.

The man's eyes revealed astonishment, however fleeting, and his dark brows drew together over his high-bridged nose. "Blackie," he snapped. "Come."

The Labrador squeezed between two overgrown laurel bushes and returned to his master, who didn't look any too pleased at his dog's affection for Jeff.

"My son has a way with animals," Robin said.

"Do you live here?" Jeff asked next. He seemed completely unaware of their new neighbor's unfriendliness.

"Next door."

"Oh, good." Jeff grinned widely and placed his right hand

on his chest. "I'm Jeff Masterson and this is my mom, Robin. We moved in yesterday."

"I'm Cole Camden. Welcome to the neighborhood."

Although his words were cordial, his tone wasn't. Robin felt about as welcome as a punk-rock band at a retirees' picnic.

"I'm getting a dog myself," Jeff went on affably. "That's why we moved out of the apartment building—I couldn't have a pet there except for my goldfish."

Cole nodded without comment.

Oh, great, Robin thought. After years of scrimping and saving to buy a house, they were going to be stuck with an ill-tempered next-door neighbor. His house was older than the others on the block. Much bigger, too. Robin guessed that his home, a sprawling three-story structure, had been built in the early thirties. She knew that at one time this neighborhood had been filled with large opulent homes like Cole Camden's. Gradually, over the years, the older places had been torn down and a series of two-story houses and trendy ramblers built in their place. Her neighbor's house was the last vestige of an era long past.

"Have you got any kids?" Jeff could hardly keep the eagerness out of his voice. In the apartment complex there'd always been plenty of playmates, and he was eager to make new friends, especially before he started classes in an unfamiliar school on Monday morning.

Cole's face hardened and Robin could have sworn the question had angered him. An uncomfortable moment passed before he answered. "No, I don't have any kids." His voice held a rough undertone, and for a split second Robin was sure she saw a flash of pain in his eyes.

"Would it be okay if I played with Blackie sometimes? Just until I get my own dog?"

"No." Cole's response was sharp, but, when Jeff flinched at his vehemence, Cole appeared to regret his harsh tone. "I don't mean to be rude, but it'd probably be best if you stayed in your own yard."

"That's all right," Jeff said. "You can send Blackie over here to visit anytime you want. I like dogs."

"I can see that." A hint of a smile lifted the corners of his mouth. Then his cool gaze moved from Jeff to Robin, his face again expressionless, but she sensed that he'd made up his mind about them, categorized them and come to his own conclusions.

If Cole Camden thought he could intimidate her, Robin had news for him. He'd broadcast his message loud and clear. He didn't want to be bothered by her or her son, and in exchange he'd stay out of her way. That was fine with her. Terrific, in fact. She didn't have time for humoring grouches.

Without another word, Cole turned and strode toward his house with Blackie at his heels.

"Goodbye, Mr. Camden," Jeff called, raising his hand.

Robin wasn't surprised when their neighbor didn't give them the courtesy of a reply.

In an effort to distract Jeff from Cole Camden's unfriendliness, she said brightly, "Hey, I'm starving. How about you?"

Jeff didn't answer right away. "Do you think he'll let me play with Blackie?"

Robin sighed, considering the dilemma that faced her. She didn't want Cole to hurt Jeff's feelings, but it wasn't likely their neighbor would appreciate her son's affinity with his Labrador. By the same token, a neighbor's dog, even one that belonged to a grouch, would ease her guilt over not being able to provide Jeff with the dog she'd promised him.

"What do you think, Mom?" Jeff prompted. "He'll probably let me play with Blackie sometimes, don't you think?"

"I don't know, honey," she whispered. "I just don't know."

Later the same day, after buying groceries to stock their bare kitchen shelves and picking up other necessities, Robin counted the change at the bottom of her purse. She needed to be sure she had money for the subway on Monday morning. Luckily she had enough spare change for BART—Bay Area Rapid Transit—to last the week, but it was packed lunches for her and Jeff until her next payday, which was in two weeks.

Her finances would've been in better shape if she'd waited another year to move out of the apartment. But interest rates were at a two-year low and she'd decided soon after the first of the year that if they were ever going to move out of the apartment this was the time.

"Mom!" Jeff crashed through the back door, breathless. "We're in trouble."

"Oh?" Robin glanced up from the salad she was mixing. A completely disgusted look on his face, her son flung himself into a chair and propped his elbows on the table. Then he let out a forceful sigh.

"What's wrong, Jeff?"

"I'm afraid we made a bad mistake."

"How's that?"

"There's nothing but girls in this neighborhood." He made it sound as though they'd unexpectedly landed in enemy territory. "I rode my bike up and down the street and all I saw were *girls*." He wrinkled his nose.

"Don't worry, you'll be meeting lots of boys in school on Monday."

"You aren't taking this seriously!" Jeff cried. "I don't think you understand what this means. There are seven houses on this block. Six of them have kids and only one has a boy, and that's me. I'm surrounded by women!"

"How'd you find all this out?"

"I asked, of course." He sighed again. "What are you going to do about it, Mom?"

"Me?" Robin asked. "Are you suggesting we move back to the apartment?"

Jeff considered this for only a moment. "I'd think we should if it wasn't for two things. We can't have a dog there. And I found a fort."

"A fort?"

"Yes," he said solemnly. "It's hidden way back in Mr. Camden's yard and covered by a bunch of brush. It's real neat there. I don't think he knows about it, because the word on the street is he doesn't like kids. Someone must've built it and I'm going to find out who. If there's a club going, I want in. I've got the right—I live closer to Mr. Camden than anyone else does."

"Agreed." Robin munched on a slice of green pepper and handed one to Jeff. "So you think it'd be all right if we stayed?"

"I guess so," Jeff conceded, "at least until I find out more about the fort."

Robin was about to say something else when the doorbell chimed.

Jeff's blue eyes met hers. "I bet it's one of those pesky girls," he said in disgust.

"Do you want me to get rid of her?"

Jeff nodded emphatically.

Robin was smiling when she answered the front door. Jeff was right; it was a girl, one who seemed to be a couple of years younger than her son. She hadn't come alone, though. Standing with the youngster was an adult.

"Hi," the woman said cheerfully, flashing Robin a warm smile. "I know you've hardly had a chance to get settled, but I wanted to introduce myself. I'm Heather Lawrence and this is my daughter, Kelly. We live next door, and we'd like to welcome you to the neighborhood."

Robin introduced herself as she opened the door and invited them in. Heather was cute and perky. Her hair was cut in a short bob that bounced when she spoke. Robin knew right away that she was going to like these neighbors. Heather's warm reception was a pleasant change from the way Cole Camden had greeted her.

"Would you like some coffee?" Robin asked.

"If you're sure I'm not interrupting anything."

"I'm sure." Robin led her into the kitchen, where Jeff sat waiting. He cast her a look that suggested she should be shot for treason, then muttered something about forgetting that mothers were really *girls* in disguise. Then he headed out the front door.

Robin reached for two matching ceramic mugs and poured coffee for herself and her new friend. She offered Kelly a glass of juice, then slid into a chair across the table from the girl and her mother. "I'm sorry about Jeff." She felt obliged to apologize. "He's at the age where he thinks girls are a plague to society."

"Don't worry about it," Heather said, smiling. "Kelly isn't keen on boys herself."

"They're creeps. I'd rather ride my bicycle than play with a boy," the girl announced. "But Mom wanted me to come over with her so she didn't look like a busybody. Right, Mom?"

Heather blushed and threw her daughter a murderous glance.

Robin laughed. "I thought it would take several weeks to get to know my neighbors and I've met two in one day."

"Someone else has already been over?"

"Cole Camden introduced himself this morning," she explained, keeping her eyes averted to hide the resentment she felt toward her unfriendly neighbor. Even now, hours later, she couldn't help thinking about the way he'd reacted to her and Jeff.

"Cole Camden introduced himself?" Heather repeated, sounding shocked. She frowned, staring into space as though digesting the fact.

"To be honest, I think he would've preferred to avoid me, but his dog wanted to make friends with Jeff."

Heather's mouth opened and closed twice. "Blackie did?"

"Is there something strange about that?"

"Frankly, yes. To say Cole keeps to himself is an understatement. I don't think he's said more than a handful of words to me in the entire two years since Kelly and I moved here. I don't know why he stays in the neighborhood." She paused to respond to her daughter, who was asking permission to go home. "Thank Robin for the juice, honey. Anyway," she went on, turning back to Robin when her daughter had skipped out the door, "he's all alone in that huge house and it's ridiculous, really. Can you imagine what his heating bills must be? Although, personally, I don't think money is much of a problem for him. But I've never heard any details."

It didn't surprise Robin to learn Cole lived alone. She'd barely met the man, but guessed that life held little joy for him. It was as though love, warmth and friendship had all been found lacking and had therefore been systematically dismissed.

"Apparently, he was married once, but he was divorced long before I came here."

Robin had dealt with unfriendly men before, but something about Cole struck her hard and deep, and she wasn't sure what it was or why he evoked such a strong feeling within her.

"He and his dog are inseparable," Heather added.

Robin nodded, hardly listening. He'd intimidated her at first, but when she'd pulled herself together and faced him squarely he'd loosened up a bit and, later, even seemed amused. But then Jeff had asked him about children, and Robin had seen the pain in his eyes.

As if by magic, her son's face appeared around the door. When he saw that Kelly was gone, he walked into the room, hands in his back pockets.

"Do you have a dog?" he asked Heather.

"Unfortunately, no. Kelly's allergic."

Jeff nodded as though to say that was exactly the kind of thing he expected from a girl. "We're getting a German shepherd soon, aren't we, Mom?"

"Soon," Robin responded, feeling wretched. After Heather left, she was going to tell Jeff the truth. She fully intended to let him have his dog, but he'd have to wait a while. She'd been practicing what to say. She'd even come up with a compromise. They could get a cat. Cats didn't seem to mind being left on their own, and they didn't need to be walked. Although she wasn't happy about keeping a litter box in the house, Robin was willing to put up with that inconvenience. Then, when she could afford to have a fence built, they'd get a dog. She planned to be positive and direct with Jeff. He'd understand. At least she hoped he would.

Heather stayed only a few more minutes. The visit had been a fruitful one. Robin had learned that Heather was divorced, worked mornings in an office and provided after-school day care in an effort to spend more time with Kelly. This information was good news to Robin, and the two women agreed that Jeff would go to the Lawrence house before and after school, instead of the community center several blocks away. The arrangement suited them both; even Jeff shrugged in agreement.

Robin would've liked to ask her new friend more about Cole, but his name didn't come up again, and she didn't want to seem too curious about him.

After Heather left, Robin braced herself for the talk with Jeff about getting a dog. Unfortunately, it didn't go well. It seemed that after waiting nearly ten years, a few more months was completely unacceptable.

"You promised!" he shouted. "You said I could have a dog when we moved into the house!"

"You can, sweetheart, but not right away."

Unusual for Jeff, tears gathered in his eyes, and he struggled to hold them back. Soon Robin felt moisture filling her own eyes. She hated disappointing Jeff more than anything. His heart was set on getting a dog right away, and he considered the offer of a cat a poor substitute.

He left the house soon afterward. In an effort to soothe his hurt feelings, Robin cooked her son's favorite meal—macaroni and cheese with sliced sausage and lots of ketchup.

She didn't see him on the pavement or the street when she went to check half an hour later. She stood on the porch, wondering where he'd gone. His bike was inside the garage, and he'd already aired his views about playing with any of the girls in the neighborhood.

It would be just like him to storm into his room in a fit of indignation and promptly fall asleep. Robin hurried upstairs to his bedroom, which was across the hall from her own.

His bed was made and his clothes hung neatly in the closet. Robin decided that in another day or two, everything would be back to normal.

It wasn't until she turned to leave that she saw the note on his desk. Picking it up, Robin read the first line and felt a swirling sense of panic.

Dear Mom,
You broke your promise. You said I could have a dog and now you say I have to wait. If I can't have a dog, then I don't want to live with you anymore. This is goodbye forever.
Love, Jeff

2

For a moment, Robin was too stunned to react. Her heart was pounding so hard it echoed in her ears like thunder, so loud it seemed to knock her off balance.

Rushing down the stairs, she stood on the porch, cupped her hands over her mouth and screamed frantically. "Jeff! Jeffy!"

Cole Camden was standing on his front porch, too. He released a shrill whistle and stood waiting expectantly. When nothing happened, he called, "Blackie!"

"Jeff!" Robin tried again.

"Blackie!"

Robin called for Jeff once more, but her voice cracked as the panic engulfed her. She paused, placed her hand over her mouth and closed her eyes, trying to regain her composure.

"Blackie!" Cole yelled. He looked furious about his dog's disappearance.

It took Robin only a moment to put two and two together. "Cole," she cried, running across the lawn toward him. "I think Jeff and Blackie might have run away together."

Cole looked at her as if she was deranged, and Robin couldn't blame him. "Jeff left me a note. He wants a dog so badly and we can't get one right now because…well, because we can't, and I had to tell him, and he was terribly disappointed and he decided to run away."

Cole's mouth thinned. "The whole idea is ridiculous. Even if Jeff did run away, Blackie would never go with him."

"Do you honestly think I'd make this up?" she shrieked. "The last time I saw Jeff was around four-thirty, and I'd bet cold cash that's about the same time Blackie disappeared."

Cole's gaze narrowed. "Then where are they?"

"If I knew that, do you think I'd be standing around here arguing with you?"

"Listen, lady, I don't know your son, but I know my dog and—"

"My name's not lady," Robin flared, clenching her hands at her sides. He was looking at her as though she were a mad-woman on the loose—which she was where her son was con-cerned. "I'm sorry to have troubled you. When I find Jeff, I'll make sure your dog gets home."

Cole's eyes shot sparks in her direction, but she ignored them. Turning abruptly, she ran back to her own house. Half-way there, she stopped dead and whirled around to face Cole again. "The fort."

"What fort?" Cole demanded.

"The one that's in the back of your yard. It's covered with brush…. Jeff found it earlier today. He wouldn't know any-where else to go and that would be the perfect hiding place."

"No one's been there in years," Cole said, discounting her suggestion.

"The least we can do is look."

Cole's nod was reluctant. He led the way to his backyard, which was much larger than hers. There was a small grove of oak trees at the rear of the property and beyond that a high fence. Apparently the fort was situated between the trees and the fence. A few minutes later, in the most remote corner of the yard, nestled between two trees, Robin saw the small wooden structure. It blended into the terrain, and if she hadn't been looking for the hideaway, she would never have seen it.

It was obvious when they neared the space that someone had taken up residence. Cole lowered himself down to all fours, peered inside, then looked back at Robin with a nod. He breathed in sharply, apparently irritated by this turn of events, and crawled through the narrow entrance.

Not about to be left standing by herself, Robin got down on her knees and followed him in.

Just as she'd suspected, Jeff and Blackie were huddled together in a corner. Jeff was fast asleep and Blackie was curled up by his side, guarding him. When Cole and Robin entered, the Labrador lifted his head and wagged his tail in greeting.

The fort wasn't much bigger than the tent Jeff had constructed the night before, and Robin was forced to pull her knees close and loop her arms around them. Cole's larger body seemed to fill every available bit of space.

Jeff must have sensed that his newfound home had been invaded because his eyes fluttered open and he gazed at Robin, then turned his head to stare at Cole.

"Hi, Mom," he said sheepishly. "I bet I'm in trouble, aren't I?"

Robin was so grateful to find him that all she could do was nod. If she'd tried to speak, her voice would've been shaking with emotion, which would only have embarrassed them both.

"So, Jeff," Cole said sternly. "You were going to run away from home. I see you brought everything you needed." He pushed the frying pan and atlas into the middle of their cramped quarters. "What I want to know is how you convinced Blackie to join you."

"He came on his own," Jeff murmured, but his eyes avoided Cole's. "I wouldn't have taken him on purpose—he's your dog."

"I'm glad you didn't...coerce him."

"All you took was a frying pan and an atlas!" Robin cried, staring at the cast-iron skillet and the atlas with its dog-eared pages.

Cole and Jeff both ignored her outburst.

"I take it you don't like living here?" Cole asked.

Jeff stiffened, then shook his head vigorously. "Mom told me that when we moved I could have a dog and now I can't. And...and she dragged me into a neighborhood filled with girls. That might've been okay if I had a dog, but then she broke her promise. A promise is a promise and it's sacred. A guy would never do that."

"So you can't have a dog until later?"

"All because of a stupid fence."

Cole nodded. "Fences are important, you know. And you know what else? Your mom was worried about you."

Jeff looked at Robin, who was blinking furiously to keep the tears from dripping down her face. The upheaval and stress of the move had drained her emotionally and she was an unmitigated mess. Normally, she was a calm, controlled person, but this whole drama with Jeff was her undoing. That and the fact she'd hardly slept the night before in his makeshift tent.

"Mom," Jeff said, studying her anxiously, "are you all right?"

She covered her face with both hands. "I slept with a dog and you ran away and all you took was a frying pan and an atlas." That made no sense whatsoever, but she couldn't help it, and once the tears started they wouldn't stop.

"I'm sorry, Mom," Jeff said softly. "I didn't mean to make you cry."

"I know," she whimpered. "I want you to have a dog, I really do, but we can't keep one locked up in the house all day and we don't have a fence and...and the way you just looked at me, I swear it was Lenny all over again."

"Who's Lenny?" Cole cocked his head toward Jeff, speaking in a whisper.

"Lenny was my dad. He died when I was real little. I don't even remember him."

Cole shared a knowing look with her son. "It might be a good idea if we got your mother back inside the house."

"You think I'm getting hysterical, don't you?" Robin burst out. "I want you both to know I'm in perfect control. A woman can cry every now and then if she wants. Venting your emotions is healthy—all the books say so."

"Right, Mom." Jeff gently patted her shoulder, then crawled out of the fort. He waited for Robin, who emerged after him, and offered her a hand. Cole and Blackie followed.

Jeff took Robin's arm, holding her elbow as he led her to the back door of their house, as if he suspected she couldn't find her way without his guidance.

Once inside, Robin grabbed a tissue and loudly blew her nose. Her composure was shaky, but when she turned to Cole, she intended to be as reasonable as a judge. As polite as a preacher.

"Have you got any aspirin?" Cole asked Jeff.

Jeff nodded, and dashed up the stairs to the bathroom, returning in thirty seconds flat with the bottle. Cole filled a glass with water and delivered both to Robin. How he knew she had a fierce headache she could only guess.

"Why don't you lie down for a few minutes? I'm sure you'll feel better."

"I feel just fine, thank you," she snapped, more angry with herself for overreacting than with him for taking charge.

"Do you have family close by?" Again Cole directed the question to Jeff, which served to further infuriate Robin. Jeff was ten years old! She, on the other hand, was an adult. If this man had questions they should be directed to her, not her son.

"Not anymore," Jeff answered in an anxious whisper. "Grandma and Grandpa moved to Arizona last year, and my uncle lives in LA."

"I don't need to lie down," Robin said forcefully. "I'm perfectly fine."

"Mom," Jeff countered, his voice troubled, "you don't look so good."

"You were talking about frying pans and sleeping with dogs in the same breath," Cole elaborated, his eyebrows raised.

"I think Mr. Camden's right," Jeff said. "You need rest—lots of rest."

Her own son had turned traitor on her. Robin was shocked. Jeff took her hand and led her into the family room, which was off the kitchen. He patted the quilted pillow on the sofa, wordlessly suggesting she place her head there. When she resisted, he pulled the afghan from the chair and draped it around her, tucking the ends behind her shoulders.

Robin couldn't believe she was allowing herself to be led around like a...like a puppy. As if reading her thoughts, Blackie wandered over to her side and lowered his bulk onto the carpet beside the sofa.

"That's a neat fort you've got there," Jeff told Cole once he'd finished tucking in the blanket. Robin watched him hurry back to the kitchen, grab a plate, then load it with macaroni and cheese and hand it to Cole, apparently wanting to share his favorite meal with their neighbor.

Cole set the plate on the counter. "Thanks anyway, Jeff, but I've got to get back to the house. In the future, if you're thinking about running away—don't."

"Yeah, I guess you're right," Jeff said with a mildly guilty look. "My mom turned into a basket case."

Cole smiled—at least, it was as close to a smile as Robin had seen. "You're both going to be fine. She intends to get you that dog, you know. Just hang on. It'll be sooner than you think."

Jeff walked to the sliding glass door with Cole. "Mr. Camden, can I ask you something important?"

"Sure."

"Is anyone using the fort?"

"Not that I know of."

Jeff's expression was hopeful. "It didn't look like anyone had been inside for a long time."

"Six years," Cole murmured absently.

"That long? How come?" Jeff asked. "It's a *great* fort. If it's all right with you I'd like to go over there sometimes. I promise not to walk in any flowerbeds or anything, and I won't leave a mess. I'll take real good care of everything."

Cole hesitated for a moment. He looked at Jeff, and Robin held her breath. Then he shook his head. "Maybe sometime in the future, but not now."

Jeff's deep blue eyes brightened; apparently the refusal didn't trouble him. "Okay. When I can use the fort, would it be all right if I took Blackie with me? He followed me today, you know. I didn't have to do anything to get him to tag along." Jeff paused and lowered his eyes. "Well, hardly anything."

"I thought as much. As your mom said, you have a way with animals."

"My dad did, too. If he hadn't died he would've gotten me a pony and everything."

There was such pride in Jeff's voice that Robin bit her bottom lip to keep from crying all over again. Jeff and Lenny were so much alike. What she'd told her son earlier was true. More and more, Jeff was starting to take on his father's looks and personality.

Cole gazed down at Jeff, and an emotion flashed in his eyes, so transient Robin couldn't recognize it. He laid his hand on Jeff's shoulder. "Since your mother explained there's going to be a delay in getting you a dog, it'd be okay with me if you borrowed Blackie every now and then. You have to stay in your own yard, though. I don't want him running in the neighborhood unless he's on a leash."

"Do you mean it? Thanks, Mr. Camden! I'll do everything you ask."

Robin had the feeling Jeff would've agreed to just about any terms as long as he could see Blackie. It wasn't a dog of his own, but it was as close as he was going to get for the next few months.

Once Cole had left, Jeff joined her on the sofa, his hands folded on his lap. "I'm sorry, Mom," he muttered, his chin buried in his chest. "I promise I'll never run away again."

"I should hope not," she said. Wrapping her arms around him, she hugged him close, kissing his cheek.

"Gee whiz," Jeff grumbled, rubbing his face. "I'd never have apologized if I'd known you were going to kiss me."

A week passed. Jeff liked his new school and, as Robin had predicted, found his class contained an equal number of boys and girls. With his outgoing personality, he quickly collected new friends.

On Sunday afternoon, Robin was in the family room reading the paper when Jeff ambled in and sat down across from her. He took the baseball cap from his head and studied it for a moment.

"Something bothering you?" she asked, lowering the paper to get a better view of her son.

He shrugged. "Did you know Mr. Camden used to be married?"

"That's what I heard," Robin said absently. But other than

Heather's remarks the previous week, she hadn't heard anything else. In fact, she'd spoken to her neighbor only when she'd gone to pick up Jeff every afternoon. The child-care arrangement with Heather was working beautifully, but there'd been little opportunity to chat.

As for Cole, Robin hadn't seen him at all. Since he'd been so kind and helpful in the situation with Jeff, Robin had revised her opinion of him. He liked his privacy and that was fine by her; she had no intention of interrupting his serene existence. The memory of their first meeting still rankled, but she was willing to overlook that shaky beginning.

"Mr. Camden had a son who died."

Robin's heart constricted. It made sense: the pain she'd seen when Jeff had asked him about children, the word on the street that Cole didn't like kids, the abandoned fort. "I... How did you find that out?"

"Jimmy Wallach. He lives two streets over and has an older brother who used to play with Bobby Camden. Jimmy told me about him."

"I didn't know," Robin murmured, saddened by the information. She couldn't imagine her life without Jeff—the mere thought of losing him was enough to tear her apart.

"Mrs. Wallach heard Jimmy talking about Bobby Camden, and she said Mr. Camden got divorced and it was real bad, and then a year later Bobby died. She said Mr. Camden's never been the same since."

Robin ached for Cole, and she regretted all the uncharitable thoughts she'd had that first morning.

"I feel sad," Jeff whispered, frowning. His face was as intent as she'd ever seen it.

"I do, too," Robin returned softly.

"Mrs. Wallach seemed real surprised when I told her Mr. Camden said I could play in Bobby's fort someday. Ever since his son died, he hasn't let any kids in the yard or anything. She said he hardly talks to anyone in the neighborhood anymore."

Heather Lawrence had said basically the same thing, but hadn't explained the reason for it. Probably because she didn't know.

"Are you still going to barbecue hamburgers for dinner tonight?"

Robin nodded, surprised by the abrupt way Jeff had changed the subject. "If you want." Next to macaroni and cheese, grilled burgers were Jeff's all-time favorite food.

"Can I invite Mr. Camden over to eat with us?"

Robin hated to refuse her son, but she wasn't sure a dinner invitation was a good idea. She didn't know Cole very well, but she'd already learned he wasn't one to socialize with the neighbors. In addition, Jeff might blurt out questions about Cole's dead son that would be terribly painful for him.

"Mom," Jeff pleaded, "I bet no one ever invites him to dinner and he's all alone."

"Sweetheart, I don't know if that would be the right thing to do."

"But we *owe* him, Mom," Jeff implored. "He let me throw sticks for Blackie twice this week."

"I don't think Mr. Camden's home," Robin said, picking up the newspaper while she weighed the pros and cons of Jeff's suggestion. Since last Sunday, Robin hadn't spoken to Cole once, and she wasn't eager to initiate a conversation. He might read something into it.

"I'll go and see if he's home." Before she could react, Jeff was out the front door, letting the screen door slam in his wake.

He returned a couple of minutes later breathless and excited. "Mr. Camden's home and he said he appreciates the invitation, but he has other plans for tonight."

"That's too bad," Robin said, hoping she sounded sincere.

"I told him we were having strawberry shortcake for dessert and he said that's his favorite."

Robin didn't want to admit it, but she was relieved Cole wouldn't be showing up for dinner. The man made her feel nervous and uncertain. She didn't know why that should be, only that it was a new and unfamiliar sensation.

"Thanks, Mom."

Robin jerked her head up from the paper. "Thanks for what?" She hadn't read a word in five minutes. Her thoughts had been on her neighbor.

Jeff rolled his eyes. "For letting me take a piece of strawberry shortcake over to Mr. Camden."

"I said you could do that?"

"Just now." He walked over to her and playfully tested her forehead with the back of his hand. "You don't feel hot, but then, with brain fever you never know."

Robin swatted playfully at her son's backside.

Laughing, Jeff raced outdoors, where his bicycle was waiting. A half hour later, he was back in the house. "Mom! Mom!" he cried, racing into the kitchen. "Did you know Mr. Camden owns a black Porsche?"

"I can't say I did." She was more interested in peeling potatoes for the salad than discussing fancy cars. She didn't know enough about sports cars to get excited about them.

Jeff jerked open the bottom drawer and rooted through the rag bag until he found what he was looking for. He pulled out a large square that had once been part of his flannel pyjamas, then started back outside. "He has another car, too, an SUV."

"Just where are you going, young man?" Robin demanded.

"Mr. Camden's waxing his car and I'm gonna help him."

"Did he ask for your help?"

"No," Jeff said impatiently.

"He may not want you to."

"Mom!" Jeff rolled his eyes as if to suggest she was overdoing this mothering thing. "Can I go now?"

"Ah... I suppose," she agreed, but her heart was in her throat. She moved into the living room and watched as Jeff strolled across the lawn to the driveway next door, where Cole was busy rubbing liquid wax on the gleaming surface of his Porsche. Without a word, Jeff started polishing the dried wax with his rag. Cole straightened and stopped smearing on the wax, obviously surprised to see Jeff. Robin bit her lip, not knowing how her neighbor would react to Jeff's willingness to help. Apparently he said something, because Jeff nodded, then walked over and sat cross-legged on the lawn. They didn't seem to be carrying on a conversation and Robin wondered what Cole had said to her son.

Robin returned to the kitchen, grateful that Cole's rejection had been gentle. At least he hadn't sent Jeff away. She peeled another potato, then walked back to the living room and glanced out the window again. This time she saw Jeff standing beside Cole, who was, it seemed, demonstrating the correct way to polish a car. He made wide circular motions with his arms, after which he stepped aside to let Jeff tackle the Porsche again. Cole smiled, then patted him on the head before walking around to the other side of the car.

Once the salad was ready, Robin ventured outside.

Jeff waved enthusiastically when he caught sight of her on the porch. "Isn't she a beaut?" he yelled.

It looked like an ordinary car to Robin, but she nodded enthusiastically. "Wonderful," she answered. "Afternoon, Cole."

"Robin." He returned her greeting absently.

He wore a sleeveless gray sweatshirt and she was surprised by how muscular and tanned his arms were. From a recent conversation with Heather Lawrence, Robin had learned Cole was a prominent attorney. And he seemed to fit the lawyer image to a T. Not anymore. The lawyer was gone and the *man* was there, bold as could be. Her awareness of him as an attractive virile male was shockingly intense.

The problem, she decided, lay in the fact that she hadn't expected Cole to look so...fit. The sight of all that lean muscle came as a pleasant surprise. Cole's aggressive, unfriendly expression had been softened as he bantered with Jeff.

Blackie ambled to her side and Robin leaned over to scratch the dog's ears while she continued to study his master. Cole's hair was dark and grew away from his brow, but a single lock flopped stubbornly over his forehead and he had to toss it back from his face every once in a while. It was funny how she'd never noticed that about him until now.

Jeff must've made some humorous remark because Cole threw back his head and chuckled loudly. It was the first time she'd ever heard him laugh. She suspected he didn't often give in to the impulse. A smile crowded Robin's face as Jeff started laughing, too.

In that moment the oddest thing happened. Robin felt something catch in her heart. The tug was almost physical, and she experienced a completely unfamiliar feeling of vulnerability....

"Do you need me to roll out the barbecue for you?" Jeff shouted when he saw that she was still on the porch. He'd turned his baseball cap around so the bill faced backward. While he spoke, his arm continued to work feverishly as he buffed the passenger door with his rag.

"Not...yet."

"Good, 'cause Mr. Camden needs me to finish up this side for him. We're on a tight schedule here, and I don't have time. Cole's got a dinner date at five-thirty."

"I see." Standing on the porch, dressed in her old faded jeans, with a mustard-spotted terrycloth hand towel tucked in the waistband, Robin felt as appealing as Ma Kettle. "Any time you're finished is fine."

So Cole Camden's got a date, Robin mused. *Of course he's got a date,* she told herself. Why should she care? And if watching Jeff and Cole together was going to affect her like this, it would be best to go back inside the house now.

Over dinner, all Jeff could talk about was Cole Camden. Every other sentence was Cole this and Cole that, until Robin was ready to slam her fist on the table and demand Jeff never mention their neighbor's name again.

"And the best part is, he *paid* me for helping him wax his car," Jeff continued, then stuffed the hamburger into his mouth, chewing rapidly in his enthusiasm.

"That was generous of him."

Jeff nodded happily. "Be sure and save some shortcake for him. He said not to bring it over 'cause he didn't know exactly when he'd get home. He'll stop by, he said."

"I will." But Robin doubted her neighbor would. Jeff seemed to be under the impression that Cole would show up at any time; Robin knew better. If Cole had a dinner date, he wasn't going to rush back just to taste her dessert, although she did make an excellent shortcake.

As she suspected, Cole didn't come over. Jeff grumbled about it the next morning. He was convinced Cole would've dropped by if Robin hadn't insisted Jeff go to bed at his regular time.

"I'll make shortcake again soon," Robin promised, hurrying to pack their lunches. "And when I do, you can take a piece over to him."

"All right," Jeff muttered.

That evening, when Robin returned home from work, she found Jeff playing with Blackie in Cole's backyard.

"Jeff," she cried, alarmed that Cole might discover her son on his property. He'd made it clear Jeff wasn't to go into his yard. "What are you doing at Mr. Camden's? And why aren't you at Heather's?" She walked over to the hedge and placed her hands on her hips in frustration.

"Blackie's chain got all tangled up," Jeff said, looking sheepish. "He needed my help. I told Heather it would be okay with you and..." His voice trailed off.

"He's untangled now," Robin pointed out.

"I know, but since I was here it seemed like a good time for the two of us to—"

"Play," Robin completed for him.

"Yeah," her son said, nodding eagerly. Jeff was well aware he'd done something wrong, but had difficulty admitting it.

"Mr. Camden doesn't want you in his yard, and we both know it." Standing next to the laurel hedge, Robin watched with dismay as Cole opened his back door and stepped outside. Blackie barked in greeting, and his tail swung with enough force to knock Jeff off balance.

When Cole saw Jeff in his yard, he frowned and cast an accusing glare in Robin's direction.

"Jeff said Blackie's chain was tangled," she rushed to explain.

"How'd you get over here?" Cole asked her son, and although he didn't raise his voice it was clear he was displeased. "The gate's locked and the hedge is too high for him to jump over."

Jeff stared down at the lawn. "I came through the gap in the hedge—the same one Blackie uses. I crawled through it."

"Was his chain really tangled?"

"No, sir," Jeff said in a voice so low Robin had to strain to hear him. "At least not much... I just thought, you know, that maybe he'd like company."

"I see."

"He was all alone and so was I." Jeff lifted his eyes defiantly

to his mother's, as if to suggest the fault was entirely hers. "I go
to Mrs. Lawrence's after school, but it's all girls there."

"Don't you remember what I said about coming into my
yard?" Cole asked him.

Jeff's nod was sluggish. "Yeah. You said maybe I could sometime, but not now. I thought... I hoped that since you let me
help you wax your car, you wouldn't mind."

"I mind," Cole said flatly.

"He won't do it again," Robin promised. "Will you, Jeff?"

"No," he murmured. "I'm sorry, Mr. Camden."

For a whole week Jeff kept his word. The following Monday, however, when Robin came home from the BART station,
Heather told her Jeff had mysteriously disappeared about a half
hour earlier. She assumed he'd gone home; he'd said something
about expecting a call.

Unfortunately, Robin knew exactly where to look for him,
and it wasn't at home. Even more unfortunate was the fact that
Cole's car pulled into the driveway just as she was opening
her door. Throwing aside her briefcase and purse, she rushed
through the house, jerked open the sliding glass door at the
back and raced across her yard.

Her son was nowhere to be seen, but she immediately realized he'd been with Blackie. The dog wasn't in evidence, either, and she could see Jeff's favorite baseball cap on the lawn.

"Jeff," she called, afraid to raise her voice. She sounded as
though she was suffering from a bad case of laryngitis.

Neither boy nor dog appeared.

She tried again, taking the risk of shouting for Jeff in a normal tone, praying it wouldn't attract Cole's attention. No response. Since Jeff and Blackie didn't seem to be within earshot,
she guessed they were in the fort. There was no help for it; she'd
have to go after him herself. Her only hope was that she could

hurry over to the fort, get Jeff and return to her own yard, all without being detected by Cole.

Finding the hole in the laurel proved difficult enough. The space was little more than a narrow gap between two thick plants, and for a distressing moment, Robin doubted she was slim enough to squeeze through. Finally, she lowered herself to the ground, hunched her shoulders and managed to push her way between the shrubs. Her head had just emerged when she noticed a pair of polished men's shoes on the other side. Slowly, reluctantly, she glanced up to find Cole towering above her, eyes narrowed with suspicion.

"Oh, hi," she said, striving to sound as though it was perfectly normal for her to be crawling into his yard on her hands and knees. "I suppose you're wondering what I'm doing here...."

"The question did cross my mind."

3

"It was the most embarrassing moment of my entire life," Robin repeated for the third time. She was sitting at the kitchen table, resisting the urge to hide her face in her hands and weep.

"You've already said that," Jeff grumbled.

"What possessed you to even *think* about going into Mr. Camden's yard again? Honestly, Jeff, you've been warned at least half a dozen times. What do I have to do? String barbed wire between our yards?"

Although he'd thoroughly disgraced himself, Jeff casually rotated the rim of his baseball cap between his fingers. "I said I was sorry."

A mere apology didn't begin to compensate for the humiliation Robin had suffered when Cole found her on all fours, crawling through his laurel hedge. If she lived to be an old woman, she'd never forget the look on his face.

"You put me on TV, computer and phone restriction already," her son reminded her.

That punishment could be another mistake to add to her growing list. At times like this, she wished Lenny were there to advise her. She needed him, and even after all these years, still missed him. Often, when there was no one else around, Robin found herself talking to Lenny. She wondered if she'd made the right decision, wondered what her husband would have done. Without television, computer or phone, the most attractive form of entertainment left open to her son was playing with Blackie, which was exactly what had gotten him into trouble in the first place.

"Blackie belongs to Mr. Camden," Robin felt obliged to tell him. Again.

"I know," Jeff said, "but he likes me. When I come home from school, he goes crazy. He's real glad to see me, Mom, and since there aren't very many boys in this neighborhood—" he paused as if she was to blame for that "—Blackie and I have an understanding. We're buds."

"That's all fine and dandy, but you seem to be forgetting that Blackie doesn't belong to you." Robin stood and opened the refrigerator, taking out a package of chicken breasts.

"I wish he was my dog," Jeff grumbled. In an apparent effort to make peace, he walked over to the cupboard, removed two plates and proceeded to set the table.

After dinner, while Robin was dealing with the dishes, the doorbell chimed. Jeff raced down the hallway to answer it, returning a moment later with Cole Camden at his side.

Her neighbor was the last person Robin had expected to see—and the last person she *wanted* to see.

"Mom," Jeff said, nodding toward Cole, "it's Mr. Camden."

"Hello, again," she managed, striving for a light tone, and realizing even as she spoke that she'd failed. "Would you like a cup of coffee?"

"No, thanks. I'd like to talk to both of you about—"

Not giving him the opportunity to continue, Robin nodded so hard she nearly dislocated her neck. "I really am sorry about what happened. I've had a good long talk with Jeff and, frankly, I understand why you're upset and I don't blame you. You've been very kind about this whole episode and I want you to know there won't be a repeat performance."

"From either of you?"

"Absolutely," she said, knowing her cheeks were as red as her nail polish. Did he have to remind her of the humiliating position he'd found her in earlier?

"Mom put me on TV, computer and phone restriction for an entire week," Jeff explained earnestly. "I promise not to go into your fort again, Mr. Camden. And I promise not to go in my backyard after school, either, because Blackie sees me and gets all happy and excited—and I guess I get all happy and excited, too—and that's when I do stuff I'm not supposed to."

"I see." Cole smiled down at Jeff. Robin thought it was a rather unusual smile. It didn't come from his lips as much as his eyes. Once more she witnessed a flash of pain, and another emotion she could only describe as longing. Slowly his gaze drifted to Robin. When his dark eyes met hers, she suddenly found herself short of breath.

"Actually I didn't come here to talk to you about what happened this afternoon," Cole said. "I'm going to be out of town for the next couple of days, and since Jeff and Blackie seem to get along so well I thought Jeff might be willing to look after him. That way I won't have to put him in the kennel. Naturally I'm prepared to pay your son for his time. If he agrees, I'll let him play in the fort while I'm away, as well."

Jeff's eyes grew rounder than Robin had ever seen them. "You want me to watch Blackie?" he asked, his voice incredulous. "And you're going to *pay* me? Can Blackie spend the night here? Please?"

"I guess that answers your question," Robin said, smiling.

"Blackie can stay here if it's okay with your mom," Cole

told Jeff. Then he turned to her. "Would that create a problem for you?"

Once more his eyes held hers, and once more she experienced that odd breathless sensation.

"I... No problem whatsoever."

Cole smiled then, and this time it was a smile so potent, so compelling, that it sailed straight through Robin's heart.

"Mom," Jeff hollered as he burst through the front door late Thursday afternoon. "Kelly and Blackie and I are going to the fort."

"Kelly? Surely this isn't the *girl* named Kelly, is it? Not the one who lives next door?" Robin couldn't resist teasing her son. Apparently Jeff was willing to have a "pesky" girl for a friend, after all.

Jeff shrugged as he opened the cookie jar and groped inside. He frowned, not finding any cookies and removed his hand, his fingertips covered with crumbs that he promptly licked off. "I decided Kelly isn't so bad."

"Have you got Blackie's leash?"

"We aren't going to need it. We're playing Sam Houston and Daniel Boone, and the Mexican army is attacking. I'm going to smuggle Blackie out and go for help. I can't use a leash for that."

"All right. Just don't go any farther than the Alamo and be back by dinnertime."

"But that's less than an hour!" Jeff protested.

Robin gave him one of her don't-argue-with-me looks.

"But I'm not hungry and—"

"Jeff," Robin said softly, widening her eyes just a bit, increasing the intensity of her look.

"You know, Mom," Jeff said with a cry of undisguised disgust, "you don't fight fair." He hurried out the front door with Blackie trotting faithfully behind.

Smiling to herself, Robin placed the meat loaf in the oven and carried her coffee into the backyard. The early evening air was filled with the scent of spring flowers. A gentle breeze wafted over the budding trees. How peaceful it seemed. How serene. All the years of pinching pennies to save for a house of their own seemed worth it now.

Her gaze wandered toward Cole Camden's yard. Jeff, Kelly and Blackie were inside the fort, and she could hear their raised voices every once in a while.

Cole had been on her mind a great deal during the past couple of days; she'd spent far too much time dwelling on her neighbor, thinking about his reputation in the neighborhood and the son he'd lost.

The tranquillity of the moment was shattered by the insistent ringing of the phone. Robin walked briskly to the kitchen, set her coffee on the counter and picked up the receiver.

"Hello."

"Robin, it's Angela. I'm not catching you at a bad time, am I?"

"No," Robin assured her. Angela worked in the same department as Robin, and over the years they'd become good friends. "What can I do for you?" she asked, as if she didn't already know.

"I'm calling to invite you to dinner—"

"On Saturday so I can meet your cousin Frank," Robin finished, rolling her eyes. Years before, Angela had taken on the task of finding Robin a husband. Never mind that Robin wasn't interested in meeting strangers! Angela couldn't seem to bear the thought of anyone spending her life alone and had appointed herself Robin's personal matchmaker.

"Frank's a really nice guy," Angela insisted. "I wouldn't steer you wrong, you know I wouldn't."

Robin restrained herself from reminding her friend of the disastrous date she'd arranged several weeks earlier.

"I've known Frank all my life," Angela said. "He's decent and nice."

Decent and *nice* were two words Robin had come to hate. Every man she'd ever met in this kind of arrangement was either decent or nice. Or both. Robin had come to think the two words were synonymous with dull, unattractive and emotionally manipulative. Generally these were recently divorced men who'd willingly placed themselves in the hands of family and friends to get them back into circulation.

"Didn't you tell me that Frank just got divorced?" Robin asked.

"Yes, about six months ago."

"Not interested."

"What do you mean you're not interested?" Angela demanded.

"I don't want to meet him. Angela, I know you mean well, and I apologize if I sound like a spoilsport, but I can't tell you the number of times I've had to nurse the fragile egos of recently divorced men. Most of the time they're emotional wrecks."

"But Frank's divorce was final months ago."

"If you still want me to meet him in a year, I'll be more than happy to have you arrange a dinner date."

Angela released a ragged sigh. "You're sure?"

"Positive."

There was a short disappointed silence. "Fine," Angela said in obvious frustration. "I'll see you in the morning."

"Right." Because she felt guilty, Robin added, "I'll bring the coffee."

"Okay."

Robin lingered in the kitchen, frowning. She hated it when her friends put her on the spot like this. It was difficult enough to say no, but knowing that Angela's intentions were genuine made it even worse. Just as she was struggling with another attack of guilt, the phone rang again. Angela! Her friend must have suspected that Robin's offer to buy the coffee was a sign that she was weakening.

Gathering her fortitude, Robin seized the receiver and said firmly, "I'm not interested in dating Frank. I don't want to be rude, but that's final!"

Her abrupt words were followed by a brief shocked silence, and then, "Robin, hello, this is Cole Camden."

"Cole," she gasped, closing her eyes. "Uh, I'm sorry, I thought you were someone else. A friend." She slumped against the wall and covered her face with one hand. "I have this friend who's always trying to arrange dates for me, and she doesn't take no for an answer," Robin quickly explained. "I suppose you have friends wanting to arrange dates for you, too."

"Actually, I don't."

Of course he didn't. No doubt there were women all over San Francisco who longed to go out with Cole. He didn't require a personal matchmaker. All someone like him had to do was look interested and women would flock to his side.

Her hand tightened around the receiver and a sick weightless feeling attacked the pit of her stomach. "I apologize. I didn't mean to shout in your ear."

"You didn't."

"I suppose you called to talk to Jeff," she said. "He's with Blackie and Kelly—Kelly Lawrence, the little girl who lives on the other side of us."

"I see."

"He'll be back in a few minutes, if you'd like to call then. Or if you prefer, I could run and get him, but he said something about sneaking out and going for help and—"

"I beg your pardon? What's Jeff doing?"

"Oh, they're playing in the fort, pretending they're Houston and Daniel Boone. The fort is now the Alamo."

He chuckled. "I see. No, don't worry about chasing after him. I'd hate to see you waylaid by the Mexican army."

"I don't think I'd care for that myself."

"How's everything going?"

"Fine," she assured him.

She must have sounded rushed because he said, "You're sure this isn't a bad time? If you have company..."

"No, I'm here alone."

Another short silence, which was broken by Cole. "So everything's okay with Blackie? He isn't causing you any problems, is he?"

"Oh, no, everything's great. Jeff lavishes him with attention. The two of them are together practically every minute. Blackie even sleeps beside his bed."

"As you said, Jeff has a way with animals," Cole murmured.

His laugh, so tender and warm, was enough to jolt her. She had to pinch herself to remember that Cole was a prominent attorney, wealthy and respected. She was an accountant. A junior accountant at that.

The only thing they had in common was the fact that they lived next door to each other and her son was crazy about his dog.

The silence returned, only this time it had a relaxed, almost comfortable quality, as though neither wanted the conversation to end.

"Since Jeff isn't around," Cole said reluctantly, "I'll let you go."

"I'll tell him you phoned."

"It wasn't anything important," Cole said. "Just wanted to let you know when I'll be back—late Friday afternoon. Will you be home?"

"Of course."

"You never know, your friend might talk you into going out with Fred after all."

"It's Frank, and there isn't a snowball's chance in hell."

"Famous last words!"

"See you Friday," she said with a short laugh.

"Right. Goodbye, Robin."

"Goodbye, Cole."

Long after the call had ended, Robin stood with her hand on the receiver, a smile touching her eyes and her heart.

"Mom, I need my lunch money," Jeff yelled from the bottom of the stairs.

"I'll be down in a minute," she said. Mornings were hectic. In order to get to the Glen Park BART station on time, Robin had to leave the house half an hour before Jeff left for school.

"What did you have for breakfast?" she hollered as she put the finishing touches on her makeup.

"Frozen waffles," Jeff shouted back. "And don't worry, I didn't drown them in syrup and I rinsed off the plate before I put it in the dishwasher."

"Rinsed it off or let Blackie lick it for you?" she asked, as she hurried down the stairs. Her son was busy at the sink and didn't turn around to look at her.

"Blackie, honestly, is that maple syrup on your nose?"

At the sound of his name, the Labrador trotted over to her. Robin took a moment to stroke his thick fur before fumbling for her wallet to give Jeff his lunch money.

"Hey, Mom, you look nice."

"Don't act so surprised," she grumbled. "I'm leaving now."

"Okay," Jeff said without the slightest bit of concern. "You won't be late tonight, will you? Remember Mr. Camden's coming back."

"I remember, and no, I won't be late." She grabbed her purse and her packed lunch, putting it in her briefcase, and headed for the front door.

Even before Robin arrived at the subway station, she knew the day would drag. Fridays always did.

She was right. At six, when the subway pulled into the station, Robin felt as though she'd been away forty hours instead of the usual nine. She found herself hurrying and didn't fully understand why. Cole was scheduled to return, but that didn't have anything to do with her, did it? His homecoming wasn't anything to feel nervous about, nor any reason to be pleased. He was her neighbor, and more Jeff's friend than hers.

The first thing Robin noticed when she arrived on Orchard Street was Cole's Porsche parked in the driveway of his house.

"Hi, Mom," Jeff called as he raced across the lawn between the two houses. "Mr. Camden's back!"

"So I see." She removed her keys from her purse and opened the front door.

Jeff followed her inside. "He said he'd square up with me later. I wanted to invite him to dinner, but I didn't think I should without asking you first."

"That was smart," she said, depositing her jacket in the closet on her way to the kitchen. She opened the refrigerator and took out the thawed hamburger and salad makings.

"How was your day?" she asked.

Jeff sat down at the table and propped his elbows on it. "All right, I guess. What are you making for dinner?"

"Taco salad."

"How about just tacos? I don't get why you want to ruin a perfectly good dinner by putting green stuff in it."

Robin paused. "I thought you liked my taco salad."

Jeff shrugged. "It's all right, but I'd rather have just tacos."

Once that was made clear, he cupped his chin in his hands. "Can we rent a movie tonight?"

"I suppose," Robin returned absently as she added the meat to the onions browning in the skillet.

"But I get to choose this time," Jeff insisted. "Last week you picked a musical." He wrinkled his nose as if to suggest that being forced to watch men and women sing and dance was the most disgusting thing he'd ever had to endure.

"Perhaps we can find a compromise," she said.

Jeff nodded. "As long as it doesn't have a silly love story in it."

"Okay," Robin said, doing her best not to betray her amusement. Their difference in taste when it came to movies was legendary. Jeff's favorite was an older kids' film, *Scooby Doo*, that he watched over and over, which Robin found boring, to say the least. Unfortunately, her son was equally put off by the sight of men and women staring longingly into each other's eyes.

The meat was simmering in the skillet when Robin glanced up and noted that her son was looking surprisingly thoughtful. "Is something troubling you?" she asked, and popped a thin tomato slice into her mouth.

"Have you ever noticed that Mr. Camden never mentions he had a son?"

Robin set the paring knife on the cutting board. "It's probably painful for him to talk about."

Jeff nodded, and, with the innocent wisdom of youth, he whispered, "That man needs someone."

The meal was finished, and Robin was standing in front of the sink rinsing off the dinner plates when the doorbell rang. Robin knew it had to be Cole.

"I'll get it," Jeff cried as he raced past her at breakneck speed. He threw open the door. "Hi, Mr. Camden!" he said eagerly.

By this time Robin had smoothed her peach-colored sweater

over her hips and placed a friendly—but not too friendly—smile on her face. At the last second, she ran her fingers through her hair, striving for the casual I-didn't-go-to-any-trouble look, then wondered at her irrational behavior. Cole wasn't coming over to see *her*.

Robin could hear Jeff chatting away at ninety miles an hour, telling Cole they were renting a movie and how Robin insisted that every show he saw had to have the proper rating, which he claimed was totally ridiculous. He went on to explain that she considered choosing the film a mother's job and apparently a mere kid didn't have rights. When there was a pause in the conversation, she could envision Jeff rolling his eyes dramatically.

Taking a deep breath, she stepped into the entryway and smiled. "Hello, Cole."

"Robin."

Their eyes met instantly. Robin's first coherent thought was that a woman could get lost in eyes that dark and not even care. She swallowed and lowered her gaze.

"Would you like a cup of coffee?" she asked, having difficulty dragging the words out of her mouth.

"If it isn't too much trouble."

"It isn't." Or it wouldn't be if she could stop her heart from pounding so furiously.

"Where's Blackie?" Jeff asked, opening the screen door and glancing outside.

"I didn't bring him over. I thought you'd be tired of him by now."

"Tired of Blackie?" Jeff cried. "You've got to be kidding!"

"I guess I should've known better," Cole teased.

Robin returned to the kitchen and took mugs from the cupboard, using these few minutes to compose herself.

The screen door slammed, and a moment later Cole appeared in her kitchen. "Jeff went to my house to get Blackie."

She smiled and nodded. "Do you take cream or sugar?" she asked over her shoulder.

"Just black, thanks."

Robin normally drank hers the same way. But for some reason she couldn't begin to fathom, she added a generous teaspoonful of sugar to her own, stirring briskly as though she feared it wouldn't dissolve.

"I hope your trip went well," she said, carrying both mugs into the family room, where Cole had chosen to sit.

"Very well."

"Good." She sat a safe distance from him, across the room in a wooden rocker, and balanced her mug on her knee. "Everything around here went without a hitch, but I'm afraid Jeff may have spoiled Blackie a bit."

"From what he said, they did everything but attend school together."

"Having the dog has been wonderful for him. I appreciate your giving Jeff this opportunity. Not only does it satisfy his need for a dog, but it's taught him about responsibility."

The front door opened and the canine subject of their conversation shot into the room, followed by Jeff, who was grinning from ear to ear. "Mom, could Mr. Camden stay and watch the movie with us?"

"Ah…" Caught off guard, Robin didn't know what to say. After being away from home for several days, watching a movie with his neighbors probably held a low position on Cole's list of priorities.

To Robin's astonishment, Cole's eyes searched hers as though seeking her approval.

"You'd be welcome… I mean, you can stay if you'd like, unless…unless there's something else you'd rather do," she stammered. "I mean, I'd…we'd like it if you did, but…" She let whatever else she might have said fade away. She was making a mess of this, and every time she tried to smooth it over, she only stuck her foot further down her throat.

"What movie did you rent?"

"We haven't yet," Jeff explained. "Mom and me had to come to an understanding first. She likes mushy stuff and gets all bent out of shape if there's an explosion or anything. You wouldn't believe the love story she made me watch last Friday night." His voice dripped with renewed disgust.

"How about if you and I go rent the movie while your mother and Blackie make the popcorn?"

Jeff's blue eyes brightened immediately. "That'd be great, wouldn't it, Mom?"

"Sure," she agreed, and was rewarded by Jeff's smile.

Jeff and Cole left a few minutes later. It was on the tip of her tongue to give Cole instructions on the type of movie appropriate for a ten-year-old boy, but she swallowed her concerns, willing to trust his judgment. Standing on the porch, she watched as they climbed inside Cole's expensive sports car. She pressed her hand to her throat, grateful when Cole leaned over the front seat and snapped Jeff's seat belt snugly in place. Suddenly Cole looked at her; she raised her hand in farewell, and he did the same. It was a simple gesture, yet Robin felt as if they'd communicated so much more.

"Come on, Blackie," Robin said, "let's go start the popcorn." The Lab trailed behind her as she returned to the kitchen. She placed a packet of popcorn in the microwave. It was while she was waiting for the kernels to start popping that the words slipped from her mouth.

"Well, Lenny, what do you think?" Talking to her dead husband came without conscious thought. It certainly wasn't that she expected him to answer. Whenever she spoke to him, the words came spontaneously from the deep well of love they'd once shared. She supposed she should feel foolish doing it, but so many times over the long years since his death she'd felt his presence. Robin assumed that the reason she talked to him came from her need to discuss things with the one other person who'd loved her son as much as she did. In the beginning she was sure she needed to visit a psychiatrist or arrange for grief counseling, but later she convinced herself that every widow went through this in one form or another.

"He's grown so much in the past year, hasn't he?" she asked, and smiled. "Meeting Cole has been good for Jeff. He lost a child, you know, and I suppose having Jeff move in next door answers a need for him, too."

About ten minutes later, she'd transferred the popcorn to a bowl and set out drinks. Jeff and Cole came back with a movie that turned out to be an excellent compromise—a teen comedy that was surprisingly witty and entertaining.

Jeff sprawled on the carpet munching popcorn with Blackie by his side. Cole sat on the sofa and Robin chose the rocking chair. She removed her shoes and tucked her feet beneath her. She was enjoying the movie; in fact, several times she found herself laughing out loud.

Cole and Jeff laughed, too. The sounds were contrasting— one deep and masculine, the other young and pleasantly boyish—yet they harmonized, blending with perfect naturalness.

Soon Robin found herself watching Jeff and Cole more than the movie. The two...no, the three of them had grown comfortable together. Robin didn't try to read any significance into that. Doing so could prove emotionally dangerous, but the thought flew into her mind and refused to leave.

The credits were rolling when Cole pointed to Jeff, whose head was resting on his arms, his eyes closed.

"He's asleep," Cole said softly.

Robin smiled and nodded. She got up to bring the empty popcorn bowl into the kitchen. Cole stood, too, taking their glasses to the sink, then returned to the family room to remove the DVD.

"Do you want me to carry him upstairs for you?" he asked, glancing down at the slumbering Jeff.

"No," she whispered. "When he wakes up in the morning, he'll think you treated him like a little kid. Egos are fragile at ten."

"I suppose you're right."

The silence seemed to resound. Without Jeff, awake and chattering, as a buffer between them, Robin felt clumsy and self-conscious around Cole.

"It was nice of you to stay," she said, more to fill the silence than because she had anything important to communicate. "It meant a lot to Jeff."

Jeff had told her Cole had an active social life. Heather Lawrence had confirmed it by casually letting it drop that Cole was often away on weekends. Robin wasn't entirely sure what to think about it all. But if there was a woman in his life, that was his business, not hers.

"It meant a lot to me, too," he said, returning the DVD to its case.

The kitchen and family room, actually quite spacious, felt close and intimate with Cole standing only a few feet away.

Robin's fingers were shaking as she placed the bowls and soda glasses in the dishwasher. She tried to come up with some bright and witty comment, but her mind was blank.

"I should be going."

Was that reluctance she heard in his voice? Somehow Robin doubted it; probably wishful thinking on her part. Half of her wanted to push him out the door and the other half didn't want him to leave at all. But there really wasn't any reason for him to stay. "I'll walk you to the door."

"Blackie." Cole called for his dog. "It's time to go."

The Lab didn't look pleased. He took his own sweet time lumbering to his feet and stretching before trotting to Cole's side.

Robin was about to open the door when she realized she hadn't thanked Cole for getting the movie. She turned, and his dark eyes delved into hers. Whatever thoughts had been taking shape fled like leaves scattering in the wind. She tried to smile, however weakly, but it was difficult when he was looking at her so intently. His gaze slipped to her mouth, and in a nervous movement, she moistened her lips. Before she was fully aware of how it had happened, Cole's fingers were in her hair and he was urging her mouth to meet his.

His eyes held hers, as if he expected her to stop him, then they slowly closed and their lips touched. Robin's eyes drifted shut, but that was the only response she made.

He kissed her again, even more gently than the first time. Robin moaned softly, not in protest, but in wonder and surprise. It had been so long since a man had kissed her like this. So long that she'd forgotten the wealth of sensations a mere kiss could evoke. Her hands crept to his chest, and her fingers curled into the soft wool of his sweater. Hesitantly, timidly, her lips trembled beneath his. Cole sighed and took full possession of her mouth.

Robin sighed, too. The tears that welled in her eyes were a shock. She was at a loss to explain them. They slipped down her face, and it wasn't until then that she realized she was crying.

Cole must have felt her tears at the same moment, because he abruptly broke off the kiss and raised his head. His eyes searched hers as his thumb brushed the moisture from her cheek.

"Did I hurt you?" The question was whispered.

She shook her head vehemently.

"Then why...?"

"I don't know." She couldn't explain something she didn't

understand herself. Rubbing her eyes, she attempted to wipe
away the evidence. She forced a smile. "I'm nothing if not
novel," she said with brittle cheerfulness. "I don't imagine many
women break into tears when you kiss them."

Cole looked as confused as Robin felt.

"Don't worry about it. I'm fine." She wanted to reassure him,
but was having too much trouble analyzing her own reactions.

"Let's sit down and talk about this."

"No," she said quietly. Adamantly. That was the last thing
she wanted. "I'm sorry, Cole. I really am. This has never happened before and I don't understand it either."

"But..."

"The best thing we can do is chalk it up to a long work-
week."

"It's not that simple."

"Probably, but I'd prefer to just forget it. Please?"

"Are you all right?"

"Emotionally or physically?" She tried to joke, but didn't
succeed.

"Both."

He was so serious, so concerned, that it was all Robin could
do not to dissolve into fresh tears. She'd made a world-class
fool of herself with this man, not once but twice.

This man, who had suffered such a tremendous loss himself,
was so gentle with her, and instead of helping, that only made
matters worse. "I'm sorry, really I am," she said raggedly, "but
perhaps you should go home now."

4

"You know what I'm in the mood for?" Angela Lansky said as she sat on the edge of Robin's desk early Monday afternoon.

"I certainly hope you're going to say food," Robin teased. They had shared the same lunch hour and were celebrating a cost-of-living raise by eating out.

"A shrimp salad," Angela elaborated. "Heaped six inches high with big fresh shrimp."

"I was thinking Chinese food myself," Robin said, "but, now that you mention it, shrimp salad sounds good." She opened her bottom drawer and took out her purse.

Angela was short and enviably thin with thick brown hair that fell in natural waves over her shoulders. She used clips to hold the abundant curls away from her face and looked closer to twenty than the thirty-five Robin knew her to be.

"I know just the place," Angela was saying. "The Blue Crab. It's on the wharf and worth the trouble of getting there."

"I'm game," Robin said.

They stopped at the bank, then headed for the restaurant. They decided to catch the Market Street cable car to Fisherman's Wharf and joined the quickly growing line.

"So how's the kid doing?" Angela asked. She and her sales-man husband didn't plan to have children themselves, but Angela enjoyed hearing about Jeff.

"He signed up for baseball through the park program and starts practice this week. I think it'll be good for him. He was lonely this weekend now that Blackie's back with Cole."

"But isn't Blackie over at your place as much as before?" Angela asked.

Robin shook her head. "Cole left early Saturday morning and took the dog with him. Jeff moped around for most of the weekend."

"Where'd your handsome neighbor go?"

"How am I supposed to know?" Robin asked with a soft laugh, hiding her disappointment at his disappearance. "Cole doesn't clear his schedule with me."

The way he'd left—without a word of farewell or expla-nation—still hurt. It was the kind of hurt that came from re-alizing what a complete fool she'd made of herself with this worldly, sophisticated man. He'd kissed her and she'd started crying. Good grief, he was probably doing backflips in order to avoid seeing her again.

"Do you think Cole was with a woman?"

"That's none of my business!"

"But I thought your neighbor said Cole spent his weekends with a woman."

Robin didn't remember mentioning that to Angela, but she obviously had, along with practically everything else. Robin had tried to convince herself that confiding in Angela about Cole was a clever way of thwarting her friend's matchmaking efforts. Unfortunately, the whole thing had backfired in her face. In the end, the last person she wanted to talk about was Cole, but of course Angela persisted in questioning her.

"Well?" Angela demanded. "Did he spend his weekend with a woman or not?"

"What he does with his time is his business, not mine," Robin reiterated. She pretended not to care. But she did. Too much. She'd promised herself she wasn't going to put any stock in the kiss or the powerful attraction she felt for Cole. Within the space of one evening, she'd wiped out every pledge she'd made to herself. She hadn't said anything to Jeff—how could she?—but she was just as disappointed as he was that Cole had left for the weekend.

"I was hoping something might develop between the two of you," Angela murmured. "Since you're obviously not interested in meeting Frank, it would be great if you got something going with your neighbor."

Robin cast her a plaintive look that suggested otherwise. "Cole Camden lives in the fanciest house in the neighborhood. He's a partner in the law firm of Blackwell, Burns and Dailey, which we both know is one of the most prestigious in San Francisco. And he drives a car with a name I can barely pronounce. Now, what would someone like that see in me?"

"Lots of things," Angela said.

Robin snickered. "I hate to disillusion you, my friend, but the only thing Cole Camden and I have in common is the fact that my small yard borders his massive one."

"Maybe," Angela agreed, raising her eyebrows. "But I could tell you were intrigued by him the very first time you mentioned his name."

"That's ridiculous!"

"It isn't," Angela insisted. "I've watched you with other men over the past few years. A guy will show some interest, and at first everything looks peachy-keen. You'll go out with him a couple of times, maybe even more, but before anything seri-

ous can develop you've broken off the relationship without really giving it a chance."

Robin didn't have much of an argument, since that was true,
but she made a token protest just the same. "I can't help it if I
have high standards."

"High standards!" Angela choked back a laugh. "That's got
to be the understatement of the century. You'd find fault with
Prince Charming."

Robin rolled her eyes, but couldn't hold back a smile. Angela was right, although that certainly hadn't slowed her matchmaking efforts.

"From the time you started talking about your neighbor,"
Angela went on, "I noticed something different about you, and
frankly I'm thrilled. In all the years we've known each other,
this is the first time I can remember you giving a man this much
attention. Until now, it's always been the other way around."

"I'm not interested in Cole," she mumbled. "Oh, honestly,
Angela, I can't imagine where you come up with these ideas. I
think you've been reading too many romance novels."

Angela waved her index finger under Robin's nose. "Listen,
I'm on to you. You're not going to divert me with humor, or
weasel your way out of admitting it. You can't fool me—you're
attracted to this guy and it's scaring you to death. Right?"

The two women gazed solemnly at each other, both too
stubborn to admit defeat. Under the force of her friend's un-
yielding determination, Robin was the one who finally gave in.

"All right!" she cried, causing the other people waiting for
the cable car to turn and stare. "All right," she repeated in a
whisper. "I like Cole, but I don't understand it."

Angela's winged brows arched speculatively. "He's attractive
and wealthy, crazy about your son, generous and kind, and you
haven't figured it out yet?"

"He's also way out of my league."

"I wish you'd quit categorizing yourself. You make it sound as though you aren't good enough for him, and that's not true."

Robin just sighed.

The cable car appeared then, its bell clanging as it drew to a stop. Robin and Angela boarded and held on tight.

Jeff loved hearing about the history of the cable cars, and Robin loved telling him the story. Andrew Hallidie had designed them because of his deep love for horses. Day after day, Hallidie had watched them struggling up and down the treacherous hills of the city, dragging heavy burdens. Prompted by his concern for the animals, he'd invented the cable cars that are pulled by a continuously moving underground cable. To Jeff and to many others, Andrew Hallidie was a hero.

Robin and Angela were immediately caught up in the festive atmosphere of Fisherman's Wharf. The rows of fishing boats along the dock bobbed gently with the tide, and although Robin had never been to the Mediterranean the view reminded her of pictures she'd seen of French and Italian harbors.

The day was beautiful, the sky blue and cloudless, the ocean sparkling the way it did on a summer day. This spring had been exceptionally warm. It wasn't uncommon for Robin to wear a winter coat in the middle of July, especially in the mornings, when there was often a heavy fog accompanied by a cool mist from the Bay. But this spring, they'd experienced some lovely weather, including today's.

"Let's eat outside," Angela suggested, pointing at a free table on the patio.

"Sure," Robin agreed cheerfully. The Blue Crab was a popular restaurant and one of several that lined the wharf. More elegant dining took place inside, but the pavement was crowded with diners interested in a less formal meal.

Once they were seated, Robin and Angela were waited on quickly and ordered their shrimp salads.

"So," Angela said, spreading out her napkin while closely studying Robin. "Tell me more about your neighbor."

Robin froze. "I thought we were finished with this subject. In case you hadn't noticed, I'd prefer not to discuss Cole."

"I noticed, but unfortunately I was just getting started. It's unusual for you to be so keen on a man, and I know hardly anything about him. It's time, Robin Masterson, to tell all."

"There's nothing to tell. I already told you everything I care to," Robin said crossly. She briefly wondered if Angela had guessed that Cole had kissed her. At the rate things were going, she'd probably end up admitting it before lunch was over. Robin wished she could think of some surefire way to change the subject.

Tall glasses of iced tea arrived and Robin was reaching for a packet of sugar when she heard a masculine chuckle that reminded her instantly of Cole. She paused, savoring the husky sound. Without really meaning to, she found herself scanning the tables, certain Cole was seated a short distance away.

"He's here," she whispered before she could guard her tongue.

"Who?"

"Cole. I just heard him laugh."

Pushing back her chair in order to get a fuller view of the inside dining area, Robin searched through a sea of faces, but didn't find her neighbor's.

"What's he look like?" Angela whispered.

Ten different ways to describe him shot through her mind. To say he had brown hair, neatly trimmed, coffee-colored eyes and was about six foot two seemed inadequate. To add that he was strikingly attractive further complicated the problem.

"Tell me what to look for," Angela insisted. "Come on, Robin, this is a golden opportunity. I want to check this guy out. I'm not letting a chance like this slip through my fingers. I'll bet he's gorgeous."

Reluctantly, Robin continued to scan the diners, but she didn't see anyone who remotely resembled Cole. Even if she did see him, she wasn't sure she'd point him out to Angela, although she hated to lie. Perhaps she wouldn't have to. Perhaps she'd imagined the whole thing. It would've been easy enough to do. Angela's questions had brought Cole to the forefront of her mind; they'd just been discussing him and it was only natural for her to—

Her heart pounded against her rib cage as Cole walked out of the restaurant foyer. He wasn't alone. A tall, slender woman with legs that seemed to go all the way up to her neck and a figure as shapely and athletic as a dancer's was walking beside him. She was blond and, in a word, gorgeous. Robin felt as appealing as milkweed in comparison. The woman's arm was delicately tucked in Cole's, and she was smiling up at him with eyes big and blue enough to turn heads.

Robin's stomach tightened into a hard knot.

"Robin," Angela said anxiously, leaning toward her, "what is it?"

Cole was strolling past them, and in an effort not to be seen, Robin stuck her head under the table pretending to search for her purse.

"Robin," Angela muttered, lowering her own head and peeking under the linen tablecloth, "what's the matter with you?"

"Nothing." Other than the fact that she was going to be ill. Other than the fact that she'd never been more outclassed in her life. "I'm fine, really." A smile trembled on her pale lips.

"Then what are you doing with your head under the table?"

"I don't suppose you'd believe my napkin fell off my lap?"

"No."

A pair of shiny black shoes appeared. Slowly, Robin twisted her head and glanced upward, squinting at the flash of sunlight that nearly blinded her. It was their waiter. Heaving a giant sigh of relief, Robin straightened. The first thing she noticed was that Cole had left.

The huge shrimp salads were all but forgotten as Angela, eyes narrowed and elbows braced on the table, confronted her. "You saw him, didn't you?"

There was no point in pretending otherwise, so Robin nodded.

"He was with someone?"

"Not just someone! The most beautiful woman in the world was draped all over his arm."

"That doesn't mean anything," Angela said. "Don't you think you're jumping to conclusions? Honestly, she could've been anyone."

"Uh-huh." Any fight left in Robin had long since evaporated. There was nothing like seeing Cole with another woman to bring her firmly back to earth—which was right where she belonged.

"She could've been a client."

"She probably was," Robin concurred, reaching for her fork. She didn't know how she was going to manage one shrimp, let alone a whole plate of them. Heaving another huge sigh, she plowed her fork into the heap of plump pink darlings. It was then that she happened to glance across the street. Cole and Ms. Gorgeous were walking along the sidewalk, engrossed in their conversation. For some reason, known only to the fates, Cole looked across the street at that very moment. His gaze instantly narrowed on her. He stopped midstride as though shocked to have seen her.

Doing her best to pretend she hadn't seen *him,* Robin took another bite of her salad and chewed vigorously. When she glanced up again, Cole was gone.

"Mom, I need someone to practice with," Jeff pleaded. He stood forlornly in front of her, a baseball mitt in one hand, a ball in the other.

"I thought Jimmy was practicing with you."

"He had to go home and then Kelly threw me a few pitches, but she had to go home, too. Besides, she's a girl."

"And what am I?" Robin muttered.

"You're a mom," Jeff answered, clearly not understanding her question. "Don't you see? I've got a chance of making pitcher for our team if I can get someone to practice with me."

"All right," Robin agreed, grumbling a bit. She set aside her knitting and followed her son into the backyard. He handed her his old catcher's mitt, which barely fit her hand, and positioned her with her back to Cole's yard.

Robin hadn't been able to completely avoid her neighbor in the past week, but she'd succeeded in keeping her distance. For that matter, he didn't seem all that eager to run into her, either. Just as well, she supposed.

He stayed on his side of the hedge. She stayed on hers.

If he passed her on his way to work, he gave an absent wave. She returned the gesture.

If they happened to be outside at the same time, they exchanged smiles and a polite greeting, but nothing more. It seemed, although Robin couldn't be sure, that Cole spent less time outside than usual. So did she.

"Okay," Jeff called, running to the end of their yard. "Squat down."

"I beg your pardon?" Robin shouted indignantly. "I agreed to play catch with you. You didn't say anything about having to squat!"

"Mom," Jeff said impatiently, "think about it. If I'm going to be the pitcher, you've got to be the catcher, and catchers have to be low to the ground."

Complaining under her breath, Robin sank to her knees, worried the grass would stain her jeans.

Jeff tossed his arms into the air in frustration. "Not like that!"

He said something else that Robin couldn't quite make out—something about why couldn't moms be guys.

Reluctantly, Robin assumed the posture he wanted, but she didn't know how long her knees would hold out. Jeff wound up his arm and let loose with a fastball. Robin closed her eyes, stuck out the mitt and was so shocked when she caught the ball that she toppled backward into the wet grass.

"You all right?" Jeff yelled, racing toward her.

"I'm fine, I'm fine," she shouted back, discounting his concern as she brushed the dampness from the seat of her jeans. She righted herself, assumed the position and waited for the second ball.

Jeff ran back to his mock pitcher's mound, gripped both hands behind his back and stepped forward. Robin closed her eyes again. Nothing happened. She opened her eyes cautiously, puzzled about the delay. Then she recalled the hand movements she'd seen pitchers make and flexed her fingers a few times.

Jeff straightened, placed his hand on his hip and stared at her. "What was that for?"

"It's a signal... I think. I've seen catchers do it on TV."

"Mom, leave that kind of stuff to the real ballplayers. All I want you to do is catch my pitches and throw them back. It might help if you kept your eyes open, too."

"I'll try."

"Thank you."

Robin suspected she heard a tinge of sarcasm in her son's voice. She didn't know what he was getting so riled up about; she was doing her best. It was at times like these that she most longed for Lenny. When her parents had still lived in the area, her dad had stepped in whenever her son needed a father's guiding hand, but they'd moved to Arizona a couple of years ago. Lenny's family had been in Texas since before his death. Robin hadn't seen them since the funeral, although Lenny's mother faithfully sent Jeff birthday and Christmas gifts.

"You ready?" Jeff asked.

"Ready." Squinting, Robin stuck out the mitt, prepared to do her best to catch the stupid ball, since it seemed so important to her son. Once more he swung his arms behind him and stepped forward. Then he stood there, poised to throw, for what seemed an eternity. Her knees were beginning to ache.

"Are you going to throw the ball, or are you going to stare at me all night?" she asked after a long moment had passed.

"That does it!" Jeff tossed his mitt to the ground. "You just broke my concentration."

"Well, for crying out loud, what's there to concentrate on?" Robin grimaced, rising awkwardly to her feet. Her legs had started to lose feeling.

"This isn't working," Jeff cried, stalking toward her. "Kelly's only in third grade and she does a better job than you do."

Robin decided to ignore that comment. She pressed her hand to the small of her back, hoping to ease the ache she'd begun to feel.

"Hello, Robin. Jeff."

Cole's voice came at her like a hangman's noose. She straightened abruptly and winced at the sharp pain shooting through her back.

"Hi, Mr. Camden!" Jeff shouted as though Cole was a conquering hero returned from the war. He dashed across the yard, past Robin and straight to the hedge. "Where have you been all week?"

"I've been busy." He might've been talking to Jeff, but his eyes were holding Robin's. She tried to look away—but she couldn't.

His eyes told her she was avoiding him.

Hers answered that he'd been avoiding *her*.

"I guess you *have* been busy," Jeff was saying. "I haven't seen you in days and days and days." Blackie squeezed through the hedge and Jeff fell to his knees, his arms circling the dog's neck.

"So how's the baseball going?" Cole asked.

Jeff sent his mother a disgusted look, then shrugged. "All right, I guess."

"What position are you playing?"

"Probably outfield. I had a chance to make pitcher, but I can't seem to get anyone who knows how to catch a ball to practice with me. Kelly tries, but she's a girl and I hate to say it, but my mother's worthless."

"I did my best," Robin protested.

"She catches with her eyes closed," Jeff said.

"How about if you toss a few balls at me?" Cole offered.

Jeff blinked as if he thought he'd misunderstood. "You want me to throw you a few pitches? You're sure?"

"Positive."

The look on her son's face defied description as Cole jumped over the hedge. Jeff's smile stretched from one side of his face to the other as he tore to the opposite end of the yard, unwilling to question Cole's generosity a second time.

For an awkward moment, Robin stayed where she was, not knowing what to say. She looked up at Cole, her emotions soaring—and tangling like kites in a brisk wind. She was deeply grateful for his offer, but also confused. Thrilled by his presence, but also frightened.

"Mom?" Jeff muttered. "In case you hadn't noticed, you're in the way."

"Are you going to make coffee and invite me in for a chat later?" Cole asked quietly.

Her heart sank. "I have some things that need to be done, and...and..."

"Mom?" Jeff shouted.

"I think it's time you and I talked," Cole said, staring straight into her eyes.

"Mom, are you moving or not?"

Robin looked frantically over her shoulder. "Oh...oh, sorry," she whispered, blushing. She hurried away, then stood on the patio watching as the ball flew across the yard.

After catching a dozen of Jeff's pitches, Cole got up and walked over to her son. They spoke for several minutes. Reluctantly, Robin decided it was time to go back in.

She busied herself wiping kitchen counters that were already perfectly clean and tried to stop thinking about the beautiful woman she'd seen with Cole on the Wharf.

Jeff stormed into the house. "Mom, would it be okay if Mr. Camden strings up an old tire from the apple tree?"

"I suppose. Why?"

"He said I can use it to practice pitching, and I wouldn't have to bother you or Kelly."

"I don't think I have an old tire."

"Don't worry, Mr. Camden has one." He ran outside again before she could comment.

Jeff was back in the yard with Cole a few minutes later, far too soon to suit Robin. She forced a weak smile. That other woman was a perfect damsel to his knight in shining armor, she thought wryly. Robin, on the other hand, considered herself more of a court jester.

Her musings were abruptly halted when Cole walked into the kitchen, trailed by her son.

"Isn't it time for your bath, Jeff?" Cole asked pointedly.

It looked for a minute as though the boy was going to argue. For the first time in recent memory, Robin would've welcomed some resistance from him.

"I guess," he said. Bathing was about as popular as homework.

"I didn't make any coffee," Robin said in a small voice. She simply couldn't look at Cole and not see the beautiful blonde on his arm.

"That's fine. I'm more interested in talking, anyway," he said. He walked purposefully to the table and pulled out a chair, then gestured for her to sit down.

Robin didn't. Instead, she frowned at her watch. "My goodness, will you look at the time?"

"No." Cole headed toward her, and Robin backed slowly into the counter.

"We're going talk about that kiss," Cole warned her.

"Please don't," she whispered. "It meant nothing! We'd both had a hectic week. We were tired.... I wasn't myself."

Cole's eyes burned into hers. "Then why did you cry?"

"I...don't know. Believe me, if I knew I'd tell you, but I don't. Can't we just forget it ever happened?"

His shoulders rose in a sigh as he threaded his long fingers through his hair. "That's exactly what I've tried to do all week. Unfortunately it didn't work."

5

"I've put it completely out of my mind," Robin said, resuming her string of untruths. "I wish you'd do the same."

"I can't. Trust me, I've tried," Cole told her softly. He smiled and his sensuous mouth widened as his eyes continued to hold hers. The messages were back. Less than subtle messages. *You can't fool me,* they said, and *I didn't want to admit it either.*

"I…"

The sense of expectancy was written across his face. For the life of her, Robin couldn't tear her eyes from him.

She didn't remember stepping into his arms, but suddenly she was there, encompassed by his warmth, feeling more sheltered and protected than she had since her husband's death. This comforting sensation spun itself around her as he wove his fingers into her hair, cradling her head. He hadn't kissed her yet, but Robin felt the promise of it in every part of her.

Deny it though she might, she knew in her heart how badly she wanted Cole to hold her, to kiss her. He must have read the longing in her eyes, because he lowered his mouth to hers, stopping a fraction of an inch from her parted lips. She could feel warm moist breath, could feel a desire so powerful that she wanted to drown in his kiss.

From a reservoir of strength she didn't know she possessed, Robin managed to shake her head.

"Please," he whispered just before his mouth settled firmly over hers.

His kiss was the same as it had been before, only more intense. More potent. Robin felt rocked to the very core of her being. Against her will, she felt herself surrendering to him. She felt herself forgetting to breathe. She felt herself weakening.

His mouth moved to her jaw, dropping small, soft kisses there. She sighed. She couldn't help it. Cole's touch was magic. Unable to stop herself, she turned her head, yearning for him to trace a row of kisses on the other side, as well. He complied.

Robin sighed again, her mind filled with dangerous, sensuous thoughts. It felt so good in his arms, so warm and safe... but she knew the feeling was deceptive. She'd seen him with another woman, one far more suited to him than she could ever be. For days she'd been tormented by the realization that the woman in the restaurant was probably the one he spent his weekends with.

She pulled away, but even to her, the action held little conviction.

In response, Cole brought a long slow series of featherlight kisses to her lips. Robin trembled, breathless.

"Why are you fighting this?" he whispered. His hands framed her face, his thumbs stroking her cheeks. They were damp and she hadn't even known she was crying.

Suddenly she heard footsteps bounding down the stairs. At the thought of Jeff finding her in Cole's arms, she abruptly broke away and turned to stare out the darkened window, hoping for a moment to compose herself.

Jeff burst into the room. "Did you kiss her yet?" he demanded. Not waiting for an answer, Jeff ran toward Robin and grabbed her by the hand. "Well, Mom, what do you think?"

"About...what?"

"Mr. Camden kissing you. He did, didn't he?"

It was on the tip of her tongue to deny the whole thing, but she decided to brazen it out. "You want me to rate him? Like on a scale of one to ten?"

Jeff blinked, uncertain. His questioning glance flew to Cole.

"She was a ten," Cole said, grinning.

"A...high seven," Robin returned.

"A high seven!" Jeff cried, casting her a disparaging look. He shook his head and walked over to Cole. "She's out of practice," he said confidingly. "Doesn't know how to rate guys. Give her a little time and she'll come around."

"Jeff," Robin gasped, astounded to be having this kind of discussion with her son, let alone Cole, who was looking all too smug.

"She hardly goes out at all," Jeff added. "My mom's got this friend who arranges dates for her, and you wouldn't believe some of the guys she's been stuck with. One of them came to the door—"

"Jeff," Robin said sharply, "that's enough!"

"But one of us needs to tell him!"

"Mr. Camden was just leaving," Robin said, glaring at her neighbor, daring him to contradict her.

"I was? Oh, yeah. Your mom was about to walk me to the door, isn't that right, Robin?"

She gaped at Cole as he reached for her hand and gently led her in the direction of the front door. Meekly she submitted, but not before she saw Jeff give Cole a thumbs-up.

"Now," Cole said, standing in the entryway, his hands heavy on her shoulders. "I want to know what's wrong."

"Wrong? Nothing's wrong."

"It's because of Victoria, isn't it?"

"Victoria?" she asked, already knowing that had to be the woman with him the day she'd seen him at the restaurant.

"Yes. Victoria. I saw you practically hiding under your table, pretending you didn't notice me."

"I... Why should I care?" She hated the way her voice shook.

"Yes, why should you?"

She didn't answer him. Couldn't answer him. She told herself it didn't matter that he was with another woman. Then again, it mattered more than she dared admit.

"Tell me," he insisted.

Robin lowered her gaze. If only he'd stop holding her, stop touching her. Then she might be able to think clearly. "You looked right together. She was a perfect complement to you. She's tall and blond and—"

"Cold as an iceberg. Victoria's a business associate—we had lunch together. Nothing more. I find her as appealing as...as dirty laundry."

"Please, don't explain. It's none of my business who you have lunch with or who you date or where you go every weekend or who you're with. Really. I shouldn't have said anything. I don't know why I did. It was wrong of me—very wrong. I can't believe we're even talking about this."

Jeff poked his head out from the kitchen. "How are things going in here?"

"Good," Robin said. "I was just telling Cole how much we both appreciated his help with your pitching."

"I was having real problems until Cole came along," Jeff confirmed. "Girls are okay for some things, but serious baseball isn't one of them."

Robin opened the front door. "Thanks," she whispered, her eyes avoiding Cole's, "for everything."

"Everything?"

She blushed, remembering the kisses they'd shared. But before she could think of a witty reply, Cole brushed his lips across hers.

"Hey, Cole," Jeff said, hurrying to the front door. "I've got a baseball game Thursday night. Can you come?"

"I'd love to," Cole answered, his eyes holding Robin's. Then he turned abruptly and strode out the door.

"Jeff, we're going to be late for the game if we don't leave now."

"But Cole isn't home yet," Jeff protested. "He said he'd be here."

"There's probably a very good explanation," Robin said calmly, although she was as disappointed as Jeff. "He could be tied up in traffic, or delayed at the office, or any one of a thousand other things. He wouldn't purposely not come."

"Do you think he forgot?"

"I'm sure he didn't. Come on, sweetheart, let's get a move on. You've got a game to pitch." The emphasis came on the last word. The first game of the season and Jeff had won the coveted position of first-string pitcher. Whether it was true or not, Jeff believed Cole's tutoring had given him an advantage over the competition. Jeff hadn't told him the news yet, keeping it a surprise for today.

"When you do see Cole, don't say anything, all right?" Jeff pleaded as they headed toward the car. "I want to be the one who tells him."

"My lips are sealed," she said, holding up her hand. For good measure, she pantomimed zipping her mouth closed. She slid into the car and started the engine, but glanced in the rearview mirror several times, hoping Cole would somehow miraculously appear.

He didn't.

The game was scheduled for the baseball diamond in Balboa Park, less than two miles from Robin's house. A set of bleachers had been arranged around the diamonds, and Robin climbed to the top. It gave her an excellent view of the field—and of the parking area.

Cole knew the game was at Balboa Park, but he didn't know which diamond and there were several. Depending on how late he was, he could waste valuable time looking for the proper field.

The second inning had just begun when Heather Lawrence joined Robin. Robin smiled at her.

"Hi," Heather said. "What's the score?"

"Nothing nothing. It's the top of the second inning."

"How's the neighborhood Randy Johnson doing?"

"Jeff's doing great. He managed to keep his cool when the first batter got a hit off his second pitch. I think I took it worse than Jeff did."

Heather grinned and nodded. "It's the same with me. Kelly played goalie for her soccer team last year, and every time the opposing team scored on her I took it like a bullet to the chest."

"Where's Kelly now?"

Heather motioned toward the other side of the field. The eight-year-old was leaning casually against a tall fir tree. "She didn't want Jeff to know she'd come to watch him. Her game was over a few minutes ago. They lost, but this is her first year and just about everyone else's, too. The game was more a comedy of errors than anything."

Robin laughed. It was thoughtful of Heather to stop by and see how Jeff's team was doing.

Heather laced her fingers over her knees. "Jeff's been talking quite a bit about Cole Camden." She made the statement sound more like a question and kept her gaze focused on the playing field.

"Oh?" Robin wasn't sure how to answer. "Cole was kind enough to give Jeff a few pointers about pitching techniques."

"Speaking of pitching techniques, you two certainly seem to be hitting it off."

Heather was beginning to sound a lot like Angela, who drilled her daily about her relationship with Cole, offering advice and unsolicited suggestions.

"I can't tell you how surprised I am at the changes I've seen in Cole since you two moved in. Kelly's been wanting to play in that fort from the moment she heard about it, but it's only since Jeff came here that she was even allowed in Cole's yard."

"He's been good for Jeff," Robin said, training her eyes on the game. Cole's relationship with her son forced Robin to examine his motives. He'd lost a son, and there was bound to be a gaping hole in his heart. At first he hadn't allowed Jeff in his yard or approved of Blackie and Jeff's becoming friends. But without anything ever being said, all that had fallen to the wayside. Jeff played in Cole's yard almost every day, and with their neighbor's blessing. Jeff now had free access to the fort and often brought other neighborhood kids along. Apparently Cole had given permission. Did he consider Jeff a sort of substitute son? Robin shook off the thought.

"Jeff talks about Cole constantly," Heather said. "In fact, he told me this morning that Cole was coming to see him pitch. What happened? Did he get hung up at the office?"

"I don't know. He must've been delayed, but—"

"There he is! Over there." Heather broke in excitedly. "You know, in the two years we've lived on Orchard Street, I can only recall talking to Cole a few times. He was always so standoffish. Except when we were both doing yard work, I never saw him, and if we did happen to meet we said hello and that was about it. The other day we bumped into each other at the grocery store and he actually smiled at me. I was stunned. I swear that's the first time I've seen that man smile. I honestly think you and Jeff are responsible for the change in him."

"And I think you're crediting me with more than my due," Robin said, craning her head to look for Cole.

"No, I'm not," Heather argued. "You can't see the difference in him because you're new to the neighborhood, but everyone who's known him for any length of time will tell you he's like a different person."

Jeff was sitting on the bench while his team was up at bat. Suddenly he leapt to his feet and waved energetically, as though he was flagging down a rescue vehicle. His face broke into a wide, eager smile. His coach must have said something to him because Jeff nodded and took off running toward the parking area.

Robin's gaze followed her son. Cole had indeed arrived. The tension eased out of her in a single breath. She hadn't realized how edgy she'd been. In her heart she knew Cole would never purposely disappoint Jeff, but her son's anxiety had been as acute as her own.

"Listen," Heather said, standing, "I'll talk to you later."

"Thanks for stopping by."

"Glad to." Heather climbed down the bleachers. She paused when she got to the ground and wiggled her eyebrows expressively, then laughed merrily at Robin's frown.

Heather must have passed Cole on her way out, but Robin lost sight of them as Jeff raced on to the pitcher's mound for the bottom of the second inning. Even from this distance Robin could see that his eyes were full of happy excitement. He discreetly shot her a look and Robin made a V-for-victory sign, smiling broadly.

Cole vaulted up the bleachers and sat down beside her. "Sorry I'm late. I was trapped in a meeting, and by the time I could get out to phone you I knew you'd already left for the field.

I would've called your cell," he added, "but I didn't have the number."

"Jeff and I figured it had to be something like that."

"So he's pitching!" Cole's voice rang with pride.

"He claims it's all thanks to you."

"I'll let him believe that," Cole said, grinning, "but he's a natural athlete. All I did was teach him a little discipline and give him a means of practicing on his own."

"Well, according to Jeff you taught him everything he knows."

He shook his head. "I'm glad I didn't miss the whole game."

"There'll be others," she said, but she was grateful he'd come when he had. From the time they'd left the house, Robin had been tense and guarded. Cole could stand *her* up for any date, but disappointing Jeff was more than she could bear. Rarely had she felt this emotionally unsettled. And all because Cole had been late for a Balboa Park Baseball League game. It frightened her to realize how much Jeff was beginning to depend on him. And not just Jeff, either....

"This is important to Jeff," Cole said as if reading her mind, "and I couldn't disappoint him. If it had been anyone else it wouldn't have been as important. But Jeff matters—" his eyes locked with hers "—and so do you."

Robin felt giddy with relief. For the first time since Lenny's tragic death, she understood how carefully, how completely, she'd anesthetized her life, refusing to let in anyone or anything that might cause her or Jeff more pain. For years she'd been drifting in a haze of denial and grief, refusing to acknowledge or deal with either. What Angela had said was true. Robin had dated infrequently and haphazardly, and kept any suitors at a safe distance.

For some reason, she hadn't been able to do that with Cole. Robin couldn't understand what was different or why; all she knew was that she was in serious danger of falling for this man, and falling hard. It terrified her....

"Have you and Jeff had dinner?" Cole asked.

Robin turned to face him, but it was a long moment before she grasped that he'd asked her a question. He repeated it and she shook her head. "Jeff was too excited to eat."

"Good. There's an excellent Chinese restaurant close by. The three of us can celebrate after the game."

"That'd be nice," she whispered, thinking she should make some excuse to avoid this, and accepting almost immediately that she didn't want to avoid it at all.

"Can I have some more pork-fried rice?" Jeff asked.

Cole passed him the dish and Robin watched as her son heaped his plate high with a third helping.

"You won," she said wistfully.

"Mom, I wish you'd stop saying that. It's the fourth time you've said it. I *know* we won," Jeff muttered, glancing at Cole as if to beg forgiveness for his mother, who was obviously suffering from an overdose of maternal pride.

"But Jeff, you were fantastic," she couldn't resist telling him.

"The whole team was fantastic." Jeff reached for what was left of the egg rolls and added a dollop of plum sauce to his plate.

"I had no idea you were such a good hitter," Robin said, still impressed with her son's athletic ability. "I knew you could pitch—but two home runs! Oh, Jeff, I'm so proud of you—and everyone else." It was difficult to remember that Jeff was only one member of a team, and that his success was part of a larger effort.

"I wanted to make sure I played well, especially 'cause you were there, Cole." Jeff stretched his arm across the table again, this time reaching for the nearly empty platter of almond chicken.

As for herself, Robin couldn't down another bite. Cole had said the food at the Golden Wok was good, and he hadn't exaggerated. It was probably the best Chinese meal she'd ever tasted. Jeff apparently thought so, too. The boy couldn't seem to stop eating.

It was while they were laughing over their fortune cookies that Robin heard bits and pieces of the conversation from the booth behind them.

"I bet they're celebrating something special," an elderly gentleman remarked.

"I think their little boy must have done well at the baseball game," his wife said.

Their little boy, Robin mused. The older couple dining directly behind them thought Cole and Jeff were father and son.

Robin's eyes flew to Cole, but if he had heard the comment he didn't give any sign.

"His mother and father are certainly proud of him."

"It's such a delight to see these young people so happy. A family should spend time together."

A family. The three of them looked like a family.

Once more Robin turned to Cole, but once more he seemed not to hear the comments. Or if he had, he ignored them.

But Cole must have sensed her scrutiny because his gaze found hers just then. Their eyes lingered without a hint of the awkwardness Robin had felt so often before.

Jeff chatted constantly on the ride home with Robin. Since she and Cole had both brought their cars, they drove home separately. They exchanged good-nights in the driveway and entered their own houses.

Jeff had some homework to finish and Robin ran a load of clothes through the washing machine. An hour later, after a little television and quick baths, they were both ready for bed. Robin tucked the blankets around Jeff's shoulders, although he

protested that he was much too old for her to do that. But he
didn't complain too loudly or too long.

"Night, Jeff."

"Night, Mom. Don't let the bedbugs bite."

"Don't go all sentimental on me, okay?" she teased as she
turned off his light. He seemed to fall asleep the instant she
left the room. She went downstairs to secure the house for the
night, then headed up to her own bedroom. Once upstairs, she
paused in her son's doorway and smiled gently. They'd both
had quite a day.

At about ten o'clock, she was sitting up in bed reading a mystery when the phone rang. She answered quickly, always anxious about late calls. "Hello."

"You're still awake." It was Cole, and his voice affected her
like a surge of electricity.

"I...was reading," she said.

"It suddenly occurred to me that we never had the chance
to finish our conversation the other night."

"What conversation?" Robin asked.

"The one at the front door...that Jeff interrupted. Remind
me to give that boy lessons in timing, by the way."

"I don't even remember what we were talking about." She
settled back against the pillows, savoring the sound of his voice,
enjoying the small intimacy of lying in bed, listening to him.
Her eyes drifted shut.

"As I recall, you'd just said something about how it isn't any
of your business who I lunch with or spend my weekends with.
I assume you think I'm with a woman."

Robin's eyes shot open. "I can assure you, I don't think anything of the sort."

"I guess I should explain about the weekends."

"No. I mean, Cole, it really isn't my business. It doesn't matter. Really."

"I have some property north of here, about forty acres," he said gently, despite her protests. "The land once belonged to my grandfather, and he willed it to me when he passed away a couple of years back. This house was part of the estate, as well. My father was born and raised here. I've been spending a lot of my free time remodeling the old farmhouse. Sometime in the future I might move out there."

"I see." She didn't want to think about Cole leaving the neighborhood, ever.

"The place still needs a lot of work, and I've enjoyed doing it on my own. It's coming along well."

She nodded and a second later realized he couldn't see her action. "It sounds lovely."

"Are there any other questions you'd like to ask me?" His voice was low and teasing.

"Of course not," she denied immediately.

"Then would you be willing to admit you enjoy it when I kiss you? A high seven? Really? I think Jeff's right—we need more practice."

"Uh…" Robin didn't know how to answer that.

"I'm willing," he said, and she could almost hear him smile.

Robin lifted the hair from her forehead with one hand. "I can't believe we're having this discussion."

"Would it help if I told you how much I enjoy kissing you?"

"Please…don't," she whispered. She didn't want him to tell her that. Every time he kissed her, it confused her more. Despite the sheltered feeling she experienced in his arms, something deep and fundamental inside her was afraid of loving again. No, terrified. She was terrified of falling in love with Cole. Terrified of what the future might hold.

"The first time shook me more than I care to admit," he said. "Remember that Friday night we rented the movie?"

"I remember."

"I tried to stay away from you afterward. For an entire week I avoided you."

Robin didn't answer. She couldn't. Lying back against the pillows, she stared at the ceiling as a sense of warmth enveloped her. A feeling of comfort...of happiness.

There was a short silence, and in an effort to bring their discussion back to a less intimate—less risky—level, she said, "Thank you for dinner. Jeff had the time of his life." She had, too, but she couldn't find the courage to acknowledge it.

"You're welcome."

"Are you going away this weekend to work on the property?"

She had no right to ask him that, and was shocked at how easily the question emerged.

"I don't think so." After another brief pause, he murmured, "When's the last time you went on a picnic and flew a kite?"

"I don't recall."

"Would you consider going with me on Saturday afternoon? You and Jeff. The three of us together."

"Yes... Jeff would love it."

"How about you? Would you love it?"

"Yes," she whispered.

There didn't seem to be anything more to say, and Robin ended the conversation. "I'll tell Jeff in the morning. He'll be thrilled. Thank you."

"I'll talk to you tomorrow, then."

"Yes. Tomorrow."

"Good night, Robin."

She smiled softly. He said her name the way she'd always dreamed a man would, softly, with a mixture of excitement and need. "Good night, Cole."

For a long time after they'd hung up Robin lay staring at her bedroom walls. When she did flick off her light, she fell asleep as quickly as Jeff seemed to have. She woke about midnight, surprised to find the sheets all twisted as if she'd tossed and turned frantically. The bedspread had slipped onto the floor, and the top sheet was wound around her legs, trapping her.

Sitting up, she untangled her legs and brushed the curls from her face, wondering what had caused her restlessness. She didn't usually wake abruptly like this.

She slid off the bed, found her slippers and went downstairs for a glass of milk.

It was while she was sitting at the table that it came to her. Her hand stilled. Her heartbeat accelerated. The couple in the Chinese restaurant. Robin had overheard them and she was certain Cole had, too.

Their little boy. A family.

Cole had lost a son. From the little Robin had learned, Cole's son had been about the same age Jeff was now when he'd died. First divorce, and then death.

Suddenly it all made sense. A painful kind of sense. A panicky kind of sense. The common ground between them wasn't their backyards, but the fact that they were both victims.

Cole was trying to replace the family that had been so cruelly taken from him.

Robin was just as guilty. She'd been so caught up in the tide of emotion and attraction that she'd refused to recognize what was staring her in the face. She'd ignored her own suspicions and fears, shoving them aside.

She and Cole were both hurting, needy people.

But once the hurt was assuaged, once the need had been satisfied, Cole would discover what Robin had known from the beginning. They were completely different people with little, if anything, in common.

6

"What do you mean you want to meet my cousin?" Angela demanded, glancing up from her desk, a shocked look on her face.

"You've been after me for weeks to go out with Fred."

"Frank. Yes, I have, but that was B.C."

"B.C.?"

"Before Cole. What happened with you two?"

"Nothing!"

"And pigs have wings," Angela said with more than a trace of sarcasm. She stood up and walked around to the front of her desk, leaning against one corner while she folded her arms and stared unblinkingly at Robin.

Robin knew it would do little good to try to disguise her feelings. She'd had a restless night and was convinced it showed. No doubt her eyes were glazed; they ached. Her bones ached. But mostly her heart ached. Arranging a date with Angela's cousin was a sure indication of her distress.

"The last thing I heard, Cole was supposed to attend Jeff's baseball game with you."

"He did." Robin walked to her own desk and reached for

the cup of coffee she'd brought upstairs with her. Peeling off the plastic lid, she cautiously took a sip.

"And?"

"Jeff pitched and he played a fabulous game," Robin said, hoping her friend wouldn't question her further.

Angela continued to stare at Robin. Good grief, Robin thought, the woman had eyes that could cut through solid rock.

"What?" Robin snapped when she couldn't stand her friend's scrutiny any longer. She took another sip of her coffee and nearly scalded her lips. If the rest of her day followed the pattern set that morning, she might as well go home now. The temptation to climb back into bed and hide her head under the pillow was growing stronger every minute.

"Tell me what happened with Cole," Angela said again.

"Nothing. I already told you he was at Jeff's baseball game. What more do you want?"

"The least you can do is tell me what went on last night," Angela said slowly, carefully enunciating each word as though speaking to someone who was hard of hearing.

"Before or after Jeff's game?" Robin pulled out her chair and sat down.

"Both."

Robin gave up. Gesturing weakly with her hands, she shrugged, took a deep breath and poured out the whole story in one huge rush. "Cole was held up at the office in a meeting, so we didn't meet at the house the way we'd planned. Naturally Jeff was disappointed, but we decided that whatever was keeping Cole wasn't his fault, and we left for Balboa Park without him. Cole arrived at the bottom of the second inning, just as Jeff was ready to pitch. Jeff only allowed three hits the entire game, and scored two home runs himself. Afterward Cole took us all out for Chinese food at a fabulous restaurant I've never heard of but one you and I will have to try sometime. Our next raise, okay? Later Cole phoned and asked to take Jeff and me on a picnic Saturday. I think we're going to Golden Gate Park because he also talked about flying kites." She paused, dragged in a fresh gulp of air and gave Angela a look that said "make something out of that if you can!"

"I see," Angela said after a lengthy pause.

"Good."

Robin wasn't up to explaining things, so if Angela really *didn't* understand, that was just too bad. She only knew that she was dangerously close to letting her emotions take charge of her life. She was becoming increasingly attracted to a man who could well be trying to replace the son he'd lost. Robin needed to find a way to keep from following her heart, which was moving at breakneck speed straight into Cole's arms.

"Will you introduce me to Frank or not?" she asked a second time, strengthening her voice and her conviction.

Angela was still watching her with those diamond-cutting eyes. "I'm not sure yet."

"You're not sure!" Robin echoed, dismayed. "For weeks you've been spouting his virtues. According to you, this cousin is as close to a god as a human being can get. He works hard, buys municipal bonds, goes to church regularly and flosses his teeth."

"I said all that?"

"Just about," Robin muttered. "I made up the part about flossing his teeth. Yet when I ask to meet this paragon of limitless virtue, you say you're not sure you want to introduce me. I would've thought you'd be pleased."

"I am pleased," Angela said, frowning, "but I'm also concerned."

"It's not your job to be concerned. All you have to do is call Fred and let him know I'm available Saturday evening for drinks or dinner or a movie or whatever. I'll let him decide what he's most comfortable with."

"It's Frank, and I thought you said you were going on a picnic with Cole on Saturday."

Robin turned on her computer, prepared to check several columns of figures. If she looked busy and suitably nonchalant, it might prompt Angela to agree. "Jeff and I will be with Cole earlier in the day. I'll simply make sure we're back before late afternoon, so there's no reason to worry."

Robin's forehead puckered. "I *am* worried. I can't help being worried. Honestly, Robin, I've never seen you like this. You're so…so determined."

"I've always been determined," Robin countered, glancing up from the computer.

"Oh, I agree one hundred percent," Angela said with a heavy sigh, "but not when it comes to anything that has to do with men. My thirteen-year-old niece has more savvy with the opposite sex than you do!"

"Mom, look how high my kite is," Jeff hollered as his box kite soared toward the heavens.

"It's touching the sky!" Robin shouted, and laughed with her son as he tugged and twisted the string. Despite all her misgivings about her relationship with Cole, she was thoroughly enjoying the afternoon. At first, she'd been positive the day would turn into a disaster. She was sure Cole would take one look at her and know she was going out with another man that evening. She was equally sure she'd blurt it out if he didn't immediately guess.

Cole had been as excited as Jeff about the picnic and kite-flying expedition. The two of them had been fussing with the kites for hours—buying, building and now flying them. For her part, Robin was content to soak up the sunshine.

The weather couldn't have been more cooperative. The sky was a brilliant blue and the wind was perfect. Sailboats scudding on the choppy green waters added dashes of bright color.

In contrast to all the beauty surrounding her, Robin's heart was troubled. Watching Cole, so patient and gentle with her son, filled her with contradictory emotions. Part of her wanted to thank him. Thank him for the smile that lit up Jeff's face. Thank him for throwing open the shades and easing her toward the light. And part of her wanted to shut her eyes and run for cover.

"Mom, look!" Jeff cried as the kite whipped and kicked in the wind. Blackie raced at his side as the sleek red-and-blue kite sliced through the sky, then dipped sharply and crashed toward the ground at heart-stopping speed, only to be caught at the last second and lifted higher and higher.

"I'm looking, I'm looking!" Robin shouted back. She'd never seen Jeff happier. Pride and joy shone from his face, and Robin was moved almost to tears.

Cole stood behind Jeff, watching the kite. One hand rested on the boy's shoulder, the other shaded his eyes as he gazed up at the sky. They laughed, and once more Robin was struck by the mingling of their voices. One mature and measured, the other young and excited. Both happy.

A few minutes later, Cole jogged over to Robin's blanket and sat down beside her. He did nothing more than smile at her, but she felt an actual jolt.

Cole stretched out and leaned back on his elbows, grinning at the sun. "I can't remember the last time I laughed so much."

"You two seem to be enjoying this," Robin said.

If Cole noticed anything awry, he didn't comment. She'd managed not to tell him about the date with Angela's cousin; she certainly didn't want him to think she was trying to make him jealous. That wasn't the evening's purpose at all. Actually she wasn't sure *what* she hoped to accomplish by dating Fred... Frank.

She mentally shouted the name five times. Why did she keep calling him Fred? She didn't know that any more than she knew why she was going out with him. On the morning she'd talked Angela into making the arrangements for her, it had seemed a matter of life and death. Now she only felt confused and regretful.

"Jeff says you've got a date this evening."

So much for her worry that she might blurt it out herself, Robin thought. She glanced at Cole. He might've been referring to the weather for all the emotion revealed in his voice.

"A cousin of a good friend. She's been after me for months to meet Frank—we're having dinner."

"Could this be the Frank you weren't going out with and that was final?"

Robin stared at him blankly.

"You answered the phone with that when I called to inquire about Blackie. Remember?"

"Oh, yes..." Suddenly she felt an intense need to justify her actions. "It's just that Angela's been talking about him for so long and it seemed like the right thing to do. He's apparently very nice and Angela's been telling me he's a lot of fun and I didn't think it would hurt to meet him...." Once she got started, Robin couldn't seem to stop explaining.

"Robin," Cole said, his eyes tender. "You don't owe me any explanations."

She instantly grew silent. He was right, she knew that, yet she couldn't help feeling guilty. She was making a terrible mess of this.

"I'm not the jealous type," Cole informed her matter-of-factly.

"I'm not trying to make you jealous," she returned stiffly.

"Good," Cole said and shrugged. His gaze moved from her to Jeff, who was jogging across the grass. Blackie was beside him, barking excitedly.

He hadn't asked, but she felt obliged to explain who'd be looking after her son while she was out. "Jeff's going to the movies with Heather and Kelly Lawrence while I'm out."

Cole didn't say anything. All he did was smile. It was the same smile he'd flashed at her earlier. The same devastating, wickedly charming smile.

He seemed to be telling her she could dine with a thousand different men and it wouldn't disturb him in the least. As he'd said, he wasn't the jealous type. Great. This was exactly the way she'd wanted him to respond, wasn't it? She could date a thousand different men, because Cole didn't care about her. He cared about her son.

"Let me know when you want to leave," he said with infuriating self-assurance. "I wouldn't want you to be late."

On that cue, Robin checked her watch and was surprised to note that it was well past four. They'd been having so much fun, the day had simply slipped away. When she looked up, she found Cole studying her expectantly. "It's... I'm not meeting Frank until later," she said, answering his unspoken question evasively while she gathered up the remains of their picnic.

An hour later, they decided to leave Golden Gate Park. Jeff and Cole loaded up the kites, as well as the picnic cooler, in the back of Cole's car. It took them another hour to get back to Glen Park because of the traffic, which made Robin's schedule even tighter. But that was hardly Cole's fault—it wasn't as if he'd *arranged* for an accident on the freeway.

Cole and Jeff chatted easily for most of the ride home. When they finally arrived at the house, both Robin and Jeff helped Cole unload the car. Blackie's barking only added to the confusion.

"I suppose I'd better get inside," Robin said, her eyes briefly meeting Cole's. She felt awkward all of a sudden, wishing Jeff was standing there as a barrier, instead of busily carrying things onto Cole's porch.

"We had a great time," she added self-consciously. She couldn't really blame her nervousness on Cole; he'd been the perfect companion all day. "Thank you for the picnic."

Jeff joined them, his eyes narrowing as he looked at Cole. "Are you gonna let her do it?"

"Do what?" Robin asked.

"Go out with that other man," Jeff said righteously, inviting Cole to leap into the argument. "I can't believe you're letting her get away with this."

"Jeff. This isn't something we should be discussing with Mr. Camden."

"All right," he murmured with a sigh. "But I think you're making a mistake." He cast a speculative glance in Cole's direction. "Both of you," he mumbled under his breath and headed for the house.

"Thanks for the wonderful afternoon, Cole," Robin said again.

"No problem," he responded, hands in his pockets, his stance relaxed. "Have a good time with Frank."

"Thanks, I will," she said, squinting at him suspiciously just before she turned toward the house. Darn it, she actually felt guilty! There wasn't a single solitary reason she should feel guilty for agreeing to this dinner date with Angela's cousin, yet she did. Cole must've known it, too, otherwise he wouldn't have made that remark about having a good time. Oh, he knew all right.

As Robin was running the bath, Jeff raced up the stairs. "Mom, I need money for the movie." He thrust her purse into her hands. "How much are you giving me for goodies?"

"Goodies?"

"You know, popcorn, pop, a couple of candy bars. I'm starving."

"Jeff, you haven't stopped eating all day. What about the two hot dogs I just fixed you?"

"I ate them, but that was fifteen minutes ago. I'm hungry again."

Robin handed him fifteen dollars, prepared for an argument. That amount should be enough to pay his way into the movie and supply him with popcorn and a soda. Anything beyond that he could do without.

Jeff took the money from her and slowly shook his head. "That's it, kid," she said in a firm voice.

"Did I complain?" Bright blue eyes gazed innocently back at her.

"You didn't have to. I could see it in your face."

Jeff was ready to leave a few minutes later, just as Robin was getting dressed. He stood outside her bedroom door and shouted that Kelly and her mom were there to pick him up.

"Have fun. I won't be any later than ten-thirty," she assured him.

"Can't I wait for you over at Cole's after the movie?"

"Absolutely not!" Robin's heart skidded to a dead stop at the suggestion. The last person she wanted to face at the end of this evening was Cole Camden. "You didn't ask him, did you?"

"No...but I'm not all that excited about going to Kelly's. I'm there every day, you know."

"Sweetie, I'm sorry. I promise I won't be late."

"You're sure I can't go over to Cole's?"

"Jeffrey Leonard Masterson, don't you *dare* bother Cole. Do you understand me?"

He blinked. She rarely used that tone with him, but she didn't have the time or energy to argue about this.

"I guess," he said with an exaggerated sigh. "But could you make it home by ten?"

"Why ten?"

"Because I don't want to do anything stupid like fall asleep in front of Kelly," he whispered heatedly.

"I'll be back as soon as I can," Robin said.

Glancing at her clock radio, she gasped at the time. She was running late. From the moment she'd made the arrangements to meet Frank, she hadn't given the reality of this evening much thought. Just forcing herself to go through with it had depleted her of energy.

Robin had always hated situations like this. Always. She was going to a strange restaurant, meeting a strange man, and for what? She didn't know.

Tucking her feet into her pumps, Robin hurried to the bathroom to spray on a little perfume. Not much, just enough to give herself some confidence. She rushed down the stairs and reached for her purse.

Her hand was on the doorknob when the phone rang. For a moment, Robin intended to ignore it. It was probably for Jeff. But what if the call was from her parents? Or Frank—calling to cancel? Ridiculous though it was, each ring sounded more urgent than the last. She'd have to answer or she'd spend all evening wondering who it was. Muttering under her breath, she dashed into the kitchen.

"Hello," she said impatiently.

At first there was no response. "Robin, it's Cole." He sounded nothing like himself. "I lied." With that the line was abruptly disconnected.

Robin held the receiver away from her ear and stared at it for several seconds. He'd lied? About what? Good heavens, why had he even phoned? To tell her he'd lied.

There wasn't time to phone him back and ask what he'd meant.

"Would you care for something to drink?" Frank Eberle asked, glancing over the wine list.

"Nothing, thanks," Robin said. Frank had turned out to be a

congenial sort, which was a pleasant surprise. He was quite attractive, with light blue eyes and a thick head of distinguished-
looking salt-and-pepper hair. Angela had once mentioned he
was "a little bit" shy, which had panicked Robin since she was
a whole lot shy, at least around men. The way she'd figured it,
they'd stare at each other most of the night, with no idea what
to say. However, they did have Angela in common. Whereas
with Cole, all she shared was—

Her thoughts came to an abrupt halt. She refused to think
about her neighbor or his last-minute phone call. She balked
at the idea of dining with one man while wistfully longing for
another—which was exactly what she was doing.

Robin studied the menu, pretending to decide between the
prime-rib special and the fresh halibut. But the entire time
she stared at the menu, she was racking her brain for a topic of
conversation.

Frank saved her the trouble. "For once," he said, "Angela
didn't exaggerate. You're a delightful surprise."

"I am?" It was amusing to hear him echo her own reaction.

Frank nodded, his smile reserved. "When Angie phoned earlier in the week, I wasn't sure what to expect. She keeps wanting
me to date her friends. And to hear her talk, she's close friends
with dozens of gorgeous women all interested in meeting me."

Robin grinned. "She should run a dating service. I can't tell
you the number of times she's matched me up with someone,
or tried to, anyway."

"But you're a comfortable person to be around. I could sense
that right away."

"Thank you. I...wasn't sure what to expect, either. Angela's
raved about you for weeks, wanting to get the two of us together." Robin glanced from the menu to her companion, then
back again. She felt the same misgivings every time she agreed
to one of these arranged dates.

"I've been divorced six months now," Frank volunteered, "but after fourteen years of married life, I don't think I'll ever get accustomed to dating again."

Robin found herself agreeing. "I know what you mean. It all seems so awkward, doesn't it? When Lenny and I were dating, I was in high school, and there was so little to worry about. We knew what we wanted and knew what we had to do to get there."

Frank sent her a smile. "Now that we're older and—" he paused "—I hesitate to use the word *wiser*...."

"More sophisticated?"

"Right, more sophisticated," Frank repeated. His hand closed around the water glass. "Life seems so complicated now. I've been out of the swing of things for so long...."

The waitress came for their order then, and from that point on the evening went smoothly. The feeling of kinship she felt with Frank astonished Robin. He was obviously at ease with her, too. Before she knew it, Robin found herself telling him about Cole.

"He sounds like the kind of guy most women would leap off a bridge to meet."

Robin nodded. "He's wonderful to Jeff, too."

"Then what's the problem?"

"His wife and son."

Frank's mouth sagged open. "He's married?"

"Was," she rushed to explain. "From what I understand, his wife left him and sometime later his son died."

"That's tough," Frank said, picking up his coffee. "But that was years ago, wasn't it?"

"I...don't know. Cole's never told me these things himself. In fact, he's never mentioned either his wife or his son."

"He's *never* mentioned them?"

"Never," she confirmed. "I heard it from a neighbor."

"That's what's bothering you, isn't it?"

The question was sobering. Subconsciously, from the moment Robin had learned of Cole's loss, she'd been waiting for him to tell her. Waiting for him to trust her enough.

Frank and Robin lingered over coffee, chatting about politics and the economy and a number of other stimulating topics. But the question about Cole refused to fade from her mind.

They parted outside the restaurant and Frank kissed her cheek, but they were both well aware they wouldn't be seeing each other again. Their time together had been a brief respite. It had helped Frank deal with his loneliness and helped Robin understand what was troubling her about Cole.

The first thing Robin noticed when she pulled into her driveway was that Cole's house was dark. Dark and silent. Lonely. So much of her life had been like that—before she'd met him.

She needed to talk to him. She wanted to ask about his phone call. She wanted to ask about his wife and the son he'd lost. But the timing was all wrong.

For a long moment Robin sat alone in her car, feeling both sad and disappointed.

Heather greeted her with a smile and a finger pressed to her lips. "Both kids were exhausted. They fell asleep in the living room almost as soon as we got back."

After Jeff's busy day, she could hardly believe he'd lasted through the movie. "I hope he wasn't cranky."

"Not in the least," Heather assured her.

Robin yawned, completely exhausted. She wanted nothing more than to escape to her room and sleep until noon the following day.

"Would you like a cup of coffee before you go?" Heather asked.

"No, thanks." Robin had been blessed with good neighbors. Heather on her right and Cole on her left....

Together Robin and Heather woke Jeff, who grumbled about his mother being late. He was too drowsy to realize it was only nine-thirty or that she'd returned ahead of schedule.

After telling Heather a little about her evening, Robin guided her son across the yard and into the house. She walked upstairs with him and answered the slurred questions he struggled to ask between wide, mouth-stretching yawns.

Tugging back his quilt, Robin urged him into his bed. Jeff kicked off his shoes and reached for the quilt. It wasn't the first time he'd slept in his clothes and it probably wouldn't be the last.

Smiling to herself, Robin moved quietly down the stairs.

On impulse, she paused in the kitchen and picked up the phone. When Cole answered on the first ring, she swallowed a gasp of surprise.

"Hello," he said a second time.

"What did you lie about?" she asked softly.

"Where are you?"

"Home."

"I'll be right there." Without a further word, he hung up.

A minute later, Cole was standing at her front door, hands in his back pockets. He stared at her as if it had been months since they'd seen each other.

"You win," he said, edging his way in.

"Win what? The door prize?" she asked, controlling her amusement with difficulty.

Not bothering to answer her, Cole stalked to the kitchen, where he sank down in one of the pine chairs. "Did you have a good time?"

She sat down across from him. "I really did. Frank's a very pleasant, very caring man. We met at the Higher Ground—that's a cute little restaurant close to the BART station and—"

"I know where it is."

"About your phone call earlier. You said—"

"What's he like?"

"Who? Frank?"

Cole gave her a look that suggested she have her intelligence tested.

"Like I said, he's very pleasant. Divorced and lonely."

"What's he do for a living?"

"He works for the city, I think. We didn't get around to talking about our careers." No doubt Cole would be shocked if he knew she'd spent the greater part of the evening discussing her relationship with *him!*

"What did you talk about, then?"

"Cole, honestly, I don't think we should discuss my evening with Frank. Would you like some coffee? I'll make decaf."

"Are you going to see him again?"

Robin ignored the question. Instead she left the table and began to make coffee. She was concentrating so carefully on her task that she didn't notice Cole was directly behind her. She turned—and found herself gazing into the darkest, most confused and frustrated pair of eyes she'd ever seen.

"Oh," she said, startled. "I didn't realize you were so close."

His hands gripped her shoulders. "Why did you go out with him?"

Surely that wasn't distress she heard in Cole's voice? Not after all that casual indifference this afternoon. She frowned, bewildered by the pain she saw in his eyes. And she finally understood. Contrary to everything he'd claimed, Cole was jealous. Really and truly jealous.

"Did he kiss you?" he asked with an urgency, an intensity, she'd never heard in his voice before.

Robin stared, frozen by the stark need she read in him.

Cole's finger rested on her mouth. "Did Frank kiss you?" he repeated.

She shook her head and the motion brushed his finger across her bottom lip.

"He wanted to, though, didn't he?" Cole asked with a brooding frown.

"He didn't kiss me." She was finally able to say the words. She couldn't kiss Frank or anyone else. The only man she wanted to kiss and be kissed by was the man looking down at her now. The man whose lips were descending on hers....

7

"So, did you like this guy you had dinner with last night?" Jeff asked, keeping his eyes on his bowl of cold cereal.

"He was nice," Robin answered, pouring herself a cup of coffee and joining him at the table. They'd slept late and were spending a lazy Sunday morning enjoying their breakfast before going to the eleven o'clock service at church.

Jeff hesitated, his spoon poised in front of him. "Is he nicer than Cole?"

"Cole's...nicer," Robin admitted reluctantly. *Nice* and *nicer* weren't terms she would've used to describe the differences between Frank and Cole, but in her son's ten-year-old mind they made perfect sense.

A smile quivered at the edges of Jeff's mouth. "I saw you two smooching last night," he said, grinning broadly.

"When?" Robin demanded—a ridiculous question. It could only have happened when Cole had come over to talk to her. He'd confessed how jealous he'd been of Frank and how he'd struggled with the emotion and felt like a fool. Robin had been convinced she was the one who'd behaved like an idiot. Before either of them could prevent it, they were in each other's arms, seeking and granting reassurance.

"You thought I was asleep, but I heard Cole talking and I wanted to ask him what he was gonna do about you and this other guy, so I came downstairs and saw you two with your faces stuck together."

The boy certainly had a way with words.

"You didn't look like you minded, either. Cole and me talked about girls once, and he said they aren't much when they're ten, but they get a whole lot more interesting later on. He said girls are like green apples. At first they're all sour and make your lips pucker, but a little while later they're real good."

"I see," Robin muttered, not at all sure she liked being compared to an apple.

"But when I got downstairs I didn't say anything," Jeff said, "because, well, you know."

Robin nodded and sipped her coffee in an effort to hide her discomfort.

Jeff picked up his cereal bowl and drank the remainder of the milk in loud gulps. He wiped the back of his hand across his lips. "I suppose this means you're going to have a baby now."

Robin was too horrified to speak. The swallow of coffee got stuck in her throat and she started choking. Trying to help her breathe, Jeff pounded her back with his fist, which only added to her misery.

By the time she caught her breath, tears were streaking down her face.

"You all right, Mom?" Jeff asked, his eyes wide with concern. He rushed into the bathroom and returned with a wad of tissue.

"Thanks," she whispered, wiping her face. It took her a moment or two to regain her composure. This was a talk she'd planned on having with him soon—but not quite yet. "Jeff, listen…kissing doesn't make babies."

"It doesn't? But I thought... I hoped... You mean you won't be having a baby?"

"I... Not from kissing," she whispered, taking in deep breaths to stabilize her pulse.

"I suppose the next thing you're gonna tell me is we'll have to save up for a baby the way we did for the house and now the fence before we get me a dog."

This conversation was getting too complicated. "No, we wouldn't have to save for a baby."

"Then what's the holdup?" her son demanded. "I like the idea of being a big brother. I didn't think much about it until we moved here. Then when we were having dinner at the Chinese restaurant I heard this grandma and grandpa in the booth next to us talking, and they were saying neat things about us being a family. That's when I started thinking about babies and stuff."

"Jeff," Robin said, rubbing her hands together as she collected her thoughts. "There's more to it than that. Before there's a baby, there should be a husband."

"Well, of course," Jeff returned, looking at her as if she'd insulted his intelligence. "You'd have to marry Cole first, but that'd be all right with me. You like him, don't you? You must like him or you wouldn't be kissing him that way."

Robin sighed. Of course she *liked* Cole, but it wasn't that simple. Unfortunately she wasn't sure she could explain it in terms a ten-year-old could understand. "I—"

"I can't remember ever seeing you kiss a guy like that. You looked real serious. And when I was sneaking back up the stairs, I heard him ask you to have dinner alone with him tonight and that seemed like a real good sign."

The next time Cole kissed her, Robin thought wryly, they'd have to scurry into a closet. The things that child came up with...

"You *are* going to dinner with him, aren't you?"

"Yes, but—"

"Then what's the problem? I'll ask him to marry you if you want."

"Jeff!" she cried, leaping to her feet. "Absolutely not! That's between Cole and me, and neither of us would appreciate any assistance from you. Is that clearly understood?"

"All right," he sighed, but he didn't look too pleased. He reached for a piece of toast, shredding it into thirds. "But you're going to marry him, aren't you?"

"I don't know."

"Why not? Cole's the best thing that's ever happened to us."

Her son was staring at her intently, his baseball cap twisted around to the back of his head. Now that she had his full attention, Robin couldn't find the words to explain. "It's more complicated than you realize, sweetie." She made a show of glancing at the clock. "Anyway, it's time to change and get ready for church."

Jeff nodded and rushed up the stairs. Robin followed at a much slower pace, grateful to put an end to this difficult and embarrassing subject.

The minute they were home from the service, Jeff grabbed his baseball mitt. "Jimmy Wallach and I are going to the school yard to practice hitting balls. Okay?"

"Okay," Robin said absently. "How long will you be gone?"

"An hour."

"I'm going grocery shopping, so if I'm not home when you get back you know what to do?"

"Of course," he muttered.

"You're Robin Masterson, aren't you?" a tall middle-aged woman asked as she maneuvered her grocery cart alongside Robin's.

"Yes," Robin said. The other woman's eyes were warm and her smile friendly.

"I thought you must be—I've seen you from a distance. I'm Joyce Wallach. Jimmy and Jeff have become good friends. In fact, they're at the school yard now."

"Of course," Robin said, pleased to make the other woman's acquaintance. They'd talked on the phone several times, and she'd met Joyce's husband once, when Jimmy had spent the night. The boys had wanted to play on the same baseball team and were disappointed when they'd been assigned to different teams. It had been Jimmy who'd told Jeff about the death of Cole's son.

"I've been meaning to invite you to the house for coffee," Joyce went on to say, "but I started working part-time and I can't seem to get myself organized."

"I know what you mean." Working full-time, keeping up with Jeff and her home was about all Robin could manage herself. She didn't know how other mothers were able to accomplish so much.

"There's a place to sit down here," Joyce said, and her eyes brightened at the idea. "Do you have time to chat now?"

Robin nodded. "Sure. I've been wanting to meet you, too." The Wallachs lived two streets over, and Robin fully approved of Jimmy as a friend for Jeff. He and Kelly had become friends, too, but her ten-year-old son wasn't as eager to admit being buddies with a girl. Kelly was still a green apple in Jeff's eye, but the time would come when he'd appreciate having her next door.

"I understand Jeff's quite the baseball player," Joyce said at the self-service counter.

Robin smiled. She poured herself a plastic cup of iced tea and paid for it. "Jeff really loves baseball. He was disappointed he couldn't play with Jimmy."

"They separate the teams according to the kid's year of birth. Jimmy's birthday is in January so he's with another group." She frowned. "That doesn't really make much sense, does it?" She chuckled, and Robin couldn't help responding to the soft infectious sound of Joyce's laughter. She found herself laughing, too.

They pulled out chairs at one of the small tables in the supermarket's deli section.

"I feel like throwing my arms around you," Joyce said with a grin. "I saw Cole Camden at Balboa Park the other day and I couldn't believe my eyes. It was like seeing him ten years ago, the way he used to be." She glanced at Robin. "Jeff was with him."

"Cole came to his first game."

"Ah." She nodded slowly, as if that explained it. "I don't know if anyone's told you, but there's been a marked difference in Cole lately. I can't tell you how happy I am to see it. Cole's gone through so much heartache."

"Cole's been wonderful for Jeff," Robin said, then swallowed hard. She felt a renewed stab of fear that Cole was more interested in the idea of having a son than he was in a relationship with her.

"I have the feeling you've *both* been wonderful for him," Joyce added.

Robin's smile was losing its conviction. She lowered her eyes and studied the lemon slice floating in her tea.

"My husband and I knew Cole quite well before the divorce," Joyce went on to say. "Larry, that's my husband, and Cole played golf every Saturday afternoon. Then Jennifer decided she wanted out of the marriage, left him and took Bobby. Cole really tried to save that marriage, but the relationship had been in trouble for a long time. Cole doted on his son, though—he would've done anything to spare Bobby the trauma of a divorce. Jennifer, however—" Joyce halted abruptly, apparently realizing how much she'd said. "I didn't mean to launch into all of this—it's ancient history. I just wanted you to know how pleased I am to meet you."

Since Cole had told her shockingly little of his past, Robin had to bite her tongue not to plead with Joyce to continue. Instead, she bowed her head and said, "I'm pleased to meet you, too."

Then she looked up with a smile as Joyce said, "Jimmy's finally got the friend he's always wanted. There are so few boys his age around here. I swear my son was ready to set off fireworks the day Jeff registered at the school and he learned you lived only two blocks away."

"Jeff claimed he couldn't live in a house that's surrounded by girls." Robin shook her head with a mock grimace. "If he hadn't met Jimmy, I might've had a mutiny on my hands."

Joyce's face relaxed into another warm smile. She was energetic and animated, gesturing freely with her hands as she spoke. Robin felt as if she'd known and liked Jimmy's mother for years.

"There hasn't been much turnover in this neighborhood. We're a close-knit group, as I'm sure you've discovered. Heather Lawrence is a real sweetie. I wish I had more time to get to know her. And Cole, well... I realize that huge house has been in his family forever, but I half expected him to move out after Jennifer and Bobby were killed."

The silence that followed was punctuated by Robin's soft, involuntary gasp. "What did you just say?"

"That I couldn't understand why Cole's still living in the house on Orchard Street. Is that what you mean?"

"No, after that—about Jennifer and Bobby." It was difficult for Robin to speak. Each word felt as if it had been scraped from the roof of her mouth.

"I assumed you knew they'd both been killed," Joyce said,

her eyes full of concern. "I mean, I thought for sure that Cole had told you."

"I knew about Bobby. Jimmy said something to Jeff, who told me, but I didn't have any idea that Jennifer had died, too. Heather Lawrence told me about the divorce, but she didn't say anything about Cole's wife dying...."

"I don't think Heather knows. She moved into the neighborhood long after the divorce, and Cole's pretty close-mouthed about it."

"When did all this happen?"

"Five or six years ago now. It was terribly tragic," Joyce said. "Just thinking about it makes my heart ache all over again. I don't mean to be telling tales, but if there's any blame to be placed I'm afraid it would fall on Jennifer. She wasn't the kind of woman who's easy to know or like. I shouldn't speak ill of the dead, and I don't mean to be catty, but Jen did Cole a favor when she left him. Naturally, he didn't see it that way—he was in love with his wife and crazy about his son. Frankly, I think Cole turned a blind eye to his wife's faults because of Bobby."

"What happened?" Perhaps having a neighbor fill in the details of Cole's life was the wrong thing to do; Robin no longer knew. Cole had never said a word to her about Jennifer or Bobby, and she didn't know if he ever would.

"Jen was never satisfied with Cole's position as a city attorney," Joyce explained. "We'd have coffee together every now and then, and all she'd do was complain how Cole was wasting his talents and that he could be making big money and wasn't. She had grander plans for him. But Cole loved his job and felt an obligation to follow through with his commitments. Jennifer never understood that. She didn't even try to sympathize with Cole's point of view. She constantly wanted more, better, newer things. She didn't work herself, so it was all up to Cole." Joyce shrugged sadly.

"Jen was never happy, never satisfied," she went on. "She hated the house and the neighborhood, but figured out that all the whining and manipulating in the world wasn't going to do one bit of good. Cole intended to finish out his responsibilities to the city, so she played her ace. She left him, taking Bobby with her."

"But didn't Cole try to gain custody of Bobby?"

"Of course. He knew, and so did everyone else, that Jennifer was using their son as a pawn. She was never the motherly type, if you know what I mean. If you want the truth, she was an alcoholic. There were several times I dropped Bobby off at the house and suspected Jen had been drinking heavily. I was willing to testify on Cole's behalf, and I told him so. He was grateful, but then the accident happened and it was too late."

"The accident?" A heaviness settled in her chest. Each breath pained her and brought with it the memories she longed to forget, memories of another accident—the one that had taken her husband.

"It was Jennifer's fault—the accident, I mean. She'd been drinking and should never have been behind the wheel. The day before, Cole had been to see his attorneys, pleading with them to move quickly because he was afraid Jennifer was becoming more and more irresponsible. But it wasn't until after she'd moved out that Cole realized how sick she'd become, how dependent she was on alcohol to make it through the day."

"Oh, no," Robin whispered. "Cole must've felt so guilty."

"It was terrible," Joyce returned, her voice quavering. "I didn't know if Cole would survive that first year. He hid inside the house and severed relationships with everyone in the neighborhood. He was consumed by his grief. Later he seemed to come out of it a little, but he's never been the same.

"The irony of all this is that eventually Jen would've gotten exactly what she wanted if she'd been more patient. A couple of years ago, Cole accepted a partnership in one of the most important law firms in the city. He's made a real name for himself, but money and position don't seem to mean much to him—they never have. I wouldn't be surprised if he walked away from the whole thing someday."

"I think you're right. Cole told me not long ago that he has some property north of here that he inherited from his grandfather. He's restoring the house, and he said something about moving there. It's where he spends most of his weekends."

"I wondered if that was it," Joyce said, nodding. "There were rumors floating around the neighborhood that he spent his weekends with a woman. Anyone who knew Cole would realize what a crock that is. Cole isn't the type to have a secret affair."

Robin felt ashamed, remembering how she'd been tempted to believe the rumor herself.

"For a long time," Joyce murmured, "I wondered if Cole was ever going to recover from Jennifer's and Bobby's deaths, but now I believe he has. I can't help thinking you and Jeff had a lot to do with that."

"I...think he would gradually have come out of his shell."

"Perhaps, but the changes in him lately have been the most encouraging things so far. I don't know how you feel about Cole or if there's anything between you, but you couldn't find a better man."

"I... I'm falling in love with him," Robin whispered, voicing her feelings for the first time. The words hung there, and it was too late to take them back.

"I think that's absolutely wonderful, I really do!" Joyce said enthusiastically.

"I don't." Now that the shock had worn off, Robin was forced to confront her anger. Cole had told her none of this. Not a single word. That hurt. Hurt more than she would've expected. But the ache she felt was nothing compared to the grief Cole must face each morning, the pain that weighed down his life.

"Oh, dear," Joyce said. "I've really done it now, haven't I? I knew I should've kept my mouth shut. You're upset and it's my fault."

"Nonsense," Robin whispered, making an effort to bring a smile to her dry lips and not succeeding. "I'm grateful we met, and more than grateful you told me about Jennifer, and about Cole's son." The knowledge produced a dull ache in Robin's heart. She felt grief for Cole and a less worthy emotion, too—a sense of being slighted by his lack of trust in her.

She was so distressed on the short drive home that she missed the turn and had to take a side street and double back to Orchard Street.

As she neared the house, she saw that Cole was outside watering his lawn. He waved, but she pretended not to see him and pulled into her driveway. Desperate for some time alone before facing Cole, Robin did her best to ignore him as she climbed out of the car. She needed a few more minutes to gather her thoughts and control her emotions.

She was almost safe, almost at the house, when Cole stopped her.

"Robin," he called, jogging toward her. "Hold on a minute, would you?"

She managed to compose herself, squaring her shoulders and drawing on her dignity.

His wonderful eyes were smiling as he hurried over. Obviously he hadn't noticed there was anything wrong. "Did Jeff happen to say anything about seeing us kiss last night?" he asked.

Her mouth was still so dry she had to swallow a couple of times before she could utter a single syllable. "Yes, but don't worry, I think I've got him squared away."

"Drat!" he teased, snapping his fingers. "I suppose this means I don't have to go through with the shotgun wedding?"

She nodded, keeping her eyes lowered, fearing he'd be able to read all the emotion churning inside her.

"You have nothing to fear but fear itself," she said, forcing a lightness into her tone.

"Robin?" He made her name a question and a caress. "Is something wrong?"

She shook her head, shifting the bag of groceries from one arm to the other. "Of course not," she said with the same feigned cheerfulness.

Cole took the bag from her arms. Robin knew she should have resisted, but she couldn't; she felt drained of strength. She headed for the house, knowing Cole would follow her inside.

"What's wrong?" he asked a second time, setting the groceries on the kitchen counter.

It was difficult to speak and even more difficult, more exhausting, to find the words that would explain what she'd learned.

"Nothing. It's just that I've got a lot to do if we're going out for dinner tonight."

"Wear something fancy. I'm taking you to a four-star restaurant."

"Something fancy?" Mentally she reviewed the contents of her closet, which was rather lacking in anything fancy.

"I'm not about to be outclassed by Frank," Cole said with a laugh. "I'm going to wine and dine you and turn your head with sweet nothings."

He didn't need to do any of those things to turn her head. She was already dangerously close to being in love with him, so close that she'd blurted it out to a woman she'd known for a total of twelve minutes.

Abruptly switching her attention to the bag of groceries,

Robin set several packages on the counter. When Cole's hands clasped her shoulders, her eyes drifted shut. "It isn't necessary," she whispered.

Cole turned her around to face him. "What isn't?"

"The dinner, the wine, the...sweet nothings."

Their eyes held. As if choreographed, they moved into each other's arms. With a groan that came from deep in his throat, Cole kissed her. His hands tangled in the auburn thickness of her hair. His lips settled on hers with fierce protectiveness.

Robin curled her arms tightly around his neck as her own world started to dip and spin and whirl. She was standing on tiptoe, her heart in her throat, when she heard the front door open.

Moaning, she dragged her mouth from Cole's and broke away just as her son strolled into the kitchen.

Jeff stopped, his brow furrowed, when he saw the two of them in what surely looked like suspicious circumstances.

"Hi, Mom. Hi, Cole." He went casually to the refrigerator and yanked open the door. "Anything decent to drink around this place?"

"Water?" Robin suggested.

Jeff rolled his eyes. "Funny, Mom."

"There are a few more sacks of groceries in the car. Would you get them for me?" He threw her a disgruntled look, until Robin added, "You'll find a six-pack of soda in there."

"Okay." He raced out of the house and returned a minute later, carrying one sack and sorting through its contents as he walked into the kitchen.

"I'll help you," Cole said, placing his hand on Jeff's shoulder. He glanced at Robin and his eyes told her they'd continue their discussion at a more opportune moment.

Robin started emptying the sacks, hardly paying attention as Jeff and Cole brought in the last couple of bags. Cole told her he'd pick her up at six, then left.

"Can I play with Blackie for a while?" Jeff asked her, a can of cold soda clenched in his hand.

"Sure," Robin answered, grateful to have a few minutes alone.

Robin cleared the counters and made Jeff a sandwich for his lunch. He must've become involved in his game with Cole's dog because he didn't rush in announcing he was hungry.

She went outside to stand on her small front porch and smiled as she watched Jeff and Blackie. Her son really had a way with animals—like his father. Every time Robin saw him play with Cole's Labrador, she marveled at how attuned they were to each other.

She smiled when she realized Cole was outside, too; he'd just finished watering his lawn.

"Jeff, I made a sandwich for you," she called.

"In a minute. Hey, Mom, watch," he yelled as he tossed a ball across the lawn. Blackie chased after it, skidding to a stop as he caught the bright red ball.

"Come on, Blackie," Jeff urged. "Throw me the ball."

"He can't do that," Robin said in astonishment.

"Sure, he can. Watch."

And just as Jeff had claimed, Blackie leapt into the air, tossed his head and sent the ball shooting into the street.

"I'll get it," Jeff hollered.

It was Cole's reaction that Robin noticed first. A horrified look came over his face and he threw down the hose. He was shouting even as he ran.

Like her son, Robin had been so caught up in Blackie's antics that she hadn't seen the car barreling down the street, directly in Jeff's path.

8

"Jeff!" Robin screamed, fear and panic choking her. Her hands flew to her mouth in relief as Cole grabbed Jeff around the waist and swept him out of the path of the speeding car. Together they fell backward onto the wet grass. Robin ran over to them.

"Jeff, how many times have I told you to look before you run into the street? How many times?" Her voice was high and hysterical.

"I saw the car," Jeff protested loudly. "I did! I was going to wait for it. Honest." He struggled to his feet, looking insulted at what he obviously considered an overreaction.

"Get into the house," Robin demanded, pointing furiously. She was trembling so badly she could barely speak.

Jeff brushed the grass from his jeans and raised his head to a dignified angle, then walked toward the house. Not understanding, Blackie followed him, the ball in his mouth, wanting to resume their play.

"I can't, boy," Jeff mumbled just loudly enough for her to hear. "My mother had some kind of anxiety attack that I'm gonna get punished for."

Cole's recovery was slower than Jeff's. He sat up and rubbed a hand across his eyes. His face was ashen, his expression stark with terror.

"Everything's all right. Jeff isn't hurt," Robin assured him. She slipped to her knees in front of him.

Cole nodded without looking at her. His eyes went blank and he shook his head, as if to clear his mind.

"Cole," Robin said softly, "are you okay?"

"I... I don't know." He gave her a faint smile, but his eyes remained glazed and distant. He placed one hand over his heart and shook his head again. "For a minute there I thought Jeff hadn't seen that car and... I don't know... If that boy had been hurt..."

"Thank you for acting so quickly," Robin whispered, gratitude filling her heart. She ran her hands down the sides of his face, needing to touch him, seeking a way to comfort him, although her heart ached at his words. So many times over the past few weeks, she'd suspected—and feared—that Cole's feelings had more to do with replacing the family he'd lost than love for her and Jeff.

With a shudder, Cole locked his arms around her waist and pulled her close, burying his face in the curve of her neck as he dragged deep gulps of air into his lungs.

"Come inside and I'll get us some coffee," Robin suggested.

Cole murmured agreement, but he didn't seem in any hurry to release her. Nor she him. Her hands were in his hair and she rested her cheek against his, savoring these moments of closeness now that the panic was gone.

"I lost my son," Cole whispered and the words seemed to be wrenched from the deepest part of his soul. His voice held an agony only those who had suffered such a loss could understand. "In a car accident six years ago."

Robin kissed the crown of his head. "I know."

Cole broke away from her, slowly raising his eyes to meet

hers. Mingled with profound grief was confusion. "Who told you?"

"Joyce Wallach."

Cole closed his eyes. "I could use that coffee."

They both stood, and when Cole wrapped his arm around her waist Robin couldn't be sure if it was to lend support or to offer it.

Inside the house, Jeff was sitting at the bottom of the stairs, his knees under his chin. Ever loyal, Blackie lay beside him.

Jeff looked up when Robin opened the front door. "I saw the car," he repeated. "You're getting upset over nothing. I hope you realize that. Hey, what's wrong with Cole?" he asked abruptly. He glanced from Robin to their neighbor and then back to his mother. "He looks like he's seen a ghost."

In some way, Robin supposed, he had.

"You all right, sport?" Cole asked. "I didn't hurt you when we fell, did I?"

"Nah." He bit his lip, eyes lowered.

Cole frowned. "You don't sound all that certain. Are you sure you're okay?"

Jeff nodded reluctantly. "I will be once I find out what my mother plans to do to me. I really was gonna stop at the curb. Honest."

The kid would make an excellent attorney, Robin thought wryly.

"I think I might've overreacted," Cole said. He held open his arms and Jeff flew into them without a second's hesitation. Briefly Cole closed his eyes, as though in silent thanksgiving for Jeff's safety.

"I didn't mean to scare you," Jeff murmured. "I would've stopped."

"I know."

"I promise to be more careful."

"I certainly hope so," Robin said.

Cole released Jeff and sighed deeply, then looked at Robin. "You said something about coffee?"

She smiled and nodded. "I'll get it in a minute. Jeff, you can go outside, but from now on if you're playing ball with Blackie, do it in the backyard. Understand?"

"Sure, Mom," her son said eagerly. "But—" he paused "—you mean that's it? You aren't going to ground me or anything? I mean, of course you're not because I did everything I was supposed to—well, almost everything. Thanks, Mom." He tossed the red ball in the air and caught it deftly with one hand. "Come on, Blackie, we just got a pardon from the governor."

Robin followed the pair into the kitchen and watched as Jeff opened the sliding glass door and raced into the backyard with Blackie in hot pursuit. Reassured, she poured two mugs of coffee while Cole pulled out one of the kitchen chairs. She carried the mugs to the table, then sat down across from him.

Cole reached for her hand, lacing her fingers with his own. He focused his concentration on their linked hands. "Bobby was my son. He died when he was ten."

"Jeff's age," Robin said as a chill surrounded her heart.

"Bobby was so full of life and laughter I couldn't be around him and not smile."

Talking about Bobby was clearly difficult for Cole, and Robin longed to do or say something that would help. But she could think of nothing to ease the agony etched so deeply on his face.

"He was the kind of boy every father dreams of having. Inquisitive, sensitive, full of mischief. Gifted with a vivid imagination."

"A lot like Jeff," she said, and her hands tightened around the mug.

Cole nodded. "Bobby used to tell me I shouldn't worry about

Jennifer—she was my ex-wife—because *he,* my ten-year-old son, was taking care of her."

Robin held her breath as she watched the fierce pain in his eyes. "You don't need to tell me this." Not if it was going to rip open wounds that weren't properly healed.

"I should've told you before this," he said, frowning slightly. "It's just that even now, after all this time, it's difficult to talk about my son. For a good many years, I felt as though part of me had died with Bobby. The very best part of me. I don't believe that anymore."

"Jeff reminds you a lot of Bobby, doesn't he?" Robin doubted Cole fully grasped that he was transferring his love from one boy to the other.

A smile tugged at the corners of his mouth. "Bobby had a huskier build and was taller than Jeff. His sport was basketball, but he was more of a spectator than a participant. His real love was computers. Had he lived, I think Bobby would have gone into that field. Jen never understood that. She wanted him to be more athletic, and he tried to please her." Cole's gaze dropped to his hands. "Jennifer and I were divorced before the accident. She died with him. If there's anything to be grateful for in their deaths, it's the knowledge that they both went instantly. I couldn't have stood knowing they'd suffered." He paused long enough to take a sip of the coffee, and grimaced once. "You added sugar?"

"I thought you might need it."

He chuckled. "I have so much to thank you for."

"Me?"

"Do you remember the afternoon Jeff ran away?"

She wasn't likely to forget it. With Jeff around, Robin always figured she didn't need exercise to keep her heart in shape. Her son managed to do it with his antics.

"I left on a business trip to Seattle soon afterward," he reminded her.

She nodded. That was when Jeff had looked after Blackie for him.

"Late one afternoon, when the meeting was over and dinner wasn't scheduled for another couple of hours, I went for a stroll," Cole said. "It was still light and I found myself on the waterfront. The sky was a vivid blue and the waters green and clear. It's funny I'd remember that, but it's all so distinct in my memory. I stood alone on the pier and watched as a ferry headed for one of the islands, cutting a path through the waves. Something brought Bobby to my mind, although he's never far from my thoughts, even now. The most amazing thing happened that afternoon. It's difficult to find the words to explain." He hesitated, as though searching for a way to make Robin understand. Then apparently he gave up the effort and shook his head.

"Tell me about it," Robin said in a quiet voice.

"Well, standing there at the end of the pier... I don't know. For the first time since I lost my son, I felt his presence more than I did his absence. It was as if he was there at my side, pointing out the Olympic Mountains and asking questions. Bobby was always full of questions. My heart felt lighter than it had in years—as though the burden of pain and grief had been lifted from my shoulders. For no reason whatsoever, I started to smile. I think I've been smiling ever since. And laughing. And feeling.

"When I got back to the hotel, I had the sudden urge to hear your voice. I didn't have any excuse to call you, so I phoned on the pretense of talking to Jeff and checking up on Blackie. But it was your voice I wanted to hear."

Robin smiled through the unexpected rush of tears, wondering if Cole realized what he was saying. It might've been her voice he *thought* he wanted to hear, but it was Jeff he'd called.

"I discovered a new freedom on that Seattle pier. It was as

if, in that moment, I was released from the past. I can't say exactly what changed. Meeting you and Jeff played a big role in it, I recognize that much, but it was more than that. It was as if something deep inside me was willing to admit that it was finally time to let go."

"I'm glad for you," Robin whispered.

"The problem is, I never allowed myself to grieve properly or deal with the anger I felt toward Jennifer. She was driving at the time and the accident was her fault. Yet deep in my heart I know she'd never purposely have done anything to hurt Bobby. She loved him as much as I did. He was her son, too.

"It wasn't until I met you that I knew I had to forgive her. I was never the kind of husband she needed and I'm afraid I was a disappointment to her. Only in the last few years of our marriage was I willing to accept that she suffered from a serious emotional and mental illness. Her addiction to alcohol was as much a disease as cancer. I didn't understand her illness, and because of that we all suffered."

"You're being too hard on yourself," Robin said, but she doubted Cole even heard her.

"After the accident, the anger and the grief were a constant gnawing pain. I refused to acknowledge or deal with either emotion. Over the years, instead of healing, I let the agony of my loss grow more intense. I closed myself off from friends and colleagues and threw myself into work, spending far more time in the office than I did at home. Blackie was virtually my only companion. And then a few years ago I started working on my place in the country. But the pleasure that gave me came from hard physical work, the kind that leaves you too tired to think." His features softened and he smiled at her. "I'd forgotten what it was like to fly a kite or laze in the sunshine."

"That's why you suggested the picnic with Jeff and me?"

He grinned and his dark eyes seemed almost boyish. "The

last time I was in Golden Gate Park was with Bobby, shortly before the accident. Deciding to have a picnic there was a giant step for me. I half expected to feel pangs of grief, if not a full-blown assault. Instead I experienced joy—and appreciation for the renewal I felt. Laughter is a gift I'd forgotten. You and Jeff helped me see that, as well."

Everything Cole was saying confirmed her worst fears.

"Mom!" Jeff roared into the kitchen with Blackie at his heels. "Is there anything to eat? Are you guys still going out to dinner? I don't suppose you'd bring me, would you?"

Cole chuckled, then leapt to his feet to playfully muss Jeff's hair. "Not this time, sport. Tonight's for your mother and me."

Two hours later, as Robin stood in front of the bathroom mirror, she had her reservations about this dinner date. She was falling in love with a man who hadn't fully dealt with the pain of losing his wife and his son. Perhaps she recognized it in Cole because she saw the same thing in herself. She loved Lenny and always would. He'd died years ago, and she still found herself talking to him, refusing to involve herself in another relationship. A part of her continued to grieve and she suspected it always would.

Examining herself in the mirror, Robin surveyed her calf-length skirt of soft blue velvet and white silk blouse with a pearl necklace.

She was fussing with her hair, pinning one side back with combs and studying the effect, when Jeff wandered in. He leaned casually against the doorway, a bag of potato chips in his hand.

"Hey, you look nice."

"Don't sound so surprised." She decided she'd spent enough time on her hair and fastened her pearl earrings. Jeff was disappointed about not joining them, but he'd been a good sport—

especially after Cole promised him lunch at a fish-and-chip place on the Wharf the following Saturday.

"You're wearing your pearls," Jeff mumbled, his mouth full.

"Yes," Robin said, turning to face him. "Do they look all right?"

Jeff's halfhearted shrug didn't do a lot to boost Robin's confidence. "I suppose. I don't know about stuff like that. Mrs. Lawrence could probably tell you." He popped another potato chip in his mouth and crunched loudly. "My dad gave you those earrings, didn't he? And the necklace?"

"For our first wedding anniversary."

Jeff nodded. "I thought so." His look grew reflective. "When I grow up and get married, will I do mushy stuff like that?"

"Probably," Robin said, not bothering to disguise her amusement. "And lots of other things, too. Like taking your wife out to dinner and telling her how beautiful she is and how much you love her."

"Yuck!" Jeff wrinkled his nose. "You really know how to ruin a guy's appetite." With that he turned to march down the stairs, taking his potato chips with him.

Robin stood at the top of the staircase. "Cole will be here any minute, so you can go over to Kelly's now," she called down.

"Okay. I put my plate in the dishwasher. Is there anything you want me to tell Kelly's mom?"

"Just that I won't be too late."

"You're sure I can't come with you?" Jeff tried one more time.

Robin didn't give him an answer, knowing he didn't really expect one. After a moment, Jeff grumbled, more for show than anything, then went out the front door to their neighbor's.

Robin returned to the bathroom and smiled into the mirror, picturing Jeff several years into the future and seeing Lenny's handsome face smiling back at her. She was warmed by the image, certain that her son would grow into as fine a young man as his father had been.

"You don't mind that I'm wearing the pearls for Cole, do you?" she asked her dead husband, although she knew he wouldn't have objected. She ran the tips of her fingers over the earrings, feeling reassured.

The doorbell chimed just as Robin was dabbing perfume on her wrists. She drew in a calming breath, glanced quickly at her reflection one last time, then walked down the stairs to answer the door.

Cole was dressed in a black pin-striped suit and looked so handsome that her breath caught. He smiled as she let him in, but for the life of her she couldn't think of a thing to say.

His eyes held hers as he reached for her hands. Slowly he lowered his gaze, taking in the way she'd styled her hair, the pearl necklace and the outfit she'd chosen with such care.

"You are so beautiful," he said.

"I was just thinking the same about you," she confessed.

His mouth tilted in a grin. "If I kiss you, will it ruin your lipstick?"

"Probably."

"I'm going to kiss you, anyway," he said in a husky murmur. Tenderly he fit his mouth to hers, slipping his fingers through her hair. The kiss was gentle and thorough and slow. A single kiss, and she was like clay ready to be molded. The realization struck her hard—when Cole touched her, Robin felt alive all the way to the soles of her feet. *Alive.* Healthy. A red-blooded woman. He released her, and she was shocked to find she was trembling. From the inside out.

"I've mussed your hair," he apologized. His hands slid under the soft cloud of hair to her nape.

"And you've got lipstick on your mouth," she said with a quaver, reaching up to wipe it away. "There. It'll only take me a moment to fix my hair," she said, picking up her purse and moving to the hallway mirror.

He stood behind her, hands on her shoulders as she brushed her hair, then carefully tucked the loose curls back into place with the tortoiseshell combs.

"Are you ready?" he asked when she'd finished.

Robin nodded, unable to speak.

Cole led her outside to his car and held the passenger door. He dropped a quick kiss on her unsuspecting lips, then hurried around the car, his movements lighthearted, and got into the driver's seat.

"You didn't tell me where we're having dinner."

"I told Heather Lawrence in case she needs to get hold of you, but otherwise it's a surprise."

Robin wasn't sure what to think. A number of San Francisco's restaurants were internationally famous, but her knowledge of fancy dining places was limited. She assumed this one was somewhere in the heart of the city, until he exited from the freeway heading south along Highway 101 toward the ocean.

"Cole?" she asked hesitantly.

"Don't worry," he said, casting her a swift glance that didn't conceal the mischievous twinkle in his eyes. "I promise you dinner will be worth the drive."

The restaurant sat high on a cliff, with a stunning view of the surf battering the jagged rocks below.

Cole parked the Porsche, then came around to help her out, taking the opportunity to steal another kiss. It was with obvious reluctance that he let her go. His arm around her waist, he directed her toward the doors leading into the elegant restaurant. The maître d' escorted them to a table that overlooked the water and with a flourish presented them with elaborate menus.

Robin scanned the entrées, impressed with the interesting variations on basic themes. She was less impressed with the prices—a single dinner cost as much as an entire week's worth of lunches. For her *and* Jeff.

"When you said fancy you weren't joking, were you?" she whispered, biting her lip.

Cole lowered his menu and sent her a vibrant smile. "Tonight is special," he said simply.

"You're telling me. If I wasn't having dinner with you, I'd probably have eaten a toasted cheese sandwich and a bowl of tomato soup with Jeff."

Their waiter appeared and they ordered wine—a bottle of sauvignon blanc. Then they each chose the restaurant's specialty—a scallop and shrimp sauté—which proved as succulent and spicy as the menu had promised.

They talked through dinner and afterward, over steaming cups of Irish coffee. It astonished Robin that they had so much to say to each other, although they hadn't touched on the issue closest to her heart. But she hesitated to broach the subject of Cole's relationship with Jeff. She didn't want to risk the delightful camaraderie they were sharing tonight. Their conversation could have gone on for hours and in fact did. They talked about books they'd read, recent movies they'd seen, music they liked. It came as a pleasant surprise to discover that their tastes were similar.

All evening they laughed, they argued, they talked, as if they'd been friends most of their lives. Cole grinned so often, it was hard for Robin to remember that at one time she'd actually wondered if the man ever smiled.

Robin told Cole about her job and how much she enjoyed accounting. She voiced her fears about not being the kind of mother she wanted to be for Jeff. "There are so many things I want to share with him that I don't have time for. There just aren't enough hours in a day."

Cole talked about his career goals and his dreams. He spoke

of the forty acres willed to him by his grandfather and how he'd once hoped to close himself off from the world by moving there.

"But you aren't going to now?" Robin asked.

"No. I no longer have any reason to hide. The house is nearly finished and I may still move there, but I'll maintain my work schedule." He stared down into his coffee. "I was approached last week about running for the state senate."

Robin's heart swelled with pride. "Are you going to do it?"

"No. I'm not the right man for politics. I'll support someone else, but a political career doesn't interest me. It never has, although I'll admit I'm flattered."

A band started playing then, and several couples took to the dance floor.

"Shall we?" Cole asked, nodding in that direction.

"Oh, Cole, I don't know. The last time I danced was at my cousin's wedding ten years ago. I'm afraid I'll step all over your feet."

"I'm game if you are."

She was reluctant but agreed to try. They stood, and she moved naturally into his embrace, as if they'd been partners for years. Robin's eyes slowly closed when Cole folded her in his arms, and in that moment she experienced a surge of joy that startled her with its intensity.

The dance ended, but they didn't leave the floor.

"Have I told you how lovely you are?" Cole asked, his mouth close to her ear.

Grinning, Robin nodded. "Twice. Once when you picked me up at the house and once during the meal. I know you're exaggerating, but..." She shrugged, then added, "When I'm with you, I feel beautiful."

"I don't think a woman's ever paid me a higher compliment."

She raised her eyes and was shocked by the powerful emotions in his.

"Do you mind if we leave now?" he asked suddenly.

"No, of course not, if that's what you want."

He frowned. "If it was up to me I'd spend the rest of the night here with you in my arms, but I have this sudden need to kiss you, and if I do it here and do it properly we're going to attract a lot of attention."

Cole quickly paid the bill and he hurried Robin to the car. The minute they were settled inside, he reached for her. He did as he'd promised, kissing her until she was breathless. Her arms clung to him as his mouth sought hers once more.

"At least I'm not making you cry this time," he said softly.

"That still embarrasses me," she told him. "It's never happened before. I still don't understand it. I don't know if I ever will."

"I don't think I'll ever forget it."

"Please do."

"No," he said, shaking his head. "It touched me in a way I can't explain. It helped me realize I was going to love you. After Jennifer and Bobby, I doubted there was any love left in me. You taught me otherwise. Jeff taught me otherwise. My heart is full and has been almost from the time we met." He took her hand and pressed her palm to his heart. "Do you feel it?"

Robin nodded. "It's beating so hard," she whispered.

"That's because I'm nervous."

"Nervous? About what?"

Cole slid a hand into his pocket and brought out a small black velvet box.

Robin's heart started to pound in double time. "Cole?" she said anxiously, not sure what she should think or how she should act.

"I love you, Robin." His voice was hoarse. "I knew it the moment I heard your voice when I called from Seattle. And every moment since has convinced me how right this is." He opened the box and revealed the largest diamond Robin had ever seen. Slowly he raised his eyes to hers. "I'm asking you to be my wife."

9

"You mean this whole evening...you arranged this whole evening because you intended to ask me to marry you?" Robin asked, pressing the tips of her fingers to her trembling lips. Despite her fears a gentle gladness suffused her heart.

"Surely it isn't that much of a surprise?" he said. "I've never made an effort to hide how I feel about you or how much I enjoy Jeff."

Contrary to what Cole might think, his proposal *did* come as a surprise. "I... I don't know what to say."

"A simple yes would suit me," Cole urged warmly.

"But... Oh, Cole, it would be so easy to marry you, so easy to join my life and Jeff's to yours and never look back. But I don't know if it would be right for us or for you. There's so much to consider, so many factors to weigh, in a decision this important. I'd like nothing better than to just say yes, but I can't."

"Are you asking for time?" Cole's eyes seemed to penetrate hers, even in the dark.

"Please." For now, that seemed the simplest thing to say, although her hesitation was based on something much deeper.

Cole had rediscovered a peace within himself since meeting her and Jeff; he'd told her so that very afternoon. She was tempted to say yes, to turn away from her doubts and agree to marry him. Cole had been so good for Jeff, so wonderful to her.

"I hate to disappoint you," she murmured sadly.

"I know exactly what you're thinking, exactly how you're feeling."

"You do?" Somehow she doubted it. But knowing she couldn't delay it any longer, she jumped in with both feet. "I was...just thinking about what you told me this afternoon. How you'd recently dealt with the loss of Jennifer and Bobby. While you were talking, I couldn't help feeling your exhilaration. You've obviously found a newborn sense of freedom. I think the question you need to ask yourself is if this rebirth you've experienced is what prompted the idea of marrying again."

"No," he said flatly. "Falling in love with you did."

"Oh, Cole," she whispered. "It must seem like fate to have Jeff and me move in next door, and it gets more complicated with Jeff being the same age as Bobby...."

"Maybe it does all appear too convenient, but if I was just looking for a woman and a child, then Heather Lawrence would've filled the bill. It's you I fell in love with."

"But how can you be so sure?" she countered quickly. "We barely know each other."

Cole smiled at her doubts. "The first time we kissed was enough to convince me I was going to love you. It was the Friday night after I returned from Seattle, remember?"

Robin nodded, wincing a little.

"I was so stunned by the effect that kiss had on me, I avoided you for an entire week afterward. If you want the truth, I was terrified. You'll have to remember, up until that time I was convinced I was incapable of ever falling in love again. One kiss, and I felt jolted to the core. You hit me hard, Robin, and

I needed time to step back and analyze what was happening. That's the reason I don't have any qualms about giving you however long you need to sort out what you're feeling. I want you to be very sure."

Robin released a pent-up sigh. Cole folded her in his arms and his chin brushed against her hair while his hands roved in wide circles across her back. The action was soothing and gentle. She was beginning to feel more confident in his love, but she had to be careful. She *wanted* him to love her, because she was so much in love with him.

Cole tucked a finger under her chin and lifted her face to his. As their eyes met, he slanted his mouth over hers in a wildly possessive kiss, a kiss filled with undisguised need.

When he broke away, Robin was trembling. She buried her face in his neck and drew several deep breaths.

"If you're going to take some time to think about things," Cole whispered against her hair, "then I wanted to give you something else to think about."

"Have you had a chance to check those figures on—" Angela began, then stopped abruptly, waving her hand in front of Robin's face.

"A chance to check what figures?" Robin asked, making a determined effort to focus. She knew she'd been acting like a sleepwalker most of the morning, but she couldn't stop thinking about Cole's proposal.

"What's with you today?" Angela demanded. "Every time I look over here, I find you staring into space with this perplexed expression on your face."

"I was...just thinking," Robin muttered.

"About what?"

"Nothing."

"Come on, girl, you know better than that. You can't fool

me." Angela leaned against the edge of Robin's desk and crossed her arms, taking her usual aggressive stance. "I've known you far too long. From everything you *haven't* said, I'd guess your handsome neighbor's involved. What's he done now?"

"Cole? What makes you ask anything so ridiculous?"

Angela frowned, shaking her head. Then she stretched out her hands and made a come-hither motion. "Tell Mama everything," she intoned. "You might as well get it over with and tell me now, because you know that sooner or later I'm going to drag it out of you. What kind of friend would I be if I didn't extract your deepest darkest secrets?"

"He took me to dinner," Robin admitted, knowing that Angela was right. Sooner or later, she'd wheedle it out of her.

"Where'd he take you?"

She shrugged, wanting to keep that to herself. "It was outside the city."

"*Where* outside the city?" Angela pressed.

"Heavens, I don't know. Somewhere along the coast on Highway 101."

Angela uncrossed her arms and started pacing. "It wasn't the Cliffhouse, was it?"

"I... I think it might have been," Robin murmured, concentrating on the task in front of her. The one she should've finished hours earlier. The one she couldn't seem to focus on, even now.

"Aha!" Angela cried, pointing her index finger at the ceiling, like a detective in a comic spoof.

"What?" Robin cried.

"If Cole took you to the Cliffhouse, he did it for a reason."

"Of course he did. The food was fabulous. By the way, you were right about Frank, he's exceptionally nice," Robin said in an effort to interrupt her friend's line of thought.

"You already told me what you think of Frank, remember?"

Angela said. "Cole took you to dinner at the Cliffhouse," she repeated slowly, as though reviewing a vital clue in a murder mystery.

"To be honest, I think his choice of restaurant had something to do with Frank," Robin inserted, tossing her sleuth friend a red herring.

"So Cole was jealous?"

"Not exactly," Robin said, leaning back in her chair. "Well, maybe a little," she amended, knowing Angela would never believe her if she denied it completely. "I mean, Cole did invite me to dinner as soon as he learned I was dining with Frank, so I guess you could say he was a *little* jealous. But not much. Cole's not the jealous type—he told me that himself."

"I see." Angela was frowning as she walked back to her desk. Her look remained thoughtful for the rest of the morning, although she didn't question Robin again. But when they left for lunch, she showed a renewed interest in the subject of Cole.

"How's Jeff?" she began as they stood in line in the employees' cafeteria.

"Fine," Robin said as she reached for a plastic tray.

"That's all you're going to say?"

"What more do you want to know?"

"I ask about Jeff once a week or so, then sit back and listen for the next fifteen minutes while you tell me about the latest craziness," Angela said heatedly. "It never fails. You've told me about him running away with a frying pan and an atlas. You've bragged about what a fabulous pitcher he's turning out to be, and you've given me a multitude of details about every game he's played. After you tell me all about his athletic ability, you generally mention how good he is with animals and all the tricks he's taught Blackie in the past week."

Robin tried to respond but Angela ignored her and kept talking. "Today I innocently ask how Jeff is, and what do I get? *Fine.* All right, Robin, tell me what happened with Cole Camden before I go crazy trying to figure it out."

"It's something I need to figure out myself," Robin said. She paused to study the salads before selecting a mound of cottage cheese and setting it on her tray.

"What are you doing now?" Angela cried, throwing her arms in the air. "You hate cottage cheese. You never eat it unless you're upset and looking for ways to punish yourself." She took the small bowl from Robin's tray and replaced it with a fresh fruit salad, shaking her head the entire time.

The problem with Angela was that she knew Robin all too well.

They progressed a little farther down the line. Robin stood in front of the entrées, but before she chose one, she glanced at her friend. "You want to pick one of these for me, too?" she asked dryly.

"Yes, I do, before you end up requesting liver and onions."

Angela picked the lasagne, thick with melted cheese and spicy tomato sauce. "If you're looking for ways to punish yourself, girl, there are tastier methods."

Despite her thoughtful mood, Robin smiled.

Once they'd paid for their lunches, Angela led her to a window table that offered a certain amount of privacy. Robin busied herself arranging her dishes and set the tray aside.

Angela sat directly across from her, elbows braced on either side of her lunch. "Are you sure there isn't anything else you'd care to tell me?"

"About what?"

"About you and Cole, of course. I can't remember the last time I saw you like this. It's as if...as if you're trapped in some kind of maze and can't find your way out."

The description was so apt that Robin felt a tingling sensation along her spine. She did feel hopelessly lost. Her mind was cluttered, her emotions confused. She had one foot in the present, one in the past, and didn't know which way to turn.

"I talked to Frank on Sunday afternoon," Angela continued, dipping her fork into a crisp green salad. "He said he enjoyed the evening you spent with him, but doubted you'd be seeing each other again because it's obvious to him that you're in love with Cole Camden. In fact, Frank said you talked about little else the entire evening."

"He said all that?"

Angela nodded. "He's right, isn't he? You are in love with Cole, aren't you?"

"I... I don't know."

"What do you mean you don't know?" Angela persisted. "It's written all over you. You've got that glazed look and you walk around in a trance, practically bumping into walls."

"You make it sound like I need an ambulance."

"Or a doctor," Angela whispered, leaning across the table. "Or maybe a lawyer... That's it!" she said loudly enough to attract the attention of several people at nearby tables. "Cole took you to bed, and now you're so confused you don't know what to do. I told you I'd stumble on the answer sooner or later." Her eyes flashed triumphantly.

"That's not it," Robin declared, half rising from the table. She could feel the color crowding into her cheeks as she glanced around the cafeteria. When she sat back down, she covered her face with both hands. "If you must know, Cole asked me to marry him."

A moment of shocked silence followed before Angela shrieked with pure delight. "That's fabulous! Wonderful! Good grief, what's wrong with you? You should be in seventh heaven. It isn't every day a handsome, wealthy, wonderful man proposes to you. I hope you leapt at the chance." She hesitated, suddenly still. "Robin? You *did* tell him you'd marry him, didn't you?"

Robin swallowed and shook her head. "No. I asked him for some time to think about things."

"Think about things?" Angela squealed. "What's there to think about? He's rich. He's handsome. He's in love with you and crazy about Jeff. What more could you possibly want?"

Tears brimmed in Robin's eyes as she looked up to meet her friend's avid gaze. "I'm afraid he's more in love with the idea of having a family than he is with me."

"Is Cole coming?" Jeff asked, working the stiffness out of his baseball mitt by slamming his fist into the middle of it several times.

"I don't know," Robin said, glancing at their neighbor's house as they walked to the car. "I haven't talked to him in the last few days."

"You're not mad at him, are you?"

"Of course not," Robin said, sliding into the driver's seat of her compact. "We've both been busy."

Jeff fingered the bill of his baseball cap, then set the cap on his head. "I saw him yesterday and told him about the game, and he said he might come. I hope he does."

Secretly Robin hoped Cole would be there, too. Over the past five days, she'd missed talking to him. She hadn't come to any decision, but he hadn't pressed her to make one, willing to offer her all the time she needed. Robin hadn't realized how accustomed she'd grown to his presence. How much she needed to see him and talk to him. Exchange smiles and glances. Touch him...

When she was married to Lenny, they were two people very much in love, two people who'd linked their lives to form one whole. But Lenny had been taken from her, and for a long time afterward Robin had felt only half alive.

All week she'd swayed back and forth over Cole's proposal,

wondering if she should ignore her doubts. Wondering if she *could* ignore them. Sleepless nights hadn't yielded the answer. Neither had long solitary walks in Balboa Park while Jeff practiced with his baseball team.

"Cole said—" Jeff started to say, then stopped abruptly as his hands flew to his head. A panicky look broke out on his face and he stared at Robin.

"What's wrong? Did you forget something?"

"My lucky hat!" Jeff cried. "It's on my dresser. We have to go back."

"For a baseball cap?" Robin didn't disguise how silly she considered that idea. "You're wearing a baseball cap. What's wrong with that one?"

"It won't work. You have to understand, Mom, it's my *lucky* hat. I've been wearing it ever since we played our first game. I had that very same hat on when I hit my first two home runs. I can't play without it," he explained frantically. "We have to go back. Hurry, or we'll be late for the game. Turn here," he insisted, pointing at the closest intersection.

"Jeff," she said, trying to reason with her son. "It isn't the hat that makes you play well."

"I knew you were going to say something like that," he muttered, "and even if it's true, I want to be on the safe side, just in case. We've got to go back and get that hat!"

Knowing it would only waste valuable time to argue, Robin did as he requested. After all, his whole career as a major-league pitcher hung in the balance!

She was smiling as she entered her driveway. Sitting in the car while Jeff ran inside for his lucky cap, Robin glanced over at Cole's place. His car was gone. It'd been gone since early that morning, and she suspected he was at the property, working on his house. Jeff would be disappointed about Cole missing his game, but he'd understand.

Jeff came barreling out of the house, slamming the front door. He leapt into the car and fastened his seat belt. "Come on, Mom," he said anxiously, "let's get this show on the road." As if *she'd* caused the delay, Robin thought to herself, amused by her son's sudden impatience.

By the time they arrived at Balboa Park, the car park was filled to overflowing. Robin was fortunate enough to find a space on the street, a minor miracle in itself. Perhaps there was something to this magic-cap business after all.

Jeff ran across the grass, hurrying toward his teammates, leaving Robin to fend for herself, which was fine. He had his precious cap and was content.

The bleachers were crowded with parents. Robin found a seat close to the top and had just settled in place when she saw Cole making his way toward her. Her heart did an immediate flip-flop and it wasn't until he sat next to her that she was able to speak.

"I thought you were working up on the property this weekend."

"And miss seeing Jeff pitch? Wild horses couldn't have kept me away." He was smiling at her with that cocky heart-stopping smile of his.

"How have you been?" she asked. She couldn't keep her eyes off him. He looked too good to be true, and his dark gaze was filled with warmth and tenderness. How could she help getting lost in eyes that generous? It seemed impossible to resist him any longer.

"I've missed you like crazy," he whispered, and the humor seemed to drain out of him as his eyes searched hers. "I didn't think it was possible to feel this alone. Not anymore."

"I've missed you, too."

He seemed to relax once she'd said that. "Thank you," he

said quietly. "Have you been thinking about what I said last weekend?"

She bowed her head. "I haven't thought of anything else."

"Then you've made up your mind?"

"No." She kept her face lowered, not wanting him to see her confusion.

He tilted her chin with one finger, forcing her to meet his eyes. "I promised myself I wouldn't ask you and then I couldn't seem to stop myself. I won't again."

She offered him a weak smile, and Cole looked around him, clearly wanting to kiss her, but not in front of such a large gathering. The funny part was, Robin didn't care about being seen. She was so hungry for the reassurance of his touch, it didn't matter to her that they were in the middle of a crowded park.

"I see Jeff's wearing his lucky hat," Cole said, clasping her hand and giving her fingers a comforting squeeze.

"You know about that?"

"Of course. Jeff tells me everything."

"He panicked when he realized he was wearing the wrong one, and I had to make a U-turn in the middle of the street because he'd left the guaranteed-to-pitch-well baseball cap on his dresser."

"You can't blame him. The luck has lasted through five games now."

"I wonder if it'll last until he reaches the pros," Robin said, sharing a smile with him.

"You're doing all right?" Cole asked unexpectedly.

She nodded, although it wasn't entirely true. Now that she was with Cole, every doubt she'd struggled with all week vanished like fog under an afternoon sun. Only when they were apart was she confronted by her fears.

"After Jeff's finished here, let's do something together," Cole suggested. "The three of us."

She nodded, unable to refuse him anything.

"Come to think of it, didn't I promise Jeff lunch? I seem to recall making a rash pledge to buy him fish and chips because we were leaving him with Heather and Kelly when we went to dinner last week."

Robin grinned. "It seems to me you're remembering that correctly," she said.

They went to a cheerful little fish-and-chip restaurant down by the Wharf. The weather had been chilly all morning, but the sun was out in full force by early afternoon. Jeff was excited about his team's latest win and attributed it to the luck brought to them by his cap.

After a leisurely lunch, the three of them strolled along the busy waterfront. Robin bought a loaf of fresh sourdough bread and a small bouquet of spring flowers. Jeff found a plastic snake he couldn't live without and paid for it with his allowance.

"Just wait till Jimmy Wallach sees this!" he crowed.

"I'm more curious to see how Kelly Lawrence reacts," Robin said.

"Oh, Kelly likes snakes," Jeff told them cheerfully. "Jimmy was over one day and I thought I'd scare Kelly with a live garden snake, but Jimmy was the one who started screaming. Kelly said snakes were just another of God's creatures and there was nothing to be afraid of. Isn't it just like a girl to get religious about a snake?"

Jeff raced down the sidewalk while Cole and Robin stood at the end of the pier, the bread and flowers at their feet.

"You look tired," Cole said, as his fingers gently touched her forehead.

"I'm fine," she insisted, gazing out at the cool green waters of San Francisco Bay. But Cole was right; she hadn't been sleeping well.

"I see so much of myself in you," Cole said softly.

His words surprised her. "How's that?"

"The pain mostly. How many years has Lenny been dead?"

"Ten. In some ways I'm still grieving him." She couldn't be less than honest with Cole.

"You're not sure if you can love another man, are you? At least not with the same intensity that you loved Jeff's father."

"That's not it at all. I... I just don't know if I can stop loving him."

Cole went very still. "I never intended to take Lenny away from you or Jeff. He's part of your past, an important part. Being married to Lenny, giving birth to Jeff, contributed to making you what you are." He paused, and they both remained silent.

"Bobby had been buried for six years before I had the courage to face the future. I hung on to my grief, carried it with me everywhere I went, dragging it like a heavy piece of luggage I couldn't travel without."

"I'm not that way about Lenny," she said, ready to argue, not heatedly or vehemently, but logically, because what he was saying simply wasn't true. She mourned her dead husband, felt his absence, but she hadn't allowed this sense of loss to destroy her life.

"Perhaps you aren't grieving as deeply as you once were," Cole amended. "But I wonder if you've really laid your husband to rest."

"Of course I have," she answered with a nod of her head, not wanting to talk about Lenny.

"I don't mean to sound unsympathetic," Cole said, his tone compassionate. "I understand, believe me I do. Emotional pain is familiar territory for us both. It seems to me that those of us who sustain this kind of grief are afraid of what lies beyond."

"You're exaggerating, Cole."

"Maybe," he agreed. "You're a lovely woman, Robin. Witty. Intelligent. Outgoing. I'm sure one of the first questions anyone asks you is how long it's been since your husband died. And I'll bet when you tell them, they seem surprised."

That was true, and Robin wondered how Cole had guessed.

"Most young widows remarry."

"Are you suggesting that because I didn't immediately fling myself back into matrimonial bliss I'm a candidate for therapy? Come on, Cole, even you must realize how ridiculous that is."

"Even me?" he asked, chuckling.

Jeff came loping toward them, his face flushed with excitement. "They're filming a movie," he cried, pointing toward a congested area farther down the pier. "There's cameras and actors and everything. Can I go watch some more?"

Robin nodded. "Just don't get in anyone's way."

"I won't. Promise. Here, Mom, hold my snake." He entrusted her with his precious package before racing back down the pier.

"He's a fine boy, Robin."

"He loves you already. You and Blackie."

"And how does his mother feel?"

The knot in her throat thickened. "She loves you, too."

Cole grinned. "She just isn't sure if she can let go of her dead husband to take on a live one. Am I right?"

His words hit their mark. "I don't know," she admitted. "Maybe it's because I'm afraid you want to marry me because Jeff reminds you of Bobby. Or because you've created a fantasy wife and think I'll fit the role."

Her words seemed to shock him. "No. You've got that all wrong. Jeff is a wonderful plus in this relationship, but it's *you* I fell in love with. It's you I want to grow old with. You, and you alone, not some ideal. If you want to know the truth, I think you're stirring up all this turmoil because you're afraid of ever marrying again. The little world you've made is tidy and safe. But is this what Lenny would've wanted for you?" He gripped her firmly by the shoulders. "If Lenny were standing beside you right now and you could ask him about marrying me, what would he say?"

"I...don't understand."

"If you could seek Lenny's advice, what would he tell you? Would he say, 'Robin, look at this guy. He's in love with you. He thinks the world of Jeff, and he's ready to embark on a new life. This is an opportunity too good to pass up. Don't be a fool. Marry him.'?"

"That sounds like something my friend Angela would say."

"I'm going to like this friend of yours—just as long as she doesn't try to set you up with any more of her divorced cousins," Cole said, laughing. His eyes grew warm as he gazed at her, and she suspected he was longing to take her in his arms and kiss her doubts away. But he didn't. Instead, he looked over his shoulder and sighed. "I think I'll go see what Jeff's up to. I'll leave you to yourself for a few minutes. I don't mean to pressure you, but I do want you to think about what I said."

"You aren't pressuring me," she whispered, staring out over the water.

Cole left her then, and her hands clutched the steel railing as she raised her eyes to the sky. "Oh, Lenny," she whispered. "What should I do?"

10

"Cole wants me to ask your advice." Robin continued to look up at the cloudless blue sky. "Oh, Lenny, I honestly don't know what's right for Jeff and me anymore. I love Cole. I love you. But at the same time I can't help wondering about Cole's motives...."

Robin paused, waiting. Not that she expected an answer. Lenny couldn't give her one. He never did; he never would. But unlike the other times she'd spoken to him, she needed a response, even though expecting one was totally illogical.

With every breath she took, Robin knew that, but the futility of it hit her, anyway. Her frustration was so hard and unexpectedly powerful that it felt like a body blow. Robin closed her eyes, hoping the heat of the sun would take away this bitter ache, this dreadful loneliness.

She felt so empty. Hollow all the way through.

Her fists were clenched at her sides as tears fell from her eyes. Embarrassed, she glanced around, grateful that the film crew had attracted most of the sightseers. No one was around to witness her distress.

Anger, which for so many years had lain dormant inside her,

gushed forth in an avalanche of grief and pain. The tears continued to spill down her cheeks. Her lips quivered. Her shoulders shook. Her hands trembled. It was as if the emotion was pounding against her chest and she was powerless to do anything but stand there and bear it.

Anger consumed her now. Consumed her because she hadn't allowed it to when Lenny was killed. It had been more important to put on a brave front. More important to hold herself together for Jeff and for Lenny's parents. More important to deal with the present than the past.

Lenny had died and Robin was furious with him for leaving her alone with a child to raise. Leaving her alone to deal with filing taxes and taking out the garbage and repairing leaking pipes. All these years she'd managed on her own. And she'd bottled the anger up inside, afraid of ever letting it go.

"Robin."

Cole's voice, soft and urgent, reached out from behind her. At the sound, she turned and walked into his arms, sobbing, needing his comfort and his love in equal measure. Needing him as she'd never needed anyone before.

She didn't know how long he held her. He was whispering soothing words to her. Gentle words. But she heard none of them over the sound of her own suffering.

Once she started crying, Robin couldn't seem to stop. It was as if a dam had burst inside her and the anguish, stored for too many years, came pouring out.

Cole's arms were securely wrapped around her, shielding her. She longed to control this outburst, longed to explain, but every time she tried to speak her sobbing only grew worse.

"Let it out," he whispered. "You don't have to say anything. I understand."

"He doesn't answer," she sobbed. "I asked him… Lenny never answers me…because he can't. He left me…"

"He didn't want to die," Cole told her.

"But he did...he did."

Cole didn't argue with her. He simply held her, stroking the back of her head as though reassuring a small child.

It took several minutes for Robin to compose herself enough to go on. "Part of me realizes that Lenny didn't want to leave me, didn't want to die. But he did and I'm so angry at him."

"That anger is what makes us human," Cole said. He continued to comfort her and, gradually, bit by bit, Robin felt her composure slip back into place.

She sensed Jeff's presence even before he spoke.

"What wrong with my mom?" he asked Cole.

"She's dealing with some emotional pain," Cole explained, speaking as one adult to another.

"Is she going to be all right?"

Robin hadn't wanted her son to see her crying and made a concerted effort to break away from Cole, to reassure Jeff herself. Cole loosened his hold, but kept his arm around her shoulders.

"I'm fine, Jeff. Really."

"She doesn't look so good."

Her son had developed the irritating habit of talking to Cole and not to her when she was upset. They'd done it that day her son had run away to the fort. Jeff and Cole had carried on an entire conversation about her while she was in their midst then, too.

Cole led her to a bench and they all sat down.

Jeff plopped down next to her and reached for her hand, patting it several times. Leaning toward Cole, he said earnestly, "Chocolate might help. One time Mom told me there wasn't anything in this world chocolate couldn't cure."

She'd actually said that? Robin started to smile. Wrapping

her arms around her son, she hugged him close, loving him so much her heart seemed about to burst.

Jeff wasn't all that keen on being cuddled, especially in public, but although he squirmed he put up with his mother's sudden need to hold him.

When she'd finished, Jeff rolled his eyes and once more directed his comments to Cole. "She gets weird like this every once in a while. Remember what happened that day I ran away?"

"I remember," Cole said, and Robin smiled at the trace of amusement she heard in his voice.

"Will you stop excluding me from this conversation? I'm going to be all right. I just had this…urge to cry, but don't worry, it's passed."

"See what I mean?" Jeff muttered to Cole.

"But Jeff's right," Robin said, ignoring her son's comment. "Something chocolaty would definitely help."

"You'll be okay by yourself for a couple of minutes?" Cole asked.

"I'll be fine. I…don't know exactly what came over me, but I'm going to be just fine."

"I know you are." He kissed her, his lips gentle against her cheek.

The two of them left and once more Robin was alone. She didn't really understand why the pain and anger had hit her so hard now, after all this time. Except that it had something to do with Cole. But the last place she would ever have expected to give in to her grief was on Fisherman's Wharf with half of San Francisco looking on.

Jeff returned less than a minute later, running to her side with a double-decker chocolate ice cream cone. "Cole's bringing two more for him and me," he explained. "I told the guy it was an emergency and he gave me this one right away."

"That was nice of you," Robin said, wondering what the vendor must have thought. Smiling, she ran her tongue over the ice cream, savoring the cold chocolate. As profoundly as she'd wept, she felt almost giddy with relief now, repressing the impulse to throw back her head and laugh.

Cole arrived, and with Jeff on her left and Cole on her right she sat on the concrete bench and ate her ice cream cone.

"I told you this would work," Jeff told Cole smugly.

"And to think I scoffed at your lucky baseball cap," she teased, feeling much better.

When they finished the cones, Cole gathered up their packages and led them back to where he'd parked his car.

Blackie was there to greet them the instant they returned to Orchard Street. Jeff ran into the backyard to play with the dog, and Cole walked Robin to her door. He accepted her offer of coffee.

"I'm probably going to be leaving soon for my property," he said, watching her closely. He sat down at the table, his hands cupping the mug as though to warm them. "Will you be all right?"

Robin nodded. She walked over and stood beside him and pressed a hand to his strong jaw. "I realize you delayed going up there today because of Jeff and his baseball game. We're both grateful."

Cole placed his hand over hers and harshly expelled his breath. "I feel responsible for what you went through there on the pier. I should never have said what I did. I'm sorry, Robin, it wasn't any of my business."

"You only said what I needed to hear."

He smiled. "If I did, it was because of what happened to me in Seattle. It's quite a coincidence that both of us would come to grips with our pain while standing on a pier—me in Seattle, you here in San Francisco. I went home with this incredible sense of release. For the first time since Bobby and Jennifer's deaths, I surrendered my grief. In a way it was as though I reached up and God reached down and together we came to an understanding."

That so completely described what Robin had been feeling that for a long moment she couldn't say anything. What Cole had said earlier about carrying the pain, dragging it everywhere, was right on the mark, too. He understood; he'd done the same thing himself. A surge of love swelled within her.

"I know you don't want to hear this," he was saying. "I honestly don't mean to pressure you. But once I returned from Seattle and realized I was falling in love with you I started thinking about having another baby." He hesitated and took a gulp of his coffee. Then he stood up abruptly, nearly knocking the chair backward. "I'd better go before I say or do something else I shouldn't."

Robin followed him into the entryway, not wanting him to leave, but not quite ready to give him what he needed.

He paused at the screen door and his eyes immediately found hers. He couldn't seem to keep himself from touching her, brushing an auburn curl from her cheek. His knuckles grazed her skin lightly, and Robin's eyes closed of their own accord at the sensation that shot through her. Her heart was full, and she seemed to have all the answers now—except to the one question that was the most important in her life. And Jeff's.

"I'll see you sometime next week," Cole said roughly, pulling his hand away. Without another word, he walked out the door, pausing at the top of the porch steps.

He called for his dog and in response both Blackie and Jeff came running.

"You're not leaving, are you?" Jeff asked breathlessly.

"I'm taking Blackie for the rest of the weekend. You think you can get along without him till Monday, sport?"

Jeff shrugged and stuck his fingers in the hip pockets of his blue jeans. "I suppose. Where are you taking him?"

"To my property." Cole didn't turn toward Robin. It was as if he had to ignore her in order to walk away from her.

"Oh, yeah!" Jeff said enthusiastically. "I remember you said something about it once. You're building a house, aren't you?"

"Remodelling one. My grandfather lived there as a boy and he left it to me, only it's been a lot of years since anyone's cared for that old house properly and there's plenty of work that needs to be done."

"I'll work for you," Jeff piped up eagerly. He made a fist and flexed his arm, revealing the meager muscles. "I know it doesn't look like much, but I'm strong. Ask anyone."

Cole tested Jeff's muscles, pretending to be impressed. "Yes, I can tell you're strong, and I'm sure I couldn't ask for a harder worker." Jeff beamed until Cole added regretfully, "I'll take you up there another time, sport."

Jeff's face fell.

Before she even realized what she was doing, Robin moved onto the porch. "Cole."

He turned to face her, but the movement seemed reluctant.

Perhaps it was because she didn't want to be separated from him any more than he wanted to be away from her. Perhaps it was the thought of Jeff's disappointment when he'd already had so many other disappointments in his life. Perhaps it was this newborn sense of freedom she was just beginning to experience.

She stepped toward Cole. "Could Jeff and I go up to the property with you?"

Jeff didn't wait for Cole to answer before leaping excitedly into the air. "Hey, Mom, that's a great idea! Really great. Can we, Cole? Blackie and I can help you, and Mom can... Well, she can do things..."

"I'll have you both know I pound a mean hammer," Robin

felt obliged to inform them. If she was going to Cole's farm, she fully intended to do her share.

Cole looked perplexed for a moment, as if he wasn't sure he'd heard her correctly. "I'd love to have you come—if you're sure that's what you want."

Robin just nodded. All she knew was that she couldn't bear to be separated from him any longer.

"Be warned—the house is only half done. The plumbing isn't in yet."

"We'll manage, won't we, Jeff?"

"Yeah," Jeff said eagerly. "Anyway, boys got it easy."

Cole laughed. "How long will it take you to pack?"

"We're ready now, aren't we, Blackie?" Jeff almost jitterbugged across the front lawn in his enthusiasm.

"Give me a few minutes to throw some things together," Robin said, grinning. Jeff was smiling, too, from ear to ear, as he dashed past her into the house and up the stairs.

Cole's eyes held Robin's in silent communication—until Jeff came bursting out of the house, dragging his sheets and quilt with him, straight from his bed.

"Jeff," she cried, aghast, "what are you doing?"

"I took everything off my bed. I can go without plumbing, but I need my sleep." He piled the bedding at their feet. "You two can go back to looking at each other. I'll get everything else we need."

"Jeff," Robin groaned, casting Cole an apologetic glance. "I'll pack my own things, thank you."

"You want me to get your sheets, too?" he called from inside the house.

"No." She scooped up the bedding and hurried into the house, taking the stairs two at a time. She discovered Jeff sitting on the edge of her bed, his expression pensive.

"What's wrong?"

"Are you ever going to marry Cole?" her son asked.

At the unexpectedness of the question, Robin's heart flew to her throat, then slid back into place. Briefly she wondered if Cole had brought up the subject with her son, but instinctively knew he hadn't. "Wh-what makes you ask that?"

He shrugged. "Lots of things. Every time I turn around you two are staring at each other. Either that or kissing. I try to pretend I don't notice, but it's getting as bad as some of those movies you like. And when you were crying on the pier, I saw something. Cole had his arms around you and he was looking real sad. Like...like he wished he could do the crying for you. It's the same look Grandpa sometimes gives Grandma when he figures out that she's upset, and she doesn't even have to talk. Do you know what I mean?"

"I think so," Robin said, casually walking over to her dresser drawer and taking out a couple of old sweatshirts. "And what would you think if I said I was considering marrying Cole?"

Robin expected shouts of glee and wild shrieks, but instead her son crossed his arms over his chest and moved his mouth in odd ways, stretching it to one side and then the other. "You're serious, aren't you?"

"Yes." She folded and refolded one of the sweatshirts, her heart pounding in anticipation. "It would mean a lot of changes for all of us."

"How many other people are involved in this?"

Robin hesitated, not understanding Jeff's concern. "What do you mean?"

"Will I get an extra set of grandparents in this deal?"

"Uh...probably. I haven't talked to Cole about that yet, but I assume so."

"That means extra gifts on my birthday and at Christmas. I say we should go for it."

"Jeffrey Leonard Masterson, you shock me!"

He shrugged. "That's how a kid thinks."

Robin shook her head in dismay at her son's suddenly materialistic attitude toward her possible marriage. She was still frowning as she stepped outside.

Cole was in his garage, loading up the trunk of his SUV when Robin joined him. She handed him one small suitcase and a bag of groceries she'd packed at the last minute.

Cole stowed them away, carefully avoiding her eyes. "I guess you said something to Jeff about us?" She could hear amusement in his voice.

"Yes. How'd you know?"

"He brought down a paper bag full of clothes and asked what kind of presents he could expect from my parents at Christmas. He also asked if there were any aunts or uncles in the deal." Robin's embarrassment must have showed, because Cole started chuckling.

"That boy's got a mercenary streak in him I knew nothing about," she muttered.

Cole was still grinning. "You ready?"

She nodded, drawing an unsteady breath, eager for this adventure to begin. Jeff and Blackie were already in the backseat when Robin slipped into the front to wait for Cole.

"Are we going to sing camp songs?" Jeff asked, leaning forward. He didn't wait for a response, but immediately launched into the timeless ditty about bottles of beer on the wall. He sang ninety-nine verses of that, then performed a series of other songs until they left the freeway and wound up on a narrow country road with almost no traffic.

Jeff had tired of singing by then. "Knock knock," he called out.

"Who's there?" Robin said, falling in with his game.

"Eisenhower."

"Eisenhower who?"

Jeff snickered. "Eisenhower late, how about you?" With that, the ten-year-old broke into belly-gripping guffaws, as if he should be receiving awards for his ability to tell jokes.

Cole's mouth was twitching and Robin had to admit she was amused, too.

"The turnoff for the ranch is about a mile up the road," Cole explained. "Now remember, this is going to be a lot like camping. It's still pretty primitive."

"You don't need to worry," Robin said, smiling at him.

A couple of minutes later, Cole slowed, about to turn down the long driveway. It was then that Robin saw the sign. Her heart jumped into her throat and her hands started to shake.

"Stop!" she screamed. "Stop!"

Cole slammed on the brakes, catapulting them forward. "Robin, what is it?"

Robin threw open the front door and leapt out of the car, running to the middle of the road. She stared at the one word on the sign even as the tears filled her eyes.

Cole's farm was named *Paradise.*

11

"Robin, I don't understand," Cole said for the third time, his dark eyes worried.

"I bet my allowance she's crying again," Jeff muttered, poking his head out the side window. "Something weird's going on with my mother. She's been acting goofy all day. Why do you think it is?"

"I'm not really sure," Cole said as he continued to study Robin.

For her part, Robin couldn't take her eyes off the sign. Jeff was right about her crying; the tears streamed unrestrained down her face. But these were tears of joy. Tears of gratitude. Tears of acknowledgment. It was exactly as Cole had described. She'd reached up and God had reached down and together they'd come to an understanding. She'd finally resolved her dilemma.

Unable to stop herself, Robin hurled her arms around Cole's neck. Her hands roamed his face. His wonderful, wonderful face.

Because her eyes were blurred with emotion, she couldn't accurately read Cole's expression, but it didn't matter. Her heart spilled over with love for him.

"Robin..."

She didn't let him finish, but began spreading a long series of kisses across his face, starting with his eyelids. "I love you, I love you," she repeated between kisses, moving from his cheek to his nose and downward.

Cole put his arms around her waist and pulled her closer. Robin was half-aware of the car door slamming and Jeff marching up the road to join them.

"Are you two getting all mushy on me again?"

Robin barely heard her son. Her mouth had unerringly found Cole's.

The unexpected sharp sound of a hand clap brought her out of her dream world. The kiss ended, and her eyes immediately went to Jeff, who was looking very much like a pint-size adult. His face and eyes were stern.

"Do the two of you know where you're standing?" Jeff demanded as though he'd recently been hired by the state police to make sure this type of thing didn't happen. "There are proper places to kiss, but the middle of the road isn't one of them."

"He's right," Cole said, his eyes devouring Robin. He clearly didn't want to release her and did so with a reluctance that tugged at her heart.

"Come with me," Jeff said, taking his mother by the hand and leading her back to the car. He paused in front of the door and frowned. "Maybe she has a fever."

"Robin," Cole said, grasping her hand, "can you explain now?"

She nodded. "It's the sign—Paradise. Tell me about it. Tell me why your grandfather named his place Paradise."

"I'm not sure," Cole said, puzzled. "He lived here his whole life and always said this land was all he'd ever needed. From what I remember, he once told me he thought of this place as the Garden of Eden. I can only assume that's why he named it Paradise."

Robin nodded, unsurprised by his explanation. "When Lenny and I were first married, we talked...we dreamed about someday buying some land and raising animals. Enough land for Jeff to have a pony and for me to have a huge garden. We decided this land would be our own piece of heaven on earth and...from that we came up with the idea of naming it Paradise."

Cole shook his head slowly, and she could tell he didn't completely understand.

"This afternoon, when I was standing on Fisherman's Wharf, you suggested I talk over my feelings about our getting married with Lenny."

"What I suggested," Cole reminded her, "was that you *imagine* what he'd say to advise you. I certainly didn't expect you to really communicate with him."

"I know this won't make any sense to you, but I've talked to Lenny lots of times over the years. This afternoon, what hit me so hard was the fact that Lenny would never answer me. That realization was what finally forced me to deal with the pain. To forgive Lenny for dying."

Jeff was looking at her in confusion, his mouth open and eyes wide.

"Here you were wanting to marry me and I didn't know what to do. I had trouble believing your proposal was prompted by anything more than the desire to replace the family you'd lost. I do love you, and I desperately wanted to believe you loved me—and Jeff. But I wasn't sure...."

"And you're sure now?"

She nodded enthusiastically. "Yes. With all my heart, I'm confident that marrying you would be the right thing for all of us."

"Of course we're going to marry Cole!" Jeff cried. "Good grief, all you had to do was ask me and I would've told you. We belong together."

"Yes, we do, don't we?" Robin whispered. "Cole," she said, taking both his hands with her own. "I'd consider it a very great honor to become your wife."

"Jeff?" Cole said, tearing his eyes away from Robin.

The boy's face shone and his eyes sparkled. "I'd consider it a very great honor to become your son."

Cole brushed his lips across Robin's and then reached for Jeff, hauling him into his arms and squeezing him tight. Blackie started barking then, wanting out of the car. Robin quickly moved to open the passenger door, and the black Lab leapt out. She crouched down and wrapped her arms around his thick neck, hugging him. "You're going to have a whole family now, Blackie," she said happily.

Two hours later, just at dusk, Robin was standing in the middle of the yard. She'd loved everything about Paradise, just as she'd known she would. The house and property were nothing like the place she and Lenny had dreamed about, but she hadn't expected them to be. The four-bedroom house was much larger than anything they'd ever hoped to own. The land was covered with Ponderosa pine, and the rocky ground was more suitable to grazing a few sheep or cattle than planting crops.

Cole was showing Jeff the barn, and Robin had intended to join them, but the evening was redolent with a sweet-smelling breeze and she'd stopped to breathe in the fresh cool air. She folded her arms and stood there, smiling into the clear sky. A multitude of twinkling stars were just beginning to reveal themselves.

Cole walked quietly up behind her, and slipped his arms around her waist, pulling her against him. "Have I told you how much I love you?"

"In the last fifteen minutes? No, you haven't."

"Then allow me to correct that situation." He nibbled the back of her neck gently. "I love you to distraction."

"I love you, too."

He sighed then and whispered hoarsely, "It was a difficult decision to marry me, wasn't it?"

Robin agreed with a nod.

"Had I given you so many reasons to doubt me?"

"No," she said quickly, turning in his arms. She pressed her palms against his jaw. "I had to be sure in my heart that you weren't trying to replace the son you'd lost with Jeff. And I had to be equally certain you loved me for myself and not because I was Jeff's mother and we came as a package deal."

He shook his head decisively. "Jeff's a great kid, don't get me wrong, but there's never been any question in my mind about how I felt. The first time we met, you hit me square between the eyes. I didn't mean to fall in love again. I didn't even want to."

"I don't think I did, either," Robin confessed.

"Past experience taught us both that loving someone only causes pain. I loved Jennifer, but I could never make her happy. When we divorced I accepted my role in the breakup."

"But she had a drinking problem, Cole. You can't blame yourself."

"I don't, not entirely, but I accept a portion of the blame for what went wrong. It tore me apart to see Bobby caught in the middle, and in an effort to minimize the pain I didn't fight for custody. He was an innocent victim of the divorce, and I didn't want him to suffer any further distress. I was willing to do anything I could to spare him. Later, when I realized how serious Jennifer's problem with alcohol had become, I tried to obtain custody, but before I could get the courts to move on it, the accident happened. Afterward, I was left facing the guilt of having waited too long.

"The thought of ever marrying again, having children again, terrified me. I couldn't imagine making myself vulnerable a second time." He paused, and a slow, gentle smile spread across his face, smoothing away the tension. "All of that changed when I met you. It was as if life was offering me another chance. And I knew I had to grab hold of it with both hands or live with regret forever."

"Oh, brother," Jeff said as he dashed into the yard. "Are you two at it again?"

"We're talking," Robin explained.

"Your mouths are too close together for talking." He strolled past them, Blackie trotting at his side. "I don't suppose you thought about making me anything to eat, did you, Mom?"

"I made sandwiches."

"Great. Are there enough for Blackie to have one?"

"I think so. There's juice and some corn chips in the kitchen, too."

"Great," Jeff repeated, hurrying into the house.

"Are you hungry?" Robin asked Cole.

"Yes," he stated emphatically, "but my appetite doesn't seem to be for food. How long will you keep me waiting to make you my wife?"

"I'll have to call my parents and my brother so we can arrange everything. It's important to me that we have a church wedding. It doesn't have to be fancy, but I'd like to invite a handful of good friends and—"

"How long?"

"To make the arrangements? I'm not sure. Three, possibly four months to do it properly."

"One month," Cole said.

"What do you mean, one month?"

"I'm giving you exactly thirty days to arrange whatever you want, but that's as long as I'm willing to wait."

"Cole—"

He swept her into his arms then and his mouth claimed

hers in a fury of desire. Robin found herself trembling and she clutched his shirt, her fingers bunching the material as she strove to regain her equilibrium.

"Cole..." She felt chilled and feverish at the same time. Needy, yet wealthy beyond her wildest dreams.

"One month?" he repeated.

"One month," she agreed, pressing her face against his broad warm chest. They'd both loved, profoundly, and lost what they'd valued most. For years, in their own ways, they'd sealed themselves off from others, because no one else could understand their pain. Then they'd discovered each other, and nothing would ever be the same again. Their love was the mature love that came when one had suffered and lost and been left to rebuild a shattered life. A love that was stronger than either could have hoped for.

"Do you see what I was telling you?" Jeff muttered to Blackie, sitting on the back porch steps. "I suppose we're going to have to put up with this for a while."

Blackie munched on a corn chip, apparently more interested in sharing Jeff's meal than listening to his comments.

"I can deal with it, if you can," Jeff continued. "I suspect I'll be getting at least one brother out of this deal, and if we're lucky maybe two. A sister would be all right, too, I guess—" he sighed deeply "—but I'll have to think about that. Girls can be a real headache, if you know what I mean."

The dog wagged his tail as Jeff slipped him another corn chip. "And you know what, Blackie? It's gonna be Father's Day soon. My very first. And I've already got a card picked out. It's got a picture of a father, a mother and a boy with a baseball cap. And there's a dog on it that looks just like you!"

★ ★ ★ ★ ★

Daddy's Little Helper

1

The new schoolteacher wouldn't last.

It didn't take Mitch Harris more than five seconds to make that assessment. Bethany Ross didn't belong in Alaska. She reminded him of a tropical bird with its brilliant plumage. Everything about her was *vivid*, from her animated expression to her sun-bleached hair, which fell to her shoulders in a frothy mass of blond. Even blonder curls framed her classic features. Her eyes were a deep, rich shade of chocolate.

She wore a bright turquoise jumpsuit with a wide yellow band that circled her trim waist. One of her skimpy multicolored sandals dangled from her foot as she sat on the arm of Abbey and Sawyer O'Halloran's sofa, her legs elegantly crossed.

This get-together was in her honor. Abbey and Sawyer had invited the members of the school board to their home to meet the new teacher.

To Mitch's surprise, she stood and approached him before he had a chance to introduce himself. "I don't believe we've met." Her smile was warm and natural. "I'm Bethany Ross."

"Mitch Harris." He didn't elaborate. Details wouldn't be necessary because Ms. Ross simply wouldn't last beyond the first snowfall. "Welcome to Hard Luck," he said almost as an afterthought.

"Thank you."

"When did you get here?" he asked, trying to make conversation. He twisted the stem of his wineglass and watched the chardonnay swirl against the sides.

"I flew in this afternoon."

He hadn't realized she'd only just arrived. "You must be exhausted."

"Not really," she was quick to tell him. "I suppose I should be, considering that I left San Francisco early this morning. The fact is, I've been keyed up for days."

Mitch suspected Hard Luck was a sorry disappointment to her. The town, population 150, was about as far from the easy California lifestyle as a person could get. Situated fifty miles north of the Arctic Circle, Hard Luck was a fascinating place with a strong and abiding sense of community. People here lived hard and worked harder. Besides Midnight Sons, the flight service owned and operated by the three O'Halloran brothers, there were a few small businesses, like Ben Hamilton's café. Mitch himself was one of a handful of state employees. He worked for the Department of the Interior, monitoring visitors to Gate of the Arctic National Park. This was in addition to his job as the town's public safety officer—PSO—which meant he was responsible for policing in Hard Luck. Trappers wandered into town now and then, as did the occasional pipeline worker. To those living on the edge of the world, Hard Luck was a thriving metropolis.

Lately the town had piqued the interest of the rest of the country, as well. But Bethany Ross had nothing to do with that. Thank heaven, although Mitch figured she'd stay about as long as some of the women the O'Halloran brothers had brought to town.

Until recently only a small number of women had lived here. Not many were willing to endure the hardship of being this far from civilization. So the O'Hallorans had spearheaded a campaign to bring women to Hard Luck. Abbey was one of their notable successes, but there'd been a few equally notable failures. Like—who was it?—Allison somebody. The one who'd lasted less than twenty-four hours. And just last week, two women had arrived, only to return home on the next flight out. Bethany Ross had actually applied for the teaching job last spring, before all this nonsense.

Unexpectedly she smiled—a ravishing smile that seemed to say she'd read his thoughts. "I plan to fulfill my contract, Mr. Harris. I knew what I was letting myself in for when I agreed to teach in Alaska."

Mitch felt the heat rise to his ears. "I didn't realize my...feelings were so transparent."

"I don't blame you for doubting me. I don't exactly blend in with the others, do I?"

He was tempted to smile himself. "Hard Luck isn't what you expected, is it?"

"I'll adjust."

She said this with such confidence he began to wonder if he'd misjudged her.

"Frankly, I didn't know *what* to expect. With Hard Luck in the news so often, the idea of moving here was beginning to worry me."

Mitch didn't bother to conceal his amusement. He'd read what some of the tabloids had written about the town and the men's scheme to lure women north.

"My dad was against my coming," Bethany continued. "It was all I could do to keep him from flying up here with me.

He seems to think Hard Luck's populated with nothing but love-starved bush pilots."

"He isn't far wrong," Mitch said wryly. If Bethany had only been in town a few hours, she probably hadn't met the pilots currently employed by Midnight Sons. He knew Sawyer had flown her in from Fairbanks.

It was after repeatedly losing their best pilots for lack of female companionship that the O'Hallorans had decided to take action.

"Midnight Sons is the flight service? Owned by the O'Hallorans?" she asked, looking flustered. "Sawyer and his brothers?"

"That's right." Mitch understood why she was confused. Immediately following her arrival, she'd been thrust into the middle of this party, with twenty or more names being thrown her way all at once. In an effort to help her, Mitch explained that Charles O'Halloran, the oldest of the three brothers, was a silent partner.

Charles hadn't been so silent, however, when he learned about the scheme Sawyer and Christian had concocted to lure women to Hard Luck. Still, he'd changed his tune since meeting Lanni Caldwell. Earlier in the week, they'd announced their engagement.

"Is it true that Abbey—Sawyer's wife—was the first woman to come here?" Her eyes revealed her curiosity.

"Yes. They got married this summer."

"But...they look like they've been married for years. What about Scott and Susan?"

"They're Abbey's children from a previous marriage. I understand Sawyer's already started the adoption process." Mitch envied his friend's happiness. Marriage hadn't been nearly as happy an experience for him.

"Chrissie's your daughter?" Bethany asked, glancing over at the children gathered around a Monopoly game.

Mitch's gaze fell fondly on his seven-year-old daughter. "Yes. And she's been on pins and needles waiting for school to start."

Bethany's eyes softened. "I met her earlier with Scott and Susan. She's a delightful little girl."

"Thank you." Mitch tried hard to do his best for Chrissie, though sometimes he wondered whether his best would ever be enough. "You've met Pete Livengood?" he asked, gesturing toward a rugged-looking middle-aged man on the other side of the room.

"Yes. He owns the grocery?"

"That he does. Dotty, the woman on his left, is another one who answered the advertisement."

Bethany blinked as if trying to remember where Dotty fit into the small community. "She's the nurse?"

He nodded. "Pete and Dotty plan to be married shortly. The first week of October, I believe."

"So soon?" She didn't give him an opportunity to answer before directing her attention elsewhere. "What about Mariah Douglas? Is she a recent addition to the town?"

"Yup. She's the secretary for Midnight Sons."

"Is she engaged?"

"Not yet," Mitch said, "but it's still pretty early. She just got here last month."

"You mean to say she's lived here an entire month without getting married?" Bethany teased. "That must be some sort of record. It seems to me the virile young men of Hard Luck are slacking in their duties."

Mitch grinned. "From what I've heard, it isn't for lack of trying. But Mariah says she didn't come to Hard Luck looking for a husband. She's after the cabin and the twenty acres the O'Hallorans promised her."

"Good for her. They've fulfilled their part of the bargain, haven't they? I read that news story about the cabins not being anywhere near the twenty acres. Sure sounds misleading to me." Fire flashed briefly in her eyes, as if she'd be willing to take on all three O'Hallorans herself.

"That's none of my business. It's between Mariah and the O'Hallorans."

Bethany flushed with embarrassment and bent her head to take a sip of her wine. "It isn't my business, either. It's just that Mariah seems so sweet. I hate the idea of anyone taking advantage of her."

They were interrupted by Sawyer and Abbey. "I see you've met Mitch," Sawyer said, moving next to Bethany.

"He's been helping me keep everyone straight," she told him with a quick smile.

"Then he's probably mentioned that in addition to his job with the Department of the Interior, he's our public safety officer."

"Hard Luck's version of the law," Mitch translated for her.

"My father's a member of San Francisco's finest," she murmured.

"Well," Sawyer said, "Mitch was one of Chicago's finest before moving here."

"That's right," Mitch supplied absently.

"I imagine your head's swimming about now," Abbey said. "I know mine was when I first arrived. Oh—" she waved at a woman just coming in the door "—here's Margaret. Margaret Simpson, the high school teacher."

Margaret, a pleasant-looking brunette in her thirties, joined them. She greeted Bethany with friendly enthusiasm, explained that she lived on the same street as Sawyer and Abbey did and that her husband was a pipeline supervisor who worked three weeks on and three weeks off.

Mitch hardly heard the conversation between Margaret and

Bethany; the words seemed to fade into the background as he found himself studying Bethany Ross.

He wanted to know her better, but he wouldn't allow himself that luxury. Although she claimed otherwise, he didn't expect her to last three months, not once the brutal winter settled in.

But she intrigued him. Tantalized him. The reasons could be as basic as the fact that he'd been too long without a woman—six years to be exact. He'd buried Lori when Chrissie was little more than an infant. Unable to face life in Chicago, he'd packed their bags and headed north. As far north as he could get. He'd known at the time that he was running away. But he'd felt he had no choice, not with guilt and his own self-doubts nipping at his heels. He was out of money and tired of life on the road by the time he reached Hard Luck.

And he'd been happy here. As happy as possible, under the circumstances. He and Chrissie had made a new life for themselves, made new friends. For Mitch, the world had become calm and orderly again, without pain or confusion. Without a woman in their lives.

He certainly hadn't expected to meet a woman like Bethany—a tropical bird—in Alaska.

She wasn't precisely beautiful, he decided. She was...striking. He struggled to put words to her attributes. Feminine. Warm. Generous. Somewhat outrageous. Fun. The kids would love her. He'd spent ten, possibly fifteen, minutes chatting with her and wanted more of her time, more of her attention.

But he refused to indulge himself. He'd learned all the lessons he ever wanted to learn from his dead wife. The new school-teacher could tutor some other man.

Bethany yawned and tried to hide it behind the back of her hand.

"You must be exhausted," Abbey said sympathetically. "I can't believe we've kept you this long. I'm so sorry."

"No, please, it was wonderful of you to make me feel so welcome." To her obvious chagrin, Bethany yawned again. "But maybe I should leave now."

"She's dead on her feet," Sawyer said to no one in particular. "Mitch, would you be kind enough to escort her home?"

"Of course." He set down his wineglass, but truth be known, he'd rather have declined. He was about to suggest someone else do the honors when he realized Bethany might find that insulting.

She studied him, and again he had the impression she could read his mind. He looked away and searched the room until he found his daughter. Chrissie was sitting near the door to the kitchen with her best friend, Susan. The two were deep in conversation, their heads close together. He didn't know what they were discussing, but whatever it was seemed terribly important. Yet another scheme to outsmart the adults, no doubt. Heaven save him from little girls.

He turned to Bethany Ross. "If you'll excuse me a moment?" he asked politely.

"Of course. I'll need a few minutes myself."

While Mitch collected Chrissie, Bethany bade the members of the school board good-night.

They met just outside the front door. He didn't have to ask where she lived—the teacher's living quarters were supplied by the state and were some of the best accommodations in town. The small two-bedroom house was located on the far side of the school gymnasium.

Mitch held open the passenger door so Chrissie could climb into the truck first. He noticed how quiet his daughter had become, as if she was in awe of this woman who would be her teacher.

"I appreciate the ride," Bethany told him once he'd started the engine.

"It's no trouble." It was, but not because of the extra few minutes' driving. But then he decided he might as well let himself enjoy her company, since the opportunity was unlikely to be repeated. Once the eligible men in Hard Luck caught sight of her, he wouldn't stand a chance. Which was probably a good thing...

"Would you mind driving me around a bit?" Bethany asked. "I didn't get much of a chance to see the town earlier."

"There's not much to see." It occurred to him that he might enjoy her company too much, and that could be dangerous.

"We could show her the library," Chrissie said eagerly.

"Hard Luck has a library?"

"It's not very big, but we use it a lot," said the girl. "Abbey's the town librarian."

Sawyer's wife had worked for weeks setting up the lending library. The books were a gift from the O'Hallorans' mother and had sat in a disorganized heap for years—until Abbey's arrival. She'd even started ordering new books, everything from bestselling fiction to cookbooks; the first shipment had been delivered a week ago, occasioning great excitement. It seemed everyone in town had become addicted to books. Mitch had heard a number of lively discussions revolving around a novel. An avid reader himself, he was often a patron, and he encouraged Chrissie to take out books, too.

"Ms. Ross should see the store," Chrissie suggested next. "And the church and the school."

"What's that building there?" Bethany asked, pointing to the largest structure in town.

"That's the lodge," he said without elaborating.

"Matt Caldwell's fixing it up." Again it was Chrissie who provided the details. "He's Lanni's brother."

"You didn't meet Lanni Caldwell," Mitch explained. "I told you about her—she's engaged to Charles O'Halloran."

"I met Charles?"

"Briefly. He was in and out."

"The tall man wearing the Midnight Sons sweatshirt?"

"That's right."

Chrissie leaned closer to Bethany. "No one lives at the lodge now 'cause of the fire. Matt bought it, and he's fixing it up so people will come and stay there and pay him lots of money."

"The fire?"

"It happened years ago," Mitch told her. "Most of the damage was at the back, so you can't see it from here." He shook his head. "The place should've been repaired or torn down long before now, but I guess no one had the heart to do either. The O'Hallorans recently sold it to Matt Caldwell, which was definitely for the best."

"Matt's going to take the tourists mushing!" Chrissie said. "He's going to bring in dogs and trainers and everything!"

"That sounds like fun."

"Eagle Catcher's a husky," Chrissie added.

Mitch caught Bethany's questioning look. "That's Sawyer's dog."

"He belongs to *Scott*," his daughter corrected him.

"True," Mitch said with a smile at Chrissie. "I'd forgotten."

"Scott and Susan are brother and sister, right?" said Bethany. "Abbey's kids?"

"Right."

Mitch could tell Bethany was making a real effort to keep everyone straight in her mind, and he thought she'd done an impressive job so far. Maybe a memory for names and faces came with being a teacher.

"Are there any restaurants in town?" Bethany asked. "I'm not much of a cook."

Mitch glanced her way. Their eyes met briefly before he looked back at the road. "The Hard Luck Café."

Bethany nodded.

"Serves the best cup of coffee in town, but then Ben hasn't got much competition."

There was a pause. "Ben?"

"Hamilton. He's a bit of a grouch, but don't let that fool you. He's got a heart of gold, and he's a lot more than chief cook and bottle washer. Along with everything else, he dishes up a little psychology. You'll like him."

"I—I'm sure I will."

Mitch drove to the end of the road. A single light shone brightly in the distance. "That's where the cabins are," he said. "Mariah's place is the one on the far left." Mitch had lost count of the number of times the youngest O'Halloran brother, Christian, had tried to convince his secretary to move into town. But Mariah always refused. Mitch was just glad *he* wasn't the one dealing with her stubbornness.

He turned the truck around and headed back toward the school. When he pulled up in front of Bethany's little house, she smiled at him.

"Thanks for the tour and the ride home."

"My pleasure."

"Chrissie," Bethany said, her voice gentle, "since I'm new here, I was wondering if you'd be my classroom helper."

His daughter's eyes lit up like sparklers on the Fourth of July, and she nodded so hard her pigtails bounced wildly. "Can Susan be your helper, too?"

"Of course."

Chrissie beamed a proud smile at her father.

"Well, good night, Chrissie, Mitch," Bethany said, then opened her door and climbed out.

"Night," father and daughter echoed. Mitch waited until she was inside the house and the lights were on before he drove off.

So, he thought, *the new schoolteacher has arrived.*

★ ★ ★

Bethany was even more exhausted than she'd realized. But instead of falling into a sound sleep, she lay awake, staring at the ceiling, fighting fatigue and mulling over the time she'd spent with Mitch Harris.

The man was both intense and intelligent. That much had been immediately apparent. He stood apart from the others in more ways than one. Bethany suspected he wouldn't have bothered to introduce himself, which was why she'd taken the initiative. She'd noticed him right away, half-hidden in a corner, watching the events without joining in. When it looked as if the evening would pass without her meeting him, she'd made the first move.

There was something about him that appealed to her. Having lived with a policeman all her life, she must have intuitively sensed his occupation; she certainly hadn't been surprised when Sawyer told her. He reminded her a little of her father. They seemed to have the same analytical mind. It drove her mother crazy, the way Dad carefully weighed each decision, considered every option, before taking action. She'd bet Mitch was like that, too.

It was one personality trait Bethany *didn't* share.

She would've liked to know Mitch Harris better, but she had the distinct impression he wasn't interested. Then again... maybe he was. A breathless moment before she'd introduced herself, she'd recognized some glint of admiration in his eye. She'd been sure of it. But now she wondered if that moment had existed only in her imagination.

All the same, she couldn't help wondering what it would be like to see his eyes darken with passion before he kissed her....

She was far too tired; she wasn't thinking clearly. Bethany closed her eyes and pounded the pillow, trying to force herself to relax.

But even with her eyes shut, all she saw was Mitch Harris's face.

She hadn't come to Hard Luck to fall in love, she told herself sternly.

Rolling onto her other side, she cradled the pillow in her arms. It didn't help. Drat. She could deny it till doomsday, but it wouldn't make any difference. There was just something about Chrissie's father....

"Ms. Ross?"

Bethany looked up from the back of her classroom. Chrissie and Susan stood by the doorway, their faces beaming with eagerness.

"Hello, girls."

"Um, we're here to be your helpers," Chrissie said. "Dad told us we'd better make sure we *are* helpers and not nuisances."

"I'm sure you'll be wonderful helpers," Bethany said.

The two girls instantly broke into huge grins and rushed inside the room. Bethany put them to work sorting textbooks. This was the first time she'd taught more than one grade, and the fact that she'd now be handling kindergarten through six intimidated her.

"Everyone's looking forward to school," Chrissie announced, "especially my dad."

Bethany chuckled. Mitch wasn't so different from other parents.

The girls had been working for perhaps twenty minutes when Chrissie suddenly asked, "You're not married or anything, are you, Ms. Ross?"

A smile trembled on her mouth. "No."

"Why not?"

Leave it to a seven-year-old to ask that kind of question. "I haven't met the right man," she explained as simply as she could.

"Have you ever been in love?" Susan probed.

Bethany noticed that both girls had stopped sorting through the textbooks and were giving her their full attention. "Yes," she told them with some hesitation.

"How old are you?"

"Chrissie." Susan jabbed her elbow into her friend's ribs. "You're not supposed to ask that," she said in a loud whisper. "It's against the human-rights law. We could get charged with snooping."

"I'm twenty-five," Bethany answered, pretending she hadn't heard Susan.

The girls exchanged looks, then started using their fingers to count.

"Seven," Chrissie breathed, as if it were a magic number.

"Seven?" Bethany asked curiously. What game were the girls playing?

"If a man's seven years older than you, is that too old?" Susan asked, her eyes wide and inquisitive.

"Too old," Bethany repeated thoughtfully. She perched on the edge of a desk and crossed her arms. "That depends."

"On what?" Chrissie moved closer.

"On age, I suppose. If I was fourteen and wanted to date a man who was twenty-one, my parents would never have allowed it. But if I was twenty-one and he was twenty-eight, it would probably be okay."

Both girls seemed pleased with her answer, grinning and nudging each other.

Bethany responded to their odd behavior with a joke. "You girls aren't thinking about dating fourteen-year-old boys, are you?" she asked, narrowing her eyes in pretend disapproval.

Chrissie covered her mouth and giggled.

Susan rolled her eyes. "Get real, Ms. Ross. I don't even know what the big attraction is with boys." Then, as if to explain her words, she said, "I have an older brother."

"Would you tell us about the man you were in love with?" This came from Chrissie. Her expression had grown so serious Bethany decided to answer, despite her initial impulse to change the subject.

"The man I was in love with," she began, "was a guy I dated while I was in college. We went out for about a year."

"What was his name?"

"Randy."

"Randy," Chrissie repeated with disgust, turning to look at her friend.

"Did he do you wrong?"

Bethany laughed at the country-and-western phrasing, although she was uncomfortable with these questions. "No, he didn't do me wrong." If anyone was to blame for their breakup, it had been Bethany herself. She wasn't sure she'd ever really loved him, which she supposed was an answer in itself. They'd been friends, and that had developed into something more—at least on Randy's part.

He'd started talking marriage and children, and at first she'd agreed. Then she'd realized she wasn't ready for that kind of commitment. Not when she had two full years of school left. Not when she'd barely begun to experience life.

They'd argued and broken off their unofficial engagement. The breakup had troubled Bethany for months afterward. But now she understood that what she'd really regretted was the loss of their friendship.

"Do you still see him?" Chrissie asked.

Bethany nodded.

"You *do*?" Susan sounded as if this was a tragedy.

"Sometimes."

"Is he married?"

"No." Bethany grew a little sad, thinking about her long-time friend. She did miss Randy, even now, five years after their breakup.

Both Chrissie and Susan seemed deflated at the news of Bethany's lost love.

"Would it be all right if we left now?" Chrissie asked abruptly.

"That's fine," Bethany told them. "Thanks for your help."

The two disappeared so quickly all that was missing was the puff of smoke.

If nothing else, the girls certainly were entertaining, Bethany thought. She returned to the task of cutting large letters out of colored paper.

The sun blazed in through the classroom windows, and she tugged her shirt loose, unfastened the last few buttons and tied the ends at her midriff. Then she pulled her hair away from her face and used an elastic to secure it in a ponytail.

Half an hour later, most of the letters, all capitals, for the word *September* were pinned in an arch across the bulletin board at the back of the room. She stood on a chair and had just pinned the third *E* when she felt someone's presence behind her. Twisting around, she saw Mitch standing in the open door.

"Hi," she said cheerfully, undeniably pleased to see him. He was dressed in the khaki uniform worn by Department of the Interior staff. His face revealed none of his emotions, yet Bethany had the feeling he'd rather not be there.

"I'm looking for Chrissie."

Bethany pinned the *R* in place and then stepped down from the chair. "Sorry, but as you can see she isn't here."

Mitch frowned. "Louise Gold told me this was where she'd be."

Bethany remembered that Louise Gold was the woman who watched Chrissie while Mitch was at work. She'd briefly met her the day before. In addition to her other duties, Louise served on the school board.

"Chrissie was here earlier with Susan."

"I hope they behaved themselves."

Bethany recalled their probing questions and smiled to herself. Pushing back the chair, she said, "They were fine. I asked Chrissie for her help, remember?"

Mitch remained as far away from her as possible. Bethany suspected he'd rather track a cantankerous bear than stay in the same room with her. It was not a familiar feeling, or a pleasant one.

"She must be over at Susan's, then," he said.

"She didn't say where she was headed."

He lingered a moment. "I don't want Chrissie to become a nuisance."

"She isn't, and neither is Susan. They're both great kids, so don't worry, okay?"

Still he hesitated. "They didn't, by any chance, ask you a lot of personal questions, did they?"

"Uh...some."

He closed his eyes for a few seconds and an expression of weariness crossed his face. He sighed. "I'll look for Chrissie over at Susan's. Thanks for your trouble."

His gaze held hers. By the time he turned away, Bethany felt a little breathless. She was sure of one thing. If it was up to Mitch Harris, she would never have left San Francisco.

Well, that was unfortunate for Mitch. Because Bethany had come to Hard Luck with a plan, and she wasn't leaving until it was accomplished.

2

"Daddy?"

Mitch looked up from the Fairbanks paper to smile at his freckle-faced daughter. Chrissie was fresh out of the bathtub, her face scrubbed clean, her cheeks rosy. She wore her favorite *Beauty and the Beast* pajamas.

His heart contracted with the depth of his love for her. No matter how miserable his marriage had been, he'd always be grateful to Lori for giving him Chrissie.

"It's almost bedtime," he told his daughter.

"I know." Following their nightly ritual, she crawled into his lap and nestled her head against his chest. Sometimes she pretended to read the paper with him, but not this evening. Her thoughts seemed to be unusually grave. "Daddy, do you like Ms. Ross?"

Mitch prayed for patience. He'd been afraid of this. Chrissie had been using every opportunity to bring Bethany into their conversations, and he knew she was hoping something romantic would develop between him and the teacher. "Ms. Ross is very nice," he answered cautiously.

"But do you *like* her?"

"I suppose."

"Do you think you'll marry her?"

It was all Mitch could do to keep from bolting out of the chair. "I have no intention of marrying anyone," he said emphatically. As far as he was concerned, the subject wasn't open for discussion. With anyone, even his daughter.

Chrissie batted her baby blues at him. "But I thought you liked her."

"Sweetheart, listen, I like Pearl, too, but that doesn't mean I'm going to marry her."

"But Pearl's old. Ms. Ross is only twenty-five. I know 'cause I asked her. Twenty-five isn't too old, is it?"

Mitch gritted his teeth. After they'd driven Bethany home that first night, Chrissie had been filled with questions about the new teacher. No doubt she'd subjected Bethany to a similar inquisition that morning.

Mitch supposed all this talk about marriage was inevitable. The summer had been full of romantic adventures. Certainly Sawyer had wasted no time in marrying Abbey; it didn't help that Abbey's daughter was Chrissie's best friend. Then Charles had become engaged to Lanni, followed by Pete and Dotty's recent announcement. To Chrissie, it must've seemed as if the whole town had caught marriage fever. Bethany, however, had been hired by the school board last spring and had nothing to do with the recent influx of women.

"I like Ms. Ross *so* much," Chrissie said with a delicate sigh.

"You hardly know her. You might change your mind once you see her in the classroom." Mitch felt he was grasping at straws, but he was growing more and more concerned. He could hardly forbid his daughter to mention Bethany's name!

He wasn't sure what the woman had done to sprout wings and a halo in his daughter's estimation. Nor did he understand why Chrissie had chosen to champion Bethany instead of, say, Mariah Douglas.

Perhaps she'd intuitively sensed his attraction to the young teacher. That idea sent chills racing down his spine. If Chrissie had figured it out, others wouldn't be far behind.

"I won't change my mind about Ms. Ross," Chrissie told him. "I think you should marry her."

"Chrissie. We've already been over this. I'm not going to marry Ms. Ross."

"Why not?"

There was something very wrong when a grown man couldn't out-argue a seven-year-old. "First, we don't know each other. Remember, sweetheart, she's only been in town two days."

"But Sawyer fell in love with Abbey right away."

"Yes..." he muttered warily.

"Then why can't you put dibs on Ms. Ross before any of the other men decide they like her, too?"

"Chrissie—"

"Someone else might marry her if you don't hurry up!"

Mitch calmed himself. It was clear that his daughter had a rejoinder for every answer. "This is different," he said reasonably. "I'm not Sawyer and Ms. Ross isn't Abbey. She came here to teach, remember? She isn't looking for a husband."

"Neither was Abbey. I *really* want you to marry Ms. Ross."

Mitch clenched his jaw. "I'm not marrying Ms. Ross, and I refuse to discuss it any further." He rarely used this tone with his daughter, but he wanted it understood that the conversation was over. He wasn't getting married. End of story. No amount of begging and pleading was going to make any difference.

Chrissie was quiet for several minutes. Then she said, "Tell me about my mommy."

Mitch felt like a drowning man. Everywhere he turned there

was more water, more trouble, and not a life preserver in sight. "What do you want to know?"

"Was she pretty?"

"Very pretty," he answered soothingly. Normally he found the subject of Lori painful, but right now he was grateful to discuss something other than Bethany Ross.

"As pretty as Ms. Ross?"

He rolled his eyes; he'd been sucker-punched. "Yes."

"She died in an accident?"

Mitch didn't know why Chrissie repeatedly asked the same questions about her mother. Maybe the child could tell that he wasn't giving her the whole truth. "Yes, your mother died in an accident."

"And you were sad?"

"I loved her very much."

"And she loved me?"

"Oh, yes, sweetheart, she loved you."

His daughter seemed to soak in his words, as if she needed reassurance that she'd been wanted and loved by the mother she'd never known.

After that, Chrissie grew thoughtful again. Mitch returned to his paper. Then, when he least expected it, she resumed her campaign. "Can I have a brother or sister someday?" she asked him. The question came at him from nowhere and scored a direct hit.

"Probably not," he told her truthfully. "Like I said, I don't plan to remarry."

"Why not?" She wore that hurt-little-girl look guaranteed to weaken his resolve.

Mitch made a show of checking his watch. He was through with answering questions and finding suitable arguments for a child. Through with having Bethany Ross offered up to him on a silver platter—by his daughter, the would-be matchmaker.

"Time for bed," he said decisively.

"Already?" Chrissie whined.

"Past time." He slid her off his knee and led her into her bedroom. He removed the stuffed animals from the bed while Chrissie got down on her knees to say her prayers. She closed her eyes and folded her hands, her expression intent.

Mitch could see his daughter's lips move in some fervent request. He didn't have to be a mind reader to know what she was asking. If God joined forces against him, Mitch figured he'd find himself engaged to the tantalizing Ms. Ross before the week was out.

Christian O'Halloran, youngest of the three brothers, walked into the Hard Luck Café and collapsed in a chair. He propped his elbows on the table and buried his face in his hands.

Without asking, Ben picked up the coffeepot and poured him a cup. "You look like you could use something stronger," he commented.

"I can't believe it," Christian moaned.

"Believe what?" Ben assumed this had to do with Christian's secretary. He didn't understand what it was about Mariah that Christian found so objectionable. Personally he was rather fond of the young lady. Mariah Douglas had grit. She had the gumption to live in one of those run-down cabins. No power. No electric lights. And for damn sure, nothing that went flush in the night.

"You won't believe what just happened. I nearly got my head chewed off by some attorney."

Now this was news. Ben slid into the chair opposite Christian's. "An attorney? Here in Hard Luck?"

Christian nodded, his face a smoldering shade of red. "I was accused of everything from false advertising to misrepresentation and fraud. *Me*," he said incredulously.

"Who hired her?"

Christian's eyes narrowed. "My guess is Mariah."

"No." Ben shook his head. Mariah might've been the cause of some minor troubles with Christian, but there wasn't a vindictive bone in her body. From everything he'd seen of her, Mariah was a sweet-natured, gentle soul.

"It isn't clear who hired the woman," Christian admitted, "but odds are it's Mariah."

"I don't think so."

"I do!" Christian snapped. "I swear to you Mariah's been looking for a way to do me in from the moment she got here. First off, she tried to cripple me."

"She didn't mean to push that filing cabinet on your foot."

"Is that a fact? I don't suppose you noticed how perfect her aim was, did you? She's been a thorn in my side from day one. Now *this*."

"Seems to me you're getting sidetracked," Ben said. He didn't want to hear another litany of Mariah's supposed sins, not when there was other, juicier information to extract. "We were discussing the attorney, remember?"

Christian plowed all ten fingers though his hair. "The lawyer's name is Tracy Santiago. She flew in from some highfalutin firm in Seattle. Let me tell you, I've seen sharks with duller teeth. This woman's after blood, and from the sound of it, she wants mine."

"And you think Mariah sent for her?" Ben asked doubtfully.

"I don't know what to think anymore. Santiago's here, and when she's through discussing the details of the lawsuit with Mariah, she wants to talk to the others. To Sally McDonald and Angie Hughes." He referred to the two most recent arrivals— Sally, who worked at the town's Power and Light company, and Angie, who'd been hired as an administrative and nursing assistant to Dottie. Both of them were living in the house owned by Catherine Fletcher—Matt and Lanni Caldwell's grandmother.

"Are you going to let her?"

Christian raised his eyes until they were level with Ben's. "I can't stop her, can I? But then, I don't think a freight train would slow this Santiago woman down."

"Where is she now? Your office?" Ben asked, craning his neck to look out the window. The mobile office of Midnight Sons was parked next to the airfield, within sight of the café. He couldn't see anything out of the ordinary.

"Yeah, I had to get out of there before I said something I'd regret," Christian confessed. "I feel bad about abandoning Duke, but he seemed to be holding his own."

"Duke?"

"Yeah. Apparently he flew her in without knowing her purpose for coming. He made the fatal mistake of thinking she might've been one of the women I hired. Santiago let him know in no uncertain terms who and what she was. By the time they landed, the two of them were at each other's throats."

That they'd been able to discuss anything during the flight was saying something, given how difficult it was to be heard above the roar of the engines.

"If I were this attorney," Christian said thoughtfully, "I'd think twice before messing with Duke."

Ben had to work hard to keep the smile off his face. When a feminist attorney tangled with the biggest chauvinist Ben had ever met, well...the fur was guaranteed to fly.

The door opened. Christian looked up and groaned, then covered his face with his hands again.

Ben turned around and saw that it was Mariah. He lumbered to his feet, reached for the coffeepot and returned to the counter.

"Mr. O'Halloran," the secretary said as she timidly approached him.

"How many times," Christian demanded, "have I asked you to call me by my first name? In case you haven't noticed, there are three Mr. O'Hallorans in this town, and two of us happen to spend a lot of time together in the same office."

"Christian," she began a second time, her voice quavering slightly. "I want you to know I had nothing to do with Ms. Santiago's arrival."

"Yeah, right."

Mariah clenched her hands at her sides. "I didn't know anything about her," she insisted, "and I certainly had nothing to do with hiring her."

"Then who did?"

Ben watched as Mariah closed her eyes and swallowed hard. When she spoke again, her voice was a low whisper. "I suspect it was my dad. He must've talked to her about my being here."

"And why, pray tell, would he do that?" Christian asked coldly.

Mariah went pale. "Would you mind very much if I sat down?"

The look Christian threw her said he would. After an awkward moment, he gestured curtly toward the seat across from him.

"You want some coffee?" Ben felt obliged to offer.

"No," Christian answered for her. "She doesn't want anything."

"Do you have orange juice?" Mariah asked.

"He has orange juice," Christian told her, "at five bucks a glass."

"Fine."

Another moment of strained silence passed while Ben delivered the four-ounce glass of juice.

"You had something you wanted to tell me?" Christian asked impatiently.

"Yes," she said, her voice gaining strength. "I'm sure my family's responsible for Ms. Santiago's visit. You see... I didn't exactly tell them I'd accepted your job offer. They didn't know—"

"You mean you were hiding from your parents?"

"I wasn't *hiding*," she argued. "Not exactly." She brushed a long strand of hair away from her face, and Ben saw that her hands were shaking badly. "I wanted to prove something to them, and this seemed the only way I could do it."

"What were you trying to prove?" Christian shouted. "How easy it is to destroy a man and his business?"

"No," she replied, squaring her shoulders. "I wanted to demonstrate to my father that I'm perfectly capable of taking care of myself. That I can support myself, and furthermore, I'm old enough to make my own decisions without him continually interfering in my life."

"So you didn't tell him what you'd done."

"No," she admitted, chancing a quick look in Christian's direction. "Not at first. It's been a while since my family heard from me, so I wrote them a letter last week and told them about the job and how after a year's time I'll have the title to twenty acres and the cabin."

"And?"

"Well, with Hard Luck being in the news and everything, Dad had already heard about Midnight Sons advertising for women. He..." She paused and bit her lower lip. "He seems to think this isn't the place for me, and the best way to get me home is to prove you're running some kind of scam. That's why he hired Ms. Santiago. I... I think he may want to sue you." She closed her eyes again, as if she expected Christian to explode.

Instead, he stared sightlessly into space. "We're dead meat," he said tonelessly. "Sawyer and I can forget everything we've ever worked for because it'll be gone."

"I explained the situation as best I could to Ms. Santiago."

"Oh, great. By now she's probably decided I've kidnapped you and that I'm holding you for ransom."

"That's not true!"

"Think about it, Mariah. Tracy Santiago would give her eye-teeth to cut me off at the knees—and all because you wanted to *prove something* to your father!"

"I'll take care of everything," Mariah promised. Her huge eyes implored him. "You don't have to worry. I'll get everything straightened out. There won't be a lawsuit unless I'm willing to file one, and I'm not."

"*You'll* take care of it?" Christian repeated with a short bark of laughter. "*That's* supposed to reassure me? Ha!"

Lanni Caldwell glanced at her watch for the third time in a minute. Charles was late. He was supposed to pick her up in front of the *Anchorage News,* where she was working as an intern. She should wait outside for him, he'd said. It had been ten days since they'd seen each other, and she'd never missed anyone so much.

They'd agreed to postpone their wedding until the first week of April. At the time, that hadn't sounded so terrible, but she'd since revised her opinion. If these ten days were any indication of how miserable she was going to be without him, she'd never last the eight months. Her one consolation was that his travel schedule often brought him to Valdez, which was only a short airplane trip from Anchorage.

Just when she was beginning to really worry, Lanni saw him. He was smiling broadly, a smile that spoke of his own joy at seeing her.

Unable to stand still, Lanni hurried toward him, threading her way through the late-afternoon shoppers crowding the sidewalk.

When she was only a few feet away, she started to run. "Charles! Oh, Charles!"

He caught her around the waist and lifted her off the ground. They were both talking at once, saying the same things. How lonely the past days had been. How eight months seemed impossible. How much they'd missed each other.

It felt so good to be in his arms again. She hadn't *intended* to kiss him right there on the sidewalk with half of Anchorage looking on, but she couldn't stop herself. Charles O'Halloran was solid and handsome and strong—and he was hers.

His mouth found Lanni's and her objections, her doubts, her misery, all melted away. She hardly heard the traffic, hardly noticed the smiling passersby.

Slowly Charles lowered her to the ground. He dragged in a giant breath; so did she. "When it comes to you, Lanni," he whispered, "I haven't got a bit of self-control."

They clasped hands and began walking. "Where are we going?" she asked.

"We have to go somewhere?" he teased.

Lanni leaned her head against his shoulder. "No, but dinner would be nice. I'm starved."

"Me, too, but I'm even more starved for you."

Lanni smiled softly. "I'm dying to hear what came of the lawyer's visit to Hard Luck. What's this about Mariah being the one who's filing the lawsuit? I don't know her well, but I can't see her doing that."

"I'll explain everything later," he promised, sliding his arm around her, keeping her close to his side.

"All I can say is that Christian deserves whatever he gets. He's been so impatient with her."

Charles's eyes met Lanni's, then crinkled in silent amusement. "Whose side are you on in this fiasco?"

"Yours," she said promptly. "It's just that I find it all rather... entertaining."

"Is that a fact?" He brought her hand to his lips and kissed her knuckles. "Christian's convinced we're in a damned-if-we-do and damned-if-we-don't situation."

"Really?" Her eyes held his. This could well be more serious than it sounded. "Is Midnight Sons in legal trouble?"

Charles held open the door of her favorite Chinese restaurant. "I don't know. Frankly, it's not my problem. Sawyer and Christian are the ones who came up with this brilliant plan to bring women to Hard Luck. I'm sure that between them they'll come up with a solution."

They were promptly seated and the waiter took their order. "Don't look so worried," Charles said, reaching across the table to take her hand. "As far as I'm concerned, this is a tempest in a teacup. Mariah's parents are the ones who started this, so I suggested we let Mariah work this out with them. Her father doesn't want to ruin Midnight Sons—all he really cares about is making sure his daughter's safe."

"I'd say Mariah can look after herself very well indeed. She's bright and responsible and—"

"Christian might not agree with you, but I do."

A smile stole across Lanni's features. "You're going to be a very good husband, Charles O'Halloran."

For long moments they simply gazed at each other. To Lanni, there was no better man than Charles. Of all the women in the world, he'd chosen to marry *her*—but then, she was convinced their falling in love had been no accident.

"I talked to your mother," she said, suddenly remembering the lengthy conversation she'd had with Ellen Greenleaf.

Ellen had remarried a couple of years ago and was now living in British Columbia.

"And?"

"And she's absolutely delighted that you came to your senses and proposed."

"I proposed?" he repeated, his eyebrows raised. "Seems to me it was the other way around."

"Does it really matter who asked whom?" she said in mock disgust. "The important thing is I love you and you love me."

Charles grew serious. "I do love you."

Lanni would never doubt him. Slowly he raised her hand to his lips and kissed her palm. The action was both sensual and endearing.

"Does your grandmother know about us?" Charles asked.

Lanni shook her head. "Her health has deteriorated in the last few weeks. Half the time, Grammy doesn't even recognize Mom. Apparently she slips in and out of consciousness. The doctors...don't expect her to live much longer."

Charles frowned and his eyes were sad. "I'm sorry, Lanni."

"I know you are."

"I spent a lot of years hating Catherine Fletcher for what she did to my family, but I can't anymore. It's because of her that I found the most precious gift of my life. You. Remember what you said a few weeks ago about the two of us being destined for each other? I believe it now, as strongly as I believe anything."

Bethany had purposely waited three days before visiting the Hard Luck Café. She'd needed the time to fortify herself for this first confrontation. The night of her arrival, Mitch had confirmed what she already knew: Ben Hamilton owned the café.

Her heart skipped, then thudded so hard it was almost painful. Her palms felt sweaty as she pulled open the door and stepped inside. If she reacted this way before she even met Ben, what would she be like afterward?

"Hello."

Ben stood behind the counter, a white apron around his middle, a welcoming smile on his lips. Bethany felt as if the wind had been knocked out of her.

"You must be Bethany Ross."

"Yes," she said, struggling to make her voice audible. "You're Ben Hamilton?"

"The one and only." He sketched a little bow, then leaned back against the counter, studying her.

With her breath trapped in her lungs, Bethany made a show of glancing around the empty room. It was eleven-thirty, still early for lunch. The café featured a counter and a number of booths with red vinyl upholstery. The rest of the furnishings consisted of tables and mismatched chairs.

"Help yourself to a seat."

"Thank you." Bethany chose to sit at the counter. She picked up a plastic-coated menu and pretended to study it.

"The special of the day is a roast-beef sandwich," Ben told her.

She looked up and nodded. "What about the soup?"

"Split pea."

Ben was nothing like she'd expected. The years hadn't been as generous to him as she'd hoped. His hair had thinned and his belly hung over the waistband of his apron. Lines creased his face.

If he hadn't introduced himself, hadn't said his name aloud, Bethany would never have guessed.

"Do you want any recommendations?" he asked.

"Please."

"Go with the special."

She closed the menu. "All right, I will."

As he walked back to the kitchen, he asked, "How are things going for you at the school?"

"Fine," she said, surprised she was able to carry on a normal conversation with him. "The kids I've met are great, and Margaret's been a lot of help." Today was Labor Day; tomorrow was her first day of teaching.

She wondered what Ben saw when he looked at her. Did he notice any resemblance? Did he see how much she looked like her mother, especially around the eyes? Or had he wiped the memory of her mother from his mind?

"Everyone in Hard Luck's real pleased to have you."

"I'm pleased to be here," she responded politely. She was struck by how friendly he was, how genuinely interested he seemed. Was that why her mother had fallen in love with him all those years ago?

The door opened and Ben looked up. "Howdy, Mitch. Said hello to the new schoolteacher yet?"

"We met earlier." Bethany thought she detected a note of reluctance in his voice, as if he regretted coming into the café while she was there.

Mitch claimed the stool at the opposite end of the counter.

"I don't think she's contagious," Ben chided from the kitchen, then chuckled. "And I'm pretty sure she doesn't bite."

Mitch cast Bethany an apologetic smile. Uncomfortable, she glanced away.

Ben brought her meal, and she managed to meet his eyes. "I... I meant to tell you I wanted to take the sandwich with me," she said, faltering over the words. "If that's not a problem."

"Not at all." He whipped the plate off the counter. "What can I get for you, Mitch?" he asked.

"How about a cheeseburger?"

"You got it." Ben returned to the kitchen, leaving Bethany and Mitch alone.

She looked at him. He looked at her. Neither seemed able to come up with anything to say. In other circumstances, Bethany would've found a hundred different subjects to discuss.

But not now. Not when she was so distracted by the battle being waged in her heart. She'd just walked up to her father and ordered lunch.

No, he *wasn't* her father, she amended. Her father was Peter Ross, the man who'd loved her and raised her as his own. The man who'd sat at her bedside and read her to sleep. The man who'd escorted her to the father-daughter dance when she was a high school sophomore.

The only link Bethany shared with Ben Hamilton was genetic. He was the man who'd given her life, and nothing else. Not one damn thing.

3

On the first day of school, Mitch swore his daughter was up before dawn. By the time the alarm sounded and he struggled out of bed and into the kitchen, Chrissie was already dressed.

She sat in the living room with her lunch pail tightly clutched in her hand. She was dressed in her new jeans and Precious Moments sweatshirt.

"Morning, Daddy."

"Howdy, pumpkin." He yawned loudly. "Aren't you up a little early?" He padded barefoot into the kitchen, with Chrissie following him.

"It's the first day of school." She announced this as if it was news to him.

"I know."

"I'm Ms. Ross's helper," she said importantly.

Mitch had stopped counting the number of times a day Chrissie mentioned Ms. Ross. He'd given up telling her he wasn't interested in marrying the teacher. Chrissie didn't want to believe it, and arguing with her only irritated him. Eventually, she'd see for herself that there'd never be a relationship between him and Bethany.

He'd heard that Bethany had stirred up a lot of interest among the single men in town. Good. Great. Wonderful. In no time at all, she'd be involved with someone else, and his daughter would get the message.

Mitch hated to disappoint her. But, he reasoned, disappointment was part of life, and he wouldn't always be able to protect her. The sooner she accepted there'd only be the two of them, the better.

"I packed my own lunch," she told him, holding up her Barbie lunch pail.

"I'm proud of you."

She delighted in showing him what she'd chosen for her lunch. Ham-and-cheese sandwich carefully wrapped in napkins, an apple, juice, an oatmeal cookie. Mitch was pleased to see that she'd done a good job of packing a well-balanced meal and told her so.

He looked at his watch, gauging the time before they could leave. "What about breakfast?"

Although Chrissie claimed she was too excited to eat, Mitch insisted she try. "How about a bowl of cereal?" he suggested, pulling out several boxes from the cupboard. He wasn't much of a breakfast eater himself. Generally he didn't have anything until ten or so. More often than not, he picked up a doughnut or something equally sweet when he stopped in at Ben's for coffee.

"I'll *try* to eat something," Chrissie agreed with a decided lack of enthusiasm. He let her pour her own cereal and milk. His daughter was an independent little creature, which was fine with Mitch. In fact, he took pride in it.

By the time he'd finished dressing, she'd eaten her breakfast and washed and put away her bowl and spoon. She sat on the couch waiting for Mitch to escort her to school.

"Are you sure you need me, now that you're a second-grader?" Not that Mitch objected to walking his daughter to class. However, he had a sneaking suspicion that if her teacher had been anyone other than the lovely Ms. Ross, Chrissie would have insisted on walking without him.

"I *want* you to take me," she said with a smile bright enough to blind him. The kid knew exactly what she was doing. And being the good father he was, he had to go along with her. The way he figured it, he'd walk her to the school door and, if he was lucky, escape without seeing Bethany.

His plan backfired. Chrissie *had* to show him her desk.

"I'm over here," she said, taking him by the hand and leading him to the front row. "Ms. Ross let me pick my own seat." Wouldn't you know, his daughter had chosen to sit directly in front of the teacher's desk.

He tried to make a fast getaway, but Bethany herself waylaid him.

"Good morning, Mitch."

"Morning." The tropical bird was back in full plumage. She wore a black skirt with a colorful floral top; it reminded him of the shirt Sawyer had brought back from Hawaii. Her hair was woven into a thick braid that fell halfway down her back.

She did have beautiful hair, he'd say that much. It didn't take a lot of effort to imagine undoing her braid and running his fingers through the glossy strands. He could see himself with his hands buried wrist-deep in her hair, drawing her mouth to his. Her lips would feel silky soft, and she'd taste like honey and passion and—

"Are you picking me up after school?" Chrissie asked, interrupting his thoughts.

Thank heaven she had. Apparently all Chrissie's chatter about Bethany was having more of an effect on him than he'd realized. His heart pounded like an overworked piston, his pulse thumping so hard he could feel it throb in his neck.

Bethany and Chrissie were both looking at him, awaiting

his response. "Pick you up?" As a rule, Chrissie walked over to Louise Gold's house after school.

"Just for today," Chrissie said, her big eyes gazing up at him hopefully.

"All right," he agreed grudgingly. "Just for today."

Chrissie's face shone with her smile.

He would've told Bethany goodbye, but she was talking to other parents. Just as well. The sooner he got away from her, the sooner he could get a grip on his emotions.

Mitch wished he knew what was wrong with him. After vehemently opposing all talk about becoming romantically involved with Bethany Ross, he found it downright frightening to discover the effect she had on him.

Sawyer debated what exactly he should say to his brother. It wasn't often that he felt called upon to take Christian to task. But enough was enough. Christian had Mariah so unnerved the poor girl couldn't do anything right.

"She did it again," Christian muttered as he walked past Sawyer's desk to his own.

Sawyer looked up. "Who?" he asked in an innocent voice.

Seething, Christian jerked his head toward Mariah. "She can't seem to find accounts receivable on the computer."

"It's here," Mariah insisted, her fingers on the keyboard. Even from where Sawyer was sitting, it looked as though she was randomly pressing keys in a desperate effort to find the missing data. "I'm just not sure where it went."

"Don't you have it on a backup disk?" Sawyer asked.

"Yes..."

"Who knows?" Christian threw his hands in the air. "The backup disk's probably in the same place as the missing file. We could be in real trouble here." Panic edged his voice.

"She'll find it," Sawyer said confidently.

Mariah thanked him with a brief smile.

"Let me look," Christian demanded, flying out of his chair. "Before you crash the entire system."

"I lost it, I'll find it." Mariah didn't budge from her seat. The woman had long since won Sawyer's admiration, not least for the mettle she'd shown in dealing with his brother.

"Leave her be," Sawyer said.

"And risk everything?"

"We aren't risking anything. There's a backup disk."

Christian sat down at his desk, but his gaze remained on Mariah. Sawyer watched Christian. And Mariah did her level best to ignore them both.

"Fact is, I could use a break," Sawyer said. "Why don't we let Ben treat us to a cup of coffee?"

"Okay," Christian agreed reluctantly.

As Sawyer walked past Mariah's desk, she mouthed a thank-you. He nodded and steered his irritable brother out the door.

"I wish you wouldn't be so hard on her," he said the minute they were alone. It annoyed him to see Christian treat Mariah as if she didn't have a brain in her head.

"Hard on her?" Christian protested loudly. "The woman drives me insane. If it was up to me, she'd be out of here in a heartbeat. She's trouble with a capital *T*."

"She's a good secretary," Sawyer argued. "The office has never been in better shape. The files are organized and neat, and the equipment's been updated. Frankly I don't know how we managed without her as long as we did."

Christian opened his mouth, then closed it. He didn't have an argument.

"Okay, so there was the one fiasco with that attorney," Sawyer said, knowing that part of Christian's anger stemmed from the confrontation with Tracy Santiago.

Christian's mouth thinned and his eyes narrowed. "Mark my words, she'll be back."

"Who?"

His brother eyed him scornfully. "The attorney, of course. If for nothing more than pure spite. That woman's vicious, Sawyer. Vicious. And as if that's not bad enough, she took an instant dislike to all of us—especially Duke. She's out for revenge."

Sawyer didn't believe that. True, Christian had been the one who'd actually talked to her, but his brother's assessment of Tracy's plans for revenge sounded a little far-fetched.

"It's my understanding that everything was squared once Mariah talked to her. I don't think there's any real threat."

"For now," Christian said meaningfully. "But don't think we've heard the end of this. Yup, you mark my words, Santiago's gone for reinforcements."

"Don't be ridiculous. Why would she do that if no one's paying her fee? We've seen the last of her."

"I doubt it," Christian muttered.

Instead of going straight to Ben's, they strolled toward the open hangar. John Henderson, who served as a sometime mechanic and a full-time pilot, was servicing the six-passenger Lockheed, the largest plane in their small fleet.

When he saw them approach, John grabbed an oil rag from his hip pocket and wiped his hands. "Morning," he called out cheerfully.

Sawyer noticed that John had gotten his hair and beard trimmed. He wasn't a bad-looking guy when he put some effort into his appearance. Of course, there hadn't been much reason to do that until recently.

It occurred to him that Duke Porter might learn a thing or two from John. Duke might have fared better with the Santiago woman had he been a bit more gentlemanly. Sawyer had never seen any two people take such an instant dislike to each other.

"You're looking good," he commented, nodding at John, and to his surprise, the other man blushed.

"I was thinking of asking the new schoolteacher if she'd have dinner with me Friday evening," he said. Sawyer noted that John was studying Christian as if he expected him to object.

"It's Thursday, John," Sawyer pointed out. "Just when do you plan to ask her?"

"That depends." Again John studied Christian.

"What are you looking at me for?" Christian snapped, his mood as surly with John as it had been earlier with Mariah.

"I just wanted to be sure you weren't planning on asking her yourself."

"Why would I do that?" The glance Christian gave Sawyer said he had more than enough problems with *one* woman.

John's face broke into a wide grin of unspoken relief.

Christian grumbled something under his breath as he headed out the other side of the hangar. Sawyer followed him to the Hard Luck Café.

As they sat down at the counter, Ben stuck his head out from the kitchen. "It's self-service this morning, fellows."

"No problem." Sawyer walked around the counter and reached for the pot. He filled two mugs. Meanwhile, Christian helped himself to a couple of powdered-sugar doughnuts from under the plastic dome.

"Getting back to Mariah," Sawyer said when he'd finished stirring his coffee. He felt obliged to clear this up; in his opinion, Christian's attitude needed adjustment.

"Do we have to?"

"Yes, we do. She's proved herself to be a capable secretary."

"The woman's nothing but a nuisance. She can't type worth a damn, she misfiles correspondence, and she habitually loses things. The accounts-receivable disaster this morning is a prime example."

"I've never had any trouble with her," Sawyer countered. "I've found Mariah hardworking and sincere."

"She makes too many mistakes."

"Frankly I don't see it. If you ask me, *you're* the problem. You make her nervous. She's constantly worried that she's going to mess up—it's a self-fulfilling prophecy, Christian. Besides," Sawyer added, "she's gone to a lot of trouble to work things out with her family and settle this lawsuit business. I admire her for that."

Christian obviously didn't share his admiration. "I wish they'd talked her into returning to Seattle. That's where she belongs."

Sawyer merely shrugged. "Face it—Mariah's going to stay the entire year. It's a matter of pride with her, and that's something we can both understand."

Christian looked away.

"She isn't so bad, you know." Sawyer slapped his brother affectionately on the back. "There's one thing you seem to have conveniently forgotten."

"What's that?"

Sawyer grabbed one of Christian's doughnuts. He grinned broadly. "You must've liked *something* about her. After all, you're the guy who hired her."

"In other words, I don't have anyone to blame but myself."

"You got it." With that Sawyer walked out of the café, leaving his brother to foot the bill.

In two weeks Bethany hadn't seen even a glimpse of Mitch Harris. The man made himself as scarce as sunlight in an Alaskan winter. He must be working overtime, and she had to wonder if it was—at least partly—in an effort to avoid her.

Bethany could accept that he wasn't attracted to her if that was indeed the case. But the night they'd met and each time

afterward, she'd sensed a growing awareness between them.
She knew he felt it, too, even though he doggedly resisted it.
Whenever they were in a room together, no matter how many
people were present, their eyes gravitated toward each other.
The solid ground beneath Bethany would subtly shift, and she'd
have to struggle to hide the fact that anything was wrong.

"Can I clean the blackboards for you, Ms. Ross?" Chrissie
asked, interrupting her musings. The youngster stood next to
Bethany's desk. It would be very easy to love this child, she
thought.

Chrissie had been her student for two weeks, and it became
increasingly difficult not to make her a teacher's pet. The seven-
year-old was so willing to please and always looked for ways to
brighten Bethany's day.

If Bethany had any complaints about Mitch's daughter, it
was the number of times Chrissie introduced her father into
the conversation. Clearly the girl adored him.

"Can I?" she asked again, holding up the erasers.

"Certainly, Chrissie. How thoughtful of you to ask. I'd be
delighted if you cleaned the boards."

Chrissie flushed with pleasure. "I like to help my dad, too.
He needs me sometimes."

"I'll bet you're good at helping him. You've been a wonderful assistant to me."

Once again the child glowed at Bethany's approval. "My dad
promised to pick me up after school today," she said; she seemed
to be watching for Bethany's reaction to that news. From other
bits of information Chrissie had dropped, Bethany knew that
Mitch occasionally collected his daughter after school. She herself hadn't seen him.

"With your dad coming, maybe you should skip cleaning the
boards this afternoon," Bethany said. She didn't want Mitch to

be kept waiting because Chrissie was busy, nor did she want to force him to enter the classroom.

"It'll be all right," Chrissie said quickly. "Don't worry, Dad'll wait."

Still, Bethany wasn't confident that she was doing the right thing, especially since Mitch seemed to be avoiding her so diligently.

The little girl was busy with the blackboards, standing on tiptoe to reach as far as she could, when Mitch walked briskly into the classroom. His movements were filled with impatience. His body language said he didn't appreciate having to come and look for his daughter.

As had happened before, his eyes flew to Bethany's, and hers to his. Slowly she rose from behind her desk. "Hello, Mitch."

"Bethany."

"Hi, Dad! I'm helping Ms. Ross. I'm almost done," Chrissie said lightheartedly. "All I have to do is go outside and get the chalk out of the erasers. I'll be back in a minute."

Mitch opened his mouth as though to protest, but before he could utter a word, Chrissie raced out the door.

Bethany and Mitch were alone.

They couldn't stop staring at each other. Bethany would've paid good money to know what he was thinking. Not that she was all that clear about her own feelings. Their attraction to each other *should* have been uncomplicated, since neither of them was involved with anyone else.

True, John Henderson, one of the bush pilots employed by Midnight Sons, had asked her to dinner. She'd accepted; there was no point in sitting around waiting for Mitch to ask her out, and John seemed pleasant.

The silence between them grew. Mitch's face was stern, his features set. Bethany sighed, uncertain how to break the ice.

"I hear you're going out to dinner with John Henderson this evening," Mitch surprised her by saying.

"Yes." She wasn't going to deny it.

"I think that's an excellent idea."

"My having dinner with John?"

"Yes."

Their eyes remained locked. Finally she swallowed and asked, "Why?"

"John's a good man."

It was on the tip of her tongue to ask the reason Mitch hadn't asked her out himself. Mitch was attracted to her, and she to him. The force of that attraction was no small thing. Surely it would be better to discuss it openly, even if they didn't act on their feelings. She longed to bring up the subject and see where it took them. But in the end she said nothing. Neither did Mitch.

Chrissie reentered the classroom, and Bethany slowly moved her gaze from Mitch to his daughter.

"The erasers are clean," Chrissie announced. Her eyes were huge with expectation.

"Thank you, sweetheart."

"You're welcome. Can I clean them again next Friday?"

"That would be very helpful."

"Have a nice evening," Mitch said as he walked out the door, his hand on his daughter's shoulder.

"I will, thank you," she called after them, but she didn't think he heard.

The encounter with Mitch left Bethany feeling melancholy. She accompanied Margaret Simpson to her house for a cup of coffee, hoping that a visit with the other teacher would cheer her up; however, she was distracted during their conversation. Once she arrived home, she turned on her CD player and lay down on the living room carpet, listening to Billy Joel—which said a great deal about her state of mind.

Instead of being excited about her dinner date, she was bemoaning the fact that it wasn't Mitch taking her out. It was time to face reality: he wasn't interested in seeing her. She told herself it didn't matter. There were plenty of other fish in the sea. But her little pep talk fell decidedly flat.

Because John was afraid he might get back late from a flight into Fairbanks, he'd asked if they could meet at the Hard Luck Café. Bethany didn't object. She showered and changed into a knee-length, chocolate-brown skirt, an extra-long, loose-knit beige sweater and calf-length brown leather boots. To dress up the outfit, she wove a silk scarf into her French braid. She looked good and she knew it. Her one regret was that Mitch wouldn't see her. She'd like him to know what he was missing!

To her astonishment, there were only two other people in the café when she arrived. The men, whom she didn't recognize, were deeply engrossed in conversation. They sat drinking beer at one of the tables.

"My, my, don't you look pretty," Ben hailed her when she took a seat in a booth near the window. Apparently he knew she was meeting John, because he filled two water glasses and tucked a couple of menus under his arm.

"Thank you."

"I heard John's got his eye on you."

Bethany didn't comment. Although she'd been in the café a number of times since her first visit, she was never completely comfortable with Ben. She'd moved to Hard Luck with an open mind about him. She had no plan other than getting to know this man who'd fathered her.

She'd learned about him only a year ago. Despite the initial shock, this new knowledge didn't change her feelings toward either her mother or Peter Ross. She just wanted to discover for herself what kind of man Ben Hamilton was. She certainly didn't intend to interfere in his life. Nor did she intend to embarrass him with the truth. The year might well come to a close without his ever finding out who she was.

In all honesty, Bethany couldn't think of a way to casually announce that she was his daughter. For a giddy moment, she was tempted to throw open her arms and call him Daddy. But no—he'd never been that.

Ben lingered at the table. "If you want the truth, I was surprised you were coming here with John."

"Really." Bethany picked up her water glass.

"I kinda thought you were sweet on Mitch."

The glass hit the table with an unexpected thunk, garnering the attention of the restaurant's two other occupants.

Ben rubbed the side of his face. "What I've seen, Mitch is taken with you, as well."

Bethany stared down at the table and swallowed nervously. "I'm sure that isn't true."

Low laughter rumbled in Ben's chest. "I've seen the way you two send looks at each other. I'm not blind, you know. Yes, sir, I see plenty—lots more than people think." He tapped his finger against his temple to emphasize the point. "I might be a crusty old bachelor, but I—"

"You never got married?" she interrupted him.

"No."

"Why not?" She turned the conversation away from herself, at the same time attempting to learn what she could about his life.

"I guess you could say I never found the right woman."

His answer irritated Bethany. Her mother was one of the finest women she'd ever known. The desire to defend her mother, tell this character about the heartache he'd caused, burned in the pit of her stomach.

"How...how long have you been in Alaska?" she asked instead.

Ben seemed to need time to calculate his answer. "It must be twenty years now. The O'Halloran boys were still wet behind the ears when I made my way here."

"Why Hard Luck?" she asked.

"Why not? It was as good a place as any. Besides," he said, flashing her a grin, "there's something to be said for having the only restaurant within a four-hundred-mile radius."

Bethany laughed.

The door opened and John Henderson rushed in, a little breathless and a whole lot flustered. He hurried over to the table, and his eyes lit up at the sight of her. He seemed speechless.

"Hello again," Bethany said.

John remained standing there, his mouth open.

Ben slapped him on the back. "Aren't you going to thank me for keeping her company?"

John jerked his head around as if suddenly noticing Ben. "Uh, thanks, Ben."

"No problem." He turned to walk back to the kitchen, but before he did, Bethany's eye caught his and they shared a secret smile. For the first time Bethany felt she'd truly communicated with the man she'd come three thousand miles to meet.

Dinner turned out to be more of an ordeal than Bethany had expected. By the time he'd paid for their meal, Bethany actually felt sorry for John. During the course of their dinner, he'd dripped gravy down the front of his shirt, knocked over the sugar canister and spilled his coffee, most of which landed on her skirt. The man was clearly a nervous wreck.

"I'll walk you home," John said.

She waited until they were outside before she thanked him.

Although they were only halfway through September, there was a decided coolness, and the hint of snow hung in the air. Bethany was glad she'd worn her coat.

"Thank you, John, for a lovely evening."

The pilot buried his hands in his jacket pockets. "I'm sorry about the coffee."

"You didn't do it on purpose."

"What about your skirt?"

"Don't worry—I'm sure it'll wash out."

"You didn't get burned?"

She'd assured him she hadn't at least a dozen times. "I'm fine, John, really."

"I want you to know I'm not normally this clumsy."

"I'm sure that's true."

"It's just that it isn't often a woman as beautiful as you agrees to have dinner with me."

There was something touching about this pilot, something endearing. "What a sweet thing to say. Thank you."

"Women like to hear that kind of stuff, don't they?" John asked. "About being pretty and all."

Bethany hesitated, wondering where the conversation was heading. "I think it's safe to say we do."

It was difficult to keep from smiling. With someone else, she might have been irritated or worse. But not with John. Besides, the evening was so beautiful. The sky danced with a brilliant display of stars, and the northern lights seemed to sizzle just over the horizon. Bethany couldn't stop gazing up at the heavens.

"Is it always this beautiful here?"

"Yup," John said without hesitation. "But then they say that beauty's in the eye of the beholder."

"That's true." Bethany shrugged, a little puzzled.

"It won't be long now before the rivers freeze," he explained soberly.

"So soon?"

"Yup. We're likely to have snow anytime."

Bethany could hardly believe it. "Really?"

"This is the Arctic, Bethany."

"But it seems as if I just got here. It's still summer at home."

"Maybe in California, but not here." He looked worried. "You aren't going to leave, are you?"

"No. I signed a contract for this school year. Don't worry, I'm not going to break my commitment because of a little snow and ice."

They strolled past the school, and she glanced at the building with a sense of pride. She already loved her job and her students.

Soon her house was in sight. Bethany was deciding how to handle the awkwardness that might develop when they reached her front door. She didn't plan to invite John in.

"Thank you," Bethany said again when at last they stood on the stoop.

"The evening would've been better if I hadn't…you know."

"Stop worrying about a little coffee."

"Don't forget the sugar." He grinned as if he'd begun to find the entire episode amusing.

"Despite a few, uh, mishaps, I really did enjoy dinner," she told him.

John kicked at the dirt with the toe of his shoe. "I don't suppose you'd go out with me again."

Bethany wasn't sure how to respond. She liked John, but just as a friend, and she didn't want to mislead him into thinking something more could develop between them. She'd made that mistake once before.

"You don't need to feel guilty if you don't want to," he said, his eyes avoiding hers. He cleared his throat. "I can understand why someone hand-delivered by the angels wouldn't want to be seen with someone like me." He glanced shyly at her.

Tempted to roll her eyes at that remark, Bethany managed a smile. "How about if we have dinner again next Friday night?" she asked.

John's head shot up. "You mean it?"

Bethany nodded. "This time it'll be my treat."

His smile faded and he folded his arms across his chest. "You want to buy *me* dinner?"

"Yes. Friends do that, you know." A car could be heard in the distance, driving slowly down the street.

"Friends?" The car was coming closer.

"Yes." She leaned forward and very gently pressed her lips to his cheek. As she backed away, she saw that the car had stopped.

Silhouetted against the moonlight sat Mitch Harris. He'd just witnessed her kissing John Henderson.

4

October 1995

The first snowfall of the year came in the third week of September. Thick flurries drifted down throughout the day, covering the ground and obscuring familiar outlines. Mitch thought he should've been accustomed to winter's debut by now, but he wasn't. However beautiful, however serene, this soft-looking white blanket was only a foretaste of the bitter cold to follow.

He looked at his watch. In a few minutes he'd walk over to the school to meet Chrissie. He'd gotten into the habit of picking up his daughter on Friday afternoons.

Not because she needed him or had asked him to come. No, he wryly suspected that going to the school was rooted in some masochistic need to see Bethany.

He rationalized that he was giving Chrissie this extra attention because he worked longer hours on Friday evenings, when Diane Hestead, a high school student, stayed with her. That was the only night of the week Ben served alcohol. Before the women had arrived, a few of the pilots and maybe a trapper or two wandered into the Hard Luck Café. But with the news of women coming to town, Ben's place had begun to fill up, not only with pilots but pipeline workers and other men.

For the past three Friday nights, John Henderson and Bethany had dined at the café. They came and left before eight, when Ben opened the bar.

From the gossip circulating around town, Mitch learned they'd become something of an item, although both insisted they were "only friends."

Mitch knew otherwise. On Bethany's first date with John, he'd happened upon them kissing. Friends indeed! Even now, his gut tightened at the memory.

For the thousandth time he reminded himself that he'd been the one to encourage her to see John. He couldn't very well reveal his discontent with that situation when she'd done nothing more than follow his advice.

He'd tried to convince himself that discovering John and Bethany together—kissing—had been sheer coincidence. But it hadn't been.

As the public safety officer, Mitch routinely checked the streets on Friday nights. He'd seen them leave Ben's place on foot that first evening and had discreetly followed them. On subsequent Fridays he'd continued his spy tactics, always making sure he was out of sight. He wasn't particularly proud of himself, but he found it impossible to resist the compulsion.

Except for their first date, when he'd seen them kissing outside her house, she'd invited John in. The pilot never stayed more than a few minutes, but of course Mitch knew what the two of them were doing.

He kept telling himself he should be pleased she was dating John; Henderson was a decent sort. But Mitch *wasn't* pleased. At night he lay awake staring at the four shrinking walls of his bedroom. Still, he knew it wasn't the walls that locked him in, that kept him from building a relationship with Bethany.

It was his guilt, his own doubts and fears, that came between him and Bethany. This was Lori's legacy to him. She'd died and in that moment made certain he'd never be free of her memory.

Mitch checked his watch a second time and decided to head over to the school. The phone rang as he closed and locked the door, but he resisted the temptation to answer it. The machine would pick up the message, and he'd deal with the call when he returned to the office.

Mitch could hear excited laughter in the distance as the children frolicked in the snow. Chrissie loved playing outside, although there'd be precious little of that over the next few months.

By the time Christmas came, Hard Luck would be in total darkness. But with the holidays to occupy people's minds and lift their spirits, the dark days didn't seem nearly as depressing as they might have.

Mitch had just rounded the corner to the school when he saw Bethany. She was half trotting with her head bowed against the wind, her steps filled with frantic purpose. She glanced up and saw him and stopped abruptly.

"Mitch." Her hand pushed a stray lock of hair away from her face, and he noticed for the first time how pale she was. "It's Chrissie. She's been hurt."

The words hit Mitch like a fist. He ran toward her and gripped her by the elbows. *"What happened?"*

"She fell on the ice and cut herself. The school tried to call you, but you'd already left the office."

"Where is she?"

"At the clinic…" Bethany's voice quavered precariously. "I knew you were probably on your way to the school. Oh, Mitch, I'm so afraid."

It was bad. It had to be, otherwise Bethany wouldn't be this pale, this frightened. Panic galvanized him and he began running toward the clinic. He'd gone half a block before he realized that Bethany was behind him, her feet slipping and sliding on the snow. Fearing she might stumble and fall, he turned back and stretched out a hand to her. She grasped his fingers with surprising strength.

Together they hurried toward the clinic. It couldn't have taken them more than two or three minutes to reach the building, but it felt like a lifetime to Mitch. He couldn't bear the thought of something happening to Chrissie. His daughter, his joy. She'd given his life purpose after Lori's death. She'd given him a reason to live.

He jerked open the clinic door, and the first thing he saw was blood. Crimson droplets on the floor. Chrissie's blood. He stopped cold as icy fingers crept along his backbone.

Dotty Harlow, the nurse who'd replaced Pearl Inman, was nowhere in sight; neither was Angie Hughes.

"Dotty!" he called urgently.

"Daddy." Chrissie moaned his name, and the sound of her pain pierced his heart.

Dotty stepped out of a cubicle in the back. Her soothing voice calmed his panic as she explained that Chrissie had required a couple of stitches, which she was qualified to do.

Angie, who'd been talking to Chrissie, stepped aside when he came into the room. Chrissie sniffled loudly and her small arms circled his neck; when she spoke, her words came in a staccato hiccupping voice. "I...fell...and cut my leg real...bad."

"You're going to be fine, pumpkin." He pressed his hand to the side of her sweet face and laid his cheek on her hair.

"I want Ms. Ross."

"I'm here," Bethany whispered from behind Mitch.

Chrissie stretched out her arms and Bethany hugged her close. Watching the two of them together threatened his resolve, as nothing else could have, to guard his heart against this woman.

"You were very brave," Dotty told Chrissie, as she put away the medical supplies, and Bethany helped his daughter back into her torn jeans.

"I tried not to cry," Chrissie said, tears glistening in her eyes, "but it hurt too bad."

"She's going to need to take this medication," Dotty said, distracting Mitch. The nurse rattled off a list of complicated-sounding instructions. Possibly because he looked confused and uncertain, Dotty wrote everything down and reviewed it with him a second time.

"I can take her home?" he asked.

"Sure," Dotty said. "If you have any questions, feel free to call me or Angie."

"Thanks, I will."

"Can I go home now?" Chrissie asked.

"We're on our way, pumpkin."

"I want Ms. Ross to come with us. Please, Daddy, I want Ms. Ross."

Any argument he might have offered died at the pleading note in Chrissie's voice. There was very little he could have denied his daughter in that moment.

When they arrived at the house and went inside, Chrissie climbed on Bethany's lap, and soon her eyelids drifted shut.

"How'd it happen?" Mitch asked tersely, sitting across from Bethany. Even now, the thought of losing his child made him go cold with the worst fear he'd ever experienced. When he'd found Lori dead, he hadn't felt the panic that overcame him when a terrified Bethany had told him his daughter was hurt.

"I'm not sure," Bethany said. "As she always does on Fridays, Chrissie offered to clean the boards and erasers. My guess is that she took them outside and slipped. She must have cut her leg on the side of the Dumpster. One of the other children came running to get me."

"Thank God you were close at hand."

Bethany squeezed her eyes shut and nodded. When she opened them again, he noticed how warm and gentle they were as she looked down at Chrissie. "I don't mind telling you, it shook me, finding her like that," Bethany admitted. "You have a very special child, Mitch."

"I know." And he did. He felt a strange and unfamiliar blend of emotions as he gazed at the two of them together. One he loved beyond life itself. The other he *wanted* to love, and couldn't. He had nothing to offer her—not his heart, not marriage. And it was because he'd failed Lori, just as she'd failed herself. And failed him, failed her daughter. Day in and day out, his wife had grown more desperate, more unhappy. After Chrissie's birth, she'd fallen into depression. Nothing he said or did seemed to help, and he realized now that he hadn't paid enough attention, hadn't understood the reality of her despair. Mitch blamed himself; his lack of awareness had cost Lori her life.

"She's fast asleep," Bethany whispered, smoothing Chrissie's hair away from her temple. Her words freed him from his bitter memories and returned him to the present.

Mitch stood, lifting his daughter from Bethany's arms. He carried her into her room while Bethany went ahead to turn down the covers, then placed his daughter in her bed.

As soundlessly as possible they left the room, keeping the door half-open.

There was no excuse for Bethany to linger. She had a date with another man—but Mitch didn't want her to leave.

"I suppose you have to get ready for your dinner with John?" he said, tucking his hands in his back pockets.

"No." Her eyes held his and she slowly shook her head.

He was about to ask why, but he quickly decided he shouldn't question the unexpected gift that had been dropped in his lap.

"Chrissie and I rented a video to watch tomorrow," he said, hoping to hide his eagerness for her company. "We generally do that on weekends. This week's feature presentation is a three-year-old romantic comedy. Not my choice," he told her. "Pete Livengood's movie selection isn't the most up-to-date, but I think you'd enjoy it. Would you care to stay and watch it with me?" Heaven knew, Mitch wanted her to stay. About as much as he'd wanted anything in his life.

She gave a small, tentative smile and nodded. "But if it's supposed to be Chrissie's movie..."

"I'll get her another one tomorrow. Or—" he grimaced comically "—I'll watch this one again."

"Okay, then. How about some popcorn?" she asked.

He grinned almost boyishly. "You got it."

It wasn't until the kernels were sizzling in the hot oil that he realized they hadn't bothered with dinner. It didn't matter. He'd fix something later if they were hungry. He had several free hours before his patrol, and he didn't intend to waste them.

When the corn had finished popping, he drenched it with melted butter, then carried the two heaping bowls into the living room. Bethany followed with tall, ice-filled glasses of soda. He placed the bowls on the coffee table and reached for the remote control.

Normally he would've sat in the easy chair and propped his feet on the ottoman. He chose to sit next to Bethany, instead. For this one night, he was going to indulge himself. He needed her.

The movie began, and he eased closer to her on the comfortable sofa. He found himself laughing out loud at the actors' farcical antics and clever banter, which was something he didn't do often. Very rarely did he see the humor in things anymore.

When he ran out of popcorn, Bethany offered him some of hers. Soon his arm was around her, and she was leaning her head against his shoulder. This was about as close to heaven as he expected to get anytime within the next fifty years.

Curiously time seemed to slow, not that Mitch objected. During one comical scene in the movie, Bethany glanced at him, laughing. Her eyes were a remarkably rich shade of brown. He wondered briefly if their color intensified in moments of passion.

He swallowed hard and jerked his head away. Such thoughts were dangerous and he knew it. He reverted his attention to the television screen. Another mistake. The scene, between the hero and heroine, played by two well-known actors, was the final one of the movie, and it was a love scene.

Mitch watched as the hero's lips moved over the heroine's, first in a slow, easy kiss, then with building passion. The actors were good at their craft. It didn't take much to convince Mitch that the characters they played were going to end up in the bedroom.

His breathing grew shallow as a painful longing sliced through him. The scene reminded Mitch of what he would never have with Bethany. In the same second, he realized with gut-wrenching clarity how much he wanted to kiss her.

As though neither of them could help it, their eyes met. In Bethany's he read an aching need. And he knew that what he saw might well be a reflection of his own.

There was a long silence as the credits rolled across the screen.

It was either throw caution to the winds and kiss her—or get out while he could still resist her. Almost without making a conscious decision, Mitch leapt from the sofa.

He buried his hands deep in his pockets, because he couldn't trust them not to reach for her. "Good movie, wasn't it?" he asked.

"Wonderful," she agreed, but she couldn't hide the disappointment in her voice.

★ ★ ★

"Mom, I'm so sorry." Lanni Caldwell stood in the doorway of the Anchorage hospital room. Her grandmother had died there only an hour before. "I came the minute I heard."

Kate looked up from her mother's bedside, her eyes brimming with tears, and smiled faintly. "Thank you for getting here so quickly." Lanni's father stood behind his wife, his hand on her shoulder.

Lanni gazed at Catherine Fletcher, the woman on the bed. *Grammy.* A term of affection for a woman Lanni barely knew, but one she would always love. Her heart ached at the sight of her dead grandmother. Over the past three months, Catherine's health had taken a slow but steady turn for the worse. Yet even in her failing physical condition, Catherine had insisted she'd return to Hard Luck. Dead or alive.

She would return.

Not because it was her home, but because Catherine wanted to go back to David O'Halloran, the man she'd loved for a lifetime. The man who'd left her standing at the altar more than fifty years earlier, when he'd brought home an English bride. The man she'd alternately loved and hated all these years.

"My mother's gone," Kate whispered brokenly. "She didn't even have the decency to wait for me. Like everything else in her life, she had to do this on her own. Alone. Without family."

After spending the summer in Hard Luck, Lanni better understood her mother's pain. For reasons Lanni would never fully grasp, Catherine Fletcher had given up custody of Kate when she was only a toddler. At a time when such decisions were rare, Catherine had chosen to be separated from her daughter. Chosen, instead, to stand impatiently on the sidelines waiting for David's marriage to Ellen to disintegrate. When that didn't happen, Catherine had decided to help matters along. But Ellen and David had clung steadfastly to each other, and in the end, after David's untimely death, Catherine had let her bitterness and disillusionment take control.

All her life, Kate Caldwell had been deprived of her mother's love. She'd known that her mother had married her father on the rebound. The marriage had lasted less than two years, and Kate's birth had been unplanned, a mistake.

"Matt's on his way," Lanni told her parents. She'd spoken to her brother briefly when he phoned to give her his flight schedule. Sawyer O'Halloran was flying him into Fairbanks, and he'd catch the first available flight to Anchorage that evening. Lanni had arranged to pick him up at the airport.

After saying her own farewell to her grandmother, Lanni moved into the room reserved for family to wait for her parents. Her heart felt heavy, burdened with her mother's loss more than her own.

Footsteps alerted her to the fact that she was no longer alone. When she glanced up, she saw Charles O'Halloran.

"Oh, Charles," she whispered, jumping to her feet. She needed his comfort now, and before another moment had passed, she was securely wrapped in his embrace.

The sobs that shook her came as a shock. Charles held her close, his strength absorbing her pain, his love quieting her grief.

"How'd you know?" Although tempted, she hadn't phoned him, even though he was currently working out of Valdez.

"Sawyer."

She should've guessed his brother would tell him.

"Why didn't you call me?" he asked.

"I...didn't think I should."

Her answer appeared to surprise him. "Why not?"

"Because... I know how you still feel about Grammy. I don't blame you. She hurt you and your family."

They sat down together and Charles took both of Lanni's hands in his own. "I stopped hating her this summer. How could I despise the woman who was ultimately responsible for giving me you?"

Lanni swiped at the tears on her cheeks and offered a shaky smile to this man she loved.

"And after my mother told me the circumstances that led to her marrying my dad," Charles went on, "I have a better understanding of the heartache Catherine suffered. My father made a noble sacrifice when he married Ellen. I know he grew to love her. But in his own way, I believe he always loved Catherine."

"I'd like to think they're together now," Lanni said. Charles's father and her grandmother. "This time forever."

"I'd like to think they are, too," Charles said softly, and he dropped a gentle kiss on the top of her head.

Lanni pressed her face against his shoulder and closed her eyes.

"The memorial service will be in Hard Luck?" he asked.

"Yes. And Grammy asked that her ashes be scattered on the tundra next spring."

He nodded. "Do you know when the service is?"

"No." The details had yet to be decided. Lanni lifted her head and looked up at him. "I'm glad you came."

"So am I," he said. "I love you, Lanni. Don't ever hold anything back from me, understand?"

She nodded.

He stood, giving her his hand. "Now let's go see about meeting your brother's plane."

Mitch heard via the grapevine that Bethany had a date with Bill Landgrin. Bill's pipeline crew was working at the pump station south of Atigun Pass. The men responsible for the care and upkeep of the pipeline usually worked seven days on and seven days off. During his off-time, Bill occasionally made his way into the smaller towns that dotted the Alaskan interior.

What he came looking for was a little action. Gambling. Drinking. Every now and then, he went in search of a woman.

Mitch didn't know when or how Bill Landgrin had met Bethany. One thing was sure—Mitch didn't like the idea of his seeing Bethany. In fact, he didn't want the man anywhere near her.

Mitch understood Landgrin's attraction to Bethany all too well. It had been hard enough to sit idly by and watch her date John Henderson. The pilot was no real threat; Bill Landgrin, on the other hand, was smooth as silk and sharp as a tack. A real conniver, Mitch thought grimly.

There was no help for it. He was obligated to warn Bethany of Bill's reputation. *Someone* had to.

He bided his time, waiting until two days before she was said to be meeting Bill. As if it was a spur-of-the-moment decision, he'd stop by to see her after school. He'd make up some fiction about being concerned with Chrissie's grades—which were excellent.

He waited until he could be sure there was no chance of running into Chrissie. The last thing he needed was to have his daughter catch him seeking out Bethany's company. The kid might get the wrong idea.

Mitch had intentionally avoided Bethany since the night of Chrissie's accident. There was only so much temptation a man could take, and that evening had stretched his endurance to the breaking point.

He found Bethany sitting at her desk. Her eyes widened as he walked into the classroom. "Mitch, hello! It's good to see you."

He smiled slightly. "I hope you don't mind my dropping in like this."

"Of course not."

"It's about Chrissie," he said hurriedly, for fear Bethany

would get the wrong impression. "I've been a little, uh, concerned about her grades."

"But she's excelled in all her subjects. She's getting top marks."

He was well aware that his excuse was weak. From the day school had started, he hadn't had to hound Chrissie to do her homework. Not once. She would've gladly done assignments five hours a night if it meant pleasing Ms. Ross.

"I've been wondering about her grades since the accident," he said.

"They're fine." Bethany flipped through her grade book and reviewed the most recent entries. "I've kept a close eye on her, looking for any of the symptoms Dotty mentioned, but so far everything's been great. Is there a problem at home—I mean, has she been dizzy or anything like that?"

"No, no," he was quick to reassure her.

"Oh, good." She seemed relieved, and he felt even more of a fool.

Mitch stood abruptly and turned as if to leave. "By the way," he said, trying to make it sound like an afterthought, "I don't mean to pry, but rumor has it you're having dinner with Bill Landgrin this Friday night."

"Yes." She stared at him. "How'd you know that?"

"Oh," he said with a nonchalant shrug, "word gets around. I didn't know you two had met."

"Only briefly. He was on a flight with Duke and stopped in at the café the same time I was there," she explained.

"I see," he said thoughtfully. He started to leave, then turned back with a dramatic flourish. "What about John? Do you often date men you've just met?"

"What about him?"

"Why aren't you seeing him anymore?"

Bethany hesitated. "I don't think I like the tone of your question, Mitch. I have every right to date whomever I wish."

"Yes, of course. I didn't mean to imply anything else. It's just that, well, if you must know, Bill has something of a... reputation."

She stiffened. "Thank you for your concern, but I can take care of myself."

He was making a mess of this. "I didn't mean to offend you, Bethany. It's just that I'm all this town's got in the way of law enforcement, and I thought it was my duty to warn you."

"I see." She snapped the grade book shut. "And I'm a policeman's daughter. As I told you earlier, I can take care of myself." She made a production of looking at her watch. "Now if you'll excuse me?"

"Yes, of course," he said miserably, turning to go. And this time he left.

Bethany wasn't sure why she was so angry with Mitch. Possibly because he was right. She had no business having dinner with a man she barely knew. Oh, she'd be safe enough. Not much was going to happen to her in the Hard Luck Café with half the town looking on.

It went without saying that she'd agreed to this dinner for all the wrong reasons. John Henderson had started seeing another woman recently. One of the newer recruits, a shy young woman named Sally McDonald.

After nearly six weeks here, Bethany had to conclude that Mitch didn't want to become romantically involved. The night of Chrissie's accident, she'd felt certain they'd broken through whatever barrier was separating them. She remembered the way his eyes had held hers after the love scene in the movie. Bethany knew darn well what he was thinking, because she was thinking it, too. Then, when things looked really promising, Mitch had leapt away from her. Since that night, he'd had nothing to say—until now. Bethany was left feeling frustrated and confused.

When Bill Landgrin had asked her out, she'd found a dozen reasons to accept. She'd always been curious about the Alaska pipeline. It was said to stretch more than eight hundred miles across three mountain ranges and over thirteen bridges. Having dinner with a man who could answer her questions seemed innocent enough.

In addition, it sent a message to Mitch, one he'd apparently received loud and clear. He didn't like the idea of her dating Bill Landgrin, and frankly she was glad. Unfortunately, Mitch had to use his daughter's injury as an excuse to talk to her about Bill. That was what irritated Bethany most.

Mitch honestly tried to stay away from Bethany on Friday night. Chrissie was spending the night at Susan's, and the house had never seemed so empty. By seven o'clock, the walls were closing in on him. He'd had to grab his coat and flee.

He tried to look casual and unconcerned when he walked into Ben's café. A quick look around, and his mouth filled with the bitter taste of disappointment. Bethany was nowhere in sight.

"Looking for the new teacher, are you?" Ben asked as he dried a glass with a crisp linen cloth.

"What gives you that idea?" Mitch growled. He was in no mood for conversation. "I came here for a piece of pie."

"I thought you decided to cut back on sweets."

"I changed my mind," Mitch said. If he'd known Ben was going to be such a pain in the butt, he would've stayed home.

Ben brought him a slice of apple pie. "In case you're interested, she left not more than twenty minutes ago."

"Who?" he asked, pretending he didn't know.

"She wasn't alone, either. Bill insisted on seeing her home."

Agitated, Mitch slapped his fork down on the plate. "Who Bethany Ross dates is her own business."

"Maybe," Ben said, bracing both hands on the counter, "but I don't trust the man, and you don't either, otherwise you wouldn't be here. My feeling is that maybe one of us should check up on Bethany—see that everything's the way it should be."

Mitch was convinced there was more to this scenario than Ben was telling him. His blood started to heat.

"Since you're the law in this town, I think you ought to go make sure she got home all safe and sound."

Mitch wiped his mouth with the back of his hand. Ben was right. If anything happened to Bethany, Mitch would never forgive himself. In the meantime, if he did meet up with Bill, he'd impress upon the man that he was to keep away from Bethany Ross.

"So, are you going to see her?"

No use lying about it. "Yeah."

"Then the pie's on the house," Ben said, grinning.

Mitch drove to Bethany's, grateful to see that the lights were still on. He knocked loudly on the door and would have barged in if she hadn't opened it when she did.

"Mitch?"

"May I come in?"

"Of course." She stepped aside.

He walked in and looked around. If Bill was there, he saw no evidence of it.

She'd been combing her hair, and the brush was still in her hand. She didn't ask Mitch why he'd come.

He suspected she knew.

"Did Landgrin try anything?" Mitch demanded.

Her eyes narrowed as if she didn't understand the question.

"Landgrin. Did he try anything?" he repeated gruffly.

She blinked. "No. He was a perfect gentleman."

Mitch shoved his fingers though his hair as he paced the confines of her small living room. He didn't need anyone to tell him what a fool he was making of himself.

"Will you be seeing him again?"

"That's my business."

He closed his eyes and nodded. He had no argument. "Sorry," he said. "I shouldn't have come." He stalked toward the door, eager to escape.

"Mitch?"

His hand was on the doorknob. He stopped but didn't turn around.

"I won't be seeing Bill Landgrin again."

Relief coursed through him.

"Mitch?"

She was close, so very close. He could feel her breath against the back of his neck. All he had to do was turn and she'd be there. His arms ached to hold her. His hand tightened on the doorknob as though it were a lifeline.

"I won't see Bill again," she said in a voice so soft he had to strain to hear, "because I'd much rather be seeing you."

5

A week after Catherine Fletcher's death, the town held a memorial service. Although she'd never met Catherine, Bethany felt obliged to attend. She slipped into the crowded church and took a place in the last row, one of the only seats left. It seemed everyone in Hard Luck wanted to say a formal goodbye to the woman who'd had such a strong impact on their community.

When news of Catherine's death had hit town, it was all anyone could talk about. Apparently the woman's parents had been the second family to settle in Hard Luck. Bethany knew that Catherine had grown up with David O'Halloran, although a lot of the history between the two families remained unclear to her. But it was obvious that Catherine had played a major role in shaping the town. Folks either loved her or hated her, but either way, they respected her feisty opinions and gutsy spirit.

The mood was somber, the sense of loss keen. Hard Luck was laying to rest a piece of its heart.

A number of people attending the service were strangers to Bethany. The members of Catherine's family had flown in for the memorial, including an older couple she assumed was Catherine's daughter and son-in-law. Matt Caldwell, Catherine's grandson, lived in Hard Luck. Bethany had met him one Saturday afternoon at Ben's café. She remembered that Matt had bought the partially burned lodge from the O'Hallorans and was currently working on the repairs.

When they'd met, Matt had told her he planned to open the lodge in time for the tourist traffic next June. Bethany was tempted to ask *what* tourist traffic, but she hadn't.

Matt's younger sister, Lanni, sat in the front pew, as well, Charles O'Halloran close by. Bethany had heard that they were engaged, with their wedding planned for sometime in April. Even from this distance, she could see how much in love they were. It was evident from the tender looks they shared and the protective stance Charles took at his fiancée's side.

Abbey had told her about Charles and Lanni, and a little of the story about the O'Halloran brothers' father and Catherine Fletcher. Bethany gathered that for many years there'd been no love lost between Catherine and the O'Hallorans. Then again, she thought, perhaps that *was* the problem between the two families. *Love lost.* Maybe, just maybe, it had been found again through Charles and Lanni.

Silently Bethany applauded them for having the courage to seek out their happiness, despite the past.

Reverend Wilson, the circuit minister, had flown in for the service. He stepped forward, holding his Bible, and began the service with a short prayer. Bethany solemnly bowed her head. No sooner had the prayer ended than Mitch Harris slipped into the pew beside her.

He didn't acknowledge her in any way. She could have been a stranger for all the attention he gave her. His attitude stung. It hurt to realize that if there'd been anyplace else to sit, he would have taken it.

As the service progressed, Bethany noticed how restless Mitch became. He shifted position a number of times, almost as though he was in some discomfort. When she dared to look in his direction, she saw that his eyes were closed and his hands tightly clenched.

Then it hit her.

She knew little of his life, but she did know he was a widower.

Reverend Wilson opened his Bible and read from the Twenty-Third Psalm. "'Yea, though I walk through the valley of the shadow of death, I will fear no evil: for thou art with me; thy rod and thy staff they comfort me.'"

Mitch had traversed that dark valley himself, and Bethany guessed that he hadn't found the comfort the pastor spoke of. But it wasn't Catherine Fletcher Mitch mourned. It was his dead wife. The woman he'd loved. And married. The woman who'd carried his child. The woman he couldn't forget.

How foolish she'd been! Mitch didn't want to become involved with her. How could he when he remained emotionally tied to his dead wife? No wonder he'd been fighting her so hard. He was trapped somewhere in the past, shackled to a memory, a dead love.

Bethany closed her eyes, shocked that it had taken her so long to see what should have been obvious. True, he was attracted to her. That much neither could deny. But he wasn't free to love her. Maybe he didn't *want* to be free. He probably hated himself for even thinking about someone else. His behavior at this memorial service explained everything.

Mitch leaned forward, supporting his elbows on his knees, and hid his face in his hands. He was in such unmistakable pain that Bethany couldn't sit idly by and do nothing. Not knowing whether her gesture would be welcome, she drew a deep breath and laid her hand on his forearm.

He jerked himself upright and swiveled in his seat to look at her. Surprise blossomed in his eyes. Apparently he'd forgotten he was sitting next to her. She gave him a quick smile, wanting him to know only that she was his friend. Nothing more.

Mitch blinked, and his face revealed a vulnerability that tore at her heart. She wanted to help, but she didn't know how.

As if reading her thoughts, Mitch reached out and grasped her hand. The touch had nothing to do with physical desire. He'd come to her in his pain.

He let go of her almost immediately, then rose abruptly and hurried out of the church. Bethany twisted around and watched him leave, the doors slamming behind him.

Mitch stalked into his office, his chest heaving as if the short walk had demanded intense physical effort. His heart hammered wildly and his breathing was labored.

He'd decided at the last minute to attend the memorial service. He hadn't known Catherine Fletcher well, but appreciated the contribution she and her family had made to the community.

Mitch had talked with her only a few times in the past five years. Nevertheless he'd seen his attendance at the service as a social obligation, a way of paying his respects.

But the minute he'd walked into the church, he'd been bombarded with memories of Lori. They'd come at him from all sides, closing in on him until he thought he'd suffocate.

He remembered the day he'd met her and how attracted he'd been to the delightful sound of her laughter. They'd been college sophomores, still young and inexperienced. Then they'd gotten married; they'd had the large, traditional wedding she'd wanted and he'd never seen a more beautiful bride. They were deeply in love, blissfully happy. At least he had been. In the beginning.

When they learned she was pregnant, a new joy, unlike anything he'd experienced before, had taken hold of him. But after Chrissie was born, their lives had quickly slid downhill. Mitch covered his head. He didn't want to remember any more.

He continued to pace in the silence of his office. Attending the memorial service had been a mistake. He'd suffered the backlash caused by years of refusing to deal with the pain, the guilt. Years of denial. Now he felt as if he was collapsing inward.

He'd never felt so desperate, so out of control.

"Mitch."

He whirled around. Bethany stood just inside the office, her eyes full of compassion.

"Are you all right?"

He nodded, soundlessly telling her nothing was wrong. Even as he did, he realized he couldn't sustain the lie. "No," he said in a choked whisper.

Slowly she advanced into the room. "What is it?"

He shook his head. His throat clogged. He stood defenseless as his control crumpled.

Bethany's hand fell gently on his arm. He might have been able to resist her comfort if she hadn't touched him. His body reacted instantly to the physical contact, and he lurched as if her hand had stung him. Only it wasn't pain he felt, but an incredible sense of release.

"Let me hold you...please," he said. "I need... I need you." He didn't wait for her permission before he brought her into his arms and buried his face in her shoulder. She was soft and warm. Alive. He drew in several lungfuls of air, hoping that would stabilize his erratic heart.

"Everything's all right," she whispered, her lips close to his ear. "Don't worry."

Her arms were his shelter, his protection. The first time he'd met Bethany, he'd promised himself he wouldn't become involved with her. Until now he'd steadfastly stuck to that vow.

But he hadn't counted on needing her—or anyone—this badly. She was his sanity.

He knew he was going to kiss her in the same moment he

acknowledged how desperate he'd been for her. With a hoarse groan that came from deep in his throat he surrendered to a need so strong he couldn't possibly have refused it.

Their lips met, and it was like a burst of spontaneous combustion. He'd waited so long. He needed her so badly. One hand gathering the blond thickness of her unbound hair, he kissed her repeatedly, unable to get enough.

He was afraid his need had shocked her, and he sighed with heartfelt relief when she kissed him back as avidly as he was kissing her.

He moaned, wanting to tell her how sorry he was. But he was unwilling to break the contact, to leave her for even those short seconds.

Bethany coiled her arms tightly about his neck. Again and again he ran his hands down the length of her spine, savoring the feel of this woman in his arms. Their mouths met urgently, frantically. He felt insatiable, and she responded with an intensity that equaled his own.

Mitch broke off the kiss when it became more than he could physically handle. He felt that the passion between them might never burn itself out. At the rate things had progressed, the kiss would quickly have taken them toward something more intimate. Something neither of them was ready to deal with yet.

Bethany gasped in an effort to catch her breath, and she pressed her hand over her heart as though to still its frenzied beat. Her lips were swollen. Mitch raised his finger and stroked the slick smoothness of her mouth.

Slowly he raised his head and studied her.

She blinked, looking confused. Or dazed.

He felt a surge of guilt—and regret. "That should never have happened," he whispered.

She said nothing.

"I promise you it won't happen again."

Her eyes flickered with...anger? Before another second had passed, she'd turned and rushed out of his office.

Matt had found the day long and emotionally exhausting. He'd attended the services for his grandmother and the wake that followed.

His mother mourned deeply, and in his own way Matt did, too. His grief surprised him. Matt had barely known Catherine—Grammy, as Lanni called her. There hadn't been many visits over the years.

She'd always sent a card with a check for his birthday. Money again at Christmas. A Bible when he graduated from high school and later, she'd established a trust fund for him. This was the money he'd used to buy the lodge from the O'Halloran brothers.

His grandmother had never known how he'd used the money in the trust fund. By the time he was able to collect it this past summer, her health had disintegrated so much she no longer recognized him. Somehow Matt felt she would have condoned his choice. He liked to think she would have, anyway.

The memorial service and wake had gone well. Virtually all the townspeople had offered condolences, and many had inquired about his progress with the lodge.

The people of Hard Luck had been open and friendly since his arrival, but Matt tended to keep to himself. He was too busy getting the lodge ready to socialize much. He didn't dare stop and think about everything that needed to be done before he posted an Open sign on the front door. The multitude of tasks sometimes overwhelmed him.

Readying the lodge was a considerable chore, but his success depended on a whole lot more than making sure the rooms were habitable.

He'd have to convince people to make the journey this far

north, and he'd have to provide them with activities. Wilderness treks, fishing, dogsledding. If his first order of business was getting the lodge prepared for paying customers, his second was attracting said customers.

He'd do it. Whatever it took, he'd do it. He had something to prove to—

His thoughts came to an abrupt halt.

Karen.

He worked fifteen-hour days for one reason, and that reason was Karen. Just saying her name produced an aching sensation in his heart, an ache that had started the day she'd filed for divorce.

What kind of wife filed for divorce without discussing the subject with her husband first? Okay, so maybe she'd mentioned once or twice that she was unhappy.

Well, dammit, he was unhappy, too!

He'd be the first to admit she had a valid complaint—but only to a point. True, he'd changed careers four times in about that many years. He was a man with an eye to the future, and opportunities abounded. But Karen had accused him of being self-indulgent and irresponsible, unable to settle down. That wasn't true. He'd always moved on to something new when the challenge was gone, when a job no longer held his interest.

He supposed he could understand her discontent, but he'd never thought she'd actually *leave* him. To be fair, she'd threatened it, but he hadn't believed her.

If she truly loved him, she would've stuck it out.

Matt shook his head. There was no point in reviewing the same issues again. He'd gone over what had led to the divorce a thousand times without solving anything.

The final blow had been when she left Alaska. Oh, he'd fully expected her to do well in her career. She was an executive secretary for some highfalutin engineering company. Great job. Great pay. When they'd offered her a raise and a promotion, she'd leapt at the chance. Without a word, she'd packed her bags and headed for California.

California? Even now he had trouble believing it.

He reached for a magazine and idly flipped through the pages, then slapped it shut. Thinking about Karen was unproductive.

California! He hoped she was happy.

No, he didn't. He wanted her to be miserable, as miserable as he was. The simple truth was...he loved her. And he missed her.

A year. You'd think he'd be over her by now. He should be seeing new women, going out, making friends. He might have, too, if he wasn't so busy working on the lodge. But if he had any free time and if there were single women available—like that new teacher, maybe—he'd start dating again.

No, he wouldn't.

Matt wasn't going to lie to himself. Not after today when he'd stood with his family and mourned the loss of his grandmother. His parents had been married for nearly thirty years now. Lanni and Charles had stood on his other side. Together.

Losing Grammy had been difficult for Lanni. Having spent part of the summer in Hard Luck cleaning out their grandmother's home, Lanni felt much closer to Catherine than he did. She grieved, and Charles was there to lend comfort.

The way his father comforted his mother.

But Matt stood alone.

It hurt to admit how much he'd yearned to have Karen beside him. His agony intensified when he was forced to recognize how deeply he still loved her.

He wondered if it would always be like this. Would he ever learn to let her go? Not that he had any real choice. The truth was, any day now he expected to hear she'd remarried.

There wasn't a damn thing to stop her. The men in California would have to be blind not to notice her. It wouldn't take long for her to meet some executive who'd give her the stability she craved. There wasn't a man alive who could resist her, he thought morosely. He should know.

His ex-wife was beautiful, talented, generous and spirited. Was she spirited!

A smile cracked his lips. Not many people knew that the cool, calm Karen Caldwell loved to throw things—mainly at Matt. She'd hurled the most ridiculous objects, too.

His shirt. A newspaper. Potato chips. Decorator pillows.

When her anger reached this point, there was only one sure method to cool her ire. One method that had never failed him.

He'd make love to her. The lovemaking was wild and wicked, and soon they'd both be so caught up in the sheer magic of it she'd forget whatever it was that had angered her.

Matt remembered the last time Karen had expressed her fury like a major-league pitcher. His smile widened as he leaned back in his chair and clasped his hands behind his head.

He'd quit his job. All right, he should've discussed it with her first. But he hadn't *planned* to go in and resign that day. It had just...happened.

Karen had been furious with him. He tried to explain that he was going to find something better. Accounting wasn't for him—he should've realized it before. He'd been thinking about a job more suited to his talents.

She wouldn't give him a chance to explain. Ranting and raving, she'd started flinging whatever she could lay hands on. Matt had ducked when she'd sent her shoes flying in his direction. The saltshaker had scored a direct hit, smacking him in the chest.

That had given her pause, he recalled, but not for long. Braving her anger, he'd advanced toward her. She'd refused to let him near her. When she ran out of easy-to-reach ammunition, she'd walked across the top of the sofa and leapt onto the chair, all the while shouting at the top of her lungs and threatening him with the pepper mill.

It hadn't taken much to capture her, and he'd let her yell and struggle in his arms for a few minutes. Then he did the only thing he could to silence Karen—kiss her.

Soon, the pepper mill had tumbled from her hands and onto the carpet, and they were helping each other undress, their hands as urgent as their need.

Afterward, he remembered, Karen had been quiet and still. While he lay there, appreciating the most incredible sex of his life, his wife had been planning their divorce. Less than a week later, she moved out and he was served with the papers.

The smile faded as the sadness crept back into his heart.

He modified his wish. He didn't want Karen to be miserable. If someone had to be blamed, then fine, he'd accept full responsibility for their failure. He deserved it.

He missed her so much! Never more than now. Whatever happened in the future with this lodge and the success of his business venture seemed of little consequence. Matt would go to his grave loving Karen.

Like his grandmother before him, he would only love once.

"You seem pensive," Sawyer said as he sat on the edge of the bed and peeled off his socks.

With her back propped against the headboard, Abbey glanced over the top of her mystery novel. "Of course I'm pensive," she muttered, smiling at her husband. "I'm reading."

"You're pretending to read," he corrected. "You've got that look again."

"What look?" she asked him with an expression of pure innocence.

"The one that says you're plotting."

Abbey made a face at him. How could Sawyer know her so well? They hadn't been married all that long. "And what exactly am I plotting?" She'd see if he could figure *that* one out.

"I don't know, but I'm sure you'll tell me sooner or later."

"For your information, Mr. Know-It-All, I was just thinking about Thanksgiving."

Sawyer cocked his head to one side, as if to say he wasn't sure he should believe her. "That's almost a month away. Tell me what could possibly be so important about Thanksgiving that it would occupy your mind now?"

"Well, for one thing, I was thinking we should ask Mitch and Chrissie to join us." She glanced at her husband in order to gauge his reaction.

Sawyer didn't hesitate. "Good idea."

"And Bethany Ross."

A full smile erupted on Sawyer's handsome face as he pointed his finger at her. "What did I say? You're plotting!"

"What?" Once more she feigned innocence.

"You want to invite Mitch *and* Bethany to Thanksgiving dinner?"

"Right," she concurred, opening her eyes wide in exaggerated wonder that he could find anything the *least* bit underhand in such a courtesy. "And what, pray tell, is so devious about that?"

His finger wagged again as he climbed into bed. "A little matchmaking, maybe? You've got something up your sleeve, Abbey O'Halloran."

"I most certainly do not," she said with a touch of righteous indignation.

"I notice you didn't suggest inviting John Henderson."

"No," she admitted.

"Isn't he the one Bethany's been having dinner with for the past few weeks?"

"They're friends, that's all."

"I see." Sawyer leaned over and deftly reached for one end of the satin ribbon tying the collar of her pajama top. He slowly tugged until it fell open.

"Besides, I heard from Mariah that John's interested in someone else now."

Sawyer idly unfastened the first button. "Is that right?"

Her husband's touch was warm, creating feathery sensations that scampered across her skin.

Sawyer's eyes dropped to her mouth, and his voice lowered to a soft purr. "Mitch has lived here for a few years."

"True." Her second button gave way as easily as the first.

"If he was interested in remarrying, he'd have done something about it before now, wouldn't you think?"

Abbey closed her book and set it blindly on the table next to the bed. "Not necessarily."

"Do you think Mitch is interested in Bethany?" Sawyer slipped his hand inside the opening he'd created.

Abbey closed her eyes at the feel of her husband's fingers. "Yes." The word sounded shockingly intimate.

"As it happens," Sawyer said in a husky whisper, "I agree with you."

"You do?" Her voice dwindled to a whisper. With her eyes still closed, she swayed toward him.

Sawyer's kiss was long and deep. The conversation about Mitch Harris and Bethany Ross stopped there. Instead, Sawyer and Abbey continued their dialogue with husky sighs and soft murmurs.

Bethany walked into the Hard Luck Café shortly after ten on Saturday and sat at the counter. The place was empty. Ben wasn't in sight, either, which was fine; she wasn't in any hurry. Tired of her own company, she'd decided to take a walk and sort through what had happened between her and Mitch. Ha! she thought sourly. As if that was even possible.

There wasn't anyone she could ask about Mitch's past. And apparently *he* wasn't going to volunteer the information. He hadn't said one word about his life before Hard Luck, and no one else seemed to know much, either.

As for what had happened at the memorial service, Bethany had given up any attempt to make sense of it. For whatever reason, Mitch had turned to her. He'd kissed her with such intensity, such hunger.... Never before had she felt that kind of joy.

Then he'd apologized. And she'd realized he had simply needed someone. Anyone. Any woman would have sufficed. She just happened to be handy. The minute he saw what he'd done, he regretted having touched her.

"Bethany, hello! How are you this fine day?" As always, Ben greeted her with a wide smile as he bustled up to the counter. "We missed you at the wake after Catherine's memorial service. The women in town put on a mighty fine spread."

There was probably some psychological significance in the fact that she'd sought Ben out now, Bethany decided. If she wasn't so sick of analyzing the situation between her and Mitch, she might have delved into *that* question. As it was, she felt too miserable to care.

"I'm fine."

"Is that so?" Without her asking, Ben filled a mug with coffee. "Then why those little lines between your eyes?"

"What lines?"

"When I'm stewing about something, these lines always appear. Right there." He pointed to his own forehead. "Three of them. Seems to me you're cursed with the same thing. Can't fool a living soul, no matter how hard I try." He smiled, encouraging her to talk.

Bethany resisted the urge to tell him she'd come by those

lines honestly. Inhaling a deep breath, she eyed him, wondering how much she dared confide in him about her feelings for Mitch. Darn little, she suspected. That she'd even wonder was a sign of how desperate she'd become. Still, maybe he could fill in a few details about Mitch's background. With no other customers present, this was the optimum time to ask.

"What can you tell me about Mitch?" she began.

"Mitch? Mitch Harris?" All at once, Ben found it necessary to wipe down the counter. He ran a rag over the top of the already spotless surface. "Well, for one thing, he's a damn good man. Decent, caring. Loves his daughter."

"He's lived in Hard Luck for how long?" She already knew the answer, but she wanted to ease Ben into the conversation.

"Must be around five years now."

She nodded. "I heard he worked for the police department in Chicago before that."

"That's what I heard, too."

"Do you know how his wife died?" Since Ben wasn't inclined to share any real information, she'd have to pry it out of him.

"Can't say I do." His mouth twisted to one side, as if he was judging what he should and shouldn't tell her. "I don't think Mitch has ever talked about her to anyone. Hasn't mentioned her to me."

Bethany heard the door open behind her. Their conversation was over, not that she'd gleaned any new facts.

"If you're curious about his wife," Ben whispered, "I suggest you ask him yourself. He just walked in."

For the briefest of seconds, she felt like a five-year-old caught with her hand in the cookie jar.

To her surprise, Mitch sat on the stool next to hers. He studied her for what seemed like minutes. "Hello, Bethany," he finally said in a low voice.

"Mitch." She refused to meet his eyes.

"I'm glad I ran into you."

Well, that was certainly a change.

Ben strolled over and Mitch asked for coffee.

"I'd like to talk to you, Bethany." He gestured toward one of the booths, the steaming mug in his hand.

She followed him to the farthest booth, and they sat across from each other. For a long moment, he didn't say anything, and when he lifted his head to look at her, his eyes were bleak.

"Bethany, I can't tell you how sorry I am. I don't know what else to say. I've lain awake nights worrying what you must think of me."

Confused and hurt, Bethany said nothing.

He gestured helplessly. "I'm sorry. What more can I say? Talk to me, would you? Say something. Anything."

"What are you sorry for?" she asked, her voice almost a whisper. "Kissing me?"

"Yes."

Even now he didn't seem to realize she'd been a willing participant. "You needed me. Was that why?"

"Yes," he said, as if this was his greatest sin.

She hesitated, searching for the words. "Any other woman would have done just as well. Isn't that what you're really saying? It wasn't *me* you were kissing. It wasn't *me* you needed. I just happened to...be available."

He didn't disagree.

6

"**Y**ou're going to do it, aren't you?" Duke Porter asked John for the second time. An incredulous look contorted the pilot's features. "You're *actually* going to do it?"

"Yes," John said, irritated. He jerked the grease rag from his back pocket and brusquely wiped his hands.

Duke followed him to the far end of the hangar while John put away the tools he'd used. "You're *sure* this is what you want?"

John didn't hesitate. "I'm absolutely, positively sure."

"But you hardly know the woman."

"I know everything I need to know," he muttered. Duke was good at raising his hackles, but nothing was going to ruin this day. The engagement ring was waiting in his pocket. His eagerness to propose was nothing compared to the way he felt about Sally.

This time it was *his* turn. Earlier, he'd fallen all over himself in an attempt to court Abbey Sutherland. What he hadn't known was that Sawyer O'Halloran had stolen her heart without giving any of the others a chance.

Then there was Lanni Caldwell. John had never seriously considered her wife material, believing she'd only be in town for the summer. Duke might've been more interested in striking up a relationship with her, but once again they'd been beaten out by one of the O'Hallorans.

John liked Mariah Douglas well enough, but it was plain as the nose on your face that she had eyes only for Christian. Besides, the last thing he wanted to do was tangle with *her*. Daddy Douglas just might sic that attorney on him.

He'd had a shot with Bethany, the schoolteacher. In the beginning he was quite drawn to her. He knew she didn't share his enthusiasm, but he'd figured that, given time, their friendship might grow into something more.

Then Sally McDonald had arrived.

Sally, with her pretty blue eyes and her gentle smile. He'd taken one look at her and his heart had stopped beating. In that moment, he'd recognized beyond any doubt that she was the one for him. After John had met Sally, he didn't resent Sawyer for stealing Abbey away from him and the others. It seemed unimportant that Lanni was marrying Charles, or that Bethany Ross wasn't as keen on him as he'd been on her. Sally was the one for him.

"If you want my opinion..."

John glared at Duke. "I didn't ask for it, did I?"

"No," Duke said, "but I'm going to give it to you anyway."

John sighed loudly. "All right. If it's so important, tell me what you think."

"I can understand why you'd want to marry Sally—" Duke began.

"But you're thinking about her for yourself!" This explained why Duke was poking into something that was none of his concern.

"No way," Duke said, raising both hands. "I'm off women.

Too many of 'em are like that lawyer, looking for any excuse to chew a man's butt."

"Tracy Santiago wasn't like that." John grinned broadly at the memory of their clashes. To be fair, he wasn't interested in her for himself, but he kinda liked the way she'd cut Duke down to size. "She was doing her job, that's all."

"Listen, if you don't mind, I'd rather not discuss her. She's gone, at least for now, and all I can say is good riddance."

John swallowed a laugh. He'd never seen Duke get this riled up over a woman. It seemed to his inexperienced eye that his friend protested too much. He figured that, this time, Duke had met his match. Too bad Tracy lived in Washington State and Duke in Alaska.

"About Sally…" The other pilot broached the topic again.

John could see there was no escaping his friend's unwanted counsel. "All right," he said, giving in. Duke was going to state his opinion whether John wanted to hear it or not. He might as well listen—or pretend to.

"Don't get me wrong here," Duke said, shoving his hands into his pockets as though he found this difficult. "I like Sally. Who wouldn't? She's a real sweetheart."

"Exactly."

"The thing that concerns me is…she's young."

"Not that much younger than Bethany. Or Lanni."

"True, only Sally's led a more sheltered life than either of them."

John couldn't argue with that. Sally had been raised in a British Columbia town with a population of less than a thousand. From what he understood, her family was a closeknit one. She'd attended a small, private high school and a church-affiliated college. When finances became too tight for her to continue her education, she'd gotten a job working in an accounting office in Vancouver. That was where she'd read Christian's newspaper ad and applied for the job with Hard Luck Power and Light.

"You know why she came to Hard Luck, don't you?"

"Yeah." John knew, and frankly he was surprised Duke did, too. After moving to Vancouver, Sally had become involved with a fast-talking man who'd ultimately broken her heart. He'd been married; she'd found out because his wife had shown up at her door.

According to what she'd told him, Sally had walked away from the relationship feeling both heartsick and foolish. When she read about Midnight Sons offering land, housing and jobs, she'd jumped at the opportunity to start over. This time she'd do it in a small-town environment, the kind of place she was comfortable with.

"Are you sure she's over this other guy?" Duke asked.

"I'm sure." Although he made it sound like there could be no question, John wasn't entirely convinced. He was grateful Duke didn't challenge his response.

"What about her family?" the other pilot asked instead.

"What about them?" John said defensively. He didn't much like where Duke's questions were leading.

"From what you've said, they're the old-fashioned sort. If you're serious about marrying their daughter, the thing to do is talk to her father first. Meet him face-to-face and tell him you love Sally and—"

"How am I supposed to do that?" John wanted to know. "Sal's dad lives in some dinky town on the coast. It's not like I can leave here. Especially now."

Winter had set in full force. Temperatures had dipped into the minus range every day for a solid week. Whenever it fell to minus thirty, Midnight Sons had to cancel all flights. The stress to the aircraft was too great a risk.

Snow accumulations measured forty inches or more in the

past month alone. Thanksgiving was two weeks away, and there didn't seem to be any break in the weather ahead. In a word, they were snowed in. No matter how much he wanted to meet Sally's family, for the time being it was impossible.

"First," Duke said, and held up his hand. He folded down one finger. "You got a woman who's only recently turned twenty-one, so she's young. Younger than any of the others who've come to Hard Luck. Secondly—" he bent down another finger "—she moved here on the rebound, hoping to cure a broken heart."

"Third," John said, fighting back his frustration, "she comes from a family who wouldn't appreciate their daughter marrying a man they haven't personally met and approved."

"If you start out on the wrong foot with her parents, it could take years to make up for it," Duke said. "If you truly love her—"

"I do," John insisted, then added in a lower voice, "I've never felt so strongly about anyone."

His friend nodded in understanding. "Then do this right. I can't think of a single reason to rush into marriage, can you?"

John could list any number of reasons to marry Sally that very day, but said nothing.

"If she's the one for you, then everything will work out the way it's supposed to, and you've got nothing to worry about."

John shrugged. He didn't like it, but Duke had a valid point. The engagement ring could continue to wait in his pocket until he'd had a chance to square things with Sally's father. Until he could be sure she loved him for himself—and not as an instant cure for a broken heart.

"Daddy, I don't feel good." Chrissie came slowly into the kitchen, clutching her Pooh bear to her chest. The stuffed animal was a favorite from her preschool days. Now she sought it out only on rare occasions.

Worried, Mitch slid the casserole into the oven, then pressed the back of his hand against his daughter's forehead. She did feel warm. Her face was flushed and her eyes were unusually solemn.

"What's wrong, pumpkin?"

She shrugged. "I just don't feel good."

"Does your tummy hurt?" There'd been lots of flu going around.

Chrissie nodded.

"Do you have a sore throat?"

She bobbed her head and swallowed. "It hurts, too."

"You'd better let me take your temperature."

Her eyes flared wide. "No! I don't want that thing in my mouth."

"Chrissie, it isn't going to hurt."

"I don't care. I don't want you to take my temperature. I'll... I'll just go to bed."

Mitch had forgotten how unreasonable his daughter could be when she was ill. "Don't you feel like eating dinner?"

"No," she answered weakly. "I just want to go to bed. Don't worry about me. I won't die."

Mitch sighed. He didn't know if she was being dramatic or was expressing some kind of anxiety about death. She'd known about Catherine's funeral, and maybe that had made her think about Lori....

"Will you tuck me in?"

"Of course." He followed her down the narrow hallway to her bedroom. While he pulled back her covers, Chrissie knelt on the floor and said her prayers. It seemed to take her twice as long as usual, but Mitch pretended not to notice.

Once she was securely tucked beneath the blankets, Mitch

sat on the edge of her bed and brushed the hair away from her forehead. Her face still seemed a little warm.

"Stay with me, okay?" she asked in a voice that suggested she was fading quickly.

Mitch reached for the Jack London story he'd been reading to her. Chrissie placed her hand on his forearm to stop him. "I want you to read the story about the Princess Bride. That's my favorite."

Mitch figured he'd read the book about a thousand times. Chrissie could recite parts of it from memory, and Mitch knew he could repeat whole sections of it himself without bothering to turn the pages. Although his daughter was quite capable of reading on her own, there were certain stories she insisted he read to her.

He picked up the book and flipped it open. He made it through the first page by merely glancing at it now and then.

"Daddy."

"Yes, pumpkin?"

"Are we going to Susan's for Thanksgiving?"

Mitch closed the book. "Sawyer asked this afternoon if we'd join them for dinner." Naturally Susan would've said something to Chrissie. Sawyer had also let it drop that Bethany would be there, then waited for his reaction. So Mitch had smiled politely and said he looked forward to seeing her again. Actually it was true.

"Did you tell Sawyer we'd come?"

Mitch nodded.

Chrissie's eyes lit up, as if this confirmation had given her a reason to live. "I hope I won't be sick then." She made a show of swallowing.

"You won't be."

Mitch didn't know what was wrong with his daughter, but he had a sneaking suspicion it wasn't nearly as serious as she'd like him to believe. He sat with her for a few more minutes, then moved into the kitchen to check on dinner.

"Daddy!"

He made his way back down the hallway and stuck his head in her bedroom door. "Now what?"

"I want Ms. Ross."

Mitch's heart rate accelerated. "Why?"

Chrissie nodded. "I just want to talk to her, all right?"

Mitch hesitated. Of all the things he'd expected Chrissie to ask of him, Bethany wasn't it. A game of checkers. A glass of juice. Anything but her teacher.

"Please, oh, please, Daddy. Ms. Ross will make me feel *so* much better."

If Mitch was looking for an excuse to call Bethany, then his daughter had just offered it to him. He and Bethany hadn't seen much of each other in the past few weeks, but *she* seemed to be the one avoiding him. Embarrassed by what had happened in his office during Catherine Fletcher's service, Mitch had decided to leave her alone. He'd done enough damage.

But it didn't change the way he felt about her. They couldn't be in the same vicinity without his heartbeat accelerating frantically. It had been years since he'd felt this vulnerable with a woman, and it made him nervous.

Since their meeting at Ben's place, they'd greeted each other cordially—nothing personal. Just noncommittal chitchat, of the kind he might have exchanged with a near stranger.

None of that, however, was enough for Mitch to forget the feel of Bethany in his arms, Bethany's lips on his, warm and welcoming. And so blessedly giving that he wanted to kick himself every time he thought about the way he'd treated her.

"Daddy." Chrissie gave him a long look. "Will you call Ms. Ross?"

He nodded helplessly. Walking into the kitchen, he reached

for the phone. Chrissie couldn't possibly realize what she'd asked of him. Even while that thought formed in his mind, he admitted he was grateful for the excuse to call Bethany.

He punched out the phone number and waited. Bethany answered on the second ring.

"Hello."

Now that he heard her voice, he felt a moment's panic. What could he say? He didn't want to exaggerate and make it sound as if Chrissie was seriously ill, nor did he wish to make light of her request.

"It's Mitch."

No response.

"I'm sorry to trouble you."

"It's no trouble." She sounded friendly, but not overly so.

"Chrissie seems to have come down with the flu." Then, on a stroke of genius, he invented the reason for his call. "Did she mention not feeling well at school today?"

"No, she didn't say a word." Concern was more evident in her voice than irritation.

"It's probably nothing more than a twenty-four-hour virus," he said.

"Is there anything I can do?" she asked.

He'd been born under a lucky star, Mitch decided. Without his having to say a word, she'd volunteered.

"As a matter of fact, Chrissie's feeling pretty bad at the moment and she's asking for you. I don't want you to go out of your way—"

"I'll be there in ten minutes."

"No." He wouldn't hear of her walking that far in weather this cold. "I'll come for you on the snowmobile."

She hesitated. "Fine. I'll watch for you."

Mitch went back into Chrissie's bedroom. "I talked to Ms. Ross."

"And?" Chrissie nearly fell out of the bed she was so eager to hear the outcome of the conversation.

"She'll come, but I didn't want her walking over here in the cold. I'm going to pick her up on the snowmobile. You'll be all right alone for five minutes, won't you?"

Chrissie's eyes filled with outrage. "I'm not a little kid anymore!"

"I'm glad to know that." If he'd actually been upset about asking Bethany to visit, he might have pointed out that someone who wasn't a little kid anymore wouldn't ask for her teacher.

Mitch called out to Chrissie that he was leaving. He put on his insulated, waterproof jacket and wound a thick scarf around his neck, covering his mouth, before he stepped outside. The snowmobile was the most frequently used means of transportation in the winter months, and he kept his well-maintained. The minute he pulled up outside Bethany's small house, her door opened and she appeared.

She climbed onto the back of the snowmobile and positioned herself a discreet distance behind him. Nevertheless, having her this close produced a fiery warmth he couldn't escape—didn't *want* to escape.

She didn't say anything until they'd reached his house. He parked the snowmobile inside the garage and plugged in the heater to protect the engine.

Once in the house they removed their winter gear. Bethany was wearing leggings and an oversize San Francisco Police Department sweatshirt; her feet were covered in heavy red woollen socks. He stared at her, taking in every detail.

Mitch found he couldn't speak. It was the first time they'd been alone together since the scene in his office. This sudden intimacy caught him off guard, and he wasn't sure how to react.

Part of him yearned to take her in his arms and kiss her again. Only this time he'd be tender, drawing out the kiss with—

"Where's Chrissie?" Bethany asked, mercifully breaking into his thoughts.

"Chrissie... She's in her bedroom."

The oven timer went off, and grateful for the excuse to clear his head, Mitch walked into the kitchen. He opened the oven and pulled out the ground-turkey casserole to cool on top of the stove.

He entered his daughter's room and discovered Bethany sitting on the bed, with Chrissie cuddled close. The child's head rested against Bethany's shoulder as she read from the story he'd begun himself. When Chrissie glanced up to find Mitch watching, her eyes shone with happiness.

"Hi, Dad," she said, craning her neck to look up at Bethany. "Dad usually reads me this story, but you do it better because you love it, too. I don't think Dad likes romance stories."

"Dinner's ready," Mitch announced. "Are you sure you won't try to eat something, pumpkin?"

Chrissie's frown said that was a terribly difficult decision. "Maybe I could eat just a little, but only if Ms. Ross will stay and have dinner with us."

Before Bethany could offer a perfunctory excuse, Mitch said, "There's plenty, and we'd both enjoy having you." He wanted to be certain she understood that he wouldn't object to her company; if anything, he'd be glad of it.

He saw her gaze travel from him to Chrissie and then back. He leaned against the doorway, hands deep in his pockets, trying to give the impression that it made no difference to him if she joined them or not. But it did. He *wanted* her to stay.

"I... It's thoughtful of you to ask. I, uh, haven't eaten yet."

"Oh, goodie." Chrissie jumped up and clapped her hands, bouncing with glee. Then, as if she'd just remembered how ill she was supposed to be, she sagged her shoulders and all but crumpled onto the bed.

In an effort to hide his smile, Mitch returned to the kitchen and quickly set the table. By the time Chrissie and Bethany joined him, he'd brought the casserole to the table, as well as a loaf of bread, butter and some straight-from-the-can bean salad.

Dinner was...an odd affair. Exciting. Fun. And a little sad. It was as if he and Bethany were attempting to find new ground with each other. Only they both seemed to fear that this ground would be full of crevices and strewn with obstacles. He'd take one step forward, then freeze, afraid he'd said something that might offend her.

He noticed that Bethany didn't find this new situation any easier than he did. She'd start to laugh, then her eyes, her beautiful brown eyes, would meet his and the laugh would falter.

Following their meal, Chrissie wanted her to finish the story. Since Mitch was well aware of how the story ended, he lingered in the kitchen over a cup of coffee.

He'd just begun washing the dishes when Bethany reappeared.

"Chrissie's decided she needs her beauty sleep," she told him, standing at the far side of the room.

Mitch didn't blame her for maintaining the distance between them. Every time she'd attempted to get close, he'd shoved her away. Every time she'd opened her heart to him, he'd shunned her. Yet when he'd desperately needed her, she'd been there. And although she'd accused him of settling for any woman who happened to fall into his arms, *she* was the only one who could fill the need in him.

"I imagine you want to get back home," he said, experiencing a curious sadness. He dumped what remained of his coffee into the sink. The way her eyes flickered told him she might have enjoyed a cup had he offered one.

"Stay," he said suddenly. "Just for a few minutes."

The invitation seemed to hang in the air. It took her a long time to decide; when he was about to despair, she gave him a small smile, then nodded.

"Coffee?"

"Please."

His heart reacted with a wild burst of staccato beats. He poured her a mug, grabbing a fresh one for himself. His movements were jerky, and he realized it was because he felt afraid that if he didn't finish the task quickly enough, she might change her mind.

He carried the mugs into the living room and sat across from her. At first their conversation was awkward, but gradually the tension eased. He was astonished by how much they had to talk about. Books, movies, politics. Children. Police work. Life in Alaska. They shared myriad opinions and stories and observations.

It was as though all the difficulties between them had been wiped out and they were starting over.

Mitch laughed. He felt warm and relaxed, trusting. Alive. She seemed curious about his past, but her occasional questions were friendly, not intrusive. And she didn't probe for more information than he was willing—or able—to give her.

He brought out a large photo album and sat next to her on the sofa, with the album resting partially on his lap and partially on hers. Mitch turned the pages, explaining each picture.

He wondered what Bethany thought about the gap in his past. It was as if their lives—his and Chrissie's—had started when they came to Hard Luck. There wasn't a single photograph taken any earlier than that. Not one picture of Lori.

He turned a page and his hand inadvertently brushed hers. He hadn't meant to touch her, but when he did, it was as if something exploded inside him. For long seconds, neither moved.

Slowly Mitch's gaze went to hers. Instead of accusation, he found approval, instead of anger, acceptance. He released his breath, tired of fighting a battle he couldn't win. With deliberate movements, he closed the photo album and set it aside.

"Mitch?"

"We'll talk later," he whispered. He wrapped his hand around the back of her neck and gently pulled her forward. He needed this. Ached for this.

He kissed her slowly, sweetly, teasing her lips until her head rolled back against the cushion in abject surrender.

"Mitch..." She tried once more.

He stopped her from speaking by placing his finger against her moist lips. "We both know Chrissie manipulated this meeting." She frowned.

"She's no sicker than you or I."

Bethany blinked.

"Let's humor her."

Her eyes darkened. "Let's," she agreed, and wound her arms around his neck.

"Thank you so much for coming," Bethany said to Ben. It had taken a lot to convince him to speak to her students.

Ben had resisted, claiming he wasn't comfortable with children, never having had any himself. But in the end Bethany's persistence had won out.

"You did a great job," she told him.

Ben blushed slightly. "I did, didn't I?" He walked around the room and patted the top of each desk as if remembering who had sat where.

"The children loved hearing about your job," she told him. "And about your life in the navy."

"They certainly had lots of questions."

Bethany didn't mention that she'd primed them beforehand. She hadn't had to encourage them much; they were familiar with Ben and fascinated by him.

Bethany wasn't especially proud of the somewhat devious method she'd used to learn what she could of Ben's past. Still, inviting him to speak to her students was certainly legitimate; he wasn't the only community member she'd asked to do so. Dotty had been in the week before, and Sawyer O'Halloran had agreed to come after Thanksgiving. She found herself studying Ben now, looking for hints of her own appearance, her own personality.

"Haven't seen much of you lately," he said, folding his arms. He half sat on one of the desks in the front row. "Used to be you'd stop in once a day, and we'd have a nice little chat."

"I've been busy lately." In the past week, she'd been seeing a lot of Mitch and Chrissie.

"I kinda miss our talks," Ben muttered.

"Me, too," Bethany admitted. It was becoming increasingly difficult, she discovered, to talk to Ben about personal things. Her fear was that she'd inadvertently reveal their relationship. The temptation to tell him grew stronger with each meeting, something she hadn't considered when she'd decided to find him.

Ben stared at her a moment as if he wasn't sure he should go on. "I thought I saw you with Mitch Harris the other day." It was more question than statement.

She nodded. "He drove me to the library." He'd said he didn't want her walking. The piercing cold continued, but temperatures weren't as low as they'd been earlier in the week. Bethany could easily have trekked the short distance; Mitch's driving her was an excuse—one she'd readily accepted.

"Are you two seeing each other now?"

Bethany hesitated.

"I don't mean to pry," Ben said, studying her. "You can tell me it's none of my damn business if you want, and I won't take offense. It's just that I get customers now and again who're curious about you."

"Like who?"

"Like Bill Landgrin."

"Oh." It embarrassed her no end that she'd had dinner with the pipeline worker. He'd phoned her several times since, and the conversations had been uncomfortable. Not because of anything Bill said or did, but because she'd gone out with him for all the wrong reasons.

Bethany walked from behind her desk and over to the blackboard. "I don't know what to tell you about Mitch and me," she said, picking up the eraser.

Ben's face softened with sympathy. "You sound confused."

"I am." It was easy to understand why people so often shared confidences with Ben; he was a good listener, never meddlesome and always encouraging.

With anyone else, Bethany would have skirted around the subject of her and Mitch, but she felt a connection with Ben— one that reached beyond the reasons she'd come to Hard Luck. It wasn't just a connection created by her secret knowledge. Since her arrival, Ben had become her friend. That surprised her; she hadn't expected to like him this much.

"I'm afraid I'm falling in love with Mitch," she said in a breathless voice.

"Afraid?"

She lowered her gaze and nodded. "I don't think he feels the same way about me."

"Why's that?" Ben leaned forward.

"He doesn't *want* to be attracted to me. Every time I feel we're getting close, he backs away. There's a huge part of himself he keeps hidden. He's never discussed Chrissie's mother. I've never really questioned him about her or about his life before he moved to Hard Luck, and he never volunteers."

Ben rubbed one side of his face. "But we all have our secrets, don't you think?"

Bethany nodded and swallowed uncomfortably. She certainly had hers.

"Mitch lost his wife, the mother of his child. I don't know the details but whatever happened, it cut deep. I can tell you because I was living here when Mitch and Chrissie first showed up. Mitch was a wounded soul. He's kept to himself. He's been here more than five years, and I've hardly ever seen him smile. Until now... You're good for him and Chrissie. Real good."

"He and Chrissie would be easy to love."

"But you're afraid."

She nodded.

"Seems to me you two've come a long way in a short time. I could be wrong, but not so long ago all you did was send these yearning looks at each other. Now you're actually talking, spending time together." He paused. "I heard he told Bill Landgrin a thing or two recently."

"Mitch did?"

Ben grinned broadly. "Not in any words I'd care to repeat in front of a lady, mind you. Seems to me he wouldn't have done that if he wasn't serious about you himself. Give him time, Bethany. Yourself, too. You've been here less than three months."

Bethany exhaled. "Thank you for listening—and for your advice."

"No problem," Ben said. "It was my pleasure."

Smiling, she closed the distance between them and kissed his rough cheek.

Ben flushed and pressed his hand to his face.

She felt so much better, and not just because Ben had given her good advice. He'd said the things her own father would've said.

The irony of that didn't escape her.

7

December 1995

"Hi." Bethany felt almost shy as she opened her front door to Mitch that Saturday night. Chrissie was with them so much of the time that whenever Bethany and Mitch were alone together, an immediate air of intimacy enveloped them.

"Hi, yourself." Mitch unwound his scarf and took off his protective winter gear. He, too, seemed a little ill at ease.

They looked at each other, then quickly glanced away. Anyone watching them would have guessed they were meeting for the first time. Tonight, neither seemed to know what to say, which was absurd, since they often sat and talked for hours about anything and everything.

This newfound need to know each other, as well as the more relaxed tenor of their relationship, came as a result of Thanksgiving dinner with Sawyer and Abbey. The four adults had played cards after dinner. Two couples. It had seemed natural for Bethany to be with Mitch. Natural and right. Conversation had been lively and wide-ranging, and Bethany felt at home with these people. So did Mitch, judging by the way he laughed and smiled. And somehow, whatever he'd been holding inside had begun to seem less important.

They'd all enjoyed the card-playing so much that it had become a weekly event. In the past few weeks Bethany had spent a lot of time in Mitch's company, and she believed they'd grown close and comfortable with each other. But then, they were almost always with other people. With Chrissie, of course. With Sawyer and Abbey. The other O'Halloran brothers. Ben. Margaret Simpson. Rarely were they alone. It was this situation that had prompted her to invite him for dinner.

"Dinner's almost ready," she said self-consciously, rubbing her hands on her jeans. "I hope you like Irish stew."

"I love it, but then I'm partial to anything I don't have to cook myself." He smiled and his eyes met hers. He pulled his gaze away, putting an abrupt end to the moment of intimacy.

Bethany had to fight back her disappointment.

"I see you got your Christmas tree," he said, motioning to the scrawny five-foot vinyl fir that stood in the corner of her living room. She would've preferred a live tree, but the cost was astronomical, and so she did what everyone in Hard Luck had done. She'd ordered a fake tree through the catalog.

"I was hoping you'd help me decorate it," she said. It was only fair, since she'd helped him and Chrissie decorate theirs the night before. Chrissie had chattered excitedly about Susan's slumber party, which was tonight. Bethany wondered if Abbey had arranged the party so Bethany and Mitch would have some time alone. Whether it was intentional or not, Bethany was grateful.

"Chrissie said the two of you baked cookies today."

"Susan helped, too," she said. Bethany had offered to take both girls for a few hours during the afternoon; Mitch was working, and Abbey wanted a chance to wrap Christmas gifts and address cards undisturbed.

Mitch followed her into the kitchen. They were greeted by

the aroma of sage and other herbs. The oven timer went off, and she reached for a mitt to pull out a loaf of crusty French bread.

Mitch looked around. "Is there anything you need me to do?"

"No. Everything's under control." That was true of dinner, perhaps, but little else felt manageable. Mitch suddenly seemed like a stranger, when she thought they'd come so far. It was like the old days—which really weren't so old.

"I'll dish up dinner now," she said.

He didn't offer to help again; perhaps he thought he'd only be in the way. With his hands resting on a chair back, he stood by the kitchen table and waited until she could join him.

The stew was excellent, or so Mitch claimed, but for all the enjoyment she received from it, Bethany could have been eating boot leather.

"I imagine Abbey's got her hands full," she said, trying to make conversation.

"How many kids are spending the night?" Mitch asked. "Six was the last I heard."

"Seven, if you count Scott."

"My guess is Scott would rather be tarred and feathered than decorate sugar cookies and string popcorn with a bunch of girls."

"You're probably right." She passed Mitch the bread. He thanked her and took another slice.

Silence.

Bethany didn't know what had happened to the easy camaraderie they'd had over the past few weeks. Each attempt to start a discussion failed; conversation simply refused to flow. The silence grew more awkward by the minute, and finally Bethany could stand it no longer. With her mouth so dry she could barely talk, she threw down her napkin and turned to Mitch.

"What's wrong with us?" she asked.

"Wrong?"

She gulped some water. "We're so *polite* with each other."

"Yeah," Mitch agreed.

"We can hardly talk."

"I noticed." But he didn't suggest any explanations—or solutions.

Bethany met his eyes, hoping he'd do *something* to resolve this dilemma. He didn't. Instead, he set his napkin carefully aside and got to his feet. "I guess I'm not very hungry." He carried his half-full bowl to the sink.

"Oh."

"Do you want me to leave?" he asked.

No! her heart cried, but she didn't say the word. "Do...do you want to go?"

He didn't answer.

Bethany stood up, pressing the tips of her fingers to her forehead. "Stop. Please, just stop. I want to know what's wrong. Did I do something?"

"No. Good heavens, no." He seemed astonished that she'd even asked. "It isn't anything you've done."

Mitch stood on one side of the kitchen and she on the other. "It's my fault," he said in a voice so quiet she had difficulty hearing him. "You haven't done anything, but—" He stopped abruptly.

"What?" she pleaded. "Tell me."

"Listen, Bethany, I think it would be best if I did leave." With that, he walked purposefully into the living room and retrieved his coat from the small entryway closet.

Although the room was warm and cozy, Bethany felt a sudden chill. She crossed her arms as much to ward off the sense of cold as to protect herself from Mitch's words. "It's back to that, is it?" she managed sadly. From the first day in September, Mitch had been running away from her. Every time they made any progress, something would happen to show her how far they had yet to go.

His hand on the doorknob, he abruptly turned to face her.

When he spoke his voice was hoarse with anger. "I can't be alone with you without wanting to kiss you."

She stared at him in disbelief. "We've kissed before." There had been those memorable passionate kisses. And more recently, affectionate kisses of greeting and farewell. "What's so different now?"

"We're alone."

"Yes, I know." She still didn't understand.

He shook his head, as if it was difficult to continue. "Don't you see, Bethany?"

Obviously she didn't.

"With Chrissie or anyone else around, the temptation is minimized. But when it's just the two of us, I can't think about anything else!" The last sentence was ground out between clenched teeth. "Don't you realize how much I want to make love to you?"

"Is that so terrible?" she asked quietly.

"Yes." The only sound she could hear was the too-fast beating of her own heart. She could see Mitch's pulse hammering in the vein in his neck.

"I can't let it happen," he told her, his back straight, shoulders stiff.

"For your information, making love requires two people," Bethany told him simply. "I wish you'd said something earlier. We could've talked about this...arrived at some understanding. It's true," she added, "the thought of us becoming...intimate has crossed my mind—but I wouldn't have allowed it to happen. Not yet, anyway. It's too soon."

Without a word, Mitch closed the distance between them. With infinite tenderness he wove his fingers through her hair, and buried his lips against her throat. "You tempt me so much."

She sighed and wrapped her arms around him.

"Feeling this way frightens me, Bethany. Overwhelms me."

"We can't run from it, Mitch, or pretend it doesn't exist."

His hands trembled as they slid down her spine, molding her against him. His kiss was slow and melting, and so thorough she was left breathless. She rested her head against his shoulder.

"I guess this means I can put away the celery," she whispered.

"The celery?"

"When the catalog order came, I didn't receive the mistletoe. The slip said it's on back order. I talked to my mom earlier today and told her how disappointed I was—and she suggested celery as a substitute. So I nailed a piece over the doorway. Apparently you didn't notice."

Mitch chuckled hoarsely. "You know what I like best about you?"

"You mean other than my kisses?"

"Yes."

The look in his eyes was as potent as good whiskey. "You make me laugh."

She shook her head. "Don't shut me out, Mitch. I can't bear it when you shut me out of your life. There isn't anything you can't tell me."

"Don't be so sure." Mitch eased her out of his arms and stared down at her, as if testing the truth of her words.

"Mitch," she said gently, touching his face, "what is it?"

"Nothing." He turned away. "It's nothing."

Bethany didn't believe that. But she had no choice other than to end this discussion, which obviously distressed him. When he was ready he'd tell her.

"Didn't you say something about decorating your Christmas tree?" he asked with feigned enthusiasm.

"I did indeed," she said, following his lead.

"Good. We'll get to that in a moment." He took her by the hand.

"Where are we going?"

"You mean you don't know?" He grinned boyishly. "I'm taking you to the celery, er, the substitute mistletoe."

Soon she was in his arms, and all the doubts she'd entertained were obliterated the second he lowered his mouth to hers. She felt only the touch of his lips. Slow and confident. Intimate and familiar.

Christian had expected Mariah to move away from Hard Luck before December. He wasn't a betting man, but he would've wagered a year's income that his secretary would hightail it out of town right after the first snowfall. Not that he would've blamed her, living as she was in a one-room cabin. He cringed whenever he thought about her in those primitive conditions.

It wasn't the first time Mariah had shown him up. Christian was positive she stayed on out of pure spite. She wanted to prove herself, all right, but at the expense of his pride.

He walked into the office to find Mariah already at her desk, typing away at the computer. Her fingers moved so fast they were a blur.

At the sound of the door closing, she looked up—and froze.

"Morning," he said without emotion.

"Good morning," she said shyly. She glanced away, almost as if she expected a reprimand. "The coffee's ready."

"So I see." He wasn't looking forward to this, but someone had to reason with her, and Sawyer had refused to take on the task.

Christian poured himself a cup of coffee, then walked slowly to his desk. "Mariah."

She stared at him with large, frightened eyes. "Did I do something wrong again?"

"No, no," he said quickly, wanting to reassure her. "What makes you think that?" He gave her what he hoped resembled an encouraging smile.

She eyed him, apparently not convinced she could trust him.

"It seems the only time you talk to me is when I've done something wrong."

"Not this time." He sat down at his desk, which wasn't all that far from her own. "It's about you living in the cabin," he said.

He watched her bristle. "I believe we've already discussed this," she answered stiffly. "Several times."

"I don't want you there."

"Then you should never have offered the cabins as accommodation."

"I'd prefer it if you moved in with the other women—in Catherine Fletcher's house," he said, ignoring her comment. Actually, having Catherine's house available to them had been a godsend. Two women—Sally and Angie—had moved in, and the arrangement was working out well.

The pilots Midnight Sons employed lived in a dorm-size room. It was stark, without much more than a big stove for heating and several bunk beds and lockers, but the men never complained. The house was far more to the women's liking. As soon as they could, he and Sawyer were bringing in two mobile homes for the women, as well.

Until then Christian wasn't comfortable thinking about Mariah—or anyone else—living in a one-room cabin. Not with winter already here.

"I'm just fine where I am," Mariah insisted.

Sawyer thought she was all right there, too, but Christian knew otherwise. At night he lay awake, thinking of Mariah out there on the edge of town in a cabin smaller than a rich man's closet. It had no electric power and no plumbing, and was a far cry from what she'd been accustomed to.

"I'm asking," he said, being careful to phrase the words in a way she wouldn't find objectionable, "if you'd move in with Sally and Angie. Just until the spring thaw."

"Why?"

Arguing with her was an exercise in frustration. And the amount of time he wasted worrying about her! That in itself made no sense to him. The fact was, he didn't even *like* Mariah. The woman drove him crazy.

"I'm asking you to move in with them for a reason other than the cabin's primitive conditions." This, of course, wasn't true, but he had to figure out *some* way of getting her to move. He said the first thing that came to mind.

"I... I think one or two of the women are considering leaving Hard Luck," he lied. "We don't want to lose them."

"Who?"

Christian shrugged. "It's just rumors at this point. But I need someone who can encourage them to stick out the winter. Someone the others like and trust."

She looked at him as if she wasn't sure she should believe him.

"The others need someone they feel comfortable with. They like you, and I think you could help."

Mariah paused. "But I don't feel it's necessary for me to move in with them."

"I do," he answered automatically. "How often do you get a chance to talk with your friends? I can't imagine it's more than once a week." He was stabbing in the dark now.

Mariah nibbled on her lower lip and seemed to be considering his words. "That's true."

"A few of them aren't having an easy time adjusting to life in the Arctic. Will you do it, Mariah?" he pleaded. Heaven knew he'd tried every other means he could think of to get her to get out of that godforsaken cabin. "Will you move in with the other women?"

She hesitated. "I'll still get the deed to the land and the cabin at the end of the year, won't I?"

"You can have both now." It wasn't the first time he'd made that offer. The sooner she accomplished her goals, the sooner she'd leave Hard Luck.

"Giving me the title now wouldn't be right. The terms of my contract state that at the end of one year I'll be entitled to the cabin and the land. I wouldn't dream of accepting the deed a moment sooner."

"Then I'll assure you in writing that the time you spend living with the other women will in no way jeopardize our agreement. You can type up the papers yourself."

He watched her and waited. Waited while the interminable minutes passed. He couldn't believe that one small decision would require such concentration.

"Will you or won't you?" he demanded when he couldn't stand the silence anymore.

"I will," she said, "but on one condition. I want to talk to the others first and make sure I won't be intruding."

Christian groaned, resisting the urge to bury his face in his hands. "Midnight Sons is paying the rent!"

"I'm well aware of that," Mariah said coolly.

"If I wanted to move the entire French Foreign Legion into that house, then I'd do it."

"No, you wouldn't," Mariah said with a know-it-all grin. "First, Sawyer wouldn't let you and—"

"It was a figure of speech." Christian now fought the urge to pull out his hair. No one on earth could anger him as quickly as Mariah Douglas. The year she was contracted to work for him couldn't end fast enough. Not until she left Hard Luck would he be able to sleep through the night again.

A wreath hung inside the door of the Hard Luck Café. Flashing miniature lights were strung around the windows. Christmas cards were pinned to one wall in a straggling triangle. Bethany guessed the shape was supposed to represent a Christmas tree.

The thank-you notes the children had written following his visit to the classroom were taped against another wall for everyone who came into the café to see. The worn look of those notes told her Ben had read them countless times himself.

"It's beginning to look downright festive around here," Bethany said as she stepped up to the counter.

"Christmas is my favorite holiday," Ben declared. "How about a piece of mincemeat pie to go with your coffee? It's on the house."

"Actually I don't have time for either," Bethany said regretfully. She was on her way to church for choir practice and only had a few minutes. "I came to invite you to my house for Christmas dinner."

Ben's mouth opened and a look of utter astonishment crossed his face. "I thought... Me? What about Mitch and Chrissie? Aren't they spending the day with you?"

"I invited them, too. I'm sure I'm not half as good in the kitchen as you are, but I should be able to manage turkey and all the trimmings. Besides, you might enjoy tasting someone else's cooking for a change."

He frowned as though this was a weighty decision. "I like my turkey with sage dressing and giblet gravy."

"You got it. My mom always stuffs the bird with sage dressing, and my dad makes giblet gravy. I wouldn't know how to do it any other way." When he seemed about to refuse, she added, "If you want to contribute something, you can bring one of those mincemeat pies you're trying to fatten me up with."

Ben turned away from her and reached for the rag. He began to wipe the already clean countertop. "I... I don't know what to say." His eyes continued to avoid hers.

"Just say yes. Dinner's at three."

He gestured weakly. "I always keep the place open."

"Close it this year." She almost suggested he should spend the holiday with family, but managed to stop herself. Still, she felt close to Ben; she *did* feel he was family. Perhaps this was emotionally dangerous, but being with him on Christmas Day might help ease the ache of missing her parents.

"Folks generally spend Christmas Day with family," he said. It was as if he'd been able to read her thoughts. "I don't have any left," he told her in a low voice. "At least, none who'd want me dropping in unannounced at Christmas."

"I'll be your family, Ben," she offered, waiting for her heart to stop its crazy beating. He had no way of knowing how much truth there was in her words. "And you can be mine. For this one day, anyhow."

"Won't I be in the way? I mean, with you and—"

Bethany reached for his hand. "I wouldn't have invited you if that was the case."

"What about you and Mitch? You two are spending a lot of time together lately—which is good," he hastened to say. "I don't think I've ever seen Mitch look happier, and what I hear is that there's a night-and-day difference with Chrissie. She used to be a shy little thing."

Bethany had the feeling he would've rambled on for an hour if she hadn't stopped him.

"Ben!" She laughed outright. "I'm asking you to Christmas dinner. Will you come or not? I need to know how much food to prepare."

She watched his throat work convulsively. "No one ever asked me to Christmas dinner," he said in a strangled voice.

"Well, someone is now."

He met her look and his eyes grew suspiciously bright. "What time do you want me there again?"

"Dinner's at three. You come as early as you like, though."

"All right," he said with some difficulty. "I'll be there, and I'll bring one of my pies."

"Good. I'll see you Christmas Day." Having settled that, Bethany left the café.

"Bethany," Ben called, "if you need any help making that gravy, you let me know."

"I will. Thanks for offering."

Not until she was outside, with the cold clawing at her face, did she realize there were tears in her eyes. She quickly brushed them away and hurried to the church.

Christmas was supposed to be a joyous time of year. It would be, Matt Caldwell thought, if Karen was with him. He glanced around the Anchorage church. The harder he tried not to think about his ex-wife, the more difficult it became to concentrate on the hymnbook in his hands.

Perhaps it was because the last time he'd been in this church was after his grandmother's death. The sadness that had taken hold of his heart then hadn't faded in the weeks since.

Matt hadn't made church a habit of late. The fact was, he and God weren't on the best of terms. He was quite comfortable ignoring the presence of an almighty being, since evidence of God had been sorely lacking in his life these past few years.

It didn't help that he was once again the only family member who was alone. His parents stood on one side of him, and Lanni and Charles on the other. Those two were so much in love it was painful just being around them.

Although Lanni enjoyed her work with the *Anchorage News,* she hated the long separations from Charles. April couldn't come soon enough as far as she was concerned.

The Christmas Eve church services continued, and the members of the congregation lifted their voices in song. Matt wasn't in any frame of mind to join in. He'd worked hard during the past few months. Damned hard. Other than his obvious purpose of getting the lodge ready, he'd driven himself in a single-minded effort, but whether it was to impress Karen or get her out of his system, he no longer knew.

He couldn't help wondering how his ex-wife was spending

Christmas. He was pretty confident she wouldn't have a white Christmas in California.

Was she alone, the way he was? Did she feel empty inside? Was she thinking of him?

Somehow he doubted it, considering how impulsively she'd left Alaska. It still bothered him that she hadn't so much as told him she was moving. Instead, she'd contacted his sister, knowing Lanni would tell him.

Once the interminable singing ended, there was the predictable Christmas pageant. Despite his misery, Matt found himself smiling as the Sunday school children gave the performance they'd no doubt been rehearsing for months.

This year, instead of a doll, they had a newborn infant playing the role of the baby Jesus. This child was anything but meek and mild. In fact, he let out a scream that echoed through the church and started all the children giggling.

Well, that was what they got for using a real baby.

A baby.

He froze on the thought. Babies. Children. He glanced around the congregation and noticed a number of families with small children.

Karen had wanted children. They'd had more than one heated discussion on that subject. Matt had been against it; he didn't feel ready for fatherhood. Not when his future and career remained unsettled. In retrospect, he could see he'd been right. Dragging a child through a divorce would've been criminal.

Now the likelihood of his having a family was remote at best. He discovered, somewhat to his surprise, that the realization brought with it a new pain. Great. Just what he needed. Another resentment to harbor. Another casualty of his dead marriage. Something else to flail himself with.

He was relieved when the church service ended. At least he hadn't been subjected to a lengthy sermon on top of the singing and the pageant.

Once they were home, his family gathered around the Christmas tree. Traditionally they opened their gifts on Christmas Eve. It had taken some doing for him to dredge up enough energy to spring for gifts, but he'd managed it.

"How about hot apple cider?" Lanni asked.

"Sure," he said, faking a smile. It didn't seem fair to burden everyone else with his misery.

His sister brought him a cup, then sat down next to him. Their mother was busy in the kitchen and his father was talking to Charles.

"I hoped we'd have a minute alone before opening the gifts," Lanni whispered. She searched through the mound of gaily wrapped presents; beneath one of them she found what she was looking for. An envelope. She handed it to him.

Matt looked at his name on the envelope and instantly recognized the handwriting as Karen's. His heart skipped a beat, and he raised his eyes to his sister's, not sure what to think.

"How'd you get this?"

"Karen mailed a gift to me and to Mom and Dad. It was in the same package."

"I...see." His hand closed tightly over the envelope.

"There's something else," Lanni said, her gaze avoiding his.

"Yes?" He was eager to escape to his room and read what Karen had written.

"Our wedding..."

"What about it?"

"Would you mind very much if Karen served as my maid of honor?"

Matt stared at his sister, not understanding. "You want her in your wedding party?"

"Yes," she said, then quickly added, "But only if you don't object. I wouldn't want it to be uncomfortable for you, Matt. You're my brother, after all, and she was your wife—but she's still my friend."

"Why should I care?" he mumbled. "It's your wedding." With that, he left the room.

Once he was inside his old bedroom, Matt threw himself on the bed and tore open the envelope. A single sheet of paper fell from the card. Heart pounding, he unfolded it and read:

Merry Christmas, Matt.

It didn't seem right to mail gifts to Lanni and your parents and send you nothing. But at the same time, it's a bit awkward to buy my ex-husband a Christmas gift.

   I hope this card finds you well.

Sincerely,

Karen

Sincerely. She'd actually signed the note *sincerely.* As if it was some kind of business letter or he was merely a casual acquaintance. He picked up the Christmas card he'd discarded earlier and found she'd written nothing but her name.

Still, sending a Christmas card was more than he'd done for her. He supposed he'd have to add that to his long list of failures and regrets.

8

Mitch woke early Christmas morning.

Not wanting to wake Chrissie, he moved silently into the living room, where the miniature lights on the tree glittered like frosted stars. He smiled at their decorations—paper chains, strung popcorn and handmade ornaments.

He rearranged the gifts under the tree. He'd placed them there the night before, after Chrissie had gone to bed. He knew she didn't believe in Santa Claus anymore, but it was fun for both of them to keep up the pretense.

The largest present wasn't from him but Bethany. A Barbie thingamajig. Town house or some such nonsense. Only it wasn't nonsense to Chrissie; the kid took her Barbie seriously. She'd be thrilled with this. He knew Chrissie would be happily absorbed with her gifts all morning, and then later, in the afternoon, they were going to Bethany's place for a turkey dinner with all the fixings.

Bethany.

He needed these quiet early-morning moments to clear his thoughts and make sense of his feelings.

It had happened.

Despite his resistance, his best efforts to prevent it, despite his vows to the contrary, despite the full force of his determination, he'd gone and fallen in love with Bethany Ross.

He didn't *want* to love Bethany, and in the same breath, he found himself humbled that this remarkable woman had entered his life. Especially after Lori. Especially now.

Mitch paced the living room, too restless to sit. Admitting that he cared deeply for Bethany required some sort of decision. A man didn't come to this kind of realization without defining a course of action.

He knew he had nothing to offer her. While it was true that he made enough money to support a family, his financial status wasn't impressive. Somehow he doubted this would matter to Bethany, but still...

He was dismally aware, too, that he came to her with deep emotional scars and a needy child in tow. The mere thought of loving again, of trusting again, terrified him. It made him break out in a cold sweat. On top of everything else was the paralyzing fear that he'd fail Bethany the way he had Lori.

Then again, he reminded himself, he had options. He could do what he'd done since September—deny his feelings. Ignore what his heart was telling him.

He might've continued that way for months, possibly years, if it wasn't for one thing.

Chrissie.

From the moment his daughter had met Bethany, she'd set her sights on turning the teacher into her mother and his wife. Watching the two of them together had touched him from the very first. In ways he'd never fully understand, Bethany ministered to his daughter's need for a mother in the same way she satisfied his own long-repressed desire for a companion. *A wife...*

As the weeks progressed, Chrissie had started looking to Bethany for guidance more and more often. There wasn't *any-*

thing Chrissie wouldn't do to be with her—including feign flu symptoms.

What confounded him was the fact that Bethany seemed to share his feelings. He felt her love as powerfully as those brief moments of sunlight every day, brightening the world in the darkness of an Arctic winter.

Admitting his love for Bethany—to her and to himself— wasn't a simple thing. Love rarely was, he suspected. If he told her how he felt about her, he'd also have to tell her about his past.

Love implied trust. And he'd need to trust her with the painful details of his marriage. With that came the tremendous risk of her rejection. He wouldn't blame her if she *did* turn away. If the situation were reversed, he didn't know how he'd react. He was laying an enormous burden on her.

Telling her all this wasn't something he could do on the spur of the moment. Timing was critical. He'd have to wait for the right day, the right mood.

Not this morning, he decided. Not on Christmas. He refused to spoil the day's celebration with the ugliness of his past. No need to darken the holiday with a litany of his failures as a husband.

"Daddy?" Chrissie stood just inside the living room doorway yawning. She wore her pretty new flannel pajamas—the one gift he'd allowed her to open Christmas Eve.

"Merry Christmas, pumpkin," he said, opening his arms to her. "It looks like Santa made it to Hard Luck, after all."

Chrissie leapt into his embrace and he folded his arms around her, slowly closing his eyes. His daughter was the most precious gift he'd ever been given. And now, finding Bethany... His heart was full.

"I can't believe I ate the whole thing," Ben teased, placing his hands on the bulge of his stomach and sighing heavily. He eased his chair away from the kitchen table. "If anyone else finds out what a good cook you are, Bethany, I'll be out of business before I know it."

Bethany smiled, delighted with his praise. "I don't think you need to worry. Those pies of yours were fabulous, especially the mincemeat. I'd like to get your recipe."

Ben grinned. "Sure. No problem. It's one I came up with myself—I like to try new things when I cook. How about you? Have you always been this good in the kitchen?"

It was another trait she shared with her birth father, but once again this wasn't something she could mention.

She nodded. "While other little girls were playing with dolls and makeup, I was using my Betty Crocker Baking Center to concoct all kinds of cookies and cakes."

"Well, all that practice sure paid off," Mitch said.

Bethany blushed a little at the compliments. She'd done her best to put on a spread worthy of their praise. The meal had taken weeks of careful planning; she'd had to special-order some of the ingredients, and her mother had mailed her the spices. A lot of the dishes she'd made were traditional family recipes. Mashed sweet potatoes with dried apricots and lots of butter. Sage dressing, of course, and another rice-and-raisin dressing that had been a favorite of hers, one her grandmother made every year.

"You miss your family, don't you?" Mitch asked as he helped her clear the table.

"Everyone does at Christmas, don't you think?" This first year so far away from her parents and two younger brothers had been more difficult than she'd expected; this morning had been particularly wrenching. She knew they missed her, too. Bethany had spoken to her family in California at least once a day for the past week. She didn't care how high her phone bill ran.

"I must've chatted to Mom three times this morning alone,"

she told Mitch. "It's funny. For years I've helped her with Thanksgiving and Christmas dinners, but when it came to doing it on my own, I had a dozen questions."

"You need me to do anything?" Ben asked, getting up from the table. He carried his plate to the sink. "I've done plenty of dishes in my time. I wouldn't mind lending a hand, especially after a meal like that. Seems to me that those who cook shouldn't have to wash dishes."

"Normally I'd agree with you, but not today. You're my guest."

"But..."

"I should think you'd know better than to argue with a woman," Mitch chided.

Laughing, Bethany shooed Ben out of the kitchen.

"We were going to continue our game of Monopoly, remember?" Chrissie reminded him eagerly. "You said you wanted a chance to win some of your money back."

"Go play," Bethany said with a laugh. "I'll rope Mitch here into helping."

"You're sure?" Ben asked.

"Very sure," she told him, glancing over at Mitch with a smile.

Mitch mumbled something she couldn't hear. She looked at him curiously as she reached for a bowl. "What did you say?"

His eyes held hers. "I said a man could get lost in one of your smiles and never find his way home."

Bethany paused, the bowl of leftover mashed potatoes in her hands. "Why, Mitch, what a romantic thing to say."

His face tightened, as though her comment had embarrassed him. "It must be the season," he said gruffly. He turned away from her and started to fill the sink with hot, sudsy water.

Bethany smiled to herself. It was rare to see Mitch Harris flustered. She fingered the polished five-dollar gold coin he'd had made into a pendant and placed on a fine gold chain. The coin had been minted the year of her birth, and he'd had it mounted in a gold bezel. The necklace was beautiful in its simplicity. The minute she fastened it around her neck, Bethany knew this was a piece of jewelry she'd wear every day for the rest of her life.

She felt that her gift for Mitch paled in comparison. Mitch was an avid Tom Clancy fan, and through a friend who managed a bookstore in San Francisco, she'd been able to get him an autographed copy of Clancy's latest hardcover.

When Mitch had opened the package and read the inscription, he'd looked up at her as though she'd handed him the stone tablets direct from Mount Sinai.

Chrissie had been excited about her Barbie town house, too.

The one who'd surprised her most, however, was Ben. He'd arrived for dinner with not one pie but four—all of them baked fresh that morning. In addition to the pies, he'd brusquely handed her an oblong box. Bethany got a kick out of the way he'd wrapped it. He'd used three times the amount of paper necessary and enough tape to supply the U.S. Army for a year.

Inside the box was a piece of scrimshaw made from a walrus tusk. The scene on the polished piece of ivory was of wild geese in flight over a marsh. Mountains rose in the distance against a sunlit sky.

Ben had dismissed his gift as nothing more than a trinket, but Bethany knew from her brief stay in Fairbanks how expensive such pieces of artwork had become. She tried to thank him, but it was clear her words only embarrassed him.

"I would've thought you'd want to fly home for Christmas," Mitch said, rolling up his sleeves before dipping his hands in the dishwater.

"I seriously considered it." Bethany wasn't going to minimize the difficulty of her decision to remain in Hard Luck. "But it's a long way to travel for so short a time. I'll probably stay in Alaska during spring break, as well. After all, my commitment here is only for the school year."

"You're going home to California in June, then?"

"Are you asking me if I plan to return to Hard Luck for another school year?"

"Yes," he said, his back to her.

Something in the carefully nonchalant way he'd asked told her that the answer was important to him.

"I don't know," she said as straightforwardly as she could. "It depends on whether I'm offered a contract."

"And if you are?"

"I...don't know yet." She loved Alaska and her students. Most of all, she loved Mitch and Chrissie. Ben, too. But there were other factors. Several of them had to do with Ben—should she tell him he was her biological father, and what would his reaction be if she did? More and more, she felt inclined to confront him with the truth.

"Well, I hope you come back" was all the response Mitch gave her. The deliberate lack of emotion in his voice was clearly meant to suggest that they'd been talking about something of little importance.

Why, for heaven's sake, couldn't the man just say what he wanted to say?

Hands on her hips, Bethany glared at him. Mitch happened to turn around for another stack of dirty dishes; he saw her and did a double take. "What?" he demanded.

"All you can say is 'Well, I hope you come back,'" she mimicked. "I'm spilling my heart out here and *that's* all the reaction I get from you?"

He gave her a blank look.

"The answer is I'm willing to consider another year's contract, and you can bet it isn't because of the tropical climate in Hard Luck."

Mitch grinned exuberantly. "The benefits are good."

"But not great."

"The money's fabulous."

"Oh, please," she muttered, rolling her eyes. She took an exaggerated breath. "My, my, I wonder what the appeal could be."

Mitch looked at her in sudden and complete seriousness. "I was hoping you'd say it was me."

She regarded him with an equally somber look. "I do enjoy the way you kiss, Mitch Harris."

The first sign of amusement touched his lips. He lifted his soapy arms from the water and stretched them toward her. "Maybe what you need to convince you is a small demonstration of my enjoyable kisses."

A second later Bethany was in his arms. The water seeped through her blouse, but she couldn't have cared less. What *did* matter was sharing this important day with the people she loved. And those who loved her.

John Henderson wanted to do the right thing by Sally. He loved her—more than he'd thought possible. Proof of that was his willingness to delay asking her to marry him. He was determined to wait until he'd talked to her father.

He'd been carrying the engagement ring with him for weeks now. Every once in a while he'd draw it out and rub the gold band between his index finger and thumb. He figured that his patience—difficult though he found it to be patient—was a measure of his love for Sally. Still, he cursed himself a dozen times a day for listening to Duke.

John told himself that the other pilot didn't know any more about love than he did. But it wasn't true; Duke had given him good, sensible advice. John desperately wanted everything to be right between Sally and him, especially after her recent heartbreak.

It would've been selfish to rush her into an engagement and then a wedding without first knowing that she shared his feelings—and was sure of her own. He had to be certain she wasn't marrying him on the rebound. Duke was right about her family, too. Her parents were traditional, old-fashioned, even, and it was important to meet them, give them a chance to know him. Important—but the waiting had become harder with every week that passed.

Now he was ready to make his move. And ask his questions...

Naturally, John would rather have delayed this initial awkwardness. No man likes to be scrutinized by strangers, especially when he's about to ask these very people for permission to marry the most precious, beautiful woman God ever made. Their daughter.

If he were Sally's father, John thought, he wouldn't blame the man for booting him out of the house. He hoped, however, that it wouldn't come to that.

He'd bought a new suit for the occasion. It wasn't a waste of money, he'd decided, seeing he'd probably need it for the wedding and all. *If* Sally agreed to marry him, and he hoped and prayed she would.

Sally's true feelings for him seemed to be the only real question. They'd been seeing each other on a regular basis, but John had noticed certain things about her that left him wondering. Her eyes didn't light up when she saw him, the way they had in the beginning. If he didn't know better, he'd think she was avoiding him lately.

Mariah Douglas had recently moved into the house with her, and Sally seemed almost relieved to have an excuse not to invite him over so often. Of course, he'd been busy at Midnight Sons, with the holiday rush and all.

Other signs baffled him, as well. These puzzling changes in

Sally's behavior had started after he'd spent the night with her. It wasn't like they'd *planned* to make love; it had just happened. John regretted not waiting to initiate their lovemaking until after the wedding. He'd known for a long time how he felt about Sally. Immediately following their one night together, he'd gone out and bought the engagement ring, but then Duke had talked him out of proposing until he could meet her family.

It might not be such a good idea to show up unannounced on Christmas Day, but John didn't have a lot of spare time. Midnight Sons was shorthanded in the wintertime as it was. The holidays had offered him the opportunity to make the trip. That was why he was here in British Columbia, in a small town with an Indian name he couldn't pronounce, dropping in on Sally's family uninvited and clutching a somewhat travel-worn bouquet of roses.

John checked the address on the back of the Christmas card envelope and walked up to the white house with the dark green shutters and the large fir wreath on the door. He pressed the doorbell, swallowed nervously and waited.

His relief was great when Sally answered the door herself. Her eyes grew huge with surprise and, he hoped, with happiness when she saw who it was.

"John? What are you doing here?"

He thrust the flowers into her hand, grateful to be rid of them. "I've come to talk to your father," he told her.

"My dad?" she asked, clearly puzzled. "Why?"

"That's between him and me." He found it difficult not to stare at her, seeing she was as pretty as a model for one of those fashion magazines. They'd made love only that once, and although he cursed himself for his lack of self-control, he couldn't regret loving Sally. He looked forward to making love to her again. Only this time it would be when his ring was around her finger and they'd said their *I do*'s.

"John?" She closed the door and stepped onto the small porch steps, hugging herself with both arms. Her eyes questioned his. "What's this all about?"

"I need to talk to your father," he repeated.

"You already said that. Is it because I've decided not to return to Hard Luck? Who told you? Not Mariah, she wouldn't do that, I know she wouldn't."

John felt as if someone had punched him. For one shocking moment, he thought he might be sick. "You...you didn't plan on coming back after Christmas?"

"No." She lowered her gaze, avoiding his.

"But I thought... I hoped—" He snapped his mouth shut before he acted like an even bigger fool. He was about to humble himself before her father and request Sally's hand in marriage. Yet she'd walked out of his life without so much as a word of farewell.

"You mean you didn't know?"

He shook his head. "You weren't planning on telling me?"

"No." She tucked her chin against her chest. "I... I couldn't see the point. You got what you wanted, didn't you?"

"What the hell is that supposed to mean?" he shouted. Standing outside her family home yelling probably wasn't the best way to introduce himself to her father, but John couldn't help it. He was angry, and with good reason.

"You know exactly what I mean," she replied in a furious whisper.

"Are you referring to the night we made love?"

Mortified, Sally closed her eyes. "Do you have to shout it to the entire neighborhood?"

"Yes!"

Sally glared at him. "I think we've said everything there is to say."

"Not by a long shot, we haven't," John countered. "Okay, so

we made love. Big deal. I'm not perfect, and neither are you. It happened, but we haven't gone to bed since then, have we?"

"John, please, not so loud." Sally glanced uneasily over her shoulder.

His next words surprised him, springing out despite himself. "I wasn't the first, so I don't understand why you're making such a big deal of it. Too late now, anyway." He would never have said this if he hadn't felt so angry, so betrayed.

Tears leapt instantly into her eyes and John would've given his right arm to take back the hurtful words. He'd rather suffer untold agonies than say anything to distress Sally, yet he'd done exactly that.

The door behind her opened and a burly lumberjack of a man walked out onto the porch. "What's going on here?"

Sally gestured weakly toward John. "Daddy, this is John Henderson. He—he's a friend from Hard Luck."

Finding his daughter sniffling back tears wasn't much of an endorsement, John thought gloomily. He squared his shoulders and offered the other man his hand. "I'm pleased to meet you, Mr. McDonald."

"The name's Jack. I don't understand why my daughter hasn't seen fit to invite you into the house, young man." He cast an accusatory frown in Sally's direction. "Seems you've come a long way to visit her."

"It doesn't look like I was as welcome as I thought I'd be," John muttered.

"Nonsense. It's Christmas Day. Since you've traveled all this distance, the least we can do is ask you to join us and give you a warm drink."

John didn't need anything to warm him. Spending time with the McDonald family would only add to his frustration and misery, but Jack McDonald gave him no option. Sally's father quickly ushered him inside.

Swallowing his pride, John followed the brawny man up a short flight of stairs and into the living room. The festivities ceased when he appeared. Sally's father introduced him around, and her mother poured him a cup of wassail that tasted like hot apple cider.

"I don't believe Sally's mentioned you in her letters home," Mrs. McDonald said conversationally as a chair was brought out for John.

He felt his heart grow cold and heavy with pain. Forcing himself to observe basic good manners, he thanked Sally's brother for the chair. All those months while he was pining over Sally, he hadn't rated a single line in one of her letters home. Although he'd told her their making love had been no big deal, it *had* been. For him. He loved her. But apparently their relationship wasn't important enough for Sally to even mention his name.

"I told you about John," Sally said.

John wondered if that was true, or if she was attempting to cover her tracks.

"John's the bush pilot I wrote you about." Sally sat across the room from him and tucked her hands awkwardly between her knees as if she wasn't sure what to do with them.

"Oh yes, now I remember. Don't think you said his name, though." Her father nodded slowly. And her mother sent him a bright smile.

John drank the cider as fast as he could. It burned going down, but he didn't care. He drained the cup, stood and abruptly handed it to Sally's mother.

"Thank you for the drink and the hospitality, but I should be on my way."

Jack bent down to the carpet and retrieved something. "I believe you dropped this, son," he said.

To John's mortification, Sally's father held out the engagement ring.

He checked his pocket, praying all the while that there were two such rings in this world, and that the second just happened to be in Sally's home. On the floor. Naturally, the diamond Jack held was the one he'd bought for Sally. Without a word, he slipped it back inside his suit pocket.

"It was a pleasure meeting everyone," he said, anxiously eyeing the front door. He'd never been so eager to leave a place. Leave and find somewhere to be by himself.

Well, he told himself bitterly, he'd learned his lesson when it came to women. He was better off living his life alone. To think he'd been one of the men eager to have the O'Hallorans bring women north!

One thing was certain; he didn't need this kind of rejection, this kind of pain.

"John?" Sally gazed at him with those beautiful blue eyes of hers. Only this time he wasn't about to be taken in by her sweetness.

He ignored her and hurried down the stairs to the front door. He'd already grasped the door handle when he realized that Sally had followed him. "You can leave without explaining that ring, but I swear if you do I'll never speak to you again."

"I don't see that it'd matter," he told her, boldly meeting her eyes. "You weren't planning on speaking to me anyway."

He gave her ample time to answer, and when she didn't, he made a show of turning the knob.

"Don't go," Sally cried in a choked whisper. "I thought… that you'd gotten what you wanted and so you—"

"I know what you thought," he snapped.

"Maybe we could talk about this?" It sounded like she was struggling not to break into tears. He dug inside his back pocket, pulled out a fresh handkerchief and handed it to her.

"Could we talk, John?" she asked and walked down the second flight of stairs to the lower portion of the house. "Please?"

John guessed he was supposed to accompany her. He looked up to find her mother, father, brother and a few cousins whose names he'd forgotten leaning over the railing staring at him.

"You'd better go with her," Sally's younger brother advised. "It's best to do what she wants when she's in one of these moods."

"Do you love her, son?" Jack McDonald demanded.

John looked at Sally, thinking a response now would be premature, but he couldn't very well deny it, carrying an engagement ring in his pocket. "Yes, sir. I meant to ask Sally to marry me, but I wanted everything to be right with us. So I thought I'd introduce myself and ask your permission first."

"It's a good man who speaks to the father first," Sally's mother said, nodding tearfully.

"Marry her with my blessing, son."

John relaxed and grinned. "Thank you, sir." Then he figured he should give himself some room in case things didn't go the way he hoped. "In light of what's happened, I'm not sure Sally will say yes. She wasn't planning on returning to Hard Luck— I'm not sure why, but she hadn't said a word about it to me."

"I believe my daughter's about to clear away any doubts you have, young man. She'll give you plenty of reasons not to change your mind."

"Daddy!" This drifted up from the bottom of the stairwell.

John winked at his future in-laws. "That's what I was hoping she'd do," he said and hurried down the stairs, his steps jubilant. "Oh, and Merry Christmas, everyone!"

9

It shouldn't upset her. If anything, Bethany thought, she should be pleased that Randy Kincade was getting married. The invitation for the March wedding arrived the second week of January, when winter howled outside her window and the promise of spring was buried beneath the frozen ground.

Bethany wasn't generally prone to bouts of the blues. But the darkness and the constant cold nibbled away at her optimism. Cabin fever—she'd never experienced it before, but she recognized the symptoms.

Her hair needed a trim, and she longed to see a movie in a real theater that sold hot, buttered popcorn. It was the middle of January, and she'd have killed for a thick-crust pizza smothered in melted cheese and spicy Italian sausage.

The craving for a pizza brought on a deluge of other sudden, unanticipated wants. She yearned for the opportunity to shop in a mall, in stores with fitting rooms, and to stroll past kiosks that sold delights like dangling earrings and glittery

T-shirts. Not that she'd buy a lot of those things. She just wanted to *see* them.

To make everything even worse, her relationship with Mitch had apparently come to a standstill. As each week passed, it became more and more obvious that her feelings for him were far stronger than his were for her.

Whimsically she wondered if this was because God wanted her to know how Randy must've felt all those years ago when she didn't return the fervor of his love.

So now she knew, and it *hurt.*

Not that Mitch had said anything. Not directly at least. It was his manner, his new reserve, the way he kissed her—as if even then he felt the need to protect himself.

That reserve of his frustrated Bethany. It angered her, but mostly it hurt. In some ways, she felt their relationship had become more honest and open, yet in others—the important ones—he still seemed to be holding back. He seemed to fear that loving her would mean surrendering a piece of his soul, and she'd begun to wonder if he'd always keep his past hidden from her.

On another front, she increasingly felt the urge to let Ben know she was his biological daughter. Perhaps this was because she missed her family so much. Or maybe it was because she'd come to terms with Ben's place in her life. Then again, maybe it was because she felt frustrated in her relationship with Mitch. She didn't know.

This wasn't to say the soulful kisses they shared weren't wonderful. They were. Yet they often left her hungering, not for a deeper physical relationship, but for a more profound emotional one. She longed for Mitch to trust her with his past, and clearly he wasn't willing to do that.

Their times alone, she noted, seemed to dwindle instead of increase. It almost seemed as though Mitch encouraged Chrissie's presence to avoid being alone with Bethany. It almost seemed as though dating Bethany satisfied his daughter's needs, but not his own.

On this January Saturday evening, when Bethany joined Mitch and Chrissie for their weekly video night, she couldn't disguise her melancholy. She tried, she honestly tried, to be upbeat, but it had been a long, drawn-out week. And now Randy was engaged, while her own love life had stalled.

Mitch must have noticed she hadn't touched the popcorn he'd supplied. "Is something wrong?" he asked, shifting beside her on the couch.

"No," she whispered, fighting to hold back the emotion that bubbled up inside her, seeking escape. Tears burned for release. She was about to weep and could think of no explanation that would appease him. No explanation, in fact, that would even make sense.

Mitch and Chrissie glanced at each other, then at her. Mitch stopped the movie. "You look like you're going to cry. I understand this movie's a tearjerker, but I didn't expect you to start crying during the previews."

She smiled shakily at his joke. "I'm sorry," she said. Her throat closed up, and when she tried to speak again, her voice came out in a high-pitched squeak. "I—"

"Bethany, what's wrong?"

She got to her feet, then didn't know why she had. She certainly didn't have anything to say.

"I—I need a haircut," she croaked.

Mitch looked at Chrissie, as if his daughter should be able to translate that. Chrissie regarded Bethany seriously, then shrugged.

"And a pizza—not the frozen kind, but one that's delivered, and the delivery boy should stand around until he gets a tip and act insulted by how little it is." She attempted a laugh that failed miserably.

"Pizza? Insulted?" Her explanation, such as it was, seemed to confuse Mitch even more.

"I'm sorry," she said again, gesturing forlornly with her hands. "I really am." She tucked her fingers against her palms and studied her hands. "Look at my nails. Just look. They used to be long and pretty—now they're broken and chipped."

"Bethany—"

"I'm not finished," she said, brushing the tears from her face. Now that they'd started, she couldn't seem to stop them. "I feel claustrophobic. I need more than a couple of hours' light a day. I'm sick and tired of watching the sun set two hours after dawn. I need more *light* than this." Even though she knew she wasn't being logical, Bethany couldn't stop the words any more than she could the tears. "I want to buy a new bra without ordering it out of a catalog."

"What you're feeling is cabin fever," Mitch explained calmly.

"I *know* that, but..."

"We all experience it in one way or another. It's not uncommon in winter. Even those of us who've lived here for years go through this," he said. "What you need is a weekend jaunt to Fairbanks. Two days away will make you feel like a new woman."

Men always seemed to have a simple solution to everything. For no reason she could explain—after all, she *wanted* to visit a big city—Mitch's answer only irritated her.

"Is a weekend trip going to change the fact that Randy's getting married?" she muttered. Her hands were clenched and her arms hung stiffly at her sides.

It took Mitch a moment or so to ask, "Who's Randy?"

"Bethany was engaged to him a long time ago," Chrissie said in a whisper.

"Do you love him?" Mitch asked in a gentle tone.

His tenderness, his complete lack of jealousy, infuriated her beyond reason. "No," she cried, "I love *you,* you idiot! Not that you care or notice or anything." Bethany went to retrieve her coat and hat.

"Bethany—"

"You don't understand *any* of what I'm feeling, do you? Please, just leave me alone."

To add insult to injury, Mitch stepped back and did precisely as she asked.

By the time Bethany had walked home—having refused Mitch's offer of a ride—she was sobbing openly. Tears had frozen to her face. The worst part was that she *knew* how ridiculous she was being. Unfortunately, it didn't seem to matter.

She was weeping uncontrollably—because she couldn't have a pizza delivered. Mitch seemed to think all she needed was a weekend in Fairbanks. Except that he didn't suggest the two of them fly in together.

"Fairbanks," she said under her breath. "How's *that* going to help?"

Restless and discontented, Bethany found she couldn't bear to sit around the house and do nothing. She was lonely and heartbroken. This type of misery preyed on itself; what she needed was some kind of distraction. And some sympathy...

On impulse, she phoned Mariah Douglas, who was living in Catherine Fletcher's house now. She hoped she could talk Mariah into inviting her over. Mariah sounded pleased to hear from her and even said she had a bottle of wine in the fridge.

Before long, the two of them sat in the living room, clutching large glasses of zinfandel and bemoaning their sorry fate. It seemed that Mariah shared Bethany's melancholy mood. Not long afterward, Sally McDonald and Angie Hughes, Mariah's housemates, showed up and willingly raided their own stashes of wine and potato chips.

Bethany acknowledged that it felt good to talk with female friends, to divulge her woes to others who appreciated their seriousness. Soon it wasn't the lack of a decent pizza they were complaining about, but a bigger problem: the men in their lives.

"He wants me gone, you know," Mariah said, staring into her wineglass with a woebegone look. "He takes every opportunity to urge me to leave Hard Luck. I don't think August will come soon enough for him. I've...tried to be a good secretary, but he always flusters me."

Bethany knew Mariah was referring to Christian O'Halloran and wondered what prompted the secretary to stay when her employer had made his views so plain.

Then Bethany understood. Mariah was staying for the same reasons she was.

Bethany swirled the wine in her goblet. Her head swam, and she realized she was already half-drunk. A single glass of wine and she was tipsy. That said a lot about her social life.

"Let's go to Fairbanks!" she said excitedly. Although she'd rejected Mitch's suggestion out of hand, it held some appeal now. Escape by any means available was tempting, especially after a sufficient amount of wine.

"You want to leave for Fairbanks now?" Mariah asked incredulously.

"Why not?" Sally McDonald asked. Of them all, Sally was the one with the least to complain about—at least when it came to men. She and John Henderson had become engaged over the Christmas holidays.

"I don't fly. Do you?" Mariah asked. They looked at each other, then broke into giggles.

"I don't fly, either," Bethany admitted. "But we aren't going to let a little thing like the lack of a pilot stop us, are we? Not when we live in a town chock-full of them."

"You're absolutely right." Mariah's eyes lit up and she wagged her index finger. "Duke'll do it. He's scheduled for the mail run first thing in the morning and we'll tag along. Now, which of you girls is coming? No, *are* coming. No..."

There weren't any other volunteers. "Then it's just Beth and me. No, Beth and *I*..."

It was at this point that Bethany realized her friend was as tipsy as she was. "How will we get back?"

"I don't know," Mariah said, enunciating very carefully. "But where there's a way there's a will."

Bethany shut her eyes. That didn't sound exactly right, but it was close enough to satisfy her. Especially when she was half-drunk and her heart dangled precariously from her sleeve.

"He doesn't love me, you know," she said, making her own confession.

"Mitch?"

It was time to own up to the truth, however painful.

"He cares for you, though." This came from Sally.

Bethany fingered the gold coin that hung from the delicate chain around her neck. The gift Mitch had given her for Christmas. Touching it now, she experienced a deep sense of loss.

"Mitch does care," she agreed in a broken voice, "but not enough."

Mariah looked at her with sympathy and asked with forced cheer, "Who wants to go to Ben's? A few laughs, a dance or two..."

Mitch lost count of the number of times he'd tried to reach Bethany by phone. He'd left Chrissie with a high school girl who lived next door and then walked over to Bethany's house.

He stood on the tiny porch and pounded on the door until his fist hurt, despite the padding provided by his thick gloves.

Clearly she wasn't home. He frowned, wondering where she could possibly have gone.

Even as he asked the question, he knew. She'd gone to Ben's. Folks tended to let their hair down a bit on Friday and Saturday nights.

It wasn't uncommon to find Duke and John lingering over a cribbage board, while the other pilots shot the breeze, talking about nothing in particular. Every now and then, some of the pipeline workers would wander in on their way to Fairbanks for a few days of R and R. Things occasionally got a bit rowdy; Mitch had broken up more than one fight in his time. He didn't like the idea of Bethany getting caught in the middle of anything like that.

When he stepped into the Hard Luck Café, he found the noise level almost painful. He couldn't recall the last time he'd seen the place so busy.

He caught sight of Bethany dancing with Duke Porter. Mariah Douglas was dancing with Keith Campbell, a pipeline employee and friend of Bill Landgrin's. Mitch didn't trust either man.

Christian O'Halloran sat brooding in the corner, nursing a drink. Mitch noted that he was keeping a close eye on Mariah. Mitch suspected she wouldn't tolerate or appreciate Christian's interference and that Keith knew it and used it to his advantage.

Frowning, Mitch made his way into the room. He wanted to talk to Bethany, reason with her if he could. He understood her complaints far better than she knew. Her accusations had hit him like a...like a fist flying straight through time. Those were the words Lori had said to him day after day, week after week, month after month....

Before he'd really grasped that it was Bethany talking to him and not his dead wife, Bethany had left. He needed to explain to her that he *did* know what she was experiencing. He'd been through it himself.

In January, when daylight was counted in minutes instead of hours, people did feel trapped in their homes.

He wanted to sit down and tell her what had been burdening his heart for weeks now. Since Christmas. *He loved her.* So much it terrified him. He wanted to tell her about Lori; he hadn't, simply because he was afraid of her response. Most of all, he wanted to tell her he loved her.

Bill Landgrin saw him, and they eyed each other malevolently. From the look of it, Bill was more than a little put out over their last meeting. Judging by the gleam in his eyes, he'd welcome a confrontation with Mitch.

Mitch wasn't eager for a fight, but he wouldn't back down from one, either.

Bill glanced from Mitch to Bethany and then back again. He set his mug on the counter and stomped over to the other side of the café, where Bethany was sitting, now that her dance with Duke was finished. Mitch started in her direction himself, scooting around tables.

Bill got there first.

"Beth, sweetie." Mitch heard the other man greet her. "How's about a dance?"

It seemed to Mitch that she was about to refuse, but he made the mistake—a mistake he recognized almost immediately—of answering for her.

"Bethany's with me," he said, his words as cold as the Arctic ice.

"I am?" she asked.

"She is?" Bill echoed. He rubbed his forehead as though to suggest he found it hard to believe Bethany would attach herself to the likes of Mitch. "Seems to me the lady can make her own decisions."

It took Bethany an eternity to decide. "I don't think one dance would hurt," she finally said to Bill.

Mitch's jaw hardened. He didn't blame her for defying him; he'd brought it on himself. But the fact that she'd dance with another man, for whatever reason, didn't seem right. Not when she'd said she loved *him!*

He sat down in the chair she'd vacated, and as he watched Bill draw Bethany into his arms, his temperature rose. He wasn't much of a drinker, but he sure could have used a shot of something just about then.

The song seemed to drone on for a lifetime. When he couldn't bear to sit any longer, Mitch got to his feet and restlessly prowled the edges of the dance area. Not once did he let his eyes waver from Bethany and Bill.

Something that gave him cause to rejoice was the fact that she didn't seem to be enjoying herself. Her gaze met his over Landgrin's shoulder, and she bit her lip in a way that told him she was sorry she'd ever agreed to this.

He resisted the urge to cut in.

Although Bethany was in another man's arms, Mitch found himself close to laughter. She'd said she loved him and in the same breath had called him an idiot. He was beginning to suspect she was right. He *was* an idiot. Love seemed to reduce him to that.

The song was finally over, and as Landgrin escorted Bethany to her table and reluctantly left her there, the tension eased from Mitch's body.

He made a beeline for her, regretting now that he hadn't been waiting for her when she returned. But he didn't want to give her reason to think he didn't trust her.

Unfortunately Keith Campbell reached her before he did. "A dance, fair lady?" Keith asked, bowing from the waist.

Mitch ended up cooling his heels again while Bethany frolicked across the dance floor in the arms of yet another man. While he waited, he ordered a soda and checked his watch.

He'd told Diane Hestead, the high school girl staying with Chrissie, that he wouldn't be more than an hour. He'd already been gone that long, and it didn't look like he'd be getting home any time soon.

With the music blaring, he used Ben's phone and made a quick call to tell Diane he'd be longer than expected.

"Bethany certainly seems to have captured a few hearts, hasn't she?" Ben commented, slapping Mitch good-naturedly on the back.

"I don't know why she needs to do that," he grumbled. "She's had mine for weeks."

"Does she know that?" Ben asked.

"No," Mitch blurted.

"What do you expect her to do, then?"

Ben was right, of course. Mitch returned to the table to wait for her. When the dance finished, he made sure he was there. "My turn," he announced flatly the minute the two of them were alone.

Bethany's eyes narrowed; she promptly ignored him and sat down. She finished her soda and set the glass aside.

"Let's dance," he said and held out his hand to her.

"Is that a request or a command?" she asked, staring up at him.

Mitch swallowed. This was going from bad to worse. "Do you want me to put on a little performance for you the way Keith did?"

"No," she answered simply.

It was now or never. "Bethany," he said, dragging air into

his lungs, "I love you. I have for weeks. I should've told you before."

She stared at him, her eyes huge. Then, as though she doubted his words, she hastily looked away. "Why now, Mitch?"

He could hardly hear her over the music. "Why now what?"

"Why are you telling me now?" she asked, clarifying her question. "Is it because you're overwhelmed by the depth of your feelings?" She sounded just a little sarcastic, he thought. "Or could the truth be that you can't bear to see me with another man?"

He frowned, not because he didn't understand her question, but because he wasn't sure how to answer. She had a point. He might well have been content to leave things as they were if he hadn't found her dancing with Landgrin.

"Your hesitation tells me everything I need to know," she whispered brokenly. She stood then, in such a rush that she nearly toppled the chair. "Duke," she called, hurrying toward the pilot. "Didn't I promise you another dance?"

Mitch ground his teeth in frustration.

He'd started toward the door when Bill Landgrin stopped him. "Looks like you're batting zero, my friend. Seems to me the lady knows what she wants, and it isn't you."

"I blew it," Bethany muttered miserably. She'd stayed behind and was helping Ben clear the remaining tables. Mariah had disappeared hours earlier after a confrontation with Christian, and she hadn't seen her since.

"What do you mean?"

"Mitch and me."

"What's with you two, anyway?" Ben asked as he set a tray of dirty glasses on the counter.

"I don't know anymore. I thought... I'd hoped..." She felt tongue-tied, unable to explain. Slipping onto the stool opposite Ben, she let her shoulders sag in abject misery. She was still feeling a little drunk—and a lot discouraged—not to mention suffering from a near-fatal bout of cabin fever.

"Here," Ben said, reaching behind the counter and bringing out a bottle of brandy. "I save this for special occasions."

"What's so special about this evening?" she asked.

"A number of things," he said, but didn't elaborate. He brought out a couple of snifters and poured a liberal amount into each. "This will cure what ails you. Guaranteed."

"Maybe you're right." At this point she figured a glass of brandy couldn't hurt.

"Cheers," Ben said and touched the rim of his glass to hers.

"To a special...friend," she said and took her first tentative sip. The liquid fire glided over her tongue and down her throat. When it came to drinking alcohol, Bethany generally stuck to wine and an occasional beer, rarely anything stronger.

Her eyes watered, and this time it had nothing to do with her emotions.

"You all right?" Ben asked, slapping her on the back.

She pressed her hand over her heart and nodded breathlessly. Her second and third sips went down far more easily than the first. Gradually a warmth spread out from the pit of her stomach, and a lethargic feeling settled over her.

"Have you ever been in love?" she asked, surprising herself by asking such a personal question. Perhaps the liquor had loosened her tongue; more likely it was the need to hear this man's version of his affair with her mother. This man who'd fathered her...

"In love? Me?"

"What's so strange about that?" she asked lightly, careful not to let on how serious the question really was. "Surely you've been in love at least once in your life. A woman in your deep, dark past maybe—one you've never been able to forget?"

Ben chuckled. "I was in the navy, you know."

Bethany nodded. "Don't tell me you were the kind of sailor who had a woman in every port?"

He grinned almost boyishly and cocked his head to one side. "That was me, all right."

Although she'd solicited it, this information disturbed Bethany. It somehow cheapened her mother and the love Marilyn had once felt for Ben. "But there must've been one woman you remember more than any of the others," she pressed.

Ben scratched his head as though to give her question heavy-duty consideration. "Nope, can't say there was. I liked to play the field."

Bethany took another sip of the brandy. "What about Marilyn?" she asked brazenly, throwing caution to the winds. "You do remember *her,* don't you?"

"Marilyn?" Ben repeated, a look of surprise on his face. "No... I don't recall any Marilyn." He sounded as though he'd never heard the name before.

Ben might as well have reached across the counter and slapped her face. Hard. She hurt for her mother, and for herself. Before she met him, she'd let herself imagine that her mother's affair with Ben had been a romantic relationship gone tragically awry.

In the past few weeks, she'd begun to think she shared a genuine friendship with Ben. A real bond. Because of that, she'd lowered her guard and come close to revealing her secret.

Bethany clamped her mouth shut. She wanted to blame the wine. The brandy. Both had loosened her tongue, she realized, but she'd been on the verge of telling him, anyway. She shook the hair out of her face and stared past him.

"Three years ago," she began resolutely, struggling to find the right words, knowing she couldn't stop now, "the doctors found a lump in my mother's breast."

"Cancer?"

Bethany nodded.

Ben glanced at his watch. "It's getting kind of late, don't you think?"

"This story will only take a couple more minutes," she promised, and to fortify her courage, she drank the rest of the brandy in a single gulp. It raged a fiery path down her throat.

"You were talking about your mother," Ben prodded, and it seemed he wanted her to hurry. Bethany didn't know if she could. Those weeks when her mother had been so sick from the chemotherapy had been the most traumatic of her life.

"It turned out that the cancer had spread," Bethany continued. "For a while we didn't know if my mother was going to survive. I was convinced that if the cancer didn't kill her, the chemo would. I was still in college at the time. My classes usually let out around two, and I got into the habit of stopping at the hospital on my way home from school."

Ben nursed his drink, his eyes avoiding hers.

"One day, after a particularly violent reaction to the treatment, Mom thought she was going to die. I tried to tell her she had to fight the cancer."

"Did she die?" Ben asked. For the first time since starting her story she had his full attention. Either she was a better storyteller than she realized, or Ben did remember her mother.

"No. She's a survivor. But that day Mom asked me to sit down because she had something important to tell me." At this point, Bethany paused long enough to steady herself. After all this time, the unexpectedness of her mother's announcement still shocked her.

"And?"

"My mother told me about a young sailor she'd loved many years ago. They'd met the summer before he shipped out to Vietnam. By the end of their time together, they'd become lovers. Their political differences separated them as much as the war had. He left because he felt it was his duty to fight, and she stayed behind and joined the peace movement, protesting the war every chance she had. She wrote him a letter and told him about it. He didn't answer. She knew he didn't approve of what she was doing."

"Whoever this person was, he probably didn't want to read about how she was trying to undermine his efforts in Southeast Asia," Ben said stiffly.

"I'm sure that's true." Bethany's voice quavered slightly. "The problem was that when he refused to open her next letter, he failed to learn something vitally important. My mother was pregnant with his child."

The snifter in Ben's hand dropped to the floor and shattered. His eyes remained frozen on Bethany's face.

"I was that child."

The silence stretched to the breaking point. "Who took care of her?" he asked in a choked whisper.

"Her family. When she was about four months pregnant, she met Peter Ross, another student, and confided in him. They fell in love and were married shortly before I was born. Peter raised me as his own and has loved and nurtured me ever since. I never would've guessed.... It was the biggest shock of my life to learn he wasn't my biological father."

"Your mother's name is Marilyn?"

"Yes, and she named you as my birth father."

"Me," Ben said with a weak-sounding laugh. "Sorry, kid, but you've got the wrong guy." He continued to shake his head incredulously. "What'd your mother do—send you out to find me?"

"No. Neither of my parents know why I accepted the teaching contract in Hard Luck. I gave your name to the Red Cross, and they traced you here. I came to meet you, to find out what I could about you."

"Then it's unfortunate you came all this way for nothing," he said gruffly.

"It's funny, really, because we *are* alike. You know the way you get three lines between your eyes when you're troubled or confused? I get those, too. In fact, you're the one who mentioned it, remember? And we both like to cook. And we—"

"That's enough," he snapped. "Listen, Bethany, this is all well and good, but like I already said, you've got the wrong guy."

"But—"

"I told you before and I'll tell you again. I never knew any woman called Marilyn. You'd think if I'd slept with her, I'd remember her, wouldn't you?"

His words were like stones hurled at her heart. "I don't want anything from you, Ben."

"Well, don't count on a mention in my will, either, understand?"

She nearly fell off the stool in her effort to escape. She retreated a step backward. "I... I should never have told you."

"I don't know why you did. And listen, I'd appreciate it if you didn't go spreading this lie around town. I've got a reputation to uphold, and I don't want your lies—and your mother's—besmirching my character."

Bethany thought she was going to be sick.

"It's a damn lie, you hear? A lie!"

"I'm sorry. I—I shouldn't have said anything," she stammered.

He didn't answer her right away. "I don't know anything about any Marilyn."

"I made a mistake," Bethany whispered. "A terrible mistake." She turned and ran from the café.

10

In all the years Mitch had lived in Hard Luck, he'd seen very few mornings when Ben wasn't open for business.

Mitch wasn't the only disgruntled one. Christian met him outside the café. "Do you think Ben might have overslept?"

Mitch doubted it. "Ben?" he asked. "Ben Hamilton, who says he never sleeps past six no matter what time he goes to bed?"

"Maybe he decided to take the day off. He's entitled, don't you think?" Christian asked.

Mitch had thought of that, too. "But wouldn't he put up a sign or something?"

Christian considered this, then said, "Probably." He frowned at his watch. "Listen, I'm supposed to meet Sawyer over at his place."

"Go ahead." It was clear Christian had the same fears as Mitch. Something was wrong. "I'll check things out and connect with you later," he promised.

Ben's apartment was situated above the café. Mitch had never been inside, and he didn't know anyone who had. Ben's real home was the café itself. He kept it open seven days a week and most holidays. Occasionally he'd post a Closed sign when he felt like taking off for a few days' fishing, but that was about it.

The Hard Luck Café was the social center of town, the place where people routinely gathered. Ben was part psychologist, part judge, part confidant and all friend. Mitch didn't know a man, woman or child in town who didn't like him.

Growing increasingly worried, Mitch went around to the back door that led to the kitchen. After a couple of tentative knocks, he walked into the dark, silent café. Flicking on the light switch, the first thing he noticed was shattered glass on the floor.

"Ben!" Mitch called out, walking all the way inside.

Nothing.

The door to the stairs leading to Ben's apartment was open, and Mitch started up, his heart pounding in his ears. He paused halfway, afraid of what he might find. If Ben was dead, it wouldn't be the first time he'd come upon a body. The last had been when he'd found Lori.

He broke out in a cold sweat, and his breathing grew shallow. "Ben," he said again, not as loudly. It was another moment before he could continue upward.

The apartment itself was ordinary. A couch and television constituted the living room furniture. Small bath. Bedroom. Both doors had been left ajar.

"Ben?" he tried once more.

A moan came from the bedroom.

More relieved than words could express, Mitch hurried into the room. Ben was sprawled across the bedspread. It took him a full minute to sit up. He blinked as if the act of opening his eyes was painful.

"Are you all right?" Mitch asked.

Ben rubbed a hand down his face and seemed to give the question some consideration. "No," he finally said.

"Do you need me to call Dotty? Or take you to the clinic?"

"Hell, no. She can't do anything about a hangover."

"You're hung over?" To the best of his knowledge, Ben rarely drank.

Ben pressed both hands to his head. "Do you have to talk so blasted loud?" He grimaced at the sound of his own voice.

"Sorry," Mitch said in an amused whisper.

"Make yourself useful, would you?" Ben growled. "I need coffee. Make it strong, too. I'll be downstairs in a few minutes."

Mitch had the coffee brewing and had swept up the broken glass by the time Ben appeared, his eyes red-rimmed and clouded. His gaze shifted toward Mitch before he took a stool at the counter.

Mitch brought him a cup of coffee the minute it was ready.

"Thanks," Ben mumbled.

"I've never known you to get drunk," Mitch said conversationally, curious as to what had prompted Ben's apparent binge.

"First time in ten years or more," he muttered. "It was either that or... I don't know what. There didn't seem to be a whole lot of options. Fight, I guess, but there wasn't anyone around to punch. Not that it would've done any good, since I had no one to blame but myself. Damn, but I messed up."

"Can I help?" Mitch asked. He'd often gone to Ben for advice about something or other, including his feelings for Bethany. Most of his visits had been on the pretext of wanting a cup of coffee. It appeared that the tables were turned now—so to speak—and if he could assist Ben in some way, then all the better.

"Help me? No." Ben shook his head and instantly seemed to regret the movement. He closed his eyes and waited a moment before opening them again.

"You want me to make you breakfast?" Mitch asked. "I'm not a bad cook."

He couldn't tell whether Ben was taking his offer into consideration. Lowering his head, Ben muttered something Mitch couldn't hear.

Mitch leaned closer. "What did you say?"

"Have, ah...have you seen Bethany this morning?"

"No." He'd actually come to tell his friend what had happened between them last night and—once again—seek his advice.

"Have you tried calling?"

"No."

Ben gave a slight nod in the direction of the phone. "Call her, okay?"

Mitch looked at his watch. "It's a little early, isn't it?"

"Maybe, but try, anyway."

Mitch wasn't keen on the idea. "Is there anything in particular you'd like me to ask her?"

Ben propped his elbows on the counter and covered his face with both hands. He rubbed his eyes, and when he glanced at Mitch they seemed to glisten. "I didn't know," he said in a frayed whisper. "I...never knew."

"What didn't you know?" Mitch asked.

"Marilyn was pregnant."

Ben might as well have been speaking in a foreign language for all the sense he made. "Who's Marilyn?" Mitch asked in calm tones.

Ben dropped his hands. "Bethany's mother." He paused. "Bethany's my daughter. I'm the reason she came to Hard Luck, and when she told me... I pretended I never knew any Marilyn."

"You mean—"

"Yes!" Ben shouted, pounding his fist on the counter. "I'm Bethany's father."

Mitch swore under his breath.

"It was the shock. I... I never guessed. Maybe I should have... I don't know."

Mitch sat on the stool next to Ben, feeling the weight of his friend's burden as if it were his own.

"When she told me, I denied ever knowing her mother and then—" his face contorted with guilt "—I said some things I regret and sent Bethany away." Ben wiped impatiently at his eyes. "She ran out of here, and now I'm afraid she won't be back."

"I'll talk to her if you like." Although Mitch was happy to make the offer, he didn't know if he'd be a help or a hindrance. His own track record with Bethany wasn't exactly impressive.

"Would you?" Ben clung to Mitch's words like a lifeline in a storm-tossed sea.

"Sure." Mitch needed to see her for his own reasons, anyway. "I'll do it right away," he said, eager now to find her. They'd parted on such cool terms Bethany might not be as eager for his company. But Mitch was willing to risk her displeasure. She needed him. When he'd been in pain and grief, she'd been there to comfort him. Ben's rejection must have left her reeling. Mitch suddenly understood how important it was to be the one to console her.

"Tell her..." Ben hesitated, apparently not knowing how to convey his message. "Tell her..." he began again, his voice weak. His eyes brightened and he drew in a deep, shuddering breath. "That I'm proud to have her as my daughter."

In Mitch's opinion, Bethany should hear those words from Ben himself.

Mitch left the café, and Ben was alone once more to deal with the pain and the guilt that had accompanied him most of the night. Even the brandy hadn't dulled the shock.

He had a daughter.

The words still felt awkward on his tongue. Getting used

to the idea was going to require some doing. What bothered him most was the thought of Marilyn struggling alone, without him. It stung a little to know she'd married someone else so soon after his departure. But he couldn't blame her. What was she to do, pregnant with his child and unable to let him know?

Even if he'd learned the truth, he didn't think he could've helped her the way she needed. He might've been able to marry her. Maybe that could've been arranged. But he was at war, and it wasn't like he could call time-out while he dealt with his personal problems. The navy wouldn't have released him from his obligations because he got a college girl pregnant.

If there was any one thing Ben regretted most about the past, it was returning Marilyn's letter unopened. It hurt him almost to the point of being physically ill to think about her alone and pregnant, believing he didn't care. The truth of the matter was that he'd loved her deeply. It had taken him years to put his love for her behind him.

She'd done the right thing in marrying this other man, he decided suddenly. Ben wouldn't have been a good husband for her, or for any woman. He was too stubborn, too set in his own ways. It was easier to comfort himself with those reassurances, he realized, than deal with all the might-have-beens.

The fact was, he'd fathered this child. Except that Bethany wasn't a child. She was an adult, and a mighty fine one at that. Any man would be proud to call her daughter.

Bethany. Ben would give anything to take back the things he'd said to her. It was the shock. The fear, too, of her wanting something from him when he had nothing to give—emotionally or financially. He couldn't change the past or make up to Marilyn and Bethany for what he'd done—and hadn't done.

Ben poured a second cup of coffee in an attempt to clear his head. His temples still throbbed—enough to convince him not to seek solutions in a bottle again.

There was a knock at the front door. He'd forgotten that he'd left it locked. With a definite lack of enthusiasm, he shuffled across the café and unlatched the bolt. To his surprise, he saw it was Mitch.

"She's gone," Mitch announced, sounding like a man in a trance.

"Bethany gone? What do you mean, gone?"

"I just saw Christian. Duke flew her out this morning."

Pain shot through Ben's chest and he felt the sudden need to sit down. He'd only just found her and now—now he'd lost her.

The pizza had helped, Bethany decided, but not nearly enough. Sorry that Mariah had decided not to join her, after all, she sat on the big hotel bed in front of the television. She was halfheartedly watching a movie she'd seen before she'd left for Alaska and paying the same price as she had in a California theater.

Earlier in the day, she'd had her hair trimmed, and while she was at it, she'd sprung for a manicure.

Following that, she'd found a shopping mall and lingered for hours, just poking around the shops and watching the people. It didn't take long, however, for the doubts and regrets to crowd back into her mind.

She'd ruined everything. With Ben feeling the way he did, she wasn't comfortable returning to Hard Luck, and at the same time she couldn't leave. Not with everything between her and Mitch still unresolved. If the situation had been different, she could've phoned her parents, but of course neither of them knew the real reason she'd accepted the teaching assignment in Alaska. She hadn't wanted them to know.

What about Chrissie? And Susan and Scott and Ronny... She couldn't leave her students or break the terms of her contract. She had a moral and legal obligation to the people who'd hired her. The state and the town had entrusted her with these young lives. She couldn't just walk out.

On the other hand, how could she go back? It was all she could do not to hide her face in her hands and weep. She had no idea what had possessed her to confront Ben with the truth last night. Her timing couldn't have been worse. The information had come at him with the stealth and suddenness of a bomb, exploding in his life. She hadn't prepared him in any way to learn she was his daughter.

No wonder he— Her thoughts came to a crashing halt at the loud knock on her door.

"Bethany."

"Mitch?"

"Please open up."

She didn't know how he'd learned where she was staying. She scrambled off the bed and ran to open the door.

He stood on the other side, feet braced, as though he was surprised he hadn't been forced to kick the door in. He blinked, then blurted, "Don't leave."

"Leave?" She followed his gaze to her small suitcase.

"You've packed your things."

True, but only for a short stay in Fairbanks. She wondered where Mitch thought she was going. Then she understood— he assumed she was returning to California.

"Give me one good reason to stay," she invited.

He walked past her and into the room. As he moved, he shoved his fingers through his hair. Unable to stand still, he paced the area like a man possessed.

"I love you, and I'm not saying that because there's another man wanting to dance with you. I'm saying it because I can't imagine living without you." He stopped, his eyes imploring. "I need you, Bethany. I didn't know how much until I discovered you were gone."

"You love me?"

"I haven't given you much reason to believe that, have I? There are reasons… I know you don't want to listen to excuses, and I don't blame you. Bethany, I'm not saying any of this for Chrissie. I need you for *me*. I love you for *me*." He paused and dragged in an uneven breath.

All at once it didn't seem fair to mislead him any further. "I'm not going anywhere," she confessed. "I was coming back, and when I did, I planned to work all of this out with you."

He closed his eyes as if a great weight had been lifted from him.

"I need to settle things with someone else, too," she said.

"Ben." His eyes held hers. "He wants to talk to you."

Bethany struggled to control her emotions before she asked, "He told you?"

Mitch nodded. "You're his daughter."

"He admitted that?" Her eyes welled with tears.

Again he nodded.

"Is he all right? I shouldn't have said anything—you don't know how much I regret it." She found it difficult to maintain her composure. "I shouldn't have confronted him the way I did. I can only guess what he must think. Please," she begged, "tell him I don't expect anything of him. I realize he lied, but I understand. I don't blame him. Who knows what any of us would have done in similar circumstances."

"He wants to talk to you himself."

"He doesn't need to say a word. I understand. Please assure him for me that I don't want anything from him," she said again.

"You can tell him yourself. He's here."

"Here?"

"Actually he's downstairs in the bar waiting. We tossed a coin to see which of us got to speak to you first. I won."

He gestured to the bed. "Please sit," he said. "This seems to be a time for confessions." Bethany obediently perched on the edge of the bed and looked up at him expectantly.

"There's something important you need to know about me," he said. "I should've told you sooner—I'm sorry I didn't. After I've told you, you can decide what you want to do. If you'd rather not see me again...well, you can decide that later."

"Mitch, what is it?"

He couldn't seem to stay in one place. "I love you, Bethany," he said urgently. "I'm not a man who loves easily. There's only been one other woman I've felt this strongly about."

"Your wife," she guessed.

"I—I don't know where to start." Mitch threw her a look of anguish.

"Start at the beginning," she coaxed gently, patiently. She'd waited a long time for Mitch to trust her enough to tell her about his past.

He resumed his pacing. "I met Lori while we were in college. I suppose our history was fairly typical. We fell in love and got married. I joined the Chicago Police Department, and our lives settled down to that of any typical young couple. Or so I thought."

He paused, and it seemed to Bethany that the light went out of his eyes.

"I see," she said quietly. "Go on."

Moving to stand in front of her, he said, "Chrissie was born, and I was crazy about her from the first. Lori wanted to be a good mother. I believe that, and I believe she tried. She honestly tried. But she was accustomed to being in the workforce and mingling with other people, and staying home with the baby didn't suit her. About this time, I was assigned to Narcotics. From that point, my schedule became erratic. I rarely knew from one week to the next what my hours would be."

He stared somewhere above her head, as if the telling of these details was too painful to do face-to-face.

"Lori became depressed. She saw her physician about it, and he explained that post-partum depression is fairly common. He prescribed something to help her feel better. He also gave her tranquilizers. A light dose to take when she had trouble sleeping."

"Did the medication help?"

"For a while, but then Lori found she couldn't sleep nights at all. Chrissie suffered from repeated ear infections, and Lori often had to stay awake with her, which added to the problem."

He frowned. "I don't know when she started doubling up on the tranquilizers, or even how she was able to get so many of them. I suspect she went to a number of different doctors."

Bethany held out her hand to him and Mitch gripped it hard between his own. Then he sat on the bed beside her, turning his body toward her. "What's so tragic about all of this is that over and over again Lori told me how unhappy she was, how miserable. She didn't like being home. She didn't like staying with the baby all the time. She wanted me home more often. She clung to me until I felt she was strangling me, and all along she was so terribly sick, so terribly depressed."

"Did you know she was hooked on the tranquilizers?"

"I suppose I guessed. But I figured she was under a doctor's care—and I didn't want to deal with it just then. I couldn't. I was working day and night on an important case," he said, his eyes bleak with sorrow. "If she wanted to dope herself up at night with tranquilizers, what could I do? I'd cope with it when I could, but not then." He closed his eyes and shook his head. "You see, I might've saved her life had I dealt with the problem immediately, instead of ignoring it and praying she'd snap out of it herself."

"What happened?" Bethany asked. She intuitively realized there was more to the story, and that it would only grow worse.

"If the signs had been any plainer, they would've hit me over the head."

"It happens every day."

"I worked with addicts. I should've known."

It was clear that this was one thing Mitch would never forgive himself for.

"She killed herself," he said in a stark whisper. "Her family thought it was an accident, but I know better. She needed me, but I was too involved in chasing down drug dealers to help my own wife. She was depressed, unhappy and addicted to tranquilizers. I turned my back on her. I might as well have poured the pills down her throat."

"Oh, Mitch, you were under so much stress. You can't blame yourself."

"Yes, I can," he said, "and I have. I should've been able to tell what was happening to her. She paid the penalty for my neglect—with her life. I can understand if you don't want to marry me..."

"Is that what you're asking me, Mitch? To be your wife?"

"Yes." His gaze held hers. "I realize how much Chrissie loves you, but like I told you, it isn't for my daughter I'm asking. It's for me."

The lump in Bethany's throat refused to dissolve. She nodded and swallowed her tears.

"Is that a yes?" he asked, as if he was afraid of the answer.

She nodded again, more vigorously.

Mitch briefly closed his eyes. "I live a simple life, Bethany. I don't want to leave Hard Luck."

"I don't want to leave, either. My home is wherever you are."

"You're sure? Because I don't think I could let you go. Not now." He reached for her and kissed her with a hunger and a longing that left her breathless. A long time passed before he released her.

"We'd better stop while I still can," he told her. "Besides, Ben's waiting."

"Ben." She'd almost forgotten.

"He's downstairs bragging to the bartender about his daughter," Mitch said. "Would you like to join him there? I know he wants to talk to you."

"In a little while," she whispered and leaned her head against his shoulder. They'd both come to Hard Luck for a purpose. His had been to hide; hers had been to find her biological father. Together they'd discovered something far more precious than the gold that had drawn generations of prospectors to Alaska.

They'd found each other. And together they'd found love.

Epilogue

Half an hour later, Bethany made her way into the dimly lit cocktail lounge and came upon Ben sitting alone at a table, nursing a bottle of beer. His shoulders slumped forward and his head was bowed. It looked, she thought sadly, as if the weight of nearly thirty years of regret rested solidly on his back.

He raised his eyes to meet hers when she walked over to his table. "Do you mind if I sit down?" she asked, feeling tentative herself. She understood that the way she'd confronted Ben had been a mistake; she wished more than anything that they could start over.

He nodded, his expression concerned as she slid out the chair and sat across from him.

"Do you want a drink?" he asked.

"No, thanks." The wine and brandy last night had loosened her tongue. She didn't want to repeat *that* mistake. "I'm so sorry..."

"I'm the one who's sorry," Ben cut in. "I'm not proud of the way I reacted yesterday—my only excuse is shock."

"I couldn't have done a worse job of it," she said.

His face tightened, and his eyes grew suspiciously bright.

"It's so hard to believe I could have a daughter as beautiful as you, Bethany. My heart feels like it's going to bust wide open just looking at you."

Bethany smiled tremulously, close to tears herself.

"Your mother...the resemblance between you is striking. I didn't see it at first, but now I do." He took a swallow of his beer and Bethany suspected he did it to hide his emotion. He set the bottle back on the table. "How's Marilyn? The cancer?"

"She's better than ever, and there's no sign of the cancer recurring."

"She's...she's had a good life? She's happy?"

Bethany nodded. "Very happy. Mom and Dad have a good marriage. Like any relationship, it's had its ups and downs over the years, but they're still in love, and they're truly committed to each other." She paused and drew in a deep breath. "They don't know that I've—that I found you."

He lowered his head. "Do you plan on telling them?"

"Yes, and you can be assured I'll handle it a lot more diplomatically than I did with you. I accepted the teaching contract in Hard Luck because I knew you were here, but originally I'd never intended to tell you."

"Not tell me?"

"All I wanted was to get to know you, but once I'd done that, it didn't seem to be enough. We're very alike, Ben, in many important ways. But before I knew that, I was afraid of the kind of man you'd be."

He sipped from the beer bottle. "I'm probably a disappointment...."

"No," she rushed to tell him. "No! I'm *proud* to be your daughter. You're a warm, generous, caring person. Hard Luck Café is the heart of the community, and that's because of you."

"I can't be your father," Ben murmured. "Your mother's husband—Peter—he'll always be that."

"That's true. But you could be my friend."

His face brightened. "Yes. A special friend."

Bethany stretched her hand across the table and Ben squeezed her fingers. "Where's Mitch?"

"He's in the lobby waiting for us." Bethany smiled, and the happiness bloomed within her. "This seems to be a day for clearing the air."

Ben placed some money on the table and they walked out of the lounge. "Are you going to marry him?" he asked. "Put him out of his misery?"

"Oh, yes. I came to Hard Luck wanting to meet you, and instead I found *two* men I'll love for the rest of my life."

Mitch hurried toward them, and they met him halfway. Grinning widely, Ben slung an arm around their shoulders, drawing them close. "Well, my friends. This seems to be an evening to celebrate. Dinner's on me!"

★ ★ ★ ★ ★